# *The* CASTLE *in the* GLEN

# ALSO BY RHYS BOWEN

*In Farleigh Field*

*The Tuscan Child*

*The Victory Garden*

*What Child Is This*

*Above the Bay of Angels*

*The Venice Sketchbook*

*Where the Sky Begins*

*The Paris Assignment*

*The Rose Arbor*

*Mrs. Endicott's Splendid Adventure*

## Constable Evans Mysteries

*Evans Above*

*Evan Help Us*

*Evanly Choirs*

*Evan and Elle*

*Evan Can Wait*

*Evans to Betsy*

*Evan Only Knows*

*Evan's Gate*

*Evan Blessed*

*Evanly Bodies*

## Molly Murphy Mysteries

*Murphy's Law*

*Death of Riley*

*For the Love of Mike*

*In Like Flynn*

*Oh Danny Boy*

*In Dublin's Fair City*

*Tell Me, Pretty Maiden*

*In a Gilded Cage*

*The Last Illusion*

*Bless the Bride*

*Hush Now, Don't You Cry*

*The Family Way*

*City of Darkness and Light*

*The Edge of Dreams*

*Away in a Manger*

*Time of Fog and Fire*

*The Ghost of Christmas Past*

## With Clare Broyles

*Wild Irish Rose*

*All That Is Hidden*

*In Sunshine or in Shadow*

*Silent as the Grave*

*Vanished in the Crowd*

## Royal Spyness Mysteries

*Her Royal Spyness*

*A Royal Pain*

*Royal Flush*

*Royal Blood*

*Naughty in Nice*

*The Twelve Clues of Christmas*

*Heirs and Graces*

*Queen of Hearts*

*Malice at the Palace*

*Crowned and Dangerous*

*On Her Majesty's Frightfully Secret Service*

*Four Funerals and Maybe a Wedding*

*Love and Death Among the Cheetahs*

*The Last Mrs. Summers*

*God Rest Ye, Royal Gentlemen*

*Peril in Paris*

*The Proof of the Pudding*

*We Three Queens*

*From Cradle to Grave*

# *The* CASTLE *in the* GLEN

*A Novel*

RHYS BOWEN

LAKE UNION
PUBLISHING

This is a work of fiction. Names, characters, organizations, places, events, and incidents are either products of the author's imagination or are used fictitiously. Otherwise, any resemblance to actual persons, living or dead, is purely coincidental.



Published by Lake Union Publishing, Seattle

www.apub.com



EU product safety contact:
Amazon Media EU S. à r.l.
38, avenue John F. Kennedy, L-1855 Luxembourg
amazonpublishing-gpsr@amazon.com

ISBN-13: 9781662527210 (hardcover)
ISBN-13: 9781662527227 (paperback)
ISBN-13: 9781662527203 (digital)

Cover design by Jarrod Taylor
Cover images: © David Lichtneker / ArcAngel; © DEEPOL / plainpicture; © Mai / Adobe Stock

Printed in the United States of America
First edition

*This is for my Westfield Girls, who have been such wonderful friends since we first met at the age of eighteen and with whom I still have adventures. Long may we flourish!*

# CAST OF CHARACTERS

## In Iris Blackburn's book, *The Wild Girl*, 1932

- Inspector James Melrose of the Glasgow Police: Young, ambitious and thoughtful but doesn't think much of the upper-class snobs. Slim, with sandy hair.
- Inspector MacDonald of the Skye Police: In his forties. Outdoor type. A bit belligerent and doesn't want outside interference.
- Mistress MacLeod, owner of the Kings Arms Hotel in Kyleakin: Typical soft-spoken, gentle inhabitant of the island.
- Young Jock MacLeod, the taxi driver: Has taken over the taxi service from his father. An earnest, hard-working young Highlander.
- Sir Henry Hamilton, MP, laird of Dun Akyn castle: Essentially an outsider, although the family has owned the castle for centuries. He is the typical laird: arrogant, snobbish, fiercely protective of his family and with little feeling for the crofters on his estate.
- Lady Hamilton, his wife: A fragile, delicate upper-class woman. Devastated by the loss of her child.
- Roland, his son: Follows in his dad's footsteps. He is arrogant and has no regard for his social inferiors.
- Lucy, Henry Hamilton's daughter, now deceased: A sweet, intelligent and imaginative girl. She's spent her whole life shut

away in a castle and dreams of escape and romance. Pretty red-blonde hair and blue eyes. When Flora comes to stay she finally finds the sister she's been craving.

- Mr Francis Stewart, from the mainland: An earnest young labour agitator dedicated to helping the lot of the crofters. He's also a climber but not much good with boats.
- Flora MacLeod, a wild girl: Had run wild since her mother died, with her father often out at sea. Attempts to tame her had not worked until Lady Hamilton took her in as companion to Lucy and turned her into an attractive young lady. She and Lucy are inseparable, which is why the tragedy is hard to understand.
- Angus, her father: A drunken bully who drove Flora's mother to suicide.
- Mr Euan Chisholm, a landowner's son from the mainland: About the most repulsive suitor any girl would want. Thinks a lot of himself. Can't keep his hands off any female.
- Miss Isla Anderson, governess to Lucy: A gentle soul who inspired and helped Lucy until she was banished. Her sweet personality does not go unnoticed by Inspector Melrose. If her father hadn't been an invalid, who knows where that might have led.
- Morag and Agnes, maids: At the mercy of groping hands yet still loyal to the family.

## In London, 1965

- Emma Callander, a young and promising Australian author: Has come to London to pursue her literary dreams but still feels like a fish out of water.
- Jilly and Robyn, her Aussie flatmates: Jilly the flamboyant, irreverent one and Robyn, who is down to earth and kind. They keep Emma sane and give her roots in London.

- Mr David Spencer, editor at Barlow and Barlow, Publishers: An elderly literary gentleman.
- Jeremy Feathers: A rich agent to Iris Blackburn.
- Miss Cynthia Morton, Iris Blackburn's secretary/companion: A typical hearty English upper-class countrywoman. Hopelessly devoted to Iris.
- Tony Gordon, son of Iris's solicitor: Good-looking in a subdued British sort of way. To start with, he seems reserved and a bit boring. But he turns out to be quite the opposite.
- Arthur Gordon, his father. Not an easy man, but with good reason.
- Iris Blackburn, one of the most famous writers in the world: Think Agatha Christie. She came from Australia in the 1930s and found instant success with her mystery series. Now she's old, spoiled and a bit difficult. Also it seems she is losing her marbles, which is why she's hired a young writer.
- Mrs Fisk, her cook: A terrifying woman, loyal to Iris and like a bulldog to everyone else. But a divine cook.
- Maggie, her maid: A kind, long-suffering girl.

## On the Island of Skye, 1965

- Andrew Patterson, son of Ross Patterson of Craigard: Handsome and charismatic. Emma is instantly attracted but senses danger.
- Mrs Bruce, owner of the Kings Arms Hotel: A kind, older inhabitant of Skye.
- Young Jock, the taxi driver: The latest generation of a business that has been in the family since the turn of the century. Like his ancestors he is caring and loyal.
- Mr MacLeod, his father: The former Young Jock, now retired.

- Mr Graham, a laird: A relative of the unpleasant Alistair Graham.
- Ross Patterson: Andrew's father. A typical laird. Arrogant. A bully.
- Mrs Patterson, his wife: A kind, reserved woman who is not happy with her lot.
- Sir Robert Patterson, his aged father: Brother to the drowned Lily. He's carried regret and guilt all his life.
- Miss Anderson, the former governess: Now old and frail but as likeable as her fictional namesake.

## And in the Past on the Island

### *The real-life characters who inspired* The Wild Girl

- Sir Harry Patterson of Craigard.
- Lily Patterson: His daughter.
- Alistair Graham: Lily's suitor.
- Catriona MacLeod: A wild girl.
- Thomas Blaine: A young man from the mainland.

# From *The Wild Girl: Inspector Melrose's First Case*, Chapter 1

## By Iris Blackburn

***The Isle of Skye, autumn 1932***

Flora was the name her mother had given her at birth, but her mother had died before the child reached five years, a wee scrap of a bairn, and in the village of Dun Akyn she was known only as the Wild Girl. Her father was a fisherman, out at sea long hours at a time, and Flora learned quickly how to fend for herself. She helped herself to eggs from those who kept chickens. She begged a roll or two from the baker. The kind folk in the village left bowls of soup out for her and their own children's outgrown clothing. She went to school when she felt like it but was most often seen running barefoot across the heather or splashing in the tide pools, communing with the wild creatures from seals to roe deer. It was whispered that Angus MacLeod was not her father at all but that it was one of the fairy folk, or even a storm-kelpie. Whatever was true in this regard, she stayed clear of the well-meaning village women who tried to take her in hand, made no friends amongst the village children and could seemingly vanish in the blink of an eye like the fairy folk.

Either way she was destined to come to a bad end.

# Chapter 1

***London, September 1965***

Emma Callander stood at the bus stop feeling utterly miserable. Rain ran down her face and dripped under her collar. Wind whipped around her legs. A bus should have come ten minutes ago, and all she wanted to do was to get home. She toyed with the word. "Home." "I want to go home," she whispered to herself. An image sprang into her mind: the house with the veranda around it, the vineyard sloping up to blue hills of eucalyptus and bellbirds, the paddock where the wallabies came at dusk, the pond with the spoonbills. And then the golden beaches, the sun always shining . . .

"Bugger England. Bugger men," she muttered.

By the time she got off the bus at Earl's Court Road and trudged up Trebovir Road to the flat she shared with two Aussie friends, she had made up her mind. She was going back to Australia.

"My word, look what the cat dragged in," Jilly exclaimed as Emma came into the flat, leaving a trail of drips behind her. "You look like a drowned rat. So was the date at a swimming pool or in the Thames?"

Emma took off her mack and hung it over the kitchen sink. "In case you haven't noticed it's pouring out there," she said. "And the date was a horrible non-starter. Or at least he was keen to get going in the bedroom without even pausing to have a chat first. He said he had to stop at his flat to pick up a letter he was supposed to post but once inside . . ." She stopped, grimacing. "He started to . . . you know . . . come on to me, and I had to tell him I'd scream the place down if he didn't open the door that instant."

"You poor thing. What a creep!" Robyn came over to her, putting an arm around her shoulder.

"Not that old 'I've forgotten something in my room' trick!" Jilly said, shaking her head so that her Vidal Sassoon bob bounced. "I thought we'd tried to educate you in the ways of the big, wicked city by now."

"All right, so I'm not exactly experienced around men like you." Emma pushed her wet hair back from her face as she crossed the room. "I haven't had much chance to practice."

"Sit down. You need a glass of wine," Robyn said kindly. "These Aussie blokes are sex mad. I don't know what gets into them. The moment they're far from home they think they can act like animals. The London boys might be slower, but at least they're polite and expect to pay for a meal first."

"Only they forget to mention they're dating someone else at the same time." Emma sank down onto the sofa. "Three months of my life with Simon and I find he's had another girlfriend all that time." She mimicked Simon's voice. "Someone more suitable, with good family connections."

"He was a swine," Jilly agreed. "He led you along."

"He certainly did," Emma said. "I've had enough of men. In fact I've had enough of everything. I decided tonight that I'm going to go home. I've come, I've seen, I've experienced England, and now I can go back to marry a reliable sheep farmer."

"Boring, darling," Jilly said. "If you're going to marry an Aussie at least choose a lifeguard from Bondi Beach. All those muscles rippling."

"But not much up top," Robyn added.

"Anyway, you don't actually have a home any more, do you?" Jilly blurted out, rather tactlessly.

Emma winced at the words and the harsh reality. "Okay, so I don't have the family property any longer, but I can live in Sydney."

"But you can't leave now, Emmie." Jilly got up and put a hand on Emma's shoulder. "You're a darling of the literary scene. Promising young Australian writer. Isn't that what *The Sunday Times* said? You have to make the most of your fame."

Emma laughed. "Fame? A couple of reviews, and I believe I've sold perhaps five thousand copies of the book. If I'd been smart I'd have another book ready to go to build upon that recognition, but I don't. I don't even know if I can write a whole book by myself. The old man at the bookshop in Sydney, the one I told you about, he helped me so much. And frankly, I'm scared to try now that people seem to think I've got talent."

"You'll never know unless you try," Robyn said. She poured a glass of wine, handing it to Emma. "You could always have Jilly dictate some of her sexual exploits and write a steamy bestseller."

"Hey, watch it!" Jilly feigned annoyance. "I might go on dates, but I don't let them cross the line, you know. A kiss and a cuddle in the back row of the cinema, that's all. I'm saving myself for the right one."

"How will you know he's the right one?" Emma asked, relaxing a little now as she warmed up.

"He'll be rich, dahling, of course." Jilly mimicked a frightfully posh accent. "I don't intend to settle for anyone poor and humble. Oh, and a title wouldn't be bad. I see myself as Lady Blah-blah."

"And where does one meet this rich paragon?" Robyn asked. "We don't exactly frequent the posh nightclubs or go to weekend house parties. And to most British blokes we're wild colonials. Uncultured. Beneath them, progeny of convicts."

"Speak for yourself," Jilly said. "My family came over as legitimate settlers after the First World War."

"And mine have been in Australia since the eighteen hundreds," Emma said. "They started with apples, then found that grapes grow better."

"Jolly useful to grow up with wine on hand," Jilly said. "It's a wonder you're not a lush."

"I never liked the taste of it," Emma confessed. "I don't mind it now, but I still can't get used to beer."

"Well, not English beer," Robyn said. "That dark brown stuff is like poison. That's why I stick to cider. It tastes all right and has the same effect."

"It gets you drunk quite quickly, actually," Jilly said. "I remember one night with three ciders and I could hardly walk home in a straight line. If I'd been with a bloke who'd wanted to take advantage, I probably wouldn't have said no. Now I know my limits." She got up, dropping her cardigan on the back of the sofa. "Well, I'm off to bed. Early night for once. I might get a chance to do some modelling. Someone who works at Mary Quant came into the boutique today and said I had the right look. How about that. Can you see me as the next Pattie Boyd, darlings?" She strutted around the room pouting, making Emma and Robyn laugh.

*I'll miss them,* Emma thought as she went to her own room. They were good company and an important tie to her homeland. Jilly was hopelessly messy, always leaving clothes around and unwashed dishes, but she was fun and easy to get along with. Robyn was the earnest one, working at the Australian High Commission. They had become close over the last year. Was she being stupid to want to go home now? She was doing well in England. She had a good job with Barlow and Barlow, an esteemed publishing house, even if she was only an editorial assistant, which meant general dogsbody. She'd met writers like Graham Greene, and she'd had a book published. From the number of hopeful manuscripts that came in she knew how hard that was. So she must have something unique as a writer and, what's more, a publisher who actually wanted another book from her. She'd be mad to go. And yet she felt out of place; she didn't belong here.

The worst thing was that she hadn't been able to write. All her life at home she had never been short of ideas, one after another begging to be put down on paper. "Always scribbling away," as her mother put it. But since she came to London the double pressures of a strange city and good reviews for her one published novel had dried up that constant stream. She wasn't sure people wanted more books set in Australia, and yet she was still an outsider and observer in London. The terrible fear that she tried to keep at bay was that she'd never write another book.

As she lay in bed picturing home, she realized with a jolt that Jilly had been right. She didn't have a home any more. Her visions of returning to Australia were of that bungalow at the family vineyard, the blue hills beyond, waking to the sound of the magpies and kookaburras. But that house now belonged to her dad's cousin and his family. She hardly knew them. Her mother now lived on Pete Warton's farm and she had no idea whether she'd be welcome there. She was sure she could land a job with an Australian publisher, using her Barlow and Barlow credential, and maybe, just maybe, she could get back to her writing again, but she'd be alone, an outsider in her own country.

# Chapter 2

The next morning Emma awoke to one of those damp and gloomy days when you need to have the light on to get dressed. And it was only September, with a whole winter looming ahead. It wasn't exactly raining but there was enough moisture in the air to make her hair frizz. That settled it. She needed sunshine and beaches and barbie. She glanced at herself in the mirror. At home she'd always had a tan. Now she appeared horribly pale, and her blue eyes had a perpetually worried look. At home her hair had been sun-streaked strawberry blonde. Now it had subsided to a dull reddish mid brown, not red enough to be startling. She wore it long, over her shoulders, unlike Jilly with her fashionable bob. But then Jilly had Irish black hair and sparkling green eyes.

*If I go home maybe I'll get ideas for another book,* she thought. *I can still send it to Mr Spencer for them to publish in England.* Then doubt crept in. What if they had only published the first one as a favour because she was working for them? Or perhaps because they saw a hint of talent that they wanted to develop. Would she really be mad to walk away now?

Robyn was already up and eating Vegemite on toast, which came from the regular care packages from her family.

"Are you really going to go back to Australia?" Robyn asked.

Emma shrugged. "I'm not really happy here. I keep asking myself what I'm doing. I don't like big cities for one thing. I was brought up on a farm. And I do miss the sunshine. If I went home now I'd have summer ahead of me."

"So where would you actually go?" Robyn asked cautiously. "Didn't you say your mum remarried and you had to leave the farm you grew up on?"

"That's right. I was thinking that last night. Where would I go? How would I afford to live if I couldn't find a job right away? Sydney is expensive. I don't have much money saved up. I spent most of it on that trip to Paris in the summer. I'd have enough for my fare, but then I really wanted to travel through Italy first and take the ship home from there."

"I'd say you'd answered yourself," Robyn said. "You need to keep working at least until you've written another book."

"Easier said than done." Emma chewed on her lip. "I wish I knew what to write about. I don't know enough about London to set a book here, and I've come to the conclusion I know nothing about life. What if I can never write another book, Robyn?"

"You will." Robyn gave her an encouraging smile. "You're only twenty-three. Most people don't even get a book published until they're middle-aged, so you're ahead of the game."

"Thanks, Rob." Emma smiled back. "But I don't really want to stay here any longer, although I guess I'll need to keep working and try to save more. I have to pay for my passage, and I'll need some money to keep me going at home until I've found another job."

"Well, you know we don't want you to go, but if you're serious about this then I'll bring you the *Sydney Morning Herald* from work and you can take a look at the want ads," Robyn said.

"Thank you," Emma said. "Good idea." She glanced at the clock. "Oh cripes. I'd better get going. They do not tolerate lateness at Barlow and Barlow. In fact it's as bad as school."

Dead leaves from the sycamore trees along the street lay in sodden piles underfoot after last night's downpour. A van drove past, splashing up puddles and making Emma dodge aside. Sydney, she thought—with the blue water of the harbour, the ferries crisscrossing, the beach at Manly—suddenly sounded so desirable that she felt a lump in her throat.

Barlow and Barlow was housed in a tall, elegant brick building in the Bloomsbury district, just off Russell Square. Emma enjoyed working in this area. It was the way she had pictured London before she came—staid, historical, unchanged. Being the site of University College London and the headquarters of the University of London, it was always full of students, as well as tourists visiting the British Museum. It was lively but civilized in a way that the grotty streets around Earl's Court were not. Emma ran up the front steps just as a nearby clock was chiming nine.

"Ah Emma, you're here. Good."

She looked up to see Mr Spencer himself standing in the front hallway. Her heart lurched. Mr Spencer was the most senior of the editors, chummy with the one surviving Mr Barlow. Was he actually waiting for her? Waiting to catch her coming in late? Had that nasty receptionist Doris told him that she was late twice last week? She always set out on time but delays on the Tube happened all too often.

"Good morning, Mr Spencer," she said. "Did you need me for something right away?"

"I do indeed." He was looking quite cheerful and she relaxed a little. "I was wondering if you'd like a ride out to the country?"

"Me? Today?" She wondered if she'd heard right.

"Right now," he said. "I have to visit a client and I wondered if you'd like to come along. Especially if I told you the client was Iris Blackburn?"

"Iris Blackburn?" She gaped at him and stammered out the words. Iris Blackburn was the most famous writer in the country, probably in the world. It was said that her books sold better than anything but the Bible. Everyone knew of her Inspector Melrose. He had appeared in a couple of films and on the telly. Emma knew that she was a client of Barlow and Barlow and that Mr Spencer had been her editor for many decades, but she was an ethereal figure who never came in to the Barlow and Barlow offices. In fact Emma assumed that she had given up writing years ago. It was rather like being asked to meet God.

"Crikey," she said. "You're inviting me along to meet Iris Blackburn?"

He nodded, smiling as if he had offered her a surprise gift. "Since you're a fellow Australian and I'd welcome the company on the drive. My eyesight isn't what it was and you can read the road signs for me once we leave the main road."

"I'd love to, Mr Spencer," she said. "I just wish I'd known in advance. I'd have put on a better skirt."

He laughed. "I'm sure Iris won't mind what you are wearing. Right then, I'll let Doris know that we're going. The motor car is parked outside."

He opened the door for Emma to go ahead of him, then indicated an ancient Daimler, still looking sleek and expensive in spite of its age. The seat was upholstered with cream-coloured leather to match the car's exterior and Emma sank into the luxury of it. Mr Spencer climbed in beside her and they pulled away from the kerb.

"Does Iris live far from London?" she asked, wondering whether they were in for a drive to a far-flung part of the British Isles and whether they'd be required to stay the night. A small alarm bell sounded, not least that she'd brought no change of clothes or sleeping things with her.

"Not too far. Just outside Tunbridge Wells. Not much more than an hour's drive if the traffic is favourable."

He drove skilfully, negotiating the busy traffic down Kingsway, around Aldwych and over the Waterloo Bridge. The crowded area of south London with its delivery vehicles took longer to get through, and Emma noticed Mr Spencer impatiently tapping on the wheel with each hold-up.

"Iris is expecting us for lunch," he said. "I hope we don't keep her waiting."

At last city streets gave way to suburbia, semi-detached houses with neat front gardens, and then to countryside. As if on cue the clouds rolled back and the sun came out.

"So how is your own writing coming along?" Mr Spencer asked. "Do you have any time for it? Do they keep you too busy at Barlow and Barlow?"

"I haven't written anything lately." Emma chewed on her lip, looking away. "I don't have that much time and I share a flat, so it's always quite noisy." She winced at the excuse.

"Oh, that's too bad," he said. "I hope you get back to it soon. You can't leave it too long between books or your readers forget about you. We're hoping for a bright future for you."

Emma stared straight ahead. Mr Spencer thought she had a bright future. It gave her a sliver of hope, but at the same time the worry resurfaced. They left the A20 and headed up the Shoreham Valley past quaint villages. Emma took them all in with interest. She had not had a chance to see much of the countryside since she came to England. She had once visited Oxford, to see what she had been forced to give up, and she'd been to the coast at Brighton and Hastings. The shingle beaches and cold breeze had not impressed her. But this countryside was so green, so peaceful. Fields with cows and horses.

They passed a village and Emma saw her first thatched cottages.

"Oh." She let out an excited gasp.

Mr Spencer looked at her. "What's wrong?"

"Nothing," she said. "It's all perfect. Just as I always pictured it. I'm seeing England properly for the first time. I'd read about thatched cottages and here they are."

Mr Spencer smiled. "You wait till you see Iris's house. It's quite impressive."

This brought to the fore the anxious thoughts she had been holding at bay. If Mr Spencer had come down to confer about a work in progress, might she not be annoyed at an outsider being present? Emma did not want to spend the day banished to the kitchen or waiting in the car. "Mr Spencer, I gather that Iris Blackburn is a very private person. Will she be annoyed that you've brought a stranger along?"

"On the contrary," he said. "I think she might be cheered by seeing a bright young person, especially a fellow Australian."

"But she's been out of Australia for years now, hasn't she?"

"Indeed she has," he said. "She left Australia in the mid-thirties. She'd started doing well with her books there, of course, and was lured to England with the promise of more money and a bigger audience. There aren't many people in Australia, are there?"

"I suppose not," she said. "Not many more than in Greater London, so I'm told."

They drove on in silence, Emma digesting what she had just learned. "So what books did she write when she was still living in Australia?"

He gave a chuckle. "Funnily enough she started writing a couple of Victorian mysteries in the style of Sherlock Holmes, not too successful. Then she created Miss Faversham."

"Oh Miss Faversham," Emma exclaimed, smiling. "I read them all when I was growing up. They were exactly how I imagined England."

"Precisely." Mr Spencer nodded. "Stroke of genius, of course. They struck a nerve with the Australian population. The classic English village mystery with the thatched cottages, the bell ringers, the blacksmith and the old woman who seems so frail but is sharp as a tack. Of course the audience in Australia snapped them up, since many of them had memories of life in the old country. Even if they were second or third generation they'd been told about it, and Iris created the ideal England in which everything was safe and sweet and the only crimes were committed by naughty people from outside the village."

"They were also really clever crimes," Emma said. "And Miss Faversham and her cat Sparky. Well, who wouldn't love them?"

"Everyone loved them, apparently," he said. "Strangely enough they were an instant hit here, too, even though she was Australian. They did very well through the thirties and forties when times were hard and the audience wanted escape reading. But then she created Inspector Melrose. Quite different in tone and subject matter. I think she had grown tired of Miss Faversham's sweet and gentle fictional world and she wanted to stretch herself as a writer. Melrose immediately appealed to both men and women, and the rest is history. You've read some of the books, of course?"

"I've read a couple," Emma said honestly. "But they aren't really my cup of tea. A little dark and bleak for me."

"They are quite dark," he said. "The writing is very spare. Very good."

"And we know nothing of Inspector Melrose's background, apart from the fact that he is Scottish, he likes his whisky and he smokes a pipe," Emma said. "And he's very clever at solving crimes. But I'm not sure we care about him as a person."

Mr Spencer nodded. "Quite true. We know nothing of the family he left behind when he came to Scotland Yard. He's never been married. We don't even know if he's had love affairs, if he prefers men . . . He is the true outsider and observer in London. But the crimes themselves—so complex, so many shades of right and wrong, and her prose is divine."

"Have you ever asked Miss Blackburn about him, whether she actually knows about his early life?"

"Not the sort of thing you ask Iris," he said. "I did once, when I was first her editor, and do you know what she said? She said, 'He hasn't revealed that to me yet. We are just getting to know each other.' As if he was a real person. I was quite shocked."

"Do you know much about Miss Blackburn's life before she came here?"

"Very little," he said. "One gathers she had a harsh childhood in the outback."

"Gosh," Emma said. "She certainly writes like someone who is very educated."

"Indeed she does. A remarkable woman, pretty much self-taught. Iris Blackburn is a pen name, of course."

"So what's her real name?"

"I'm not sure I ever knew. She changed it legally before she came to England."

Emma digested this. "Has anyone ever written a biography of her?"

He chuckled then. "She wouldn't allow it, I'm sure. She'd probably say there was nothing worth telling. I expect there was a lot of pain that she doesn't want to share. She never had a real home, she told me. That's probably why she adores this house so much." He broke off. "Ah. Here is where we turn."

He swung the car sharply to the left down a lane so narrow that only one vehicle would fit. Hedgerows hemmed them in on either side, cutting out views of the fields beyond. Emma noted that his eyesight seemed perfectly all right and he hadn't asked her to help with directions once. After about a mile down this lane, again overhung with hazelnut bushes ripe with their green-cased treasures, they came upon an imposing gateway. On either side of wrought iron gates there were tall brick gateposts, each topped by the statue of a lion, it's paw on a ball (or was it the world?). The discreet ironwork sign incorporated into the gate read "Whitehaven."

"So we have arrived," he said. He got out of the car. Emma could see no house as yet. But before she could follow him, Mr Spencer went to the gatepost on his left and she saw some kind of metal panel in it. He pressed buttons and the gates swung silently open. He got into the car again, looking pleased with himself. "Luckily I remembered the code," he said. "Iris keeps out intruders."

A gravel driveway curved between rhododendron bushes, not in flower at this time of year, then came out to an impressive vista that made Emma gasp again. Lawns stretched down to a small lake and behind it a long white house with black shutters and a red tiled roof. On one side was a veranda, reminding Emma of home, and she thought immediately that this was more an Australian house than an English one. As they approached, a flight of white doves fluttered and dipped ahead of them, and on the lake were white swans.

"It's like a fairy tale," Emma said.

"It is rather lovely, I agree," Mr Spencer replied. "I used to enjoy visiting her more frequently when she was still actively writing. It's a beautiful setting to wake up to in the mornings."

"She hasn't written a book for some time, has she?" Emma asked. "I don't think I've heard about a new Inspector Melrose since I've been in the book business."

"Not for at least five years," he said. "Of course she doesn't need to write another word, but I gather she is doing so now."

"Iris Blackburn is writing a new book?" she asked in wonder.

"So one understands."

"Which is why she wants to meet with her editor," Emma said. "But are you sure I won't be in the way? I wouldn't want a stranger around if I was going to discuss my writing."

"I don't think we'll actually be doing any work today. More of a social call. I expect she feels a bit cut off out here and she rarely travels any more."

As they approached the house he turned to Emma. "I expect there will be other people present. I should fill you in so that you don't say the wrong thing." Emma nodded nervously. "She lives with a secretary/companion, a Miss Cynthia Morton. I don't think she is anything more than a companion, in case you are wondering. Iris bosses her around. Doesn't treat her well at all, I'm afraid, but Cynthia takes it. And there is a cook/housekeeper, Mrs Fisk. Very possessive about Iris. Can also be very bossy and rude." He glanced across at Emma and grinned. "And her agent might be there, too. Jeremy Feathers. I expect you've come across him during your time at Barlow and Barlow."

"I've heard his name mentioned," Emma said.

"He used to be a powerhouse in the business. People trembled when Jeremy came into the room. He doesn't work much any more," Mr Spencer said. "Doesn't have to, of course, with his earnings from Iris. Ah. Here we are. We have arrived safely."

The car came to a halt outside the house and Mr Spencer went to open the car door, then paused. "Oh, I should also mention that it seems Iris has been having memory problems lately. When I've spoken to her she seems quite normal but I gather there are lapses . . . Just so that you are aware."

With that he opened the car door. Emma took a deep breath before she followed him.

# Chapter 3

As Emma was getting out of the car the front door opened and a stout middle-aged woman came out. She looked, to Emma, like the classic British countrywoman, wearing a tweed skirt and a hand-knitted twin-set in a dark, muddy green that made her pale complexion look even more washed out. She wore a strand of pearls at her neck and sensible shoes. Her greying hair was cropped in a mannish bob and there was no hint of make-up on her face.

"Here you are," she said in a throaty posh-accented voice. "And you've made good time, too. Iris is waiting for you in the conservatory. I expect you're ready for a sherry." She turned her attention to Emma. "And I take it you are the young Australian writer. Your book made quite a splash, so we heard. Iris did enjoy it. I'm afraid I didn't read it. I'm not much of a reader, apart from *Country Life* and *Horse and Hound*, much to Iris's dismay. I'm Cynthia. Cynthia Morton. I'm Iris's secretary and general dogsbody." She gave a hearty laugh and pumped Emma's hand in greeting. "Come on then. In we go."

Emma stepped into a square central hall. It had a slate floor and whitewashed walls. The only adornment was a mirror above a glass-topped table on which there was a bowl of fresh flowers. A maid in a black dress with a crisp white apron and cap stepped out to greet them. "Can I take your coat, miss?" she asked.

Emma was conscious that her mack was not up to the standard of the house. She handed it over quickly, then glanced at herself in the mirror. Why hadn't she worn something different today? Her grey flannel pleated skirt, white silky blouse and navy cardigan were almost like a school uniform, making her look ridiculously young and unfashionable. Still, there was nothing she could do about it, but she wondered whether Mr Spencer asking her to accompany him had been a last minute idea or something he'd been asked to do because of her nationality. If it was the latter then he could at least have warned her ahead of time!

"This way," Cynthia Morton said. "Do you need to spend a penny before we go through?"

"No, thank you," Emma muttered.

"If you do later there's a cloakroom off the hall here. That little passageway to the left. Right then. Come on. Let's not keep Iris waiting." Cynthia took off down a long hallway with doors on either side.

At the end she turned into a sitting room with a sofa and armchairs arranged around a marble fireplace. Where French doors should have been there was now the entrance to a magnificent conservatory. The sound of conversation floated through until someone said, "Ah, the visitors have arrived," and all conversation stopped. Emma hung back, letting Cynthia and Mr Spencer go before her. The conservatory was delightfully warm and Emma noticed radiators around the walls. The furniture was white wicker and everywhere there were tropical plants. Orchids hung in baskets and in one corner was a huge palm tree. Beyond the glass walls was a terrace with a fountain. Further off a lawn led to an orchard and woodland. A huge property, Emma thought. Too much for one woman.

She glanced around quickly trying to take in the scene before her. On a wicker chaise, facing the view, was a frail-looking older woman. She must have had fine features once, with high cheekbones and a good jaw, but these now made her face look sunken. Her wrinkles betrayed too many years in the cruel Australian sunshine. Her hair must have once been reddish-blonde but was now streaked with grey and was set in immaculate curls. She wore a pale mauve cashmere jumper and a large opal brooch at her neck. She had a sheepskin rug over her knees, in spite of the warmth of the room. Emma recognized her instantly. There was a photo of her on the wall at Barlow and Barlow, receiving an MBE from the queen. Sitting in a rocking chair beside her was an older man with a shock of grey wiry hair and a round, pink and remarkably boyish face. He had a glass of sherry in his hand. Emma thought she recognized him, that he might have come to Barlow and Barlow on occasion. And on Iris's other side Emma was surprised to see a slim young man in a blazer and slacks, his dark hair neatly parted. Nobody had mentioned him and Emma wondered who he could be. She had understood that Iris had no family.

"Here they are," Cynthia said heartily.

Iris attempted to sit up and Cynthia immediately rushed to help her.

"I'm not a complete invalid yet," Iris snapped. "Don't fuss." She held out her hand to Mr Spencer. "David, my dear. How lovely to see you. It's been ages." Her voice sounded more smooth upper-class English than Australian and Emma guessed that she had worked on it over the years. David Spencer took her hand and kissed it. Then Iris's gaze moved from David and fastened on Emma. "So this is my young compatriot," she said. "Come over here, dear, don't be shy." She held out her hand. Emma wondered if she too was supposed to kiss it, but instead Iris grasped Emma's hand and pulled her forward. The hand was bony. It felt like being caught by a bird of prey.

"So you are Emma Callander," she said. "Writer of *The Blue Gum Murders*." The eyes that fastened on Emma were remarkably bright, in contrast to the old, greyish face.

"I am." Emma smiled at the old woman. "And I am so honoured to meet you, Miss Blackburn."

"Sit down, darling," Iris said. "Pull up a chair for her, dear boy."

The young man leapt out of his own chair, pulled it forward, placing it beside Iris's chaise.

"Thank you, you're a sweetheart," Iris said, giving him a beaming smile. Emma wondered for a moment if he could possibly be a toy boy, but that was too ridiculous to contemplate. But the moment the thought had flashed into her mind Iris said, "I don't think you've met Arthur Gordon, have you David?"

"I don't believe I have," David said. He broke off abruptly, realizing what he was saying and frowned. "Arthur Gordon? But he's . . ."

The young man laughed. "Arthur is my father. I'm Tony Gordon."

He had a nice laugh, Emma thought. Until then he had looked serious, almost worried, but she noticed how his eyes sparkled when he smiled. Not bad, she thought.

"Arthur's boy? All grown up?" David asked.

"That's right, sir," Tony said, still smiling. He glanced across at Emma and their eyes met for a second. "All grown up and qualified as a solicitor. My father is getting ready to retire so I'm taking over the reins of the business."

"Heavens above. How time flies. Well, congratulations." Mr Spencer turned to Emma. "Arthur Gordon was Iris's solicitor for years. He made sure all her contracts were legal."

"And favourable," Iris said, giving a throaty laugh. "Thanks to Mr Gordon I have this house." As the laughter faded Iris looked around the room. "That's my wonderful agent, Jeremy Feathers. Now who are we still missing? Dr Harkness, of course. That man is always late. Probably delivering a baby again. They breed like rabbits around here."

Cynthia leaned closer to her. "Remember Dr Harkness telephoned to say he couldn't make it today?" she said in a low whisper. "He had to go up to town for a medical conference?"

"Oh. Oh yes. Of course. No Dr Harkness then." Iris brushed it off. "That means we're all complete. Shall we go through to lunch then?"

"You haven't even offered us a sherry yet, dear lady," Mr Spencer said. "We are parched after having driven all this way."

"Oh dear me. How ungracious. I'm turning into a terrible hostess," Iris said. "It comes from living out here in the country. Give them a drink, for God's sake, Cynthia, while I talk to this delightful young lady."

Iris turned to examine Emma so critically that Emma felt herself blushing. "So tell me all about yourself, darling," Iris said. "I want to hear all about everything."

"There's not much to tell," Emma said. "I had an idyllic childhood in many ways. My family ran a vineyard in the Hunter Valley."

"Oh, the Hunter Valley. How glorious. Sauvignon blancs?"

"Exactly." Emma smiled, feeling herself relax a little. "And there were no other children within reach so I spent a lot of time alone."

"Did you do any writing in those days?"

"Yes, I did." Emma looked down at her hands. "Just silly little stories, but I was always pretending to be someone else."

"Just like me," Iris said. "My stories were my escape from what was a harsh reality. So go on. What else did you do?"

"I rode my pony, swam in the pond and read a lot of books, including your Miss Favershams, until I was sent off to boarding school when I was thirteen."

"How was boarding school? I hear they can be pretty grim, although when I was a girl I longed to go to school."

"Mine was quite nice," Emma said. "There were some rich and snooty girls who looked down on me, but on the whole I enjoyed my time there. I was all set to go to university when my father died."

"That's so sad. What was it, heart attack?"

Emma shook her head. "A horrible accident. He was killed when a piece of farm equipment rolled onto him."

"You poor little thing," Iris said. She gripped Emma's hand again. "So which university were you heading to, Newcastle or Sydney?" Iris asked.

"Actually I'd been offered a scholarship to Oxford."

"To Oxford. My my. Impressive. But you didn't take it?"

"I couldn't," Emma said. "My mother was a wreck. Someone had to look after her. And what's more we lost our home. The vineyard was owned by the family trust and my father's cousin came to run it. I suppose we could have stayed on, although it would have been really crowded with his family there. I had to find a job. So we moved down to Sydney and I worked in a bookshop."

"Good training for a writer," Iris said.

Cynthia put a glass of sherry into Emma's hand, but she hesitated to take a sip while Iris was still grilling her.

"It was. The owner was a wonderful old man, and when my mother got married again he let me live above the shop so I didn't have to pay rent." She paused. "He even helped me polish my book."

"Ah yes. The famous book," Iris said. "I found it most interesting. That little Abo boy. What a character. Where did he come from?"

Emma tried not to wince at the derogative term, obviously quite accepted in Australia in Iris Blackburn's day. "There was an aboriginal family who helped with the horses at our vineyard," Emma said. "The young son was so bright and talented and should have had a great future. But the way most people spoke to him and his family . . . it was awful. They treated them like less than human. And once there was a minor theft in the neighbourhood and immediately his family was suspected. I remember thinking at the time if he was arrested he'd get no justice from a white jury."

Iris was nodding while she spoke. "That's what gripped me about this story," Iris said. "Justice. You care about justice. You wanted to make things right. That's exactly what I do with Inspector Melrose. He has to make sure justice is served in every case. It matters to me. I've been passionate about it. That's why my books resonate with so many people. In real life there is often no justice."

She broke off, looked around, then laughed. "Listen to me, preaching away again. Drink your sherry, darling, and have one of the cheese puffs. Mrs Fisk is a whiz at cheese puffs."

Cynthia held out a plate and Emma took one. Before she could take a bite Iris asked, "So what is the next book about? Also set in Australia? Same characters?"

Emma hesitated. "I haven't started on a next book yet. Frankly I'm finding it hard, feeling so much like a fish out of water here. I can't write about London. I still don't know enough about how people think and interact, and yet Australia seems so remote now. To be honest I've been feeling quite homesick lately. I'm thinking of going back home."

"No, you can't do that!" Iris said the words so forcefully that Emma almost spilled her sherry. Iris looked around the room. "We won't let her go, will we, darlings?"

"Not until she's written the next book," Jeremy Feathers said quickly, and Emma watched him glance at Mr Spencer.

At that moment a woman appeared in the doorway. She was short and round with hair pinned back in a bun and wearing a flowery pinny. "If you don't come in for your lunch soon the soufflé will have fallen!" she announced, hands on her hips.

As they walked through to lunch Tony fell into step beside Emma. "Well done," he muttered moving closer to her. "You survived a cross-examination worse than being in court."

Emma shot him a grateful smile and he returned it.

# Chapter 4

Lunch was a most satisfying meal. The soufflé was light and fluffy, accompanied by asparagus and served with a glass of sparkling wine. The pudding that followed was a pavlova. "In your honour, my darling," Iris said, patting Emma's hand. She looked around at the other guests. "I don't think there is a single Australian home that doesn't serve a pavlova to guests on special occasions."

Emma nodded. "Ours was always with passion fruit. I do miss that."

"Ah yes. Passion fruit. So delicious, but those bloody seeds are so annoying." Iris laughed again. Emma noticed that Iris had got through two glasses of wine and that Cynthia was watching her nervously.

"So where exactly did you grow up?" Emma asked.

"Where didn't I?" Iris was still chuckling. "All over, that's the answer. Never in one place long enough to feel like it was home. My father was a bit of a drifter, I suppose you could say. He never stuck with one job for long. We'd be in Victoria and he'd hear of a mining opportunity, a new gold strike or copper or something and off we'd go again. My poor mum was very patient and never complained, at least to me. But it meant I never had proper schooling, and then they both died when I was quite young and I found myself working as a maid. What a shock that was, I could tell you. The first night on that sheep station there was a thump, and a dead sheep had been delivered to the back porch. I was told to go and skin it and butcher it. As if I had any idea how to do that! I'd never done manual work before, but do you know what? By God I did it! I went away and threw up afterwards but I did it. I wasn't going to let the buggers beat me." She wagged a finger. "I'd like to see the youth of today do that. Your generation has grown up coddled. You've never really faced a challenge."

Tony caught Emma's gaze and gave her a wink. She felt her cheeks turning hot again and was annoyed with herself for acting like a schoolgirl. He was just being friendly, she told herself, but it felt good to have an ally.

Iris took another good swig of wine. Her face grew wistful. "But we were once in the Hunter Valley. I liked it a lot. So green, and the scent of all those gum trees. And the bellbirds. Ah yes. I'd happily have stayed on there."

Emma felt the homesickness welling up at the mention of the bellbirds. She had proved that she was not a big-city girl. But would she be able to write another book if she moved back to Australia? Here she had a willing publisher, waiting for her. All she needed was inspiration.

Mrs Fisk came in carrying a tray with coffee cups on it. "I suppose you'll be wanting your coffee now," she snapped, glaring at them, then proceeded to pour the coffee.

"Now," Iris announced, when they had finished their cups, "I'm going to take my nap, same as I do every day, and you gentlemen can show Emma the grounds. Show her the sunken garden. She'll like that. I've got some Aussie plants there."

Tony Gordon stood up, but Iris gripped his sleeve, restraining him. "Not you, darling. You have to entertain Cynthia while I snooze, and I may need you later."

Tony looked puzzled but sat down again. Emma felt a stupid surge of disappointment that he wasn't coming with them.

"Shall we?" David stood and helped Emma out of her seat. "Do you need your coat? I think it's quite pleasant out there now."

The shoes Emma was wearing were not suitable for walking through wet grass, but it had been a command, not a request, so she had to comply. She was still feeling a little overwhelmed at the way Iris had taken to her, a little bit like a fraud that Iris felt her book was worth praising. Perhaps like her Iris was homesick at times and had enjoyed being taken to the Hunter Valley in Emma's story.

Jeremy Feathers had accompanied them, a big man wearing a beautifully tailored suit and a grey silk cravat. Being Iris's agent must have been profitable, Emma thought. They came out of the house to a pleasant afternoon of slanted sunlight and puffy white clouds. The men set off across the forecourt, then turned to the right. Emma wondered how far they intended to walk, since her heels would not make walking across lawns easy. Also she was not used to wine at midday and felt the effect of both wine and sherry buzzing in her head.

"Let's go this way," David said. "Iris wants to show you her prize." They followed a path around the house and then between sections of lawn and flower garden. Ahead of them was a high hedge that blocked the view of what lay beyond. As they came closer Emma saw that the hedge hid a tall brick wall with a door in it.

Jeremy turned the doorknob and motioned for Emma to go first. She gasped as she stood at the top of a shallow flight of steps. The sunken garden below was arranged in a series of flower beds with gravel paths between them. The last roses were still putting on a magnificent show, although white and yellow petals had fallen onto the raked paths. Creepers covered the old brick walls, their leaves now turning a vibrant red. The air smelled of perfume and hummed with the buzz of bees. In the centre was a fountain, splashing gently, and dotted around were white marble benches. Several white doves were bathing themselves in the fountain basin, and their cooing echoed from the high walls.

"It's like the Secret Garden!" she exclaimed.

The two men smiled. "It certainly is," Jeremy said. "I rather think Iris created it to be so. She had this house completely rebuilt to her taste, you know, and the grounds, too. It was quite a ruin when she bought it. She likes to come here when she is creating. She says it takes her out of the world and helps her think."

"I'm sure it does," Emma said. "It's absolutely lovely."

"Shall we sit?" David said, patting a bench beside him.

Emma sat and Jeremy came to sit on her other side, almost squashing her. She glanced warily. Why were they sitting together like this, all close together on one bench when there were other seats around? Was she being paranoid? she asked herself. She was alone in a walled garden with two strange men. She glanced back at the gate, still standing open. She could make her getaway if she needed to.

"You may have wondered why you were brought here," Jeremy said. He had a big, hearty voice, but he was speaking in a hushed undertone as if he didn't want any outsider to hear.

"Yes, I did wonder," she said. "I presumed it was because I'm a fellow Australian and she was curious to meet me."

"That's true," Jeremy said. "She wanted to give you the once over, to see if you'd do."

"Do what?"

Jeremy cleared his throat and looked across at David. David hesitated before saying, "I mentioned earlier that Iris is writing another book."

"Yes, you did. How wonderful."

"Not so wonderful," David said. "I also mentioned that she is having memory lapses. You probably noticed a couple at luncheon. She called Tony by his father's name. She forgot the doctor couldn't make it today."

Emma stared at him, wondering where this was leading. Did Iris now need someone to be with her? A companion? But she already had Cynthia.

"She's started the book, Emma," Jeremy said. "But she can't finish it. She can't remember what was supposed to happen. She gets very frustrated and upset and she has come to realize that she might never be able to finish it. But it's important to her. It's Inspector Melrose's first case. It's like putting a seal on the whole series. The book in which we finally get to know who Melrose really is."

Emma was still staring at Jeremy. "Why are you telling me this?"

"Because she wants you to finish the book," Jeremy said.

"Me?" The word came out unnaturally loud, causing the doves to flutter away, their wings flapping like paper. She gave an uneasy laugh. "But that's ridiculous. I'm the last person she'd want. I have written one small book. I have no experience. She could have any writer. Anyone would be honoured to work with her."

"She wants you," David said. "She is quite adamant about it."

"Why? Why on earth would she want me?" Her words echoed around the garden.

"Who can tell how Iris's mind works?" Jeremy chuckled. "She's always been a law unto herself. What other Australian would decide to write a series featuring a Scottish detective who drinks whisky when she knows nothing about either? But if you want an answer, my dear Emma, I think perhaps she sees something of herself as a young woman in you."

"And she just told you that your story resonated with her. She says she's passionate about justice," David added.

Emma shook her head fiercely. "I'm sorry but I couldn't do it. At least I couldn't do justice to an Iris Blackburn novel. You've read my book. You were the one who decided to publish it, Mr Spencer. It's a typical small first novel. You said it had promise. But promise isn't the same as being a fully-fledged writer."

When neither man said anything she went on. "I told you before that the Melrose books are not my style—the prose is too spare and the subjects a little too dark. I don't think I am the right person at all."

"Nevertheless Iris wants you, and Iris is accustomed to getting her own way."

She had been looking at David as he spoke. Jeremy touched her hand, making her jump. "You do realize that this would make you as a writer. You'd have the clout to do what you wanted after this."

Emma still shook her head, digesting the truth in this statement. "I'd be afraid of letting Iris down."

"You'll never know unless you try," Jeremy said. "And if it wasn't up to snuff, if Iris didn't like what you'd done, then who would know, apart from us? You'd go your merry way, go back to answering the morning post at Barlow and Barlow, and she'd find somebody else."

"I suppose so," Emma had to agree. "But I have to tell you I know nothing about the workings of Scotland Yard or the crime scene in London. I've only been here a short while, and I live in a little Australian enclave in Earl's Court."

"This book doesn't take place in London," David said. "I mentioned it was Melrose's first case. In this book he's a young policeman in Glasgow, solving a crime on the Isle of Skye."

Now Emma laughed. "This is even more absurd. I've never been to Scotland. I've never even met a Scottish person. All I know is that they play bagpipes, wear kilts and eat haggis."

"You'll have to go there, naturally," Jeremy said. "Go and see the location for yourself. Get the feel for the place."

Emma shifted nervously on the bench, conscious of the two men sitting close to her. "I don't think you realize that I'm living on a junior assistant's salary. The money I have saved is for my ticket home. I simply couldn't afford to travel to Scotland."

"My dear girl . . ." Jeremy shook his head as he patted her hand again. "Has it not sunk in that if you're a cowriter this book will make you awfully rich? You won't need to live in Earl's Court any more. And of course you will be advanced the funds to go to Scotland for as long as you need. Iris is adamant that you get everything right."

"Oh, I see," Emma said, still digesting this. "But a few days in Scotland is not going to make me an expert on the Scots, is it?"

"Stay as long as you like," Jeremy said. "And the good thing is that Melrose is also an outsider on the island of Skye. He's from the slums of Glasgow. It's like another world for him, too."

"Gosh. It's very tempting, I must admit," Emma said. "But as I said before I don't think I could imitate her style."

"When you go home today you will take the chapters she's written so far. I think you'll be surprised. It feels quite different from the other books. More like a very young Iris Blackburn before she found the voice that made her famous. Quite descriptive, almost flowery."

"Crikey," Emma said. "I wonder what made her do this?"

She turned to Jeremy. He spread his hands as if he was as perplexed as she was. "I can only think that she wanted to show she was more than the Melrose books. She felt trapped in his world sometimes, you know. She said to me more than once, 'Why did I ever invent that bloody man?'"

"If you want my opinion," David began, making Emma swivel towards him, "I think she wants finally to understand Melrose, where he came from. To show him as a human being. You said yourself that we don't know much about him. A Scottish outsider in London, a reclusive sort of person in a way. Smokes his pipe. Appreciates his whisky. But we have never seen a glimpse of his life before he came south. She wants to make the series complete, answer everyone's questions."

"I see," Emma said.

"Think of it as a literary swan song . . . only she's bitten off more than she can chew," David said. "She was diagnosed with dementia before she started the book, but she plunged ahead anyway, hoping to have it all on paper before her memory failed her. Now she just can't come up with the words."

"Poor thing. How horrible for her—to have a brilliant creative mind and then to know it's slipping away."

"So you'd want to help her if you could?" Jeremy asked, smiling again.

"If I could," she repeated. "But how can I possibly know how she wanted her story to end? How can I reveal Melrose's character when I hardly know anything about him?"

"You should probably work your way through the rest of the series," David said. "See what snippets of himself he reveals."

Emma nodded, chewing on her bottom lip, something she did when stressed.

"Iris will work with you, I'm sure," Jeremy said. "Maybe her memory will come back in bits and bobs and what you've written will trigger exactly what she wanted to say."

"At least this is what we hope," David said.

Emma was still fighting to stay reasonable. A small voice whispered that what they were saying was true. If she was cowriter of an Iris Blackburn novel she'd be set for life. But she tried to picture herself writing about a reclusive Scot who drank whisky, and it seemed an impossible task.

"I really don't know what to say," she said at last.

"Then don't make the decision now," Jeremy said kindly. He patted her knee, which somehow didn't seem like too familiar a gesture. "Read what she has written so far, and then you can decide whether you dare take it on. That's fair, isn't it?"

"Yes. I suppose it is," she said. Another worry surfaced. "But what about my job, Mr Spencer? How can I go off to Scotland and come down here, then write a book if I'm supposed to be at work all day?"

"My dear girl, I think Barlow and Barlow will second you to Iris for as long as she needs you. In fact, if you decide to take on the book she'll want you close at hand so she can keep up with what you're writing. There's a guest cottage by the swimming pool. Iris will put that at your disposal, so there's no need to keep coming down from London."

Emma put her hands to her cheeks. She was conscious of the splashing of the fountain and the cooing of the doves now on top of the wall. Images raced through her head: the allure of being rich and famous, the chance to sit and write in this lovely garden and above all the chance to prove herself as a writer. She'd be a fool to turn it down.

"All right," she said. "I'll read what she has written so far, and if I think I can give it a good shot, then I'll do it."

"That's our girl." Jeremy put an arm around her shoulders and hugged her to him. "I don't think you'll regret this."

# Chapter 5

When they returned to the house Emma expected Iris to be resting as she had said, but instead they heard voices from another room at the back of the house, then Iris's unmistakable laugh, an almost masculine deep-throated chuckle.

"Ah, that's where they are. The music room," Jeremy said and led the way to a room at the rear of the house. This was another sitting room on a more lavish scale although still with the country house feel—chintz-covered sofas and armchairs, low tables, potted plants and by the window a white grand piano. Iris was lounging on one of the sofas, still with the sheepskin rug over her knees, although again the room felt almost too warm. Cynthia Morton perched on the arm of the sofa, hovering protectively, and Tony Gordon sat in an armchair by the fire, smoking a cigarette.

Iris sat up as they came in.

"Well?" she asked, leaning forward like an expectant baby bird. "What does she say?"

"She needed some persuading," Jeremy said. "She said she'll read what you've already written and then see . . ."

"See what? What is there to see?" Iris's voice became shrill. Now Emma heard a hint of Australian in it.

"To see if I can do justice to it, Miss Blackburn," Emma said.

Cynthia leaned over to face Iris. "What are we talking about? Do justice to what?"

"I've decided I can't finish the book, Cindy. I want Emma to do it for me."

"You want her to finish your book? Why wasn't I told about this?" Cynthia demanded. "You went behind my back. And if you ask me, it's a stupid idea. Why ask her, of all people? A little slip of a girl who's written a tiny book and you want her to write an Iris Blackburn novel. You're losing your marbles, Iris. You should have consulted me first."

"And why would I do that?" Iris asked, staring at her calmly. "As far as I remember you are neither my publisher nor my agent."

Cynthia's face turned bright red. Emma was still standing, now feeling horribly embarrassed. Iris turned away from Cynthia and reached out a hand to Emma. "Come and sit beside me, darling. And don't be scared. You'll do beautifully, I'm sure. Together we'll finish the best Inspector Melrose novel ever."

Emma allowed herself to be led to the sofa beside Iris. "Miss Blackburn," she said, "I'm afraid you might be overestimating my talents. It's not as if I've had much experience as a writer, and I've no idea about Scotland or Scottish people for that matter. I've never even met one."

"You've told her you want her to go and see for herself, haven't you?" Iris demanded, glaring at Jeremy. "I want her to go and get the feel of the place and the people. I want her to see it as if through Melrose's eyes." She turned back to Emma, patting her hand. "I want you to feel and to see just as he did. As the outsider. The man with no preknowledge, not knowing what to expect. That's what I want. That element of surprise everywhere you go." Her fingers closed around Emma's hand, squeezing it hard. "You will do it for me, won't you? I'm placing all my hopes in you."

"I can't promise anything until I've read the pages you've already written."

"Go and get her the manuscript, Cindy," Iris said. "It's on the desk in my study."

Before Cynthia could move David said, "Remember you already gave the manuscript to me to look at, Iris. I have it with me in my briefcase. I can give it to Emma when we're back in London."

"No!" Cynthia said angrily. "Absolutely not. This is utter folly, Iris. Those pages should not leave this house. You want to give them to a strange girl you know nothing about? What is to stop her from selling them to the highest bidder? Tell her, Tony. Tell her she's being reckless and foolish."

Tony Gordon had been sitting silently until then. He cleared his throat, obviously also embarrassed by the tense scene. "It might be wise, Iris, to have Emma sign some sort of contract in which she acknowledges that you are the creator and she has no rights to the material and is forbidden to share it with anyone outside this room." He gave Emma a sort of apologetic glance. Emma realized that he was Iris's lawyer and what he said was right, but it made her feel he was not quite the ally she had first thought.

"That's not a bad idea," Jeremy said. "I'm sure Emma is a most trustworthy young person, but a flatmate or a boyfriend could seize the opportunity to make a quick bob or two."

"Very well," Iris said. "If you're all so adamant about not trusting poor Emma then she shall read the manuscript here. Make the guesthouse ready for her, Cindy. We wanted her to move in anyway once she starts writing. She can move in now, instead."

"I can't move in today, Miss Blackburn," Emma said. "I don't have any of my things with me, and I'd have to tell my flatmates. And I'd have to keep on paying my rent there. It wouldn't be fair to leave them in the lurch."

"See what I told you?" Iris said, still holding Emma's hand. "A strong sense of justice and fairness. That's what I wanted. She's going to be perfect."

Cynthia stood up. "Huh," she said. "Absolute rubbish." And she stalked out of the room.

They were forced to stay for tea, which included tiny sandwiches, scones, a Victoria sponge and Eccles cakes. Emma was still feeling full from the large lunch but felt she had to eat what was offered to her by the glowering Mrs Fisk. In spite of her hostile nature it was clear Mrs Fisk was a wonderful cook.

"They won't be staying for dinner, I take it?" she demanded. "Only I need to know now if I'm to put an extra chicken in the oven."

"Don't worry, Mrs Fisk. We have to drive back before dark," David said. Emma gave a small sigh of relief that she wouldn't have to face another meal and the pressure of expectations she hadn't even had time to process. They finally parted with Emma agreeing to return the next day, Tony agreeing to draw up a rudimentary contract to protect Iris's rights but also Emma's.

"If she reads the pages and decides not to go ahead then you should agree to compensate her for the time she's put in, Iris," he said. "You have to be fair to Emma. You're asking a lot of her." He looked across to Emma, giving her a little nod.

"Of course, dear boy. Put it all in writing. Make it legal and binding." Iris laughed. "And you, my dear, are going to show up nice and early in the morning." She wagged a finger at Emma. "Are you going to drive her again, David?"

"I'm afraid I can't, Iris. I have a meeting with another writer. Emma will have to come down on the train and then get a taxi from Tunbridge Wells."

"I can meet her at Tunbridge Wells," Tony said, getting up from his seat. "My office isn't far from the station." He fished in his top pocket. "Here's my card, Emma. Phone me from the station and I'll come to pick you up."

"That's awfully good of you," Emma said, but he waved this aside. "Not at all. I have to be at Iris's anyway with the contract to make you sign your life away." He smiled as he said it but Emma shivered. It had all gone so fast and was feeling so final and overwhelming.

Emma remained silent for a long time as they drove back to London and twilight fell. David tried to be cheerful. "That was quite a scene back there, wasn't it? Lots of drama. I'm afraid Iris does like to feed on drama—she pits Cynthia against Jeremy and both against me at times, but she's clearly taken with you."

"I just hope she doesn't have a false idea of me and my talents," Emma said.

"Don't underestimate yourself, my dear," David said. "Remember I was the one who decided to publish your book. Barlow and Barlow does not publish second-rate stuff. It was my reputation on the line, too."

They drove on. Streetlights had now come on and light reflected from the road, still wet from an earlier rain shower. Emma felt as if she were driving through a dream. None of what had happened seemed real to her.

"Why do you think Miss Blackburn wants to write about Melrose's early life and set a mystery in Scotland?" she asked. "Does she know much about Scotland herself? Has she spent a lot of time there?"

David had to smile. "Very little. She's been to speak in Edinburgh and got an honorary degree from the University of St Andrews, and I think she once did a tour of the Highlands when she first came to this country, but that's about it. I don't know how she planned to write and finish this book if you hadn't come along. She certainly isn't up to the journey to Skye herself, and I know as little about the Scots as you do. We'd all be floundering in the dark. Still, she has these whims from time to time and they've usually turned out well for her. Remember one of the Melrose books was about the discovery of artifacts from Henry VIII. She knew nothing about him or about archaeology, but she managed to write a convincing book and we didn't get any of those horrid letters pointing out all our errors. So I'm sure she would have done her research well enough to be convincing. But now you have the chance to go to Scotland in person and be a reporter. Not much will have changed on Skye since the thirties, which is when this book takes place."

"I'm actually anxious to read it now," Emma said.

"You'll find it quite intriguing," David replied. "I certainly did. When I got to the end, or rather where she simply stopped writing, I was really annoyed. I wanted to know what happened next. The sad thing is that I think Iris also wants to know and doesn't have the answer."

They made their way past the Elephant and Castle, past the Oval cricket ground, and approached Central London.

"I'll drive you home," David said.

"Oh, that's not necessary, sir," Emma said hastily. "I can easily take the Tube."

"No sense in taking you back to the office. I don't need to go there myself tonight, and I live out in Ealing. So you're on the way."

"Thank you. You're very kind." She smiled at him.

"Not at all. I have to look after Iris's latest asset," he replied.

They crossed the Thames at Chelsea Bridge with the great power station belching out white smoke beside them, then passed the Brompton Cemetery and arrived in Earl's Court. David drew up in front of the three-storey Victorian that housed Emma's flat.

"Good luck tomorrow," he said to Emma. "In spite of the volatility you've seen, I think that Iris is essentially a kind person and won't give you trouble. She's been rather spoiled and isolated for too long. It's not good to be too rich and too adored. Just remember that when you are famous."

Emma had to laugh. "I can't see that happening to me. Being famous, I mean. If Iris pays me I'll probably take the money and run straight back to Australia, buy myself a little bungalow with a couple of kangaroos out back and be very happy."

"What about a young man in your life? When does he enter into it? Don't you want a home and family?"

"Yes, I suppose I do," she said. "I've just not met the right person yet."

"You will. You're still very young. You have your whole life ahead of you. You don't want to wind up like me, a dried-up old man who spends his evenings with a book and a cup of cocoa."

"You were never married?" Emma asked.

"I was," he said. "I'm a widower now. I've got a daughter. She lives in Cornwall so we don't see each other often, but she's a dear girl. She married a farmer and they have three boys. I do enjoy going to visit. Families are important, I think. I'm sorry you lost yours."

Emma squeezed her eyes shut, afraid she would cry. She nodded. Then she took a deep breath and opened the car door. "Thank you for driving me home, Mr Spencer."

"Report in and let me know how things are going with Iris," he said.

"I will."

Emma ran up the front steps and fished for her door key as he drove away.

# Chapter 6

Music was blasting out from the record player as Emma opened her front door. Gerry and the Pacemakers. "Ferry Cross the Mersey." They were Jilly's new favourites. She had a pin-up of Gerry on her bedroom wall and kissed it.

Jilly was sitting on the couch painting her toenails, and Robyn was in the kitchenette stirring something on the stove. They both looked up as Emma came in.

"You're late tonight," Jilly said. "Did you have to work late again? I hope they pay you overtime."

"Anyway, you're just in time," Robyn said. "I've made plenty. It's a new pasta dish I'm experimenting with. I read the recipe in *Woman's Own*. Spaghetti and meatballs. I can't vouch for the meatballs."

Emma looked at them fondly, realizing how much she appreciated their presence in an otherwise hostile, strange city. And now she might be about to walk away from them, to give up this flat and their easy camaraderie.

"Thanks but I don't think I could eat another thing ever," she said. "You'll never guess where I've been today."

"Been?"

"Out into the country with Mr Spencer."

Before she could go on Jilly grinned. "Out for the day with the boss, eh? Nudge nudge, wink wink. Did you go to Brighton? Mr and Mrs Smith?"

"Shut up," Emma said, laughing. "It was all perfectly respectable. And you won't believe who I met."

"Well, don't keep us in suspense," Robyn said, coming through from the kitchenette with a spatula in her hand.

"I was taken to meet Iris Blackburn."

"Crikey," Jilly said. "That's quite an honour, isn't it? How was she?"

"Very friendly to me, because I'm a fellow Aussie, I think, but it's all rather overwhelming." She sat on the sofa beside Jilly. "I'm not sure if I'm supposed to tell you this, and you mustn't repeat it, but she's writing another book and wants me to help her finish it."

"You're joking!" Jilly gave a loud laugh. "Good one. Pull the other leg, it's got bells on."

"No, I'm not joking. I'm serious," Emma said. "She's writing her final book, only she's been diagnosed with dementia and she can't finish it. And for some ridiculous reason she's got it into her head that I'm the person to finish it for her."

"Can you do that, do you think?" Robyn came to perch on the arm of the sofa. "Is it set in Australia? Is that why she wants you?"

"No, that's the weird thing. It's set in Scotland."

Jilly put her hand up to her mouth to stifle a laugh. "Scotland? And what exactly do you know about Scotland?"

"Absolutely bugger all," Emma said. "That's what I told them."

"Them?"

"It was her agent and her editor who were given the task of convincing me to do this, not Iris herself."

"So how do you know she actually wants you to do it?"

"Oh yes, she really does. When we went back into the house—and you should see the house by the way—pretty bloody fancy—she asked, 'Well, what does she say?' in a very aggressive voice."

"So, Emmie," Robyn said. "Why do you think she's adamant about wanting you?"

Emma sighed. "It's the book I wrote. She seems quite taken with it. She says I have her strong sense of justice and that's what she wants for this book. She hasn't written anything for five or six years, you know, and she wants to wrap up her Inspector Melrose series in a way that's satisfying to her."

"So it's Melrose's last case?" Jilly asked.

"That's another weird thing. It's his first case, when he was a young man in Scotland, before he was lured south to Scotland Yard."

Emma saw a look pass between Jilly and Robyn.

"How on earth will you do it? Read *Rob Roy* in a hurry?" Jilly asked. "How does one get the feel for how the Scots sound and behave? I've only met two in my life and they were both quite brash and aggressive." She paused. "And could they knock back the booze!"

"Iris wants me to go there in person. To stay as long as it takes."

"You're going to Scotland?" Robyn asked.

Emma squirmed nervously in her seat. "I haven't said yes yet. I'm going to read the pages she's already written and see if I could possibly take a shot at writing the rest of the book. If it's really beyond me, then I'll say thanks and walk away."

Robyn got up again, dashing across to the kitchen, where the bubbling sound had become a little too intense. "Damn! The spaghetti's boiling over."

She came back into the room. "It's just dawning on me what this could mean for you, Em," she said. "If it really worked out and you cowrote an Iris Blackburn novel everyone would want a book from you."

"Is she actually going to put your name on the book as a cowriter?" Jilly asked. "Or is she going to pretend she wrote the entire thing and pay you enough to stay silent?"

"We haven't got that far yet," Emma said. "Her lawyer is drawing up a contract for me to review tomorrow morning—he's rather dishy by the way. Smooth but appealing in a British sort of way."

"Ah, now we get why she wants to do it." Jilly dug Emma in the side. "Romance at last for the virgin queen."

Emma blushed.

"Forget about romance," the ever-practical Robyn said. "They are going to pay you for this, aren't they? The whole thing is not on spec—you going to Scotland and writing a book and then finding it isn't what they wanted?"

"I think Iris will be fair," Emma replied, now wondering how much she actually knew. "She did say they'd take care of my expenses in Scotland, and Barlow and Barlow will give me a leave of absence, so at the very worst I'll get a free Scottish holiday."

"How long do you think you'll be gone?" Robyn asked, now looking worried. "What about this place and the rent? And what if you do decide to write the book with her? Can you still live here and commute?"

"No. She wants me to move into her guest cottage," Emma said. "So I'm not sure about the flat. Oh, I'll pay my rent until I know what I'm doing, and then we'll have to decide if you want another flatmate instead of me." She looked up, suddenly distraught. "I don't want to leave you guys. You're my family here."

"We don't want you to leave either. We'd have to break in a new girl," Jilly said. "That's not always easy. Luckily you were well trained from boarding school when you came to us, but I've heard horror stories."

"Like that girl who brought back blokes every night and had sex with them on the living room floor?" Robyn said and they laughed, breaking the tension.

"When do you get these pages to read?" Jilly asked.

"Tomorrow morning. I have to go down to Tunbridge Wells and Tony, her lawyer, is picking me up from the station and driving me to Iris's house."

"Crikey, that's not much time to think about it," Jilly said. "Are you going to bring back the manuscript to read here?"

Emma shook her head. "They didn't think the pages should leave Iris's house, just in case they fell into the wrong hands. I've got to move into the guest cottage while I read it. That will be good, won't it, because Iris will be there if I want to ask questions."

"Although if she's already gone gaga will she be able to give you the answers?" Robyn said dryly.

"I don't know how bad the dementia is," Emma said. "She sounded quite all there to me today, although she did forget a few things and mixed up names, but I expect that's quite normal for someone over eighty."

"Is that how old she is?" Jilly asked.

"I don't really know. She looks old. I asked if there was a biography of her and David said she wouldn't allow one."

"David? Another beau?"

"Will you shut up about beaux." Emma laughed now. "My boss. Mr Spencer. He's about seventy himself. He's been her editor since she came to this country. I thought he was rather stiff and frightening until now, but he's quite nice when you get to know him." She sat up suddenly. "Oh gosh, I've just realized. I have to pack clothes to take down to Iris's house. I want to look a bit better than today. Why did I have to wear this outfit and look like a *Belles of St Trinian's* schoolgirl?"

"Is Iris rather fashionable?" Jilly asked.

"Obviously rich," Emma said. "Not fashionable, but she wore a lovely cashmere jumper and well-tailored trousers. Of course that might be just because she was having guests to lunch."

"I always thought authors were a sloppy lot," Robyn said. "Going about in their pyjamas until the muse struck."

"I can't ever imagine Iris going about in her pyjamas, but who knows. Oh, and she has a live-in companion."

"Companion, eh?" Jilly winked.

"David said he thought she really is just a companion. Iris bosses her around. She's the classic English countrywoman—brogues and tweeds and home-knitted jumpers. I don't know anything about her yet, how long she's been with Iris or what made her take the job. I expect I'll find out if I have to live there for a while."

"At least you'll get some decent food without having to cook," Jilly said. "I've no doubt people like Iris Blackburn eat well."

"The lunch was delicious. Although the cook is terrifying. I think even Iris is afraid of her, but she does cook divinely, so yes, I'm looking forward to the food."

"Well, this will be our last night together for a while," Robyn said solemnly. "I think we should open the last bottle of plonk to celebrate, don't you?"

"Celebrate getting rid of me? Thanks a lot." Emma pretended to walk away.

"No, you dope. To celebrate our friendship and that one of us is soon going to be rich and famous."

"A likely story," Emma said. "I expect I'll read the pages she's written, decide I can't possibly write anything like it and be back here by the end of the week. Or I'll try to write the book and they'll take one look and say, 'Uh, no thanks.' Don't let my room while I'm gone."

With that she went into her bedroom to pack.

# Chapter 7

Emma woke early, lying in the warmth of her bed, the duvet up around her face, listening to the early-morning sounds of the city. The electric milk float was approaching. She heard the rattle of bottles as the milkman walked to a door nearby. Further away was the hum of traffic, already busy at this hour before dawn. She looked around the room, the ghastly wallpaper in purples and browns that she had loathed to start with, the tiny wardrobe, too small for even her dresses and coats. After almost two years it now felt like home and she was loath to leave it, or to leave the comforting presence of her flatmates.

Then she gave herself a good talking to. "Don't be such a ninny," she said. "You're going to the country for a few days. Just as long as it takes to read the book. You'll read it, decide you couldn't possibly write anything close to Iris Blackburn's brilliant prose, you'll thank her politely for the opportunity and you'll come back to London. End of story."

With those words she got up, went to wash and brush her teeth. But as she was looking at herself in the mirror the thought came to her that this opportunity would get her writing again, force her to write. It might be just the spur she needed. She was going to give it a go. She went back to the bedroom to get dressed. This time she had chosen more carefully from amongst her meagre collection of clothing. She had acquired, thanks to Jilly, who got a great discount at her boutique on Carnaby Street, a dark green pantsuit—the latest thing, according to Jilly. It was smart and businesslike and could be worn with a turtleneck jumper under it if the weather turned colder. She had also packed a couple of merino jumpers she had brought from Australia, her grey skirt, a pair of tweed slacks and her suede jacket. She left out her mack in case she had to wear it over the pantsuit, but so far the day looked bright enough. However, Emma had been in England long enough to know that the saying "fine before seven, rain by eleven" often proved to be true.

She shoved her sponge bag into her tote, along with the notebooks she was never without. Even if the writing with Iris didn't work out, she'd jot down impressions of an English country house for a potential future novel. *Murder of a Famous Writer?* she thought wickedly. She went to the kitchen and put on the kettle for a cup of tea, but she found she was so nervous that she couldn't swallow a bite of toast.

Neither Robyn nor Jilly had put in an appearance yet, and Emma wondered if she'd be wise to slip out now, to avoid embarrassing goodbyes. But she was just retrieving her suitcase when Robyn's door opened and she came out, hair tousled and looking bleary-eyed.

"Oh, you're going already?"

Emma nodded. "I thought it might be easier not to have to say goodbye."

Robyn came over to her. "You're making it sound so final. Aren't you just going for a few days?"

"That's right," Emma said. "But I'm thinking there's a chance that I like what she's written and I might want to finish her book. I'd really like to if I really believed I could do it." She put her hands on Robyn's shoulders. "Just think, Rob. If I get a cut of what Iris Blackburn earns with every book I'd be bloody rich. And if the world knew that I was the cowriter, I wouldn't have trouble selling another book ever."

"Just make sure they don't stiff you then," Robyn said, looking at her kindly. "Make sure you get a contract that suits you, that gives you a fair share of the royalties, not pays you off with a few pounds as a writer for hire."

Emma held her gaze. "You're right. Not that I think I'd have much say in the matter. If they offer me a decent sum I think I'd have to take it, but I would like some sort of credit for my contribution."

"You said she was really keen to have you as the writer," Robyn said. "Remember that. You're not the hired help, you are her rescuer."

Emma gave a nervous chuckle. "Golly. You should be doing this, not me."

"Not me, darling," Robyn said. "I have trouble writing a shopping list. You're a bloody good writer and don't you forget it. Iris Blackburn is lucky to have you." She planted a kiss on Emma's cheek. "Now go and be brilliant."

"Give my love to Jilly," Emma said. "See you soon."

Emma picked up her suitcase and off she went into the morning bustle that was the Earl's Court Road. After the Tube she negotiated the crowd surging into Victoria Station, feeling like a salmon swimming upstream, then boarded a delightfully empty train to Tunbridge Wells, arriving at nine thirty. As she approached the telephone kiosk she hesitated. Had she arrived too early? What time did solicitors start work? Then she decided that if she was early, at least it showed she was keen.

She took out Tony Gordon's card and dialed the number on it.

"Gordon and Tate, Solicitors," said a crisp female voice.

Emma asked for Mr Tony Gordon and he came to the line. "I'll be right over to pick you up," he said. "Look for a decrepit Morris Minor."

She went outside the station and stood waiting on the street. All around her the town was busy with morning commerce although not at the frantic pace of London. It seemed a pleasant place, Emma thought, as if life was simpler and slower here. Then she heard the toot of a horn and the Morris Minor drew up. Tony leaned across to open the door for her.

"Hello, you're bright and early," he said. "Jump in."

Emma climbed cautiously into a front seat with a couple of rips in the upholstery.

"You look nice," Tony said. "Fashionable. Quite Carnaby Street."

Emma gave an embarrassed smile. "Thank you. My one good outfit. My flatmate works in a boutique. I wish I'd worn something better yesterday but I wasn't given any warning."

"I thought you looked fine." He gave her that reassuring smile that made her feel warm inside.

"Sorry about the state of the car," Tony said as they drove off. "It does have a rather lived-in feel to it. I've had it since my Oxford days and plan to replace it when I officially become a partner, which should be going through as we speak."

"Congratulations," she said. "A partner in a law firm at your age. That's pretty good, isn't it?"

Tony's face became guarded. "It wouldn't have happened for quite a while if my father's health hadn't gone downhill. He's needed me to learn the business in a hurry. Luckily every solicitor's office has an old biddy working there who knows everything and secretly runs the place. You'll meet Margo and you'll see."

As he spoke they turned on to a high street. "I should warn you that we're popping in to see my father first, before we go to Iris's," Tony said. "He wants to give you the once over."

"That sounds alarming." Emma shot him an anxious look.

"Don't worry. He's always been most protective of Iris Blackburn's best interests. He probably wants to see for himself that you're not a fraud or an imposter."

"Goodness," Emma said. "I don't see how he could think that, when I was brought to Iris by David Spencer, who she's known for donkey's years. And Iris has read my book."

"I'm sure it's just a formality," Tony said. "My father does like to see for himself, to make his own judgments."

"On whether I'm trustworthy?" Emma said sharply. "Look, if this whole thing is going to be unpleasant I'll just go back to London and get on with my life. I don't need to be here."

"Hold your horses, old thing," Tony said. "Nobody wants to make it unpleasant for you, I'm sure. Just humour my father and we'll be on our way." The car pulled up outside a square brick Georgian house. A brass plate beside the front door stated "Gordon and Tate, Solicitors."

"So who is Mr Tate?" Emma asked.

"Long dead," Tony replied. "He was my grandfather's partner when they started this company, back in Edwardian days."

"But you still have his name on the business?"

"Quaint English tradition." Tony grinned as he got out, then came around to open the door for her. "I expect you've found that we're all about tradition here. Horribly stuffy, too. I expect Australia is like a breath of fresh air compared to us."

"In some ways," she agreed. "Australians believe that everybody is as good as everyone else. There's no class system. But we still cling to a lot of ties to the old country. You'll find a picture of the queen inside every pub in Australia, and they play the national anthem at the end of the cinema every night."

"That's funny," he said. "Come on. Let's go and face the dragon."

"Dragon?" Emma glanced at him apprehensively.

"My father. He can be a bit . . . well, a little bit brusque at times." He gave her an encouraging grin. "But don't worry, his bark is worse than his bite and I'll protect you!"

Tony opened the front door for Emma and they stepped into a narrow hallway. From the open door on the right came the clatter of a typewriter.

"We're here, Margo," Tony called. The clattering stopped. "Is it all right to go through to Mr Arthur?"

A face appeared in the doorway—a rather alarming-looking woman with grey hair drawn back into a severe bun, a shapeless grey cardigan, sharp, birdlike features and dark, little eyes that darted, fixing on Emma. Emma could see that she was deciding whether she was worthy to enter the inner sanctum.

"He's expecting you, Mr Tony," she said. "You may proceed."

"The royal seal of approval," Tony muttered as he led her down the hall and knocked on a door at the back of the building. "No one is allowed to venture further without Margo's approval. Woe to anyone who dares to tiptoe down the hall."

"Come!" said a sharp voice.

Tony opened the door and went in first. "I've brought the young lady from Australia, Father," he said. "You wanted to see her?"

"I do. Come in."

Emma stepped into a pleasant room with royal blue carpet and white walls, lined with bookshelves. The view beyond was of a small garden with a trellis, but the room itself was dominated by a huge mahogany desk. The man behind the desk was a commanding presence, a shock of grey hair, a strong jaw and deep frown lines giving him an aggressive expression. Emma wondered why he was planning to retire, when he still looked so vibrant.

"So you're the young lady who has created such a stir," he said. "Come in. Take a seat."

He motioned to a leather captain's chair in the window. As Emma moved towards the chair she noticed that Mr Gordon was actually sitting in a wheelchair with a rug over his knees.

"I don't think one good review in *The Sunday Times* amounts to creating a stir, sir," she said, attempting to give him a friendly smile because he was still scowling.

"I don't mean the book. I mean yesterday. Quite a kerfuffle, so I understand. Cynthia having a tantrum and not speaking to Iris."

"None of my doing, I assure you," Emma said. "Look, it was not my idea to suggest I could finish her book—in fact I'm fairly sure that I won't be able to. I'm still a very amateur writer, and it's worrying to me that Iris has got it into her head that I'm the one she wants."

Mr Gordon smiled now, making him look less formidable, and Emma realized that the frown lines might be because of pain. "You don't know Iris, my dear. I've been her solicitor since the thirties and she does get these whims. She also likes to get her own way. Once she's made up her mind she won't let go. She's like a dog with a bone. So I would say do your very best to make it happen, then we'll all have an easy life. If not, God help us."

"I will do my best, Mr Gordon, but I can't promise anything. Not every writer can write like someone else, and I've already told her that I have no clue about Scotland or the Scots. I've never met one."

"That's a lie," he said. "You've met two. Right in this room. Gordon is a Scottish name, although my family has been in the south for many generations. But we carry the ancestry and the name proudly, like all Scots do." He glanced up at his son. "Grab a chair, Tony, for God's sake. You make me nervous hovering like that."

"Sorry, Father." Tony pulled up a wooden chair, closer to the desk. Emma wondered if he was scared of his father, or was he just trying to do the right thing with Emma present?

"Now, Miss Callander," Mr Gordon said. "I just want to ask you a few questions. You have to understand that any person working with someone of the stature of Iris Blackburn has to be vetted. There is a lot of money at stake as well as her reputation, and her peace of mind. I consider myself the guardian at her gate."

When Emma nodded he went on. "Now, my dear, your full name?"

"Emma Louise Callander."

"And your date of birth?"

"September the twelfth, nineteen forty-two."

"You've just had a birthday!" He looked quite human now.

"Yes. Last week. My flatmates made a curry. It was rather a disaster." She grinned.

"Where were you born?"

"Where was I born?" She sounded amused that anyone would want to know this. "In New South Wales and to be precise in the hospital in Cessnock, not too far from my home at the winery."

"The winery is called?"

"Callander Wines," she said as if this was a silly question.

"And your father's name?" He was barking out the questions with rapid fire.

This was beginning to annoy Emma. "Rory Callander."

"His full name? Did he have a middle name?"

"I don't know." She stopped to think. "My parents were Mum and Dad. I never used their names. Hang on, wait a minute. I think his middle name was Blake."

"Blake? You're sure?"

She shrugged. "Not sure. I think I saw it written on his death certificate, but I could be wrong."

"No problem. Your mother's name?"

"Amelia May Callander. Only it's not Callander any more, it's Warton. She remarried." She stopped, frowning at him now. "Look, I don't want to appear rude, Mr Gordon, but what has any of this to do with me? My dad is dead. My mum is off somewhere married to someone else, and I'm a grown woman earning my living in London."

Arthur Gordon rested an elbow on the desk, examining her. "Mere formality, my dear. So tell me a bit about your life growing up."

"Is this really necessary?" Emma said, trying not to feel she was being backed into a corner.

He chuckled then. "Not at all. The first part was, just to make sure you are who you claim to be, but now I'm just interested, so humour a sick man, will you?"

"I'm sorry, sir," she said. "Were you in an accident?"

"No accident. A bloody war. I was in the tank regiment in North Africa. A shell landed too close and left me with useless legs. That's why I'm pushing Tony to take over more of the work." She saw the bitterness in his face now.

"I'm so sorry," she repeated.

"So am I. Bloody nuisance, if you'll pardon the language. I used to love my golf and swimming and all those things that make life worthwhile. So humour a poor old invalid, will you?"

"Of course." She smiled now. "I don't have much to tell. I had a normal childhood, quite nice, nothing special."

"You were happy?"

"Yes, happy enough. A bit lonely. There were no other kids around, so I read a lot of books, rode my pony. Tried my hand at writing my own stories."

"Ah, so you've always been a writer?"

Emma gave an awkward shrug. "I've always liked to write. I'm not sure any of it was any good but it was a great outlet for me."

"And you went to school where?"

"I was sent off to boarding school when I was thirteen, and that was quite nice, too. And in the sixth form I was about to apply to the University of Newcastle, not too far from us, when I was offered a scholarship to Oxford."

"Really. How wonderful. But you didn't take it?"

"No."

"Why miss a chance like that? Was it just too far from home at the time?"

"Not at all," she said. She looked away, staring at the view outside the window. "I would have given my eyeteeth to go, but my dad was killed in a freak accident. A farm machine ran over him. And my mum, who was never the strongest of women, completely went to pieces. She had a nervous breakdown. So I couldn't leave her."

"An admirable daughter."

"Not really. It was just the right thing to do."

He was staring at her with interest. "I can see why Iris took to you. She likes people who do the right thing."

"Anyway," Emma said. "It's all in the past now. My mother remarried and she's off living happily on someone else's estate and I'm here, so all is well."

"You don't miss her?"

"Good Lord, no." The words just came out more forcefully than Emma intended. She blushed. "I was never as close to her as I was to my dad. He was a lovely man. He enjoyed life, he loved to laugh, always very active, tennis, swimming, riding . . . You name it, he did them all. And we got along so well. He'd take me with him, show me what he was doing on the estate, and we'd talk about life. My mum . . . well, you could never get close to her. She was always a bit critical, of how I looked, what I was wearing, and I think she wasn't happy being stuck out in the country, although they did lead quite an active social life."

Arthur Gordon nodded. "So you're not homesick here?"

"On the contrary," Emma said. "I'm quite homesick at the moment; in fact if this hadn't turned up I was all set to book my passage home."

"Back to your winery?"

"Oh no." Emma stopped, frowning. "That's now occupied by Dad's cousin and his family. There's not really room for me, and anyway, what would I do out in the back of Bourke?"

"Back of Bourke?" He looked amused.

"Middle of nowhere," she explained. "An Australian expression. Bourke is a town in the outback."

"Such quaint expressions you Australians have." He looked amused. "So what would you do back in Australia?"

"Get a job in Sydney, I suppose. Go to the beach or up to the Blue Mountains. Enjoy the outdoors. That's what I miss here—blue skies, open spaces. You feel so hemmed in in London. I go to Hyde Park and walk around, but it's not the same."

"I've never been a city person myself," Arthur Gordon said and nodded in affirmation. "Well, Miss Callander, I think we've grilled you long enough. My son has a contract for you to sign when you meet with Iris. All a formality to keep her safe."

"And me?" Emma asked. "Am I to be kept safe?"

"I assure you that Miss Blackburn intends to do right by you, Emma. I don't think you'll be disappointed if you follow this through." He waved a dismissing hand. "Off you go then. You know Iris doesn't like to be kept waiting."

# Chapter 8

"Sorry about my dad," Tony said as the ancient car drove away with a slight grinding of gears. "I suspect it had nothing to do with your family and background but more to see how you reacted to being under pressure. Iris can be demanding at times. Dad wanted to make sure you didn't lose your cool and thus upset Iris. You'll find he's quite protective of her. They all are, her little team."

"That's all right," Emma said. "If Iris is going to trust me with her precious manuscript I can understand that you'd all want to know I'm not a crooked or flighty type. I expect someone has already checked into my background in Australia to make sure my story holds up."

"Quite possibly," Tony said. "And of course my dad is angry with the world. Well, who wouldn't be?"

Emma nodded. "It must be awful to be stuck in a wheelchair when you were an active person and there's nothing you can do about it. What about your mum? Does she look after him well?"

Tony frowned. "My mum left my dad in the war. When he came home wounded she decided she didn't want to be stuck with a cripple. She met an American and went off to the States with him. I hardly remember her. I was only about four at the time."

"Oh Tony. I'm so sorry." She resisted an urge to touch his arm. "She left you with your dad?"

He nodded. "She did. Obviously didn't want to be encumbered with a kid. I was actually brought up by our housekeeper. Dad wasn't exactly a fatherly type, you know, and was off doing war work once he'd recovered. Then he sent me off to school at ten."

"Crikey, that's young. Was it awful? I've read books about English schools."

He shrugged. "It was all right. Better than being at home, actually. And I've survived. So have you. And here we are. Let's enjoy the day."

Tunbridge Wells seemed to be an elegant, old-fashioned sort of town with half-timbered white-and-black houses, interesting shops and impressive civic buildings. Not quite as ancient as Oxford, which was the only historic place Emma had visited outside of London. But it had lots of Georgian houses and stately parks. Emma thought she wouldn't mind living somewhere like this if she stayed on in England. As they left the remnants of the town behind, they came out into glorious countryside. The leaves were beginning to turn to shades of yellow, red and brown and glowed in autumn sunlight.

"It's lovely here," Emma commented. "Quite different from London."

Tony smiled. "We're never satisfied with what we have. I feel as if I'm stuck in a dreary backwater of aged colonels. I'd have liked the chance to live in London."

"Where did you train as a lawyer?" she asked.

"I did my law degree at Oxford, then articled to my father," he said.

"Lucky you." She sighed. "That had been my dream, to go to Oxford."

"Yes, it was a perfect experience," he said. "I'm sorry that you couldn't take the scholarship."

"Well, it's too late now," she said.

They slowed as they came upon two young girls riding their ponies along the lane. Emma laughed. "They're so sedate. You should have seen me on my pony. I used to gallop everywhere."

"You can hardly gallop along an English road," he replied, looking at her with amusement. "I had no idea you were such a wild child." Then he broke off. "Which is an odd thing to say because that's what Iris has called her book. *The Wild Girl.*"

"*The Wild Girl*? That's interesting. Now I'm keen to read it."

"You'll identify with the main character," he said, and she glanced up, realizing he was teasing.

"I've become quite civilized since my childhood days," she replied, giving him a mock scolding frown. "Having to earn a living and take care of a sick mother at eighteen does that to you."

He blushed. "I'm sorry. That was crass of me. You must know by now that we British like to rag a bit."

"So do the Aussies," she said. "I guess it's an inherited trait." She examined him, noting the neatly clipped short, dark hair, the dark suit, pale blue shirt and old school tie. It seemed at odds with the cheeky smile and the wink he had given her the day before. Almost as if he was being forced to act as another character. "Do you always have to dress like that in your profession?" She realized as she said it that it was a rather rude question. "Sorry. We Aussies are a bit blunt sometimes."

"Like what?" He looked amused, not upset.

"Conservative—not as in the political party. I mean typical British business male. I bet you even wear a bowler hat when necessary."

He grimaced. "My dad insists I look the part. Also he wants me to look older than I am, so that the clients trust me. Actually I'd like to grow my hair a bit. Not down to my shoulders as I gather you see in London now, but at least Beatles length."

She laughed. "I don't see you as another Ringo."

"You're right. I don't play the drums. But I did play the trumpet at school. I wasn't very good." He paused, negotiating a sharp bend in the lane. "Actually my girlfriend is encouraging me to grow my hair."

*Girlfriend. Make a note of that,* she told herself, feeling stupid for what she had perceived as a developing closeness with him. Of course he had a girlfriend. He was just being friendly because Iris had told him to be nice to her. She fought back an absurd feeling of disappointment and kept her expression serene. "What's her name?"

"Isobel."

"Is her last name Ringing?" It now felt important to keep the mood light.

"What?" He gave her a questioning glance.

"Isobel Ringing?" she said.

"Oh. That was dense of me." He chuckled. "No, it's Farley. Her father is also a solicitor, and Dad has visions of the firms being joined one day."

"He wants you to marry her so that he can unite two lawyers' offices?"

"Oh, don't get me wrong," Tony said. "She's a really nice girl. Very intelligent. She's a trainee lawyer like me. And she's mad about horses. You'd probably get along well since you galloped everywhere on your pony." He glanced at Emma for affirmation. She nodded. "She goes in for these gymkhanas. Jumps fences and things." He shuddered. "Absolutely not my cup of tea. And I can't stand her horsy crowd. But what about you? Have you found a good chap in England yet, or are you still pining for someone in Australia?"

"Neither," she said, trying to sound breezy and light-hearted. "Footloose and fancy-free. It doesn't make sense to get involved when I'm going home soon."

"No. Of course not." He broke off. "So you're really going back?"

"That's the plan. I've come. I've seen. I haven't exactly conquered. Now I need my sunshine and beaches."

"Sounds good," Tony said. "I'd like to travel more, see the world."

"Don't solicitors make good money?"

"Oh yes. Eventually when you build up the client list. But I was articled until two years ago."

"What does that mean? Like an apprenticeship?"

"Exactly. So you only get paid a small stipend because you're still learning. Then you have to take the exam, and if you pass you're a qualified lawyer."

"Good for you." She looked around. "And then you can see the world." A fleeting image of Tony standing beside her at the Taj

Mahal flashed through her head. *Stop it,* she told herself. "Oh, we're nearly there."

"So we are. Good memory. Now don't talk to me. I don't want to miss the gate like I did the other day. Ah, here we are."

He pulled up at the wrought iron gate, got out and entered the code, and the gate swung open.

Emma glanced back as they drove in. She felt a shiver of apprehension. She was going to be left here, with people she had only met once, inside those gates that only opened if you knew the code. Then she told herself, *Rubbish! You've got the chance to work with the most famous writer in the world. What more could you want?*

# Chapter 9

This time there was no Cynthia Morton dashing out the front door to welcome them. Tony came around to open the car door for her—*perfect gentleman,* Emma thought, contrasting him with the Aussie guys she'd met in London. He retrieved Emma's suitcase from the back seat and carried it for her to the front door, also carrying his own briefcase. He put down the suitcase and rang the doorbell, and the door was opened by the maid Emma had met before.

"Please come in," she said. "Madam is expecting you in her study."

Emma tried to pick up her suitcase but Tony beat her to it and stood back to let Emma enter first. Without asking, the maid took Emma's mack and the suitcase from Tony and placed them by the front door. "Your things will be taken over to the guest cottage for you, miss," she said. "Now if you will follow me . . ."

She led them down a small hallway off to the right. The maid tapped and then opened a door and went in ahead of them. "Mr Tony and the young lady, madam," she said. It was all so much like a drawing room comedy that Emma stifled a grin. Until now she hadn't believed that people still lived like this in the second half of the twentieth century. Then she corrected herself—only people who had lots of money could afford to live like this. Iris had created the world for herself that she once wrote about and presumably dreamed about when she was on that sheep station in Australia.

Iris was sitting in an armchair by the fire, staring at the flames. She looked up at the sound of the maid's voice, then focused on Emma and Tony.

"Oh. Hello," she said. "What are you doing back here so soon?"

"Hello, Miss Blackburn. We've brought the papers from my father," Tony said.

"The papers?" Iris frowned. "But I don't need any papers. The maid always brings me *The Telegraph* with my morning cup of tea, although I confess I can no longer complete the crossword."

"No, I mean the papers for you to sign. The contract for Miss Callander so that she can start working on the book."

Iris's gaze seemed to clear as she looked at Emma, then she smiled. "Oh, those papers. Yes, of course. I was miles away. Thinking." She stood up. "Right, let's get down to it then." And she walked across to a small table in the window, not to her desk in the middle of the room, and pulled out a chair.

"Would you like some coffee? Maggie, tell Cook we'd like coffee and some of that ginger cake she made."

"Very good, Miss Blackburn," the maid replied, and Emma glanced around to see if she had curtseyed, but Maggie was already walking away.

Iris was now alert and focused. "You look very smart today, Emma my darling," she said. "London suit. Latest fashion. And green goes well with your colouring. Well done."

"Thank you." Emma blushed at the praise. She glanced across to see Tony looking amused. "My flatmate works in a boutique. She gets good discounts."

"Right. Let's get to work," Iris said. "I'm sure Tony's dad wants him back at the office. Take a seat please, and let's have a look at these contracts your dad has drawn up."

There were two upright chairs on the other side of the table, and Emma took the one closest to the window. Outside the wind had picked up and was swirling dead leaves across the lawn. Tony opened his brief-case, checked the papers before spreading them out before Iris. Today she wore a burgundy twinset and matching wool slacks. She didn't look as frail as she had the day before. She reached for a pair of glasses and placed them on her nose before picking up the first sheet of paper.

Tony and Emma waited in silence as Iris read it carefully, grunting or nodding occasionally. Then she put it down and looked up at them. "Yes, that all seems to make sense. Explain it to her, dear boy."

"First things first, Emma," Tony said. "We ask that you sign an agreement not to divulge anything that goes on here while you are working with Iris or any information about the book until it is published."

"That seems fair," Emma said, wincing as she remembered she had already told her flatmates about the book. It seemed wiser not to mention that.

"Good. For this preliminary period while you read and assess," he went on. "You will be paid ten pounds a day, plus room and board, up to one week. At the end of the week you make up your mind whether to give this project a try. If you decide yes, you will then go up to Scotland to do your research. There is no set amount of time that you will spend up there, but obviously you can't turn it into a long holiday at Iris's expense."

"I don't think that Scotland in late September is going to be so inviting that I'll want to linger," Emma said. "It's not like the Riviera."

Iris gave a chortle. "Good sense of humour. Aussie wit. I like that."

Tony cleared his throat. "For this period you will also be paid ten pounds a day plus expenses. Does that sound fair to you?"

"Yes. Very fair," Emma said. Ten pounds a day seemed like a fortune after living on eight pounds a week.

"Then if you'd read this through and sign and date." He pushed the sheet in front of her. He then handed it to Iris, who also signed. Tony put it back in a folder and handed a second sheet to Iris, who took longer to read this one, frowning as she concentrated. Eventually she put it down. "Too complicated, dear boy. Can't take it all in right now. You explain it."

Tony had a worried look on his face as he took back the paper.

"This contract is to protect Iris," he said. "It states that you, Emma Callander, have no claim to the finished product, the character or the series. You are being taken on in what is called work for hire, which means you'll be paid a fee, if Iris is satisfied with your work, and that will be that. The book will be published under Iris's name."

"Wait a second," Emma interrupted. "I'm not to get a credit as a cowriter?"

Tony looked slightly uncomfortable. "The book is part of the Inspector Melrose series, known around the world as Iris Blackburn's creation. My father felt it would diminish the value of the product if it was thought that Iris did not write this book herself."

"Then, if you don't mind my saying so, what sort of protection do I have?" Emma asked, surprised at how sharp her voice sounded. "I won't be able to use this as a stepping stone without my name on the cover. I'm not going to get a cut of the royalties if the book is a major bestseller? Look, I could work on this for three months, and Iris could decide one day that she didn't want me around any more. The book would eventually be published with my writing, my words in it, but I'd get no credit and nobody would ever know. She might even get out of paying me, if she decides she's not satisfied with my work. So why would I want to give up months of my life for something that will only bring in a little more money than my current job? I could be writing my own book in that time and actually furthering my career."

"She's right, you know," Iris said. "There is very little in this for her, apart from the honour of working with me." She gave Emma what was almost a wink, making Emma realize it was self-deprecating humour. "I say we have another think about the finished product when we see how things are progressing. We're getting ahead of ourselves at the moment. We don't know if Emma wants to do it. We don't know if she can do it to my satisfaction. We don't know if we can work together. I say we take the first step with the contract that Emma has signed. She reads the pages I've written and we go from there."

"If that's your wish." Tony gave something between a nod and a little bow. "Fair enough. I'll take this one back to my father and tell him we're going to hold off until we can see the light ahead." He put the paper back into the folder and the folder into the briefcase. "Then I'll wait until we hear from you, Iris. I wish you good luck, Emma. It was nice talking to you."

He gave another curt little bow and left the room. Emma sat, feeling uncomfortable. It seemed unlike the friendly person with whom she had been getting on so well. Had he now switched to full solicitor mode? Then it occurred to her that he was probably carrying out his father's instructions whether he agreed with them or not. Mr Gordon's words echoed in her head. "You're the young lady who has created such a stir." *I was supposed to agree and submit,* she thought and wondered if she had blown her big chance.

When the front door slammed Iris turned back to Emma. "Left in a huff, if you ask me. I expect you've already found out that no man likes being corrected by a woman. They take it for granted that you'll smile sweetly and say, 'Yes dear, whatever you say is right.'"

Emma gave her a delighted grin. "I really didn't mean to make a fuss," she said.

"No. You were absolutely right. Stick up for what you want in life. I always have. We'll talk about the next contract when you've finished reading. As a matter of fact I'm interested to see what you think so far. To be truthful I can't quite remember what I've already written. I find it comes and goes these days. Some days it's all lovely and clear in my head and I want to surge ahead with the book, and other days I stare at the page and it's as if a stranger has written it. Or I try to write and the words just won't come."

Emma looked at her with compassion.

"I'm so sorry. That must be awful for you, when the words have come so easily all your life."

"You're right. It's bloody awful," Iris said. "I don't know what to do about it, but I can tell you I'm going to fight it with every fiber of my being."

"Not go gently into that good night," Emma said softly, and Iris smiled. "Too right, mate," she said. "You see, the trouble is with all the Melrose books I just let him do what he wants and I put it down on paper, but in this book it felt different, as if he didn't know what he wanted himself. You'll see. It's there in the cottage, waiting for you. Go and take a look. Don't bother to come over for lunch. There is a telephone connection to the house. Just ring when you want food and someone will bring it across."

"I don't want to be a nuisance," Emma said. "I'm afraid I've already made an enemy of Miss Morton."

"Miss Morton is far too possessive of me," Iris said. "She thinks of me as her pet spaniel to be cosseted. Her behaviour has nothing to do with reading and writing my book. She's just worried that an outsider has been brought into our little circle. She fears that I'll give my attention to someone else. She's been with me far too long. It's not healthy. Now." She picked up a little bell on the table. "Maybe you'd like some coffee first. Shall I ring for some?"

"You already asked your maid to bring coffee when we first arrived," Emma said.

"Did I? Ah. Well, I expect it will soon turn up then." Even as she said the words there was a rattle of cups and spoons in the hallway and the maid, Maggie, came in, carrying a tray with cups, saucers, a pot of coffee and one of hot milk, plus a plate with slices of cake on it.

"Cook wants to know if the visitors are going to stay for lunch?" she said as she put the tray down in front of Iris.

Iris sighed. "I told Cynthia to tell her that the young lady will be occupying the guesthouse and will be wanting her meals. I expect she'll have dinner with us but someone will need to take over her breakfast and lunch. Cynthia can do it if you're too busy."

Maggie's face took on a worried look. "I don't think Miss Morton will be happy with that. She wasn't at all happy at having to get the cottage ready." Then she went red, as if she'd been telling tales.

"Miss Morton will just have to lump it," Iris said. "So go and let everyone know what the plan is, and Miss Callander and I will enjoy a quiet cup of coffee with no fuss."

Emma did not relish what lay ahead—facing two dragons.

"Look, Miss Blackburn, I really don't want to cause a problem," she said. "I can come to the house and take my meals whenever or wherever you want. I'm sure it's too much trouble for someone to have to walk across to bring me food."

"Bloody rubbish," Iris said. "Cynthia goes out for walks all the time. She can just swing by the cottage on her way. She's just being difficult to punish us for making plans that don't include her. And Mrs Fisk, well, Mrs Fisk is always a pain in the neck. But I put up with it because she's the best cook I'll ever find and she knows it. Try the cake."

Emma took a slice. It was moist and gingery and full of raisins. "It's really good," she said. She finished the slice of cake, finished her coffee, then got to her feet. "I should get started then," she said. "Which direction is the cottage?"

"I'll have Cynthia take you." She picked up a little brass bell in the shape of a Victorian lady and rang it imperiously. The tap of shoes approached. Cynthia came in, today wearing baggy wool slacks and a loose navy cardigan.

"Ah, there you are, my dear," Iris said. "Miss Callander has had her coffee and is ready to get to work. Please take her to the cottage and show her how everything works over there."

"Come on then," Cynthia said coldly. "We'll go out of the side door."

She walked fast and Emma had to break into a trot to keep up. "Look, Miss Morton," she gasped as she was a little out of breath, "you really don't have to be angry with me. I didn't ask to be here. I don't even know that I'm capable of what Iris wants, but if it helps her and she can finish a book that means a lot to her, then that's a good thing, isn't it? We both want her to be happy, and who knows how long she has to live?"

Cynthia glanced back at her. "How long she has to live? That old biddy will live forever. She has the constitution of an ox. You weren't here for the flu epidemic in the fifties, were you? Everyone else got the most awful flu. People died. Mrs Fisk and I were both laid low for ages. Iris cooked for us and waited on us and never got sick. Unfortunately it's only her memory that's going, and there's nothing I can do about that."

"We can help her finish the book," Emma said.

They went out a small door on the left side of the house, and Cynthia set off across a lawn on the opposite side from the sunken garden. The first thing Emma saw was the swimming pool, a wonderful, pristine blue. And behind it, in a stand of trees, was a cottage that looked as if it belonged in a fairy tale. Emma half expected to see a dwarf or two peering out of the window. Cynthia opened the front door that was just high enough for them to enter without bending.

"Did Iris have this built?" she asked.

"No. It was already here. I gather it was some kind of Victorian fantasy. Iris pulled down much of the big house and had it rebuilt to her taste but she left the cottage. It appealed to her sense of whimsy."

Emma expected to find the sort of furniture the three bears might have used, but instead she stepped into a perfectly ordinary, almost shabby room with a simple wooden table and chairs and a sofa in front of a fireplace. In the window was a small oak desk with a typewriter and brown paper package on it. The room was dark, with only the one paned window at the front. The fire had been laid but not lit and the room felt cold and damp. On one side a door led to a small bedroom with a single bed, chest and wardrobe. On the other was a tiny kitchenette with a two-burner stove and a sink and behind that a bathroom with a shower, not a tub. Not the most hospitable of places.

"I expect Cook can give you supplies to make your own tea, and maybe some of her biscuits," Cynthia said. "I gather your meals are to be brought to you."

"Only if that's convenient," Emma said. "I don't want to be any trouble."

"There's a phone on this table. It connects to the main house. Just pick it up and you can ask for your meals."

"Or someone could ring me from the main house and I'll come across," Emma said.

Cynthia frowned. "Iris does not want you to be disturbed too much, and Iris gets what Iris wants. She rules the roost here. So I'll leave you to it then."

"Are there matches to light the fire?" Emma asked. "It's cold in here."

"I expect you'll find a box beside the stove in the kitchen," Cynthia said. And with that she walked out, leaving Emma staring after her.

Emma found the matches and got the fire going. On further inspection she found an electric fire in the bedroom and also one in the main room. She plugged this latter one in and waited for the wood fire to heat up. She suspected that Cynthia had been asked to light the fire ahead of time but had chosen not to. She probably wanted to make Emma so uncomfortable that she'd leave. In the bedroom Emma unpacked the clothes she had brought with her, then changed from her pantsuit into more comfortable sweatpants. Then she laid out her hairbrush and cosmetics on the chest of drawers, and took her sponge bag through to the bathroom.

By this time the fire was crackling merrily. Emma put a big log on it and went over to examine the paper parcel sitting on the desk. It had to be the manuscript, but it was thinner than she had expected. She undid the brown paper and saw the title on the folder. *The Wild Girl*, in what Emma assumed was Iris's own aggressive handwriting. In spite of herself she felt a shiver of excitement. All her life she had lived for books, and now she was about to read a book in its early stages of creation by one of the greatest authors in the world. She hardly dared to touch it. She would have liked to take it over to curl up on the sofa near the fire, but it seemed sacrilege to move it.

As she pulled out the chair to sit at the desk she noticed a low bookcase along the far wall and saw it contained Iris's books. She remembered David suggesting that she read through the series to get the feel of Inspector Melrose. Emma pulled one out and went over to the sofa with it, switching on the standard lamp beside it to give her more light.

*In a Dark Place: An Inspector Melrose Mystery*, she read on a dated and rather lurid cover. She opened it at random:

> *The alleyway was narrow, dark and slick from evening rain. Melrose's footsteps echoed from the brick walls on either side. It smelled strongly of cigarette smoke and dog urine. From above his head somewhere came the sound of a woman sobbing. Probably the alleged victim. God, he hated these sorts of cases. He had no idea how to handle weeping women. Why didn't they hire more female officers for cases like this? A woman would know what to say, how to comfort. He'd only stare at her distraught face, tears running down cheeks that were often bruised or swollen, and feel helpless and angry and useless. And then there was her assailant, either grovelling in a corner—"I didn't mean it. I just lost my cool."—or standing defiant, fists at the ready, saying, "She shouldn't have pushed me so far. She had it coming."*
>
> *Melrose had no qualms about how to handle him.*

Emma put the book down hurriedly. There was no way she could write this sort of stuff. She'd have to get into the head of a tough Scottish policeman, one who probably didn't think too much of women. And yet Iris had just expressed an opinion about the way women were treated by men that echoed Emma's own. She got up, returned the book to its place on the shelf and went back to the desk. The thought of working her way through Iris's shelf of books before she tackled the manuscript was not an appealing one, and frankly she was really curious now to see the new manuscript. Perhaps she'd know after one or two pages that the task was not for her. Then she toyed with this thought. Was that what she wanted? To leave this place, go back to the safety of the flat and her job at Barlow and Barlow?

"Don't be a bloody fool," she said out loud. Wasn't this what she'd dreamed of? Her own little cottage and a chance to write again? She'd been given the chance to do something exciting, something that might lead to establishing her own career in some way. And she was being paid decently for the time she spent reading and researching. Her job in London would be waiting for her when she finished. She had nothing to lose and a lot to gain.

She opened the folder, turned to the title page, neatly typed and centred.

*The Wild Girl: Inspector Melrose's First Case*

By Iris Blackburn

Trembling a little with excitement, she turned the page.

# Chapter 10

## *The Wild Girl: Inspector Melrose's First Case*, Chapter 1

***The Isle of Skye, autumn 1932***

Flora was the name her mother had given her at birth, but her mother had died before the child reached five years, a wee scrap of a bairn, and in the village of Dun Akyn she was known only as the Wild Girl. Her father was a fisherman, out at sea long hours at a time, and Flora learned quickly how to fend for herself. She helped herself to eggs from those who kept chickens. She begged a roll or two from the baker. The kind folk in the village left bowls of soup out for her and their own children's outgrown clothing. She went to school when she felt like it but was most often seen running barefoot across the heather, or splashing in the tide pools, communing with the wild creatures from seals to roe deer. It was whispered that Angus MacLeod was not her father at all, but that it was one of the fairy folk, or even a storm-kelpie. Whatever was true in this regard, she stayed clear of the well-meaning village women who tried to take her in hand, made no friends amongst the village children and could seemingly vanish in the blink of an eye like the fairy folk.

Either way she was destined to come to a bad end. This was what Detective Inspector James Melrose was told when he arrived on the Isle of Skye and journeyed to the remote village of Dun Akyn, perched on the shore south of the harbour town of Kyleakin. He was a tall, slim young man, with the pale skin and ginger hair of the Celt. He was currently attempting to grow a moustache to make him look older, but the result was a disappointing layer of sandy fuzz on his upper lip. At the time he had just turned thirty, a young detective inspector, recently promoted from detective sergeant and with no experience at all of life in the wilder parts of Scotland. He was born and raised in Glasgow, in the slums called the Gorbals. His father worked in the shipyards, his mother in a laundry. At least they had jobs, which was unusual at that time, and they had paid for their son to go to a better school than the one around the corner where the law of the bully and the schoolmaster's strap reigned and the only aim was to turn out young thugs at the age of fourteen who might possibly be able to read and write.

Inspector Melrose had repaid his parents' sacrifice well. He had excelled at school and it had been suggested that he might go on to the University of Glasgow. But that seemed like an idea too far above his station. Instead he had joined the Glasgow Police, proudly worn the uniform until his superiors felt he was the right material to move across to the Criminal Investigation Department. He had been attached to an older inspector from whom he learned the ropes. Coming from the Gorbals himself he was not afraid to deal with the gangs. Then one day the older inspector collapsed and died of a heart attack, and at the age of thirty James Melrose found himself promoted. He didn't adjust to the inspector rank easily . . . all too aware of those early days in the two-up two-down house with no inside bathroom and the times when he'd come home with a bloody nose from fighting.

So when the superintendent told him that he was being sent out to the island of Skye to look into a perplexing case that might be a multiple murder he did not jump at the chance, especially since the case involved an aristocratic family who lived in a castle. Melrose had little patience with aristocrats—those who spent their idle days shooting and fishing while poor sods like his father got up at dawn to work in the shipyards that these people owned. But he was not given the option to refuse.

"We don't have too many details," his superintendent said. "The telephone line from the islands isn't that great, and you know what these toffs are like. You are summoned and you go. I expect you'll figure it out when you get there."

"How long ago did this happen?" Melrose asked.

"Three days ago now. They expected you to be there immediately, so you'd better get moving."

He had his marching orders, made his way up through the Highlands towards Mallaig, where he could board the ferry to the island of Skye.

As Melrose had grown up in the big city of Glasgow, the Highlands were as unfamiliar to him as they would have been to a Londoner. His family had no money for fancy excursions, no summer holidays when he was a boy. He had only been that far north once before, on a school trip to the site of the Battle of Culloden. He had journeyed there in a coach with a group of rowdy boys and had needed to pay too much attention to missiles being launched at him, from spitballs to small rocks from peashooters, to pay much attention to the scenery. All he remembered of it was feeling coach-sick and hoping he didn't disgrace himself and vomit. Now, as the train took him towards Fort William, he stared, almost in disbelief, at the scenery unfolding before him. Mountains rose, one behind the other, their bare slopes covered in yellow-green grass dotted with great strands of brilliantly purple heather. The only trees were along the sides of small streams that plunged through the valleys, or a couple of Scots pines behind a lonely white cottage, planted to block the worst of the wind. Every now and then they passed above a loch—a thin strip of shining water, deep in a valley. As he looked out at uninhabited land stretching as far as the eye could see he felt overawed, almost afraid. This was hostile country, unforgiving, unwelcoming, and he was going in as the outsider.

He had been offered the use of a police vehicle, but he was glad now that he had refused as he boarded the second train, from Fort William to the ferry port of Mallaig, and saw the narrow road across the hillside snake down in a series of zigzags. Again, having grown up in a crowded city, he had little experience in driving. Luckily, at the turn of the century a train line had been built to

Mallaig. The train route was a feat of impressive engineering over spectacular scenery, starting at the high point of Fort William, with the magnificent Ben Nevis mountain rising up to one side, then passing one loch after another, flying over steep glens on amazing bridges as it wound down to the sea and the port. Mallaig was one of the most prosperous herring fishing ports in Scotland, and Melrose saw, and smelled, this for himself the moment he stepped down from the train. Kippering shacks lined the waterfront and the smell of their smoking wood chips mingled with the overpowering stench of fish. Seagulls wheeled overhead and dived for scraps. Their screaming cries were deafening. Several fishing boats were tied up at the quayside, one in the process of being unloaded, and the shouts of the men competed with the cries of the seagulls. Trays of kippers waited, stacked on the platform for the train to take them south to the big cities and to England.

When Melrose saw the size of the car ferry he was even more grateful that he had not accepted the offer of a vehicle. This car ferry was a flat-bottomed crate that didn't look seaworthy, with space for only two cars at once. He watched a driver trying to manoeuvre his delivery van on board while the swell of the sea lifted the ramp up and down.

To his relief he found that the passenger ferry to the island was a bigger craft, a proper steamer that looked seaworthy. He paid his fare and walked on board, taking a seat at the prow. Across a strait of shining silver water he saw the island, a low shoreline rising to a chain of slate-blue mountains in the distance. It was a fine, blustery autumn day and whitecaps dotted the sea. Remembering the way his stomach had reacted on that coach ride to Culloden as a boy he hoped he was not prone to seasickness. It would be ironic since his father had spent his life building boats, although to Melrose's knowledge his dad had never actually been on one.

Exactly on the hour the gangplank was raised, the engine sputtered to life and the boat moved away from the dock. As it met the oncoming waves it rose and fell, sending fine spray over the side and making Melrose hastily move into the centre. He held his breath, waiting for the seasickness to strike. When it didn't he looked around, rather surprised. Two women with shopping baskets and local tweed shawls wrapped over their heads and shoulders sat across from him. Facing them was a man with a suitcase and an older couple, all chatting easily as if this crossing on the wild seas was the most normal thing in the world. Melrose heard the soft sounds of their speech, so different from the harsh Glasgow dialect. It took him a while to realize they weren't speaking English but Gaelic, and he found himself wondering if he'd be able to communicate once he got to Skye. Surely all schoolchildren had to learn English, didn't they?

Once away from shore the boat settled into a more gentle rhythm, rocking from side to side as it turned towards the island, as if it were a giant cradle. Unbidden, the words of a song came to Melrose—a song learned by every school child in Scotland. *Speed bonny boat like a bird on the wing, onward the sailors cry. Carry the lad who was born to be king over the sea to Skye.*

"The Skye Boat Song," telling of Bonnie Prince Charlie, escaping from the English after his failed attempt to gain the throne. He'd been assisted by the local people, including one Flora MacDonald, and got away safely after risking the stormy sea crossing, remaining a romantic figure for all Scots. Anyone that defied the English was treasured here in Scotland, where they were still seen as the invaders and conquerors after all those hundreds of years. As Melrose hummed along to the rocking of the boat a strange feeling came over him. His first time leaving the shores of his birth, being transported, like Bonnie Prince Charlie, over the sea to Skye. It almost felt like a rite of passage, as if he were leaving the shackles of his past life behind him and somehow being reborn, free to be the person he wanted. He shook aside this fanciful notion as the island came closer and those hazy mountains came into focus, barren and rocky foothills with sharper peaks rising up behind them. An inhospitable place if ever he'd seen one! As the boat approached the shore he saw that the lower ground was tree covered, softer and green, but showed no signs of human habitation, no smoke rising from crofters' chimneys. Still the boat headed towards the shore and then slipped into a little bay. A few cottages nestled together near the ferry dock.

"Is this Portree?" he asked, having been told that was the name of the biggest town, where he'd find the police station.

"No, this is Armadale, mo ghaol," one of the women said, standing now and ready to disembark. "You need to stay on board while the boat goes all the way up the coast. You've a long trip before you. Better go into the cabin and make yourself comfortable. That's what I would do. Get yourself a cup of tea. Have a little snooze."

"Oh." Melrose looked concerned. "Would it not be quicker to disembark here and take the road to Portree?"

This made the women laugh. "The road, as you call it, is little more than a track through the heather, with streams running across it, sheep every few yards, oh, and a couple of mountains in the way. I believe it would take you three hours or more, if you found anyone daft enough to drive you. The bus only goes on Tuesdays and Fridays."

Since today was Wednesday Melrose resigned himself to his fate, went into the cabin where there were wooden benches and settled into a corner while the boat made its way around the coast of the island. He had not realized how big Skye was. The coast, with its many inlets and promontories, seemed to stretch on forever. They passed through a narrow point where the mainland came close with only a channel separating Skye from the bleak hillsides on the other side. *Why the devil didn't they put the ferry here?* he wondered, but there were no villages in sight on either side. Not even a lone cottage. A little further along, where the channel opened up again, there was a promontory jutting out from the mainland, and he saw another ferry, annoyed now to find it would also have been a short crossing.

As they came around to the north, leaving the mainland behind, the swell picked up, and soon he really did feel a little nauseous, making him go outside into the brisk wind. Other islands appeared, off to their right, low-lying mounts of grey-green, heather covered and uninhabited, apart from the sheep that dotted the hillsides. Skye itself became more stark and menacing as they pushed north. Clouds moved in from the Atlantic, covering the most northerly of the peaks on the island, and the air held the promise of rain. Melrose began to wonder whether this assignment was in fact a pat on the back for his promotion at such a young age, or a punishment for getting above himself. He decided on the latter.

# Chapter 11

Emma put the pages down, staring at them thoughtfully. David had been right. This book had an entirely different feel to it. Immediately Iris was revealing the vulnerability of Melrose, a young man still unsure of himself, unsure of what he wants from life. And the prose was wordy, descriptive, almost lyrical. Melrose was seeing the Isle of Skye as a magical place, where anything might happen. She felt compelled to read on:

## *The Wild Girl*, Chapter 2

By the time Detective Inspector Melrose had landed in Portree evening had fallen, the clouds had settled in and the first raindrops spattered onto the quayside. That chain of mountains that had seemed so formidable from the boat had now vanished into mist and cloud. All he saw was a row of small houses along the quayside, lights already twinkling in some windows as the daylight faded early here, so far north. He stepped ashore unsteadily, still feeling the movement of the boat as he walked. He had not succumbed to seasickness but his insides still felt horribly delicate, partly from hunger. He hadn't thought to bring food with him, and there had been nothing more on the boat than cups of tea and dry biscuits. He checked his watch and saw that it was too late to present himself at the police station, so he headed for the one guesthouse that had lights in the windows.

The proprietor was a diminutive Mistress MacDonald, who seemed surprised that anybody from the mainland would be stupid enough to come to Skye now that the darkness was settling in for the winter, but she admitted she did have a room available, although she'd not be serving him his supper. But there was the pub where he could no doubt find something hot. She led him up a flight of stairs and along a narrow, unlit hallway. "Bathroom's at the end of the hall," she said. "Hot water available from six to eight in the mornings if you've a mind for a wash." With this cheery warning she opened a door for him and left.

The room was spartan in the extreme, not unlike the prison cells he had visited: apparently unheated since there was no fireplace or radiator, with a single bed with a hand-stitched quilt on it, a small chest of drawers, a couple of hooks on the wall and over the bed a sampler with a biblical quote: *It is easier for a camel to pass through the eye of a needle than for a rich man to enter the kingdom of heaven.* He had to smile as he read it. *At least that doesn't apply to me,* he thought. He'd never get rich on a policeman's salary, unless he accepted kickbacks and bribes, as it was whispered some of the higher-ups did.

He chose not to freshen up with cold water, put on his mack and went out into the rainy darkness to the pub in a back street behind the harbour. It was a rough and ready place, populated by fishermen and heavy with pipe smoke.

Melrose ordered a pint of Belhaven Black, which the men watching him seemed to approve of. And he was told that they could no doubt find him a bit of fish pie if he had a mind to try it.

"You'll be here for the fishing, I've no doubt," the barman ventured. "The trout have been jumping most satisfactorily this past week if you're doing the rough fishing."

"I'm afraid I'm here to work," Melrose said. He did not mention that he was a policeman.

"But you're no a Sassenach? Not one of those Englishmen who come here with their noses in the air, ordering us around. You sound like a true Scot to me."

"I'm from Glasgow," he said, smiling.

"Ah. Glasgow. I hear it's a big city right enough," another of the men commented. "Did you not go there yourself once, Lachy?" He addressed an old fellow dressed in an oilskin jacket with a shapeless tweed hat on his head.

"Aye but I did. I had to appear in some courtroom over fishing rights. Och, but it was a terrible place."

"The courtroom?" Melrose asked.

"The city. All those people and air so thick ye could nae even breathe. I don't know how people can live there. It sucks the verra life out of you. Turns humans into ants, scurrying about their anthill, that's what it does."

Melrose nodded agreement. "It does. You're right. But for me, born and raised in the city, it's the openness of places like this I find intimidating."

"You'll get used to it, laddie, if you stay here long," one of them said. "And then you'll nae be wanting to leave."

The fish pie was placed in front of him, a generous portion accompanied by boiled cabbage. It proved to be quite filling and tasty, with plenty of chunks of haddock and salmon in a cheesy white sauce under crisp potato crust. The local ale went down well too and once he was back in his room, he fell asleep with no problem. He awoke to strange unearthly screams, jumped up and looked out of his window to see that a fishing boat had come in, with gulls swirling and diving around it, fighting off each other with their harsh cries. The rain of the night had cleared and the morning was crystal clear.

*Not a bad place,* he thought, managed a quick wash and shave with warm water, then went downstairs to breakfast, served in a small dining room with six tables. He was the only occupant and resigned himself to cornflakes or toast. He was then pleasantly surprised when Mistress MacDonald served him a huge bowl of porridge followed by eggs, bacon, black pudding, baked beans and fried bread. Feeling rather too full, and guilty that the old lady had gone to such trouble just for him, he prepared to get to work.

"Will you be staying another night then?" she wanted to know.

"I'm not sure yet. I have to meet with the local police and find out where I'm needed."

"You're after being a policeman yourself then, is it?" she asked in her sweet and lilting voice. "I'd never have taken you for it. You look to me like a bonnie gentle laddie. Nae fierce enough looking for a policeman."

He had to smile. "I'm a detective," he said. "Sent up from Glasgow. Homicide squad."

"Oh." She gave him a knowing look. "So you'll be here about the murder, no doubt. Shocking business, that. That poor wee lassie and a fine young man, although he was from the mainland."

"Oh, you've heard about it then?"

"There are not many people on Skye," she said with a sweet smile. "We generally know each other's business."

"So it happened near Portree?"

"Oh no, mo ghràidh," she said, again using words he didn't know. "It's a wee way from here. You'll no doubt be using the police motor car. They only got one two years ago. Awful proud of it they are, so you'd better not scrape it or bump into a sheep."

"I think I'll have one of the local boys drive me," he said. "I was told I'd be given assistance."

He bade her good morning and stepped out into the clear, bracing air. The harbour was still bustling, with a line of seagulls perched on the wall, waiting hopefully. But the sea beyond was smooth as glass, shining silver with blue islands dotting the horizon. Melrose stood to admire it, thinking he'd never seen anything as grand. And the air—freshness with a tang of salt and seaweed. It was almost intoxicating after the perpetual smokiness of Glasgow, fuelled by thousands of coal fires as well as heavy industry. He nodded to himself in satisfaction, glad he had come.

He walked along the quayside until he found a street going inland, followed it and came to the police station. It was a humble affair, a whitewashed building with a slate roof and the obligatory blue light in front. Inside smelled of damp wool and cigarette smoke. A young policeman in uniform jumped up from behind the counter as he came in. Melrose saw that he'd been reading a child's comic book, *Boy's Own*.

"Can I help you, sir?" Again the soft Highland voice.

"I'm Detective Inspector Melrose," he said. "Your governor is expecting me."

The boy's eyes opened wider. "Oh aye. They said a man was being sent up from Glasgow. So you're he then? I'll go and tell the inspector. Wait here."

Melrose found this funny, as if he might want to run away. He heard an extended conversation in the back room and then a slightly older man came out. He had the weathered face of an outdoorsman and carried himself like one who is fit and might have been a former rugby player.

"Inspector Melrose," he said, holding out his hand. "Delighted to meet you. Welcome to Skye. I'm MacDonald . . . Don't look surprised," he added. "We're all MacDonalds here, unless we're MacLeods.

Anyone called something different is an outsider, an interloper." He gave a friendly smile and Melrose relaxed. He had worried that he was being thrust upon them against their will and would not be welcome.

"Come into my office," Inspector MacDonald said, lifting a section of the counter to let him through. They went back into a small, dark room with one high window. It would make an ideal interrogation room, Melrose thought and wondered how often they had to bring somebody in for questioning. Not too often, he thought. The occasional sheep stealing would be about the worst crime he could think of on the island. On the table was an ashtray filled with cigarette butts, on the wall a map of the island with pins stuck in it as well as a portrait of the king.

"Take a seat." MacDonald indicated the one chair beside the desk, then went around to take his own captain's chair. "You've come about the murders. Nasty business. We're not used to murders here. In fact the only ones we've had in my time here, and that's now going on twenty years, don't take that many brains to solve. A man drinks too much whisky, finds his wife with another man and clobbers her to death. The last time that happened the chap turns himself in, hands me the club and says, 'I won't say I'm sorry, because I'm not.

She was a right cow.'" He laughed. "Not too much actual detective work, which is why Glasgow thought we might need a little expert guidance." He took a cigarette out of a Player's packet, offered one to Melrose, who refused politely, then lit his own, taking a long drag, all the time not taking his eyes off Melrose. Melrose could see him thinking that this boyish person would not be up to the job.

"Tricky business, this will be. Dealing with gentry," he went on. "They still hold a lot of power in these regions, you know. The crofters on their estates actually belong to them, more or less. They pay rent to the laird but it's more than that. It's the old feudal system still working. The laird can commandeer them to work for him when he feels like it. And take away their livelihood if he gets a mind to as well."

He took a long drag on his cigarette, then went on. "Back a while the laird on the mainland around Mallaig decided he wanted the land for himself to run sheep . . . wool prices being high at the time. No more of these annoying crofters. So he built a dock and village at Mallaig and sent everyone down there to be fishermen. Told them they'd be more prosperous, which probably they were, but it was still an upheaval from the old ways. And you know what? They had no say in the matter because it was the laird's land."

Melrose had heard the story before but he gave a sympathetic nod. He could see that the inspector liked to chat. He waited until the man took another drag of his cigarette before saying, "So this murder involves a laird?" He was confused about what he'd heard so far. In Glasgow he was told he was dealing with the gentry, but the landlady had talked of a poor wee lassie.

"Aye, it does. The laird's own daughter, you know. And the tricky thing is that the prime suspect is also of the aristocracy. The son of the landowner across the water near Kyle of Lochalsh. Euan Chisholm. He was staying with the family, the Hamiltons, when the tragedy occurred." He took another drag on his cigarette, blew out the smoke, then stood up. "Look, why don't I fill you in on this while we drive? I thought I should come with you, just in case there was resistance to an outsider being brought in. There probably will be. We like to take care of things ourselves on the island, you know. And you being so young . . ." He paused. "I thought they'd have sent a senior man. One with experience in solving murders. But you can't be more than a couple of years in long trousers, yourself."

"I've just turned thirty," Melrose said, indignant now. "I've been on the force since I was eighteen. Seven years in uniform on the streets of Glasgow and now five years in plain clothes. Believe me, you grow up quickly when you have to patrol the Gorbals, Inspector MacDonald. More than one of our boys has been stabbed or beaten up on a dark night. You learn to observe and keep your wits about you or you don't survive."

"So you've handled murder cases before?"

"I have," Melrose said smoothly, not willing to admit that he'd been the junior officer on previous cases and that most murder cases in the big city involved domestic violence or someone being bashed on the head or stabbed after a pub fight. Nothing tricky or complicated about them. He had never had to tackle the type of case you read about in crime novels with multiple suspects and tantalizing clues. He rather looked forward to this one, even if he felt a little apprehensive. If he solved it, it would prove that the super had not made a mistake in promoting him.

Inspector MacDonald stubbed out his cigarette. "Well then let's get going, shall we? The motor car is parked round the back."

# Chapter 12

Emma finished the chapter. She went over to the desk and picked up the new notebook and pen. She realized she'd need to make notes if she was not allowed to remove the manuscript. She headed the first page *Character names/role in story.*

*Inspector Melrose. First name? James. Parents' names?*

*Mistress MacDonald. Owns B and B.*

*Inspector MacDonald. Runs police station in Portree. Big healthy type.*

At this she paused. If everyone on the island was called MacDonald it would soon be confusing to the reader. She realized that such remote places would have members of the same clan, but she'd talk to Iris about it, see how they could make things clearer. With this thought came the realization that she was already accepting that she would be working on this book.

On the next page she wrote: *Known facts about the murder.*

*Local laird. His daughter victim? Unknown man victim? Confused. Suspect son of laird across on mainland. Euan Chisholm.*

Then she closed the notebook again, anxious now to read on.

## *The Wild Girl*, Chapter 3

The motor car was a new Morris Cowley, looking as if it had not been out of the garage much. Melrose collected his belongings from the boarding house and paid Mistress MacDonald, as the police chief had suggested he stay nearer to the crime scene, rather than have to make this journey. Melrose could see why, as the narrow road hugged the rocky shore, winding in and out of sea lochs, then swung inland over treeless hills, covered in windswept grass with streaks of faded heather and dying bracken, before dropping down to the next bay. He had survived the sea crossing without feeling sick, but after an hour of swinging around bends he felt a little queasy. He hoped and prayed that he'd make it to their destination without having to admit to his weakness. He could tell the chief already thought he might not be up to the job, that he was too young and inexperienced, and he was determined to prove the man wrong.

After miles of seeing no sign of life except sheep and an occasional fishing boat out to sea they came to a small hamlet and slowed as they went along the quayside. Melrose thought that a cup of tea and a bun might be nice and would settle his stomach, but MacDonald showed no signs of stopping. Melrose was not going to show any sign of weakness by asking to stop. So on they went, now with the waves breaking on a rocky shore beside them. From time to time small islands appeared, some green and closer to shore and some just hazy blue shapes in the distance. Melrose wondered how far along in the journey they were and when he'd get a first glimpse of the mainland. When he ventured to ask, the chief inspector shook his head. "Not for a wee while yet," he said.

Melrose stifled a little sigh. He wished he had not had the big, fatty breakfast. That black pudding sat like a stone in his stomach. After more twists and turns in the road they came into the first signs of civilization. Melrose let out that sigh he had been holding. "Is this it now?" he asked.

"Nae, laddie, this is Broadford. And yon mountains behind the town are the Red Cuillin. Quite a challenge if you've a mind to climb one. I was quite a keen climber in my younger days. Of course the harder climbs are in the Black Cuillin to the west of here. Some nasty rock faces. There are climbers killed every year on Skye, with the changeable weather we have. They think our mountains are not that tall, but they are unforgiving, I can tell you. I've had a few scares myself."

"Well, I can assure you that I don't plan to do any climbing," Melrose said.

"Are you more of a rugby man or would it be football?"

"I used to play football at school," Melrose said, feeling inadequate that he no longer played anything other than the occasional snooker or darts. "Now I just follow the Rangers."

"Ah, a Rangers man. Good. We've those around here who follow the Celtics. Leads to blows in the pub sometimes." He chuckled. "My wee son Robbie is verra keen on his football. Practices all the time. Thinks he's going to be a pro someday. 'Don't be so daft,' I tell him. 'Ye might be a good player for Skye, but you've nae seen the outside world.'" He glanced across at Melrose. "Don't get me wrong, I think he is going to be good. And no doubt he'll be off the island as soon as he can. That's what most of the young folk do these days. We'll wind up with only old folk, and then there will be no need for policemen. They always behave themselves, don't they? Too tired to be naughty or too short-sighted to shoot anyone." And he laughed at his own joke before asking, "So do you have wee bairns of your own?"

"No, I'm not married," Melrose said.

"You have a young lady in mind, I've no doubt?"

Melrose shook his head. "No one at the moment. There was a bonnie girl a few years ago, but she died. She was a nurse at the Glasgow Royal Infirmary, but she was nursing during an outbreak of typhoid. She caught it and died. I've not found anyone since to match up to her."

"I'm sorry," MacDonald said, "but then you're still young. Plenty of time to play the field, eh? I rather wish I hadn't rushed into it myself, but there was a reason to speed things up, if you get my meaning." He gave a knowing grin.

While he had been talking the coast of the mainland had come into view. Melrose took in the range of mountains, clear and blue in the morning light, rising up behind a steep and rocky shore and a jagged promontory jutting into the sea. As he watched, a ferry boat left the mainland and started across the narrow strait. They were finally nearing their destination.

"So this is Kyleakin," MacDonald said. "It's the ferry port and it has a decent little hotel where we'll check you in. The village we're going to is a mile or two beyond."

Melrose was calculating mentally. "Are you planning to stay down here while I do my investigation?"

"No, laddie. I'm needed back in Portree. I was just driving you down to fill you in on the details so far."

Melrose noted that the chief inspector insisted on addressing him as laddie. This might have been to show friendliness, or how people spoke to one another on Skye. On the other hand it might have been talking down to him because of his age, when in fact he was an equal in rank.

He decided not to be patronized. "In that case how am I to get from my hotel to the site of the crime? I don't plan on walking a mile or two each day, and you say the primary suspect is from the mainland. I presume you've had officers over there checking out his family and friends?"

"Most of the investigative work was waiting for you to come up from Glasgow," MacDonald said. "Frankly we'd have let this be, not considered it a crime, if the laird wasn't involved. Sir Henry Hamilton. He's a big noise in these parts. Local member of Parliament. It was his daughter who died, you see."

"Let me get this straight. There were two murders? I wasn't told that much before I set out. I heard the laird's daughter, but did you not say it was a young man from the mainland?"

"Aye. A lower-class man from the mainland and the laird's daughter. They were running off together so it seems. Somebody made sure their boat would capsize and sink. The jealous suitor would be the primary suspect then, wouldn't he?"

"That's the son of the gentry on the mainland who was the jealous suitor, is it?"

"Aye. That's the one. Nobody's seen hide nor hair of him since. We've sent a description out to all the police stations in the area, but so far nobody has reported seeing him. It's my belief he got away in a boat, before the tragedy happened, probably in Ireland now, or on his way to France."

"I see," Melrose said. His thoughts were racing. How was he supposed to do anything if the main suspect was known and had vanished? Without a police vehicle he couldn't go chasing all over Scotland. "So you didn't answer my question about how I'm going to get around if you take the motor car back."

"Dinnae fash yourself, laddie," MacDonald said. "I've already arranged with Young Jock MacLeod to have the local taxi at your disposal when you need it. His father, Old Jock, had the first taxi on the island, and now his son has taken over the business. He's not too busy at this time of year. Not many people daft enough to try the mountains when the rain can turn to snow at any moment."

When Melrose nodded, he added, "So I'll drive you over to Dun Akyn. But first let's get you checked into the hotel, then we'll go together to visit Sir Henry. As I said, it will make things easier for you if I introduce you. I don't think he'd take kindly to an outsider butting in."

"I'm sure he'd be glad to have the death of his daughter solved by a professional detective," Melrose said.

MacDonald gave a small snort. "Professional detective, is it? I suppose all that Glasgow training gives you the edge over us poor souls stuck in the back of beyond with only our wits and experience to guide us."

Melrose felt his fair skin flushing. "I did not mean to insult you in any way, Inspector," he said. "I meant that men like Sir Henry would expect to be sent top-level help, and that means the biggest city within reach."

"Aye, you're maybe right on that," MacDonald agreed. "And you see yourself as a top-level man, I take it?"

"I see myself as competent," Melrose replied, refusing to take the bait. He still had not made out Inspector MacDonald. At one moment quite friendly and chatty and then next questioning whether Melrose was up for the job.

They had arrived at the point at the same time as the ferry. Melrose noticed that this one was a proper steamer although flat bottomed to carry motor cars. The village of Kyleakin itself was no more than a few white cottages lining the waterfront and dotting the hillside above the port plus a couple of larger buildings. One of these was the Kings Arms Hotel, a long, low building that looked like an overgrown cottage.

"Oldest hotel on the island," MacDonald said. "I hear it dates from the sixteen hundreds. But no doubt they've put in a few upgrades since then. You might even find an inside WC if you're lucky." Again he laughed heartily at his own joke. Melrose smiled.

"I'll leave you to get on with it then," MacDonald said. "I'll be waiting in the motor."

Inside, the reception area was pleasantly warm, thanks to a big, open fire at the back of the lounge. The counter connected to the back of the bar so that one person could check in guests and then swing around to pour a pint. At this time of day the pub was closed, drinking hours being strictly observed in Scotland. A pleasant grey-haired woman greeted Melrose and said she'd been warned that a gentleman from the big city would be coming to help with the investigation. "Such a terrible thing to happen to that sweet girl," she said, shaking her head. "I don't know what she was thinking, running off with that stranger. If you ask me, I'd wager he kidnapped her. Else why would she be leaving that fine, young Euan Chisholm, son of the laird from over across the strait? She'd not have made herself a better match."

"It is indeed perplexing," Melrose said. "But let's hope we can get to the bottom of it quickly."

"But you're such a young man," she said. "Will your superior nae be joining you on the case?"

"I am the detective inspector sent from Glasgow," he said. "I may look young but I can assure you this is not my first murder case."

"Well then, they must think highly of you to send you to Sir Henry. He's not an easy man to please, I can tell you. Spends half his life down in London at Westminster and stops in here quite frequently. And do we hear it if the beer is too warm or too cold, or if the ferry crossing was too rough for his liking—as if we have the power to calm the waves for him like the Blessed Lord."

Melrose decided that islanders liked to talk—make that gossip. He nodded attentively as the woman produced a hotel register and a key.

"Inspector Melrose, is it then?" she asked.

"And you'd be Mrs MacDonald?" he replied jovially.

"Oh no, mo ghaol." She frowned. "I'm Mistress MacLeod. You'll find as many MacLeods on the island as there are MacDonalds. And a number of Hamiltons, too." She looked up with a cheeky smile. "But you'd be the first Melrose we've had."

With that she handed him a key. "Number twenty, at the end of the hall. I've put you away from the noise of the bar and close to the bathroom," she said. "You'll be taking your evening meal in the bar at this time of year. We don't open the dining room when the summer tourists have gone home. Breakfast at eight. And if you don't mind my saying so, I hope you do a good job and find whoever did that to the lovely young lady. A wicked shame that was. A truly evil deed."

# Chapter 13

Emma startled as the big log on the fire settled, sending out a flurry of sparks. For a moment she had forgotten where she was, her mind now firmly on the island of Skye and already making notes on what she had learned. The first thing she needed was a map of Scotland and, more importantly, a map of Skye. She drew what she had pictured from the descriptions. Kyleakin on a point adjoining a similar promontory on the mainland and the town of Kyle of Lochalsh.

She didn't know enough about the circumstances of the crime yet to make more notes on that, but she added a Mistress MacLeod to the character list. As she was about to tackle the fourth chapter the telephone rang. She looked around the room and saw the phone on a small round table by the front door. She went over and picked it up cautiously.

"Hello?"

"It's Miss Morton," said the throaty voice. "Cook wishes to know when you would be requiring your luncheon to be brought to you."

Emma glanced at her watch and saw it was almost one o'clock. "Look, I can easily come across. I don't want to cause an inconvenience," she said. "Besides it would be good for me to stretch my legs."

"As you wish," Miss Morton said and replaced the receiver.

Emma stacked the pages she had read in a neat pile, then put another log on the fire before going through to the bathroom to wash her hands. The water that came out of the tap was ice cold. She let it run for a long time before admitting it was not going to heat up. Surely there was supposed to be hot water in a guest cottage? She dried her hands, then noticed through the bathroom window that the sky had darkened. The first raindrops were already falling as she opened the front door, making her go back for her mack. Perhaps going across for lunch was not such a good idea after all. She could wait until the rain passed over. But then she realized she was hungry. She'd only had that slice of cake to eat all day. It wasn't raining too hard. As she made a dash across the heavens opened, and by the time she came in through the side door she was truly soaked.

"Oh my dear. What bad timing. You could have waited until this passed over." Cynthia Morton met her in the hallway, presumably having watched her mad dash.

"I thought you meant that lunch was being served now," Emma said, realizing how hard she was trying not to put a foot wrong.

"You should have stayed put," Cynthia said. "We could have sent Maggie over with your food."

"There's no reason Maggie should get wet instead of me," Emma replied. "Besides, it's only water. I'll dry."

"Leave your wet coat here on the hook in the hall, and come through to the kitchen," Cynthia said. "I'll have Cook give you a bowl of soup to warm you up."

Emma followed her into a big, modern kitchen with a row of pans hanging over an AGA cooker. In the centre was a scrubbed pine table, and on this a plate and cutlery had been laid.

"You can sit here, if you don't mind," Cynthia said. "Iris is not feeling too well and will have her lunch in her room, so it didn't seem worth laying the table in the dining room just for us."

"It's fine," Emma said. "Nice and warm in here."

"Thanks to the AGA," Cynthia said. "I insisted that Iris have one installed. What a wonderful invention. Do they have them in Australia?"

"I don't think it would be a good idea for us," Emma said, smiling. "It heats the whole room nicely, doesn't it? We spend most of our time trying to keep cool."

Mrs Fisk turned from the cooker and gave Emma a withering stare. "There's leek and potato soup," she said. "Is that all right for you?"

"Thank you. Sounds very nice, Mrs Fisk," Emma said and watched the woman's expression soften just a little.

"I'm afraid there's nothing fancy today. The mistress just wanted a boiled egg. So for us it's nothing more than cold ham and pickles."

While she talked she ladled soup into an earthenware bowl. She put this on the table in Emma's place, then carried over a board with a basket of rolls, slices of ham, a hunk of cheddar cheese and a jar of piccalilli.

"Get that lot inside you and you won't do too bad," she said.

The soup was warm and rich, the rolls crusty and the lunch satisfying. Emma felt self-conscious sitting there to eat alone. She wondered if the others had already eaten or would eat later. She knew that English hours were much later than Australian ones. At the winery they had their evening meal at six, whereas in England they thought nothing of dining at eight.

While Emma was eating, Cynthia Morton returned to the kitchen, poured herself a cup of tea from the pot on the AGA and pulled out a stool opposite Emma at the table. "So have you taken a look at the book yet? Had a chance to get started?"

"I have," Emma said.

"And what do you think so far? Is it good enough? Is it going to be good enough to publish? That's what's worrying me. I don't know how the dementia is affecting her writing, and I'm no reader. Besides, she wouldn't show it to me."

"I think it's going to be very good," Emma said.

"You do? You're not just saying that to be polite or kind?" Cynthia's expression became quite hopeful.

"I'm absolutely riveted so far. But it is very different from her usual books. Much more descriptive, and it gives us more insight into Inspector Melrose than we've had before."

"Interesting," Cynthia said. "I've no idea why she suddenly got this bee in her bonnet to write another book. And Scotland of all places. What does she know about Scotland? I thought she was quite happy to retire gracefully and live on the spoils of her royalty checks."

"Maybe it had to do with her diagnosis," Emma said. "She wanted to prove she could still write a book before it was too late."

"Which of course she couldn't," Cynthia said sharply. "I thought it was an absolutely absurd idea and I told her so. I said at the beginning that it would only lead to tears. 'Rest on our laurels,' I told her. 'You've more laurels to rest on than any other damned person on this planet. You've nothing to prove to anyone.' But she wouldn't listen to me. Never does, of course. Just plunges ahead. Typical Iris."

"I haven't got far enough to know if she's thought through the plot logically," Emma said. "So far she's just setting the scene. We've got a murder and apparently some suspects, but I'm already hooked, and I like the young Melrose. He's in many ways more human than the later one. More vulnerable."

"Well that's a blessing." Cynthia gave a derisive snort. "I never did take to that man. I always found him too clever by half, patronizing and supercilious."

"Maybe that was a defence mechanism in his later years," Emma suggested. "He was always a bit of an outsider in London, wasn't he?"

Cynthia drained her cup. "I can't really tell you. As I say, I've never read much of them. Iris made me try a few times. Not my cup of tea." She stood up. "Well, I'd better let you get back to work. Iris will want a full report in the morning when she's feeling better, I'm sure. Come across for supper at about seven. We'll eat in the kitchen again, I expect."

As she went Emma remembered. "Oh, by the way, Miss Morton. There doesn't appear to be any hot water in the cottage."

"Oh no. Silly me. I forgot to turn on the boiler. I'll come over and do it this afternoon, when I have a moment." Then she walked out before Emma could say another word. Emma detected the hint of a smile on her face. *She's enjoying making things difficult for me. First she didn't light the fire and now there's no hot water,* she thought. *Is she trying to scare me off, or just punish me for being here?* She shook her head, trying to understand Cynthia's motivation. Shouldn't she be glad if Iris wanted to finish another book while she still could? Was it just that she felt Emma wasn't up to the task and wouldn't do Iris's work justice, or was she so attached to Iris that she resented any intruder claiming Iris's attention? She suspected there might be a romantic attachment on Cynthia's side even if Iris did not reciprocate. But then Iris had never married either, so . . .

Emma shrugged, got up and carried her plates over to the sink.

"Just leave them," Mrs Fisk snapped. "There's no need for you to do kitchen work. You're here to help the mistress, although if you ask me, she's bitten off more than she can chew."

# Chapter 14

The rain had subsided to a drizzle as Emma returned to the cottage. The log was glowing on the fire, and the room felt warm and cosy. *My little cottage,* Emma thought and savoured those words. She felt as if she had made a step forward with her life; she was a professional writer, here to work with another author. It was the sort of place she had dreamed about when she had lived in the tiny room above the bookshop and written her novel at night. It had all gone so smoothly for her since coming to England: the publishing job, the novel accepted and now this. A dream fulfilled. Then the doubt crept in again. What if she couldn't write well enough to do Iris's work justice?

She glanced at the pile of pages on the desk. It didn't look very thick. Just how far had Iris gone with the story? Would Iris's dementia show in the logic of the writing? Emma had seen a couple of times that morning when Iris seemed to lose a train of thought, only to come back quickly to reality. What did Iris expect of her? Would they talk through the plot together, would she give Emma suggestions for where she wanted the story to go, or would she expect Emma to take what she had and get on with it? Going to Scotland was a necessity, that was clear. She found it hard to picture what Skye looked like. Those rugged Cuillin mountains—were they tall and sharp like the Alps? Or were they more like the mountains in Australia—rounded slopes, not appearing particularly high at all?

*I'm jumping ahead of myself,* she thought. *Let me get through Iris's pages and talk the plot through with her before I go up to Scotland.* All the same, it was exciting to think about, getting on the train, then a ferry, and being in a very different sort of place. Following in the footsteps of Inspector Melrose.

She went back to the pages and read on:

## *The Wild Girl*, Chapter 4

The hotel room proved to be spacious and well appointed, with a gas fire in the old fireplace and a view over the strait to the mainland. Melrose left his suitcase on the bed, conscious that he shouldn't keep MacDonald waiting. When he came out the inspector was deep in conversation with the landlady, and Melrose heard the soft notes of the Gaelic speech. That might be a disadvantage, he thought, if everyone could say things he couldn't understand. But then he decided that it was unlikely that Sir Henry Hamilton, MP, spoke the local tongue.

"Right then, let's get going while the weather holds," MacDonald said, giving a nod to Mistress MacLeod.

Since the day had been bright and blustery a few minutes ago, Melrose felt that this was a trifle pessimistic, but on coming out of the hotel he noticed a bank of dark clouds covering the northern part of the island. The wind had picked up and the water in the strait was flecked with whitecaps. The ferry was just departing, and he watched spray breaking over the front of the boat, glad that he wasn't on it. He climbed into the passenger seat beside MacDonald and they set off, driving up the hill past simple white cottages. As they left the settlement behind the scenery became stark again. Not a tree in sight and the land rising up to a formidable cone-shaped hill.

"That ahead is Sgurr na Coinnich," MacDonald said.

Melrose had no idea what he was talking about.

"Yon mountain. Not as big or imposing as the Cuillin, but a fair size. An easy tramp to the top, though. No real climbing there."

They continued upward, not encountering any vehicle or indeed any living thing apart from a bird of prey that drifted in the upcurrents above them. At the crest the scenery opened up before them: a series of bays and inlets along the coast to the left with the mainland beyond, and ahead to their right the mountains, the formidable Cuillin, now outlined sharp and dark in the approaching storm.

"So let's go over the facts, shall we?" he asked MacDonald as the road began to descend to the next cove. "Sir Henry

Hamilton. He's an MP. He lives in the village of Dun Akyn?"

"He lives in Dun Akyn castle," MacDonald said. "That's right. A proper fortress of a place, jutting out on a headland. I certainly wouldnae want to live there. He's only there part of the year. Down in London doing his job as an MP some of the time. Then there's his wife, she's down in the south with him sometimes, actually as often as she can, her being a Sassenach and not from here. They have—correction, had—two children. Their son, Roland, is twenty-one. He's been to the university in Edinburgh. Not sure what he plans to do with his life, but he's home again at the moment. Then there was the daughter, Lucy. She was eighteen, and she had been educated at home by a governess."

"So rather sheltered until now," Melrose said.

"Very sheltered, I'd say. Raised as girls were in the old days to make a good match."

"And this Euan Chisholm, he was the one her parents had selected for her, or had she chosen him?"

"Definitely the parents," MacDonald said. "This young man's father, Lord Chisholm, owns a vast estate across the strait on the mainland. Having the two linked by marriage would be extremely profitable to both. One could run sheep and the other cattle."

"Did the daughter agree to this match? Was she happy about it?"

"From what I gather the courting was only in the early stages. Chisholm had come to stay at Dun Akyn so that the young people could get to know each other. According to her mother it seemed to be going well. He was quite a charming young man, good-looking, nothing really for Lucy not to like."

"But then an outsider arrived?" Melrose asked.

MacDonald nodded. "A Mr Francis Stewart. He came to the island ostensibly to do some climbing, but it turns out he was a bit of a Communist agitator, and he was going around trying to tell the crofters their rights when Sir Henry wanted to move them off their land."

"I thought the expulsion of the crofters happened in the last century?" Melrose said. "That's what we were taught in school. The big landowners wanted the crofters gone so that they could farm sheep."

"True. That happened in most places but not so much on the islands. It's only recently that meat prices have risen in London and Sir Henry got it into his head to raise black Angus cattle on the island. So he's been gently persuading some of his crofters to move out so he can turn their land back into grazing."

"Gently persuading?" Melrose raised an eyebrow.

"Aye. Sometimes not so gently. And there was even one cottage that burned down mysteriously."

"So this young man—Stewart, you said—he was causing a bit of trouble for the laird."

"You could say that. Not only talking to the locals but he wrote a couple of articles for the newspapers in Glasgow and Edinburgh, exposing the injustice here."

"So Sir Henry would have every reason to want to get rid of him?"

"Definitely. But I don't think he'd resort to drowning his own daughter. He thought the world of her."

MacDonald slowed the motor car as a sheep stood in the middle of the road, eyeing them defiantly. MacDonald gave a toot on the horn and the animal wandered off, in no hurry.

"So let me get this straight," Melrose said. "Stewart was apparently running away with the laird's daughter, fleeing by boat to the mainland, is that correct?"

"Quite correct. He had come over in his own small sailing boat. As you can see the distance is not great at this point."

"Do we know if she was leaving willingly with him, or if he was kidnapping her for some reason? Was there a romantic entanglement? Had she fallen for him?"

"Quite possibly. He was, after all, quite a dashing outsider, and as we've said, she had been so sheltered."

"But someone got word of it and didn't want them to go?"

MacDonald nodded. "Someone made damnty sure they would not make the crossing. The mainsail had been cut to shreds. Clearly slashed through with a knife. They'd have been at the mercy of the current and the waves."

"Would they not have noticed this when they raised the sail?"

"It was dark, remember. They wouldn't have seen the rips in the sail."

Melrose had taken a small notebook from his breast pocket and was jotting down the odd word, not too easily as the car rattled and shook over the rough surface of the road.

"So the jilted suitor would be our obvious suspect. He finds his intended is running off with a bloke of lower class and decides to stop them."

"That would be my first thought," MacDonald said. "Especially since Chisholm's now disappeared. We can't find hide nor hair of him. Nobody remembers seeing him leave the island. It's even possible he's still hiding out in one of the wilder parts of the western shore. Quite uninhabited there, you know. Or easy enough to bribe a boatman to take him to one of the nearby islands. We've still got men on the look-out for him."

"It seems like an open-and-shut case then," Melrose said. "Unless . . ."

"Unless?" MacDonald turned to look at him.

"Unless the laird knew that Stewart was about to leave and wanted to make sure he never reached the mainland, not knowing about his daughter's romantic feelings for the young man and that she'd be going with him."

"That's a possibility," MacDonald said. "But you'll never be able to prove that one. In my experience of the gentry they close ranks when necessary, and men like Sir Henry wield a lot of power in these parts. If you so much as hinted he had anything to do with his daughter's death you'd be taken off the case instantly."

"Sounds like a charming assignment ahead for me then," Melrose said.

# Chapter 15

As Emma put down the last sheet she had read, a sudden thought hit her.

"Wait. What about the Wild Girl?" She said the words out loud. "You start off the book with her, and you haven't mentioned her since. You've called the book *The Wild Girl*, for Pete's sake. Where does she fit in? When is she going to come into the story?"

Now feeling annoyed and frustrated she grabbed the next chapter.

## *The Wild Girl*, Chapter 5

They came around a bend at the top of the hill, and MacDonald slowed the car. "There it is," he said. "That's Dun Akyn."

Melrose stifled a little gasp. The castle was a veritable fortress, jutting out into the sea on a narrow promontory. A medieval keep of high, impenetrable walls with slits for windows. Behind it was a wood of Scots pine trees, making it truly isolated from the string of cottages that lined the little cove beyond. From this viewpoint it reminded him of the sort of wooden castle his dad had made for him when he was a boy. He'd never liked it much, not being the sort of child who found wars exciting and heroic. He'd been old enough to see what the carnage of the Great War had done—a neighbour blinded by mustard gas, an uncle coming home without a leg and others not coming home at all.

MacDonald put the car into a low gear as they descended the steep hill. "You see the channel is quite narrow here," he said. "So the journey should not have been hard for a sailing boat. Just along there is where they swim the cattle across."

"Swim the cattle?" Melrose wondered if he'd heard right.

"Aye. Every year for hundreds of years they've swum the cattle across to market on the mainland. They put a rope through the nose of the first one, tie them together and lead them behind a boat. It's quite a sight."

"I bet it is," Melrose said. He was taking in stone cottages with smoke curling from their chimneys, tiny cultivated fields, peat stacked and left to dry, just as it must have been for hundreds of years.

Melrose held on as the car negotiated one bend after another and tried to concentrate on the scenery. To their right the land rose to the first outcrops of the Cuillin, sharp and black against a darkening sky. Not incredibly tall mountains but ominous in their way. Melrose moved uncomfortably in his seat. Why was he here? What on earth could he achieve? Either the suitor committed the murders and had fled somewhere safe, or his family was hiding him, presumably in a castle like this one, or Sir Henry had it done and would never confess. It felt hopeless, and he had to stop himself from telling MacDonald to turn the car around and take him back to the ferry.

They entered the small settlement: simple whitewashed cottages. Not even a pub. Waves splashed up against a wharf where fishing nets were drying.

"Oh, there is one thing I almost forgot to mention," MacDonald said. "I'm not sure where it fits in, or rather where she fits in, but it might be relevant."

"She? Who are we talking about?"

"The Wild Girl," MacDonald said.

Melrose looked sharply at him as if he suspected MacDonald was pulling his leg. "Wild Girl?"

"That's what the villagers call her. Her mother died when she was little. Her father is a fisherman and often out at sea, leaving the child to run wild, no proper schooling, no one to make sure her clothes are clean. The local people have suggested that she is not entirely human, but one of the fairy folk."

Melrose gave a nervous chuckle. Now he was sure he was being spun a tale.

"Oh yes. Can she fly?"

"I'm deadly serious, man," MacDonald said. "Anyway, a few years ago the laird's wife took pity on her and took her in. You might say she tamed her. Educated her with her own daughter. The girls became bosom friends and did everything together. And now apparently she has gone missing, too. Or rather she has vanished. Well, she might if she was half fairy, I suppose."

Still Melrose wasn't sure whether this islander was having a laugh at his expense. He'd wait until Melrose questioned the owners of the castle about a wild girl who could vanish and then he would watch them all chuckle. Melrose was determined to tread warily and let these folks know that he might look young but he was a trained and competent member of the Criminal Investigation Department.

They left the last cottage behind as they approached the castle. MacDonald brought the car to a halt where the road ended at a small harbour, nestled into the rocks. Two fishing boats were tied up but there was no sign of life there.

"Easier to walk from here," he said. "There are steps up to the castle. Otherwise we have to drive up and around through the wood, and there's no guarantee the main gates won't be locked. They were last time. Damnty nuisance."

Melrose got out, to be met by the wind, cold and damp. He realized that even the narrow crossing here, where the wind was funnelled between the mountains on either side, would be dangerous for a sailing boat if the weather turned nasty. What if the deaths were just a tragic accident? The boat had capsized because of an inexperienced sailor and an unexpected wave. Wouldn't it be best to leave it at that for now? He turned up his coat collar as he felt the first raindrops, then trudged after MacDonald, who was already ascending the path up to the castle. As they rose higher the wind hit them full in the face. Melrose looked up at those granite walls towering above him and shivered. What on earth would it be like, actually having to live in such a bleak and inhospitable place? He wondered how it coloured the temperament of the people inside that granite fortress. Once up on the promontory they followed the outer wall around to a gateway leading to the inner keep. This gate was open and they went inside, up to a most formidable front door. Solid oak, studded with iron, it wasn't the type that could be breached.

MacDonald brought the knocker crashing down, turning to grin at Melrose with satisfaction at the noise it made. "That'll wake them up if they're asleep," he said.

They did not have to wait long before the door was opened by an elderly man with white hair, wearing a black morning coat with tails, high starched collar and pin-striped trousers. Melrose had never met a butler before, but he had read of them in crime novels and recognized this as the real article.

"Ah, Inspector MacDonald," the butler said in his soft Highland tones. "I see you have brought the gentleman from Glasgow with you. Please do come in. I shall inform the master that you are here."

They stepped into a dark, cavernous hallway. On one side a stone staircase ascended to a landing above, now bathed in gloom. On the walls weapons and bits of armour of various shapes and sizes were displayed: pikes and shields and a wicked-looking axe. Melrose thought it would have been a foolish person who decided to pick a fight with the Hamiltons. Before he had time to take it all in the butler opened a door to their right.

"In here if you please, gentlemen."

They stepped into a room that was warmed by a fire in a huge stone fireplace. The furniture was what you might find in any household: a chintz-covered sofa, large leather armchairs, even a potted plant struggling to survive in the corner. An ordinary, comfortable living room that might have been his parents' if not for the tall, narrow windows set into two-foot-thick walls giving just a glimpse of the loch below. The men remained standing, not saying anything, and soon they heard male voices echoing in that entrance hall and a man came in. He was a commanding presence—a big, powerful man in his fifties, sporting a red beard flecked with grey. He wore a tweed jacket and corduroy slacks like any of his crofters, but there was no mistaking that this was the laird, Sir Henry Hamilton.

"Oh, you're back," he said. His gaze swept over Melrose, his look one of arrogant disdain. "I thought we were supposed to be getting a homicide chappie from Glasgow."

Melrose cleared his throat and stepped forward. "I am Inspector Melrose from the homicide squad in Glasgow," he said. "How do you do, sir."

"You? You're the so-called experienced man I requested? Is this a joke? It's my daughter's murder we are investigating, man. Not a missing pussy cat."

Melrose met his gaze and did not blink. "I can assure you, sir, that I have the necessary experience. I will do a thorough job for you."

"Experience? What are you, twenty-one? How many years can you possibly have had on the force?"

"As a matter of fact it's now almost twelve years," he said. "Five of those with the CID."

"Well, I am not at all satisfied," Sir Henry said. "Bloody well disgusted. If this is the way that the Glasgow Police treat a Scottish member of Parliament then heaven help us all. I should have bypassed you and gone straight to Edinburgh, or even down to Scotland Yard."

"We definitely have our share of murders in Glasgow," Melrose said. "And I have taken and passed the required courses." He was tempted to say that he didn't think Scotland Yard would consider the deaths of two people in an overturned sailing boat, which might turn out to be an accident, important enough to send a team to the wilds of Scotland. But wisely he stayed silent.

"I can assure you, Sir Henry, that we of the island police will be entirely at Inspector Melrose's disposal to make sure this case is dealt with thoroughly and fairly," MacDonald said.

"Hmmpf," Sir Henry snorted. "A lot of help that will be. You haven't apprehended the blaggard so far, have you?"

"Who are you talking about, Sir Henry?" Melrose asked.

"Why that Chisholm fellow," Sir Henry bellowed. "I invite him into my home thinking we've found the ideal suitor for my daughter. And now my daughter is dead and the bugger has disappeared. He obviously found out that my daughter was planning to run away with that no-good Communist agitator and killed them both. Now he's probably already on his way to South America, God rot his guts."

Melrose frowned. "Do you have any reason to believe that he was the one to blame for this tragedy?"

"Why else would he have disappeared?" Sir Henry snapped.

Melrose took a deep breath. "Maybe we could all sit down and talk this through, starting at the beginning. I've only heard snippets of what happened and why so far. I'd prefer to know all the details from you, Sir Henry."

Without being asked he took a seat in one of the armchairs and took out his notebook.

# Chapter 16

## *The Wild Girl*, Chapter 6

Sir Henry gave a grunt of impatience. "Bloody waste of time. You should be out there looking for Chisholm not chatting like some woman with me."

"I can't proceed if I don't have the facts, sir," Melrose said.

"Oh, very well." Sir Henry sighed and took a seat in the armchair across from him while MacDonald perched on an upright ladder-back chair near the window, clearly wanting to be as far away from this conversation as possible.

"Now," Melrose said. "Should we not invite your wife to be present?"

"My wife is a delicate creature, and I don't want to put her through more grief. She's already devastated with the loss of her daughter, even though I'm sure she finds it hard to forgive her for running off so inexplicably and ungratefully." He winced as if this admission pained him.

"And with that nobody, that lower-class Communist agitator. I'll never understand it ever."

When Melrose said nothing he went on. "Maybe it was partially our fault. We sheltered her too much. We wanted to protect her, to keep her safe from the temptations of the outside world, and to find her a good husband. That's how it had worked for my wife, and she was perfectly happy with the arrangement. Lucy never showed any signs of being unhappy. It's true she didn't take to young Chisholm to start with, but what did she know about men? She would have come to love him."

"So your daughter had been living here, in this castle, all her life? She had not gone away to school or to a finishing school? You weren't going to have her presented at court?"

"Absolutely not," Sir Henry said. "Both are a total waste of money. Why educate a girl beyond the basics? We hired a decent governess for her who taught her to read, write and do arithmetic. Some geography, history and French. That's all a young woman needs. And as for being presented at court—why would I want to expose my daughter to a lot of young Englishmen when it was clear she had to marry a fellow Scot? I'm proud of my Scottish blood. I can trace my ancestry back before the Vikings.

And I intend to keep that bloodline pure. Chisholm would have been ideal for her."

"And ideal for you, too, so I understand," Melrose said.

"Meaning what by that?" Sir Henry glared.

"I understood that his estate on the mainland is just across from yours. Convenient for both of you, I'd imagine."

"Damned cheek." Sir Henry's face flushed beet red. "Do you not think I wanted the best for my daughter?"

"I'm sure you did, sir," MacDonald said quickly. Melrose stayed silent, telling himself to watch his mouth or he'd make the man into an enemy before they'd even started.

"So Chisholm arrived to meet your daughter, but she didn't take to him, is that correct?" he asked.

"I'm not sure. You can never tell with young women. They are inclined to be flighty, aren't they? I'm sure she would have liked him just fine and been prepared to go ahead with the match if that damned interloper had not shown up on our doorstep." Melrose noted how Sir Henry had clenched his fist.

"He arrived here, claiming to be a climber and asking for advice on best routes up various mountains. I had been a keen mountaineer in my youth, so naturally I took to the boy, showed him around the Cuillin, the best climbs, and eventually invited him to stay. Big mistake! It turned out he was going around to our tenants, telling them about their so-called rights. Stirring up trouble. He was a labour agitator, that's what he was. More likely a Communist agitator trained by Russia, determined to ruin all the landowning families. He didn't understand how we have to survive here. If beef cattle can make a profit for us, then we have to run beef. Instead we've these tiny crofts, dividing my land into useless parcels and not giving me access to any decent grazing. I was going to pay to relocate my tenants, set them up with new homes. Better homes. Indoor plumbing."

"And he had designs on your daughter?"

"I had no idea," Sir Henry said. "Not the least idea that that was going on behind my back. I must say they were damned good at hiding it. I say 'they' because I have to consider that she might have not been quite innocent in this matter. Well, I suppose I can understand it. I mean, she was an impressionable young girl. He wasn't bad-looking, not badly spoken for a lower-class person, and he represented all that her parents hated. But as for running off with him—who could ever have foreseen that? A harmless little flirtation is one thing. But running away from her family, from all that she held dear? Choosing a life of poverty and disgrace?

I'll never understand that. Never." He brought his fist crashing down on the arm of his chair. Melrose got a clear glimpse of why a daughter would want to run away from such a household.

"So when was the first moment you realized your daughter was gone?" Melrose asked.

"Around lunchtime the next day. Her maid reported that Lucy's bed had not been slept in."

"Was the castle door not kept locked at night?" Melrose asked. "You don't have any servants on guard?"

Sir Henry gave a derisive chuckle. "My good man, what reason would we have for locking doors here? The Viking raids, for which this castle was built, are long gone. The people who live around us are all our tenants. They owe their livelihood to us. Besides, crime on this island is limited to the occasional sheep stealing, wouldn't you agree, Inspector MacDonald?"

"Oh definitely, Sir Henry," MacDonald said. "If it's not sheep stealing, it's getting into a fight after too much whisky. But I'd say that robbery, burglary, are almost unheard of here. For one thing we know our neighbours. For another where would you run to when you live on an island and the only way off is the ferry where you'd be recognized?"

"And yet Mr Chisholm apparently managed to get away quite easily, and the young couple would have managed to elope had it not been for disaster befalling their boat," Melrose said.

"That's true enough. As for Chisholm, he may have stolen or borrowed a boat to take him to the mainland. He may have paid one of our fishermen enough to buy his silence. They have a difficult winter ahead of them. When there are weeks of storms they can't go out and fish. Money would certainly be tempting, and Chisholm had plenty of it." He paused, grimacing. "My daughter would have wanted for nothing. She would have lived in luxury all her days. What on earth drove her to this reckless decision?"

Melrose waited until Sir Henry had finished his outburst. "So to get back to the night she disappeared. It was only the next day that the maid found her bed had not been slept in?"

"That is correct," Sir Henry said. "We take our breakfast when we feel like it and do not always cross paths in the breakfast room. Lucy was of delicate constitution and sometimes would only have a sliver of toast and marmalade in the mornings, or even have her maid bring her a cup of tea to her bedroom. So the fact that nobody had seen her that morning was not unusual."

"And when did you notice that Chisholm was missing?"

"I gather he told one of the servants that he wasn't feeling well the evening before and would not be joining us for dinner. We had housed him in one of the cottages, not the main house, you understand. It would not have been proper to be under the same roof as my daughter before they were engaged. But the servants took good care to see he wanted for nothing, and he took his meals with us. So it was only after we found Lucy missing that the servants said they hadn't seen Mr Chisholm all morning, and we found his bed had not been slept in either. Naturally we leapt to the conclusion that he had fled in a hurry. Most of his clothes were still hanging in the wardrobe."

Melrose looked across at MacDonald. "You said that your men had checked the ferries and he had not been seen aboard?"

"That is correct," MacDonald said. "I suppose it's possible he might have gone down to the Mallaig ferry, where he would not have been recognized so easily, but that would indeed be a long walk during a dark night. And as yet, he has not been spotted on the mainland either."

"I expect we'll find that the blaggard got someone to take him to another island and from there across to Ireland." Sir Henry's face was an angry red. "That's what I would do if I was trying to flee. I presume you've been in touch with the Irish police?"

"It's never easy dealing with the Irish, sir," MacDonald said.

"Damned Irish. We should never have let them have their independence. Too weak by half."

Melrose thought it wise not to point out that the part of Ireland where Chisholm would have landed would have been in Northern Ireland and therefore still part of Britain. He felt they were getting off track. He was here to do an investigation on the island. He had no way of chasing after a fugitive who might be abroad by now. He paused, thinking through what he had already been told. He cleared his throat. "I understand there was another person who might have been involved. This so-called Wild Girl? Was I not told that she was living with you these days?"

"Flora, you mean? Yes, they did call her the Wild Girl down there in the village. The poor child was left to fend for herself while her father was out at sea. My wife and I talked about it for some time. We felt so badly for her, running barefoot through the countryside like that. It wasn't natural. And when she started to grow into a young woman and we saw the young men in the village eyeing her, my wife finally decided we had to act. The girl was quite unschooled, innocent, unaware of the world. She'd be an easy target for any young man with bad designs on her. So we persuaded her to come and live with us. We did it with good intentions. Whether that was wise or not, I can't say."

"What do you mean by that, sir?" Melrose asked.

"I suppose I'm asking myself whether Flora turned out to be a bad influence in any way. Whether she might have put the idea into Lucy's head to run off with a man. I'm sure it would never have occurred to my daughter before that girl came here." He paused again, staring out of the window, lost in thought.

"So your daughter became friendly with her?"

He nodded. "As it happened Lucy took to her instantly. I suppose she had been lacking in female friendship. Her brother was off at university. She had a governess but was getting too old for lessons, so a companion was what she craved. The girls became bosom friends. Inseparable. Flora slept in the small maid's room adjacent to Lucy's suite."

"You say the girls were close. Did Lucy not confide in her what she planned to do? Did she not notice Lucy slipping away in the night?"

"That's just the problem," Sir Henry said. "Flora is gone and she wasn't here when Lucy ran away. A day earlier she had heard that her father was poorly—caught a chill out at sea—and said she had to go and visit him. So off she went with some broth from the kitchen. She does tend to come and go, when the mood takes her. She has to be out running through the heather or climbing over the rocks like a wild creature. That's why she's called the Wild Girl, and I don't think we've ever fully tamed her. My wife worries about her—that she'll come to some kind of bad end. Her mother wasn't exactly a saint. For all we know she could be meeting men, doing what comes naturally to her. Believe me, we've had many a heated discussion on what happens next."

"Meaning when Lucy got married and moved away?" Melrose asked.

"Precisely." Sir Henry thumped the arm of his chair again. "Do we still look after her when Lucy goes? What would become of her? Ideally she would have moved with Lucy to the mainland and lived as her companion, but she wouldn't abandon her father—although the man does not deserve her devotion. He hardly paid her a scrap of attention all the while she was growing up. When he wasn't out fishing, he was at the pub, staggering home late and full of whisky. Flora would help him off with his shoes and put him to bed when she was a tiny scrap of a girl."

"So she is currently down with her father in his cottage?" Melrose asked.

"That's right. She went a couple of days ago."

"Have the police talked to her yet?" Melrose looked across at MacDonald.

"We have not," MacDonald said. "When one of my men went to the cottage nobody was there. The father was out at sea apparently, and the girl . . . well, there was no sign of her. Maybe she saw the police car coming and went to hide. She has a deep distrust of the law, like most people around here."

"So we will need to find her and talk to her as soon as possible," Melrose said. "She would be the one person who Lucy would have confided in."

"If she confided in anyone," Sir Henry said. "My daughter has always kept her feelings to herself. And she probably paid for this with her life."

"Do you have any reason to believe that Flora was in league with Chisholm then? You called her a wild creature earlier."

Sir Henry hesitated, frowning. "No, I suppose I was overwrought. I had not noticed Chisholm paying any attention to her. In fact, given his nature I cannot believe he'd have any interest in someone who is clearly his social inferior. She was Lucy's companion. Not worth a second glance."

"Do you happen to have any photographs of the people involved?" Melrose asked. "It would be helpful if I knew who I was looking for."

"I suppose so." Sir Henry got up and left the room. Melrose and MacDonald glanced at each other.

"I don't know how you'll ever get to the bottom of this," MacDonald said. "Rather you than me, my friend. As soon as we've finished up here, I'll be back to Portree and then it's all up to you."

He looked rather smug.

# Chapter 17

A squall of rain hit the window, rattling the panes alarmingly. Emma looked up and glanced at her watch. Almost three o'clock. She wondered if she'd have time to finish the pages today. She was anxious to discuss the story with Iris Blackburn. She didn't see how it could be in any way complicated. Two suspects, either Chisholm or the Wild Girl, if it wasn't an accident—which it surely could not be, since this was a crime novel. Emma sighed, jotted down more notes, then picked up the next sheaf of papers.

## FROM *THE WILD GIRL*, CHAPTER 7

They didn't have to wait long before Sir Henry reappeared, carrying several photographs in leather frames.

"Here," he said. "These should give you some idea." He passed the first photograph to Melrose. It was a posed portrait of a young girl, sitting holding a bunch of flowers and looking shyly at the camera.

"That was taken on her sixteenth birthday," he said. "That was our daughter."

Melrose thought she was extremely pretty, with wide eyes that showed a hint of amusement and soft curls falling over her shoulders. His immediate reaction was that he would like to have known her.

"Here are some snapshots taken recently," Sir Henry said, handing over some smaller photographs. The first was of several figures standing outside in dappled shade. Two men and two girls. Melrose recognized Lucy, then focused on the other girl. She looked remarkably similar, not only in dress and hairstyle but in features, too. Melrose realized that she was obviously wearing Lucy's clothes and emulating her benefactor. However there was nothing submissive about her. She stared at the camera defiantly. The Wild Girl. Only she did not look as Melrose had imagined her. She could have passed as a family member, he thought. They had tamed her after all. He looked up.

"One of these young men is your son?"

"The one on the right. Next to Flora."

Melrose saw the family resemblance. A bigger, brawnier version of Lucy. The same wide eyes and high forehead. "And the other man? This is Chisholm?"

Sir Henry nodded. Chisholm was tall, good-looking in an effete sort of way—hair parted in the middle and slicked down, neat Ronald Colman moustache and staring at the camera with the same air of arrogance that

Sir Henry displayed. In fact he looked quite pleased with himself—smug, Melrose thought, and he noted he had an arm around Lucy's waist. Her expression, as far as he could tell, conveyed that she did not like this. She was gritting her teeth and looked like she wanted to be away from him. She must have felt trapped, Melrose thought. Pushed into a marriage her father wanted with a man she clearly loathed. No wonder she had latched on to Stewart as her chance to escape.

"Do you have a picture of Stewart? The young man who drowned?" he asked.

"Why would I waste good film on a stranger?" Sir Henry asked. "Besides, you'll see him for yourself. His body is laid out in our game larder. It's one place guaranteed to be cold enough. I'll have you taken there when we are through with the questions."

Melrose was wondering what more he should ask, how to wind up this interview and have a chance to speak with the other family members, when he heard the sound of light feet tapping down the hallway. The door opened and Lady Hamilton came in. At least Melrose surmised it must be she—a fine-boned, middle-aged woman with flawless skin and hair in neat waves. Her forehead was creased with frown lines, although Melrose couldn't tell if these were from grief. She wore a severe black dress with a black shawl over her shoulders which made her pale complexion look almost ghostlike. In fact she almost looked like a ghost as she crossed the room, a figure detached from reality.

Sir Henry frowned. "My dear, the police are here. I'm sure you don't want to go through this again. Why don't you wait in the morning room until we are finished?"

"Oh no, Henry," she said and her voice sounded surprisingly strong. "I want to know everything, hear everything. I want to find out who killed my daughter."

Melrose gave a nodding bow in her direction. "Lady Hamilton. I am Detective Inspector Melrose from Glasgow, and I will do my very best to get to the truth for you."

She examined him critically, as her husband had done. "You are not much older than my son, Roland," she said. "How is it that they sent you and not an experienced man?"

"Exactly what I said, my dear." Sir Henry spat out the words.

"And I explained to your husband that I might look young but I have worked on murder investigations and feel that I am capable of doing the job. So now that you are here, might I ask you a few questions, your Ladyship?"

Lady Hamilton went over to the fireplace and perched at the edge of the sofa.

"I don't know what I can tell you that my husband has not already said. We had no idea that our daughter was in any way unhappy with our arrangement for her. Or that she was in any way attached to this stranger."

"Was your daughter chaperoned all the time? Would she have had time and opportunity to meet with this young man alone?"

"She wasn't a prisoner, Inspector," Lady Hamilton said. "Although she wasn't the type to crave solitude. She went out riding, usually with her brother."

"Was she close to her brother, Lady Hamilton?"

For a second she smiled, the lines vanishing from her face. "As children they were inseparable. They did everything together, including getting up to mischief. Lucy could run and climb as well as any boy. Her governess kept trying to insist that she learn to behave like a lady, and do you know what she said? She said, 'When I'm old enough to be a lady, I'll learn to be one.' She had a ready tongue, my dear child. Always stood up for herself."

The smile faded. "But Roland went away to university. When he came back I saw that their relationship had changed. He was still extremely protective of her, but she did not want to be smothered, as she put it. She resented the fact that he was allowed to study and she was not. She felt it highly unfair when her brain was as good as his. Recently she became much closer to Flora."

"Ah yes. Flora. The Wild Girl," Melrose said.

"Don't call her that. So many unkind things have been said about that child. It really wasn't her fault that she was allowed to run wild and was given no care at all. We worked hard to civilize her when she came to us, and she seemed to take well to all instruction. A good brain, that's for sure. And she clearly loved Lucy. We let her wear Lucy's clothes and she soon learned that it was nice to get approval by looking pretty. They looked like two peas in a pod when they went out. Both of them with their reddish curls. So delightful."

She broke off, fished for a handkerchief in her pocket and dabbed at her eyes. "They went everywhere together. You asked how Lucy would have had time to meet this man alone, and I really don't know. As I said, she and Flora were inseparable. They went for walks together. But apart from that, her former governess was still in residence until very recently. We have groundsmen and ghillies who would surely have noticed our daughter trying to meet this man in secret outside the castle. Nobody has reported observing such meetings." She gave a deep sigh. "But none of this is relevant. The fact is that she did run off with this person and that somebody did deliberately sabotage their boat, thus drowning both."

"We are sure of that, are we?" Melrose asked. "It is absolutely clear that it was deliberate? I understand that the sail was ripped. Could that not have happened to old canvas with the force of the wind?"

"It was clearly slashed with a knife, Inspector," Sir Henry said. "Slashed to pieces."

Melrose frowned. "So I'm no sailor," he said, "but if they raised the sail would they not have noticed this and thus not left the harbour?"

"It's a tight manoeuvre to get out of the harbour here," Sir Henry said. "A small boat like that would have only hoisted the mainsail once in clear water."

"Even so," Melrose said. "If the sail was damaged, wouldn't it just flap uselessly and they wouldn't go anywhere?"

"True," Sir Henry said, "but I understand one of the sheets was also cut through."

"Sheets?" Melrose pictured laundry flapping.

"Nautical term for ropes. If a sheet that controlled the mainsail was cut through, the sail would swing wildly and easily capsize such a small boat."

"I see." Melrose tried to collect his thoughts as he spoke. "The slashed sail indicates an impulsive action, a momentary anger. But cutting the rope so the sail cannot be controlled, that is more calculated."

Sir Henry nodded. "I agree with that."

"You say the boat was in the harbour. Did nobody notice someone damaging the sail and cutting the rope?"

"I suspect it was done under cover of darkness that night. And you should note it was not that big a boat, Inspector. We are not talking about a yacht here. It was pathetically small. A mere dinghy, ample for the short crossing but certainly not seaworthy. And I suspect horribly easy to capsize and sink."

"Was there rough weather that night?" Melrose asked.

"There was a stiff breeze apparently. No moon. A black night if ever there was one. But they could have made the crossing if the man was an experienced sailor. Quite possibly he was not and that contributed to the tragedy."

"So when was the tragedy discovered?"

"That next morning as the fishing boats went out they found the boat upside down and no sign of the sailors. They towed it in to shore and soon afterward Stewart's body was found on some rocks nearby. It wasn't until lunchtime that we discovered our daughter was missing. We asked in the village, of course, and one woman thought she saw a couple walking along the waterfront late at night. The woman wearing a hooded cape. She couldn't see who they were. So we then had to assume that Lucy had gone with him.

"We searched Lucy's cupboards and found that she had taken some of her things, including her jewellery. That's when we knew. We had every boat in the harbour out and searching for her. It wasn't until a day later that her body was found, floating in the shallows on the mainland side. The sea creatures had already got at her." He closed his eyes and gave a shudder. "My poor daughter. Poor little Lucy. What a horrible death."

Melrose nodded, wondering where to go with his questioning next. "It seems to me that the person who might have some answers for us is this Flora. If your daughter was as close to her as you say, she will have confided in her. I'll go and try to find her. And I'd also like to take a look at the boat and examine both of the bodies."

"Naturally," Sir Henry said. "I'll have my son take you."

MacDonald stood up. "I really should be getting back to my duties in Portree," he said. "Can I ask your son to deliver

Inspector Melrose back to the Kings Arms when you are finished here today?"

Melrose gave him an inquiring glance. "I thought you said a driver was to be put at my disposal?"

"Aye. Jock from Kyleakin. The local taxi. He should be available unless there's an emergency."

"I might need more local assistance to locate Flora," Melrose said. "Do you have any officers stationed down here?"

"The nearest police station is at Broadford. We've two men there."

"But I can recruit some of my crofters for a search if it's needed," Sir Henry said. "Mind you, if the girl doesn't want to be found you've little chance of finding her. She knows these hills like the back of her hand. She can probably survive out in the wild until winter sets in."

Melrose stifled a sigh. "Let's take a look at the bodies and the boat, then head for her cottage, shall we?" He was getting a feeling that nobody wanted to be particularly helpful. Were they now trying to shield Flora? Did they suspect she had something to do with Lucy's and Stewart's deaths?

# Chapter 18

Emma broke off, looking up from the pages. This was a new twist. Was the writer suggesting that Flora had caused the fatal accident? Because she hadn't wanted Lucy to leave her behind? Surely if she was close to Lucy, bosom friends as Sir Henry had suggested, she wouldn't want her harmed or killed. But she was the Wild Girl. She clearly didn't play by the rules of society.

Emma considered Chisholm. He was the more likely suspect. Described as arrogant and smug. Lucy was his conquest. If he married her, he'd acquire more land and more power. So if she had rejected him and he found she was fleeing with a man he considered his social inferior, he would have been angry enough to make sure they never made that crossing. And staying in a cottage rather than the main house would have given him the freedom to come and go without being noticed.

She jotted down more notes, satisfied that the case could now be easily solved. There were not too many more pages. She would finish it by the end of the day, and then she could tell Iris that she felt confident enough to tie the remaining threads together and finish the book. And she was looking forward to going to Scotland, seeing for herself the scenes described, although it wasn't strictly necessary. Iris had described it all well enough. She picked up the next set of pages off the pile:

## *The Wild Girl*, Chapter 8

"So I can safely leave you in good hands then?" MacDonald said as they followed Sir Henry out of the room. "As soon as we've taken a look at the bodies."

Lady Hamilton still sat by the fire, not moving. The look on her face was one of blank despair.

The butler appeared in the hall in that uncanny way that butlers had of knowing when someone was about to leave.

"Ah, Cummings, go and find Mr Roland and tell him he's wanted. Tell him he'll find us in the game larder."

"Very good, Sir Henry." The elderly man went up the stairs with surprising agility.

"Right. Follow me. This way." They stepped out into a fine, misty rain. Sir Henry didn't seem to notice the rain or go back for an umbrella. Instead he led them around the side of the keep to several low stone outbuildings. He opened the door to one of these. Melrose reacted to the smell. In spite of the cold temperature inside, the bodies were beginning to decay.

There was a stone slab on each side and a cruel-looking hook hanging from the ceiling at the back. It looked like a house of horrors to Melrose. The two bodies were lying on the slabs, each covered in a white sheet. Sir Henry went ahead and drew back the first sheet. The young man looked greenish-white but quite peaceful. He had had a pleasant face, but there was no trace of expression. He resembled a large porcelain doll.

"You have had a doctor examine both of them?" Melrose asked. His voice echoed from the stone walls and floor. "And he signed a death certificate?"

"Of course. The cause of death was drowning. That's obvious enough isn't it? No sign of trauma on either body, so nobody knocked them into the water. The boat capsized. They went in."

"Could your daughter not swim?"

"She could not," Sir Henry said. "With the temperature of the water here there is little need for swimming lessons. And I gather that Stewart could not swim either."

"It's interesting to me that Stewart was found near the boat and your daughter down the coast on the mainland," Melrose said.

"The currents are strong in the channel," Sir Henry said. "Maybe Stewart was able to cling to the boat for a while before he became too cold and lost his grip while Lucy went under and was carried away."

Melrose covered Stewart again, then went across to the other body.

"It's not a pretty sight," Sir Henry said. "She was face down in a rock pool for quite a while. The crabs must have gone to work on her."

He pulled back the sheet and Melrose swallowed hard. Part of her face and neck were eaten away. "I don't need to see more," he said, hastily covering her again with the sheet. "At least she was dead before . . ." He shuddered.

"You wanted me, Father?" A voice from the doorway made them turn around. Roland Hamilton was indeed a young version of his father. Striking red hair, a strong chin and blue eyes. A remarkably good-looking family, Melrose thought. Even at twenty-one Roland had that same air of arrogance. Did all aristocrats look like that? Melrose wondered. Were they born that way or did they acquire the expression from ordering other people around all their lives and having servants bowing and scraping to them?

"Ah yes, Roland, my boy," Sir Henry said. "This is Inspector Melrose, sent to us from Glasgow. He wants to take a look at the wrecked boat and to find Flora."

"I don't know what good either of those things will do," Roland said, giving Melrose a look of dislike. Or was it disdain?

"The boat capsized. And Flora wasn't even here when it happened."

"Your sister may have confided in her about her plans to run away," Melrose said.

"My sister was quite a private person," Roland said. "I doubt she would have confided in a peasant girl who was only here out of the goodness of my mother. Mother wanted to educate the girl. I doubt that it did much good. They say her own mother was wild, too. Slept with any sailor who came into port. The locals say she was part kelpie. Ridiculous superstition, of course. Primitive people."

"That's enough, Roland," Sir Henry said, his voice echoing in the chamber. "The girl is not to be judged on her mother. I'd say my wife and Lucy did a fine job of educating her. Miss Anderson said she had a good brain and a willingness to learn. Anyway, I'm asking you to fetch the estate car and drive the inspector where he needs to go—unless you have more pressing matters?"

"I do. Plenty of pressing matters. Didn't you tell me I should be studying for my law exams?" Roland scowled at the two policemen. "Do the police not have their own motor cars on this island?"

"We do, but I'm needed elsewhere," MacDonald said. "I can't put a police vehicle at the inspector's disposal for the entire time he is here. I need to be back at headquarters."

"Headquarters?" Roland gave a derisive chuckle. "That shack in Portree? Come now, man. What major crimes are you expecting to find committed in the next few days? I take it this man from Glasgow will only need to be here for a day or so. He's not going to find Chisholm on the island, is he? And if anyone damaged the boat, it will have been he." He turned to Melrose. "I suggest we call this a horrible mistake, an accidental drowning, so we don't embarrass another important family, and let us give my sister a decent burial."

"And if somebody did deliberately send your sister to a watery grave, do you not want them apprehended and punished?" Melrose held his gaze. The young man eventually shrugged and looked away. "You'll never find him," he said. "He has money and a powerful family. They'll have spirited him off somewhere. He'll be in the colonies by now."

"Well, get going then," Sir Henry said. "Go with Roland. He'll drive you."

"Father, I really don't . . . ," Roland began, but Sir Henry cut him off. "Now, Roland. Get cracking."

Another thought had come to Melrose. "Perhaps I should speak to the other members of the household first. The governess? Your daughter might have confided in her."

"The governess was let go recently. When Euan Chisholm arrived to court Lucy it was clear that her school days were behind her and the governess was no longer needed."

"Where would I find her now?" Melrose asked.

"I presume she moved back in with her parents on the mainland," Sir Henry said. "Her father was the local schoolmaster in Kyle of Lochalsh, on the other side of the ferry. Miss Anderson assisted him at the school before coming to us. I understand she was quite well educated. Her father had been to the university and imparted his knowledge to her. At least she was educated enough to teach Lucy the basics she needed to know."

Melrose made a note that he should take the ferry across to Kyle and speak with the lady as soon as he could.

"I'll be on my way then." MacDonald thumped him on the shoulder. "You'll be able to reach me by telephone if you need me. There is a telephone at the hotel where you're staying. Perhaps Mr Roland will be kind enough to drive you back to your hotel, and they can summon Jock and his taxi when you need him."

"Come on, if you're coming," Roland said. "The garage is this way."

Melrose remembered his manners. "Thank you for your time, Sir Henry. I'll keep you updated on any developments," he said. "And if anything else occurs to you, please pass along any information to me at the Kings Arms."

"What information is there likely to be?" Sir Henry said, giving him a scornful look. "Somebody caused my daughter's death. She drowned. Nothing you do can bring her back. But I would like the person responsible for this caught."

He stumped off towards the front steps. Melrose followed Roland past several outbuildings to what had clearly been the old stables but now housed a Daimler and a shooting brake. Melrose waited as Roland started the latter up and drove it out of its parking space, then got in beside him.

"So are you supposed to be some bright new hope of the police force?" Roland asked. "All the new forensic techniques and that sort of thing? Did they send you to college?"

"I have been trained in the latest methods, yes," Melrose replied civilly although he could tell the other man's tone was derisive. "But you can't beat experience on the streets, dealing with real criminals and solving real cases. I had a good mentor who had been on the force for thirty years. There wasn't anything about the criminal mind he didn't know."

"Such a pity we're not dealing with criminal minds here then," Roland said.

"If Euan sank the boat it was in a mad fit of rage and jealousy. He was a spoiled little boy, you know. He'd have a tantrum if he didn't get what he wanted, and he wanted my sister and all that came with her. He wouldn't have given up without a fight."

"Did you ever see your sister and Chisholm have any sort of confrontation?"

"Not a confrontation," Roland said. "But she made it quite clear she didn't like him. He was patronizing, too smarmy. She liked people to be straightforward, not say things they didn't mean."

"Would the match have gone ahead anyway, even if your sister didn't want it?" Melrose asked.

"Would my parents have forced her to marry him?" Roland frowned. "I don't think so, but they were of the opinion that she was young and sheltered. That she would have come to like him when she got to know him better."

"Do you think that would have happened?"

"Probably not. My sister was strong-minded, even though she came across as dainty and meek. We had some good old fights when we were young."

"Did you and your sister get along well?"

"When we were children we were very close. We did everything together. Then I was sent off to school and then university, and the relationship was never the same. And when Flora came Lucy turned all her attention and affection to her. She became the sister Lucy never had."

"Do you believe she was involved in this . . . tragedy?"

"Flora?" Roland shrugged. "Who can say? Flora is a law unto herself. She doesn't abide by the rules like the rest of us."

"Do you think we'll find her?"

Roland shrugged again. "If she hears there's a policeman from Glasgow come to Skye I reckon she'll be off and away into the hills."

# Chapter 19

## *The Wild Girl*, Chapter 9

As they talked Roland manoeuvred the estate car through the pine wood and then down the narrow track until it reached the road. He drove rather fast, as someone who knows the road well, and Melrose had to hang on around the sharp bends. Once on the tarmacadam he put his foot down and the vehicle sped forward. Melrose could see Roland smirking and waiting to find out if he was scared. He stared resolutely forward and asked, in the calmest voice possible, "So how far away is this boat being kept?"

"Not far. Only at the other end of the village," Roland said, slowing down as they approached the line of cottages and drove along the waterfront. "It's at the old lifeboat slip. They moved the lifeboat further down the coast. Not much use for it here. The water's not too treacherous."

"Except that particular night," Melrose said.

"I don't believe it was any worse than usual. If the boat was compromised and the man was a poor sailor it would be easy enough to capsize it, and the water temperature here is pretty frigid."

As they drove past the cottages Melrose was aware of curtains being pulled back, curious glances. Word would be all around the place by now that he had arrived. He felt that he should question them all. Someone might have glanced out of a window on that dark night and seen something.

"Where was the boat docked when they set off?"

"In the harbour below the castle," Roland said. "That's where all the boats are moored here."

"So what did you think of Stewart? Did you have much to do with him?"

"He was a pleasant enough chap to talk to," Roland said. "Educated. Went to Edinburgh on a scholarship. And seemed interested in the local fauna and geology. Of course we didn't find out until later that he was really stirring up our tenants, telling them their rights and how to stand up to my father if he wanted to evict them from their land. Damned cheek of the man—accepting our hospitality, too. Not batting an eyelid when he sat down to dinner with us. My father was livid when he found out."

"When did your father find out?"

"That morning. He had a good old shouting match with Stewart and told him he wanted him out of his house and off the island or it would be the worse for him."

"Interesting," Melrose said.

Roland looked at him sharply. "I don't know what you are implying, but my father would never have done anything underhand like damaging a boat. He wanted the man gone. If he got in his boat and sailed away that would have been enough. He would not have been foolish enough to have come back again. Here we are." He pulled up at a shed balanced at the top of a slipway into the water. The words "Lifeboat Station" were still visible, painted on the side of the building. They got out. The rain had now picked up and stung Melrose's cheeks. Living in the city he had never realized what an impact weather had when you lived in the country. Roland Hamilton did not seem to be in the least perturbed by it. He was wearing a tweed jacket like his father, and Melrose reasoned that it kept out the rain as well as his Burberry. They went around to the back of the building, bordering the road, and Roland opened the door, which had not been locked. Inside was gloomy, with only high, narrow windows along either side.

A cold dampness hung in the air. There were shelves along the walls but the floor space was entirely empty save for one boat that lay on its side, its mainsail spread out on the floor. It was indeed nothing more than a dinghy—twelve feet maybe? A simple wooden craft, barely big enough for two people. Melrose stepped forward to examine it in the shaft of light from the open door.

"Not much to see, is there?" Roland said. "Sail torn pretty badly."

Melrose could see that. Several great horizontal slashes across it. But not ripped to shreds. Could the boat still have functioned with that amount of damage to the sail? Surely Stewart or Lucy would have noticed the moment it was hoisted outside the harbour. Why hadn't they turned back at that moment? He knew the answer as soon as he posed the question. Because they were both desperate to get away before they were caught. They decided to risk it. Perhaps she had held the sail together enough for the boat to move, but when they encountered high winds mid-channel, it was ripped from her hands and tore even more because one of the ropes that controlled it had been cut through.

"I gather the rope that held the sail had also been damaged?"

"So I heard," Roland said. He didn't sound particularly interested.

Melrose fished around and found one. It had frayed and snapped but it was hard to tell if the cut had been deliberate. It appeared to have been in part cleanly cut through.

"I'm no sailor," he said. "Do you know much about boats?"

"Not that much," Roland said. "I have sailed, but it's not an interest of mine. I'm more into the proverbial huntin', shootin' and fishin' that we gentry are supposed to like. And frankly I am looking forward to moving to the city and becoming a lawyer, only please don't tell my father because he assumes I'll take over the estate one day. Which perhaps I will when I've made my pile, married well and produced the son and heir. But now that Lucy is gone, I'll probably have to stick around for my mother's sake. Have you talked to her? She's absolutely devastated, as you can imagine. She adored Lucy. We all did. I can't tell you how terrible I feel."

Melrose nodded at this sudden opening up. Roland was little more than a boy, and he had just lost a beloved sister. He felt more kindly towards him.

He felt duty bound to examine the rest of the boat but saw nothing suspicious, at least to his untrained eye.

"I don't see what else we could do here," he said. "Why don't we go and try to locate Flora."

Roland gave him an amused glance. "Only if you're willing and equipped to go tramping over the hills in the rain," he said. "Or even climbing halfway up the Cuillin. That girl can go up a rock face like a lizard. When the locals say there's something not quite natural about her, I have to agree, although if you talk to her now she sounds like any refined young Scottish girl. She's certainly learned to copy my sister in how to behave in polite society. She could probably make a good match for herself if she wishes." He paused, thinking. "I've no idea what will become of her now."

They came out into stinging, horizontal rain.

"Beastly day," Roland said. "Are you sure you want to do this? I could drive you back to your hotel."

"Thanks, but I feel I should press on as quickly as possible. Your parents and my boss expect me to be working hard, trying to get to the bottom of this."

"Come now, man," Roland said. "Surely there is nothing hard to unravel. Chisholm learned they were eloping, fell into a fit of rage, slashed the sail, cut the sheet, and when they drowned he realized he could be found guilty of murder and managed to get away. Have your people send messages to be on the lookout for him at all the ports, although it's probably too late."

"You don't think his family could be hiding him then?"

"I didn't say that. Quite possibly they are. But since the Chisholm place is about as impenetrable as ours and their lands are a few hundred acres of mountainside I'd say good luck in finding him."

A feeling of despair engulfed Melrose as he climbed back into the car. His first solo case and he was doomed to fail. The books would be closed without any arrest and sentencing. And he found himself wondering whether someone in the Glasgow force was unhappy with his rapid promotion and wanted to make sure he failed.

They drove off, the tires sending up a sheet of spray. The last houses of the village were left behind, and the road swerved up the next hillside, cresting at last with what would have been a sweeping view of the land beyond, except it was all hidden in dark grey mist. Any mountains had ceased to exist. The shoreline lay there as an indistinct line through the rain. The road had turned into an unpaved track and they slithered through mud as they came down the hill.

"Where does this lead?" Melrose asked.

"Not anywhere much," Roland said. "This part of the shore is scarcely populated, apart from our crofters."

"And Flora's father? He's one of your crofters?"

"He's a fisherman and a law unto himself. He is beholden to nobody. You'll see his cottage ahead of you as we come around this bend." As he spoke he swung the wheel, and Melrose had a view down a steep drop to the shoreline. A stream tumbled down the hillside onto the rocks in a small waterfall. One solitary cottage perched amongst the rocks. An outcropping provided a tiny natural harbour, and a boat bobbed at anchor there. So it seemed that the fisherman was at home. A few minutes later they came to a halt in a front yard littered with lobster pots, bits of timber, the skeleton of a rowing boat, old tins, tubs and fish crates.

"Watch what you say," Roland said. "He's not the easiest of men, not the best of tempers, and he owns a shotgun."

With those cheerful words he got out of the estate car.

# Chapter 20

## *The Wild Girl*, Chapter 10

The cottage had a slate roof, although some slates were missing. The grey stone of the walls wasn't whitewashed like many of the others and blended in, almost as if it was part of the rocks behind it. Tattered curtains hung in the one window that faced them. Roland went ahead of Melrose and banged on a rough front door. He waited, then banged harder. At last shuffling steps were heard and the door was wrenched open.

"What do you want?" Flora's father stood there, not the most attractive sight in a greyish woolen undershirt and braces. From his bleary-eyed stare it looked as if he had been awoken from a sleep.

"I'm sorry to disturb you, Mr MacLeod," Roland said, "but we wondered if we could have a word with your daughter."

"Daughter? I don't have a daughter," he said, blinking as he stared at them as if the light hurt his eyes.

"Your daughter Flora." Melrose stepped forward. "I am Detective Inspector Melrose from Glasgow, and we need to speak to your daughter as soon as possible. Withholding evidence of her whereabouts is a criminal offence and you could be locked up."

The man gave an amused snort. "Locked up now, is it? Have the police now turned into bully boys? Do you know what? Sometimes being locked up sounds pretty good to me. Three meals a day and a warm cell and no need to go out on the high seas in the worst weather. Well, I'm sorry to disappoint you, but you'll get nothing from me because I know nothing. Flora's not here, nor has been these past few months. I lost my lassie when your family lured her away with the promise of new clothes, your fancy food and the chance of book learning." His gaze focused on Roland and was not friendly.

"I was told that your daughter came to visit you a few days ago," Melrose said. "They said you had been poorly and she brought you a bowl of broth from the castle."

"Poorly? When have I ever been poorly?" the man demanded. "If I don't fish, I don't eat. I've been out there in a storm with a fever and a bad chest before now. And these past few days I've been out at sea all day and every day. You can ask the other fishermen along the coast. They'll have seen my boat. They'll know."

"So Flora would not have found you home if she brought you a bowl of broth?"

"She would not, unless she came in the middle of the night. And that she did not do. I tell you, I've only caught the least glimpse of her these past months. As far as I can tell she doesn't care whether her old father lives or dies."

"Might we come in?" Melrose asked. "I'm sure you've heard that there has been a great tragedy and the laird's daughter has drowned."

"And what's that to do with me?" MacLeod asked. "If the laird's daughter wants to go running off with a trouble-making nobody it's not my concern. She got what she deserved for not obeying her parents. I said the same thing to my daughter, although . . ." He paused. "I always did right by her, didn't I?"

He stood at the doorway with one arm barring entrance. Melrose thought it was clear that they were not about to be invited in and wondered if Flora was inside at this moment. From what Melrose had heard the man had completely neglected his daughter, but Roland had warned him to keep his mouth shut, so instead he said, "We just wondered where we might find Flora now. I've been told that she and Miss Lucy were close friends. I thought that maybe Lucy had confided in her about her plans to run away."

"And what if she had. A lot of good it would do now, with the young lady lying on a slab like a piece of fish, from what I've been told."

"We need to find out who did this terrible thing, Mr MacLeod," Melrose said. "Who tried to wreck their sailing boat so they couldn't make the crossing to the mainland. Someone must have known they were going, and made sure they didn't reach the other side."

"And you're trying to hint it was my wee lassie? I can tell you one thing, Mr Policeman from Glasgow, my lassie adored Miss Lucy. She thought the sun shone out of her head. She'd have done anything for her. Anything at all. And she'd not have harmed her in any way."

"Thank you, Mr MacLeod," Melrose said. "That is good to hear. So please be assured that your daughter is not in any kind of trouble, but we would wish to have a word with her. Do you have any idea where we might find her?"

The old man stared up towards where the mountains had now vanished into cloud. "She could be anywhere," he said. "She knows every inch of the land around here. She's probably got any number of secret hideouts. Even when she was a little girl she'd be gone for days. Everyone worried about her, and then she'd turn up, right as rain, as if nothing had happened. You should see the way she ran through that heather, like a little sprite, she was, as if she weighed nothing at all. And the way she'd communicate with the animals and birds. They trusted her as if she was one of them, you know."

Melrose realized how keen he was to meet the elusive Flora.

"Are you not going to invite us in for a wee strupak, Angus?" Roland said. "We're getting fair drenched standing out here."

"Then you'd best be back to your motor car, hadn't you?" Angus MacLeod said. "Because I've nothing more to tell you."

"Did Flora not keep any of her possessions in your cottage still?" Melrose asked.

Angus MacLeod shrugged. "She might have left a few things in an old trunk—clothes that were not suitable for the fine life at the castle. A stuffed rabbit my wife made for her before she died. Maybe some shells she found on the beach."

"Could we just take a look?" Melrose asked.

The old man shrugged. "I can see you're determined to come in. Well, come on then. No doubt I can find you a cup of tea and an oatcake, but I can't vouch for the state of the place. I'm no housekeeper, and since my lassie went I've not had the time or inclination to do much."

He opened the door to let them enter. Immediately Melrose wished he hadn't suggested this. The smell was almost overpowering: a mixture of unwashed clothing, unwashed body, fish and spoiled food mingled with the pleasant aroma of peat smoke. The fire glowed in the hearth and a kettle stood on the hob.

"Sit yourselves down then," Angus MacLeod said.

There was a bench made of an old board running along the wall beside the table and one rickety-looking chair. Roland gave Melrose a look of disgust as they both chose the bench. Angus took the kettle off the hob and poured water into an old brown teapot.

Melrose looked around the room, taking in the unwashed dishes, the items of discarded clothing lying on the floor. There was no trace of a woman's presence, no sampler or picture on the walls, nothing to hint that a young girl had ever lived here.

"Your tea." MacLeod put chipped earthenware cups in front of the two men, along with a plate of oatcakes.

"So does your daughter not come home to help you around the place any more?" he asked. He took a swig of horribly strong, sweet tea and followed it with a bite of dry and elderly oatcake.

"She does, occasionally," MacLeod said, pulling up a stool opposite them. "When the mood takes her. But not in a while. Too busy with the things that you fine folks get up to at the castle to see her poor old father."

Melrose did feel for him. He imagined his parents if he moved away and they didn't see him again. "Could I take a look at her things in the trunk?"

"Aye, I suppose so, if you've a mind to." MacLeod crossed the room and pulled out a battered sea chest from beneath several pegs hung on the wall, holding oilskins, a scarf and hat. Melrose went over and opened it. His instinct was to shut it again. This felt like an intrusion on privacy. Apart from a couple of well-worn jumpers and skirts there were only childhood treasures: a cardboard box of shells and pebbles, interesting shapes of driftwood, and the toy rabbit, the plush now worn almost shiny with being handled. He closed it again.

"You'll not find nought of interest here." MacLeod dragged the trunk back to its position in the corner. "She's long gone. Long gone from my life, too."

Melrose wondered if the man actually missed his daughter or missed having someone to keep house for him. He couldn't imagine that Flora had had a happy life here, or that the man had shown her much affection. And now what would happen to her? Would the Hamiltons still welcome her at the castle with their daughter gone? Would they want Lucy's clothes back? Would she have a chance to find herself a job on the mainland, or would she return to her old life in this dismal cottage?

One thing was sure—there was no indication that Flora had been here recently, and Melrose could see no large vessel that could have carried broth from the castle. Wherever Flora went a few days ago, it was not to see her father.

Emma looked up, startled by a hammering on the door. For a second she felt she was in the cottage on the rocks and wondered if this was Flora. Then she realized where she was, got up and answered the door. Maggie the maid was standing there.

"The mistress thought you'd be needing your tea, and she didn't want you to break off what you are doing to come to the house for it," she said. She came in, carrying a tray. She put it down on the table.

"I'm to tell you that dinner is at seven and you don't need to get dressed up for it. It's just us tonight."

"Thank you," Emma said. When she had closed the door behind Maggie she examined the tea tray. Beside the teacup there was a small Chinese teapot, milk jug, sugar basin, a plate of egg-and-cress sandwiches covered in a white cloth, a slice of malt bread and butter and a piece of Victoria sponge cake. All most satisfactory, except Emma didn't feel hungry and was keen to keep on reading. She knew there was no rush. Nobody was forcing her to finish, but now she had to know the truth about who had damaged the boat and where the Wild Girl had gone. She poured herself a cup of tea, picked up a sandwich and went back to the book.

# Chapter 21

## *The Wild Girl*, Chapter 11

Inspector Melrose dearly wished Roland had not requested the strupak, which seemed to be the local word for a bite to eat. It had prolonged the visit. They left having extracted a promise from MacLeod that he'd let them know if his daughter turned up. "Please tell her she's in no kind of trouble," he emphasized. "We just need her help to find out who might have wanted to harm Miss Lucy."

"I'll tell her." MacLeod sniffed. "If and when I see her." He didn't sound too hopeful.

"I'm not volunteering to help you look for her in this weather," Roland said as they drove off. "She'll have sought shelter somewhere. There are caves in the mountains and sheep bothies. She may even be watching us and stay hidden until you take the ferry back."

*So what next?* Melrose asked himself. "I suppose I should question the other villagers," he said. "Surely somebody would have noticed the events of that night?"

Roland snorted. "Have you ever been on the island at night, Inspector? If there is no moon the blackness is complete. You're lucky if you can see your hand in front of your face. We've no electric lights, no streetlamps. Everyone goes to bed soon after it gets dark here. They close the curtains and shut out the night."

"All the same, I should speak with them."

Roland was staring straight ahead as the windscreen wipers tried valiantly to keep the rain off the glass. "What we're going to do right now is to go back to your hotel. My father asked me to show you the boat and then take you to your hotel. That's what I'm doing. If the police can't provide their own transportation then that's too bad. I can't be expected to play chauffeur to every visiting policeman."

Melrose sat staring ahead as cloud and mist shifted and parted. He felt miserable and frustrated. His hat was sodden, his hair was wet, his feet were freezing and he was wishing fervently that he had never accepted this assignment. But then he realized he had had no choice. An order was an order.

They drove in silence back to Kyleakin and pulled up outside the Kings Arms. Melrose thanked Roland and went inside. A pleasing warmth and the smell of something frying, possibly fish and chips, reminded him that he hadn't eaten since breakfast.

"Well, here you are then, Inspector." Mistress MacDonald appeared from a side room. "And it's what we say here is 'tha i fliuch.' A wet day and no denying it. You look positively soaked. Take your coat and hat and put them in front of the fire while I go and find you a nice cup of tea. And no doubt you'll be wanting something to eat?"

"That would be lovely," he said. "Thank you very much."

"What had you in mind? A sandwich?"

"I need warming up," he said. "Do you have something hot?"

"A bowl of cock-a-leekie then," she said.

Clearly the frying was for someone else, and he didn't have the nerve to ask her for some of that. Besides, a bowl of stew was just what he needed right now. He spread out his hat and coat to dry, took a seat and waited. Mistress MacDonald came out, carrying a tray with the stew, a roll and butter and a cup of tea.

"Get those inside you and you'll not do too badly," she said, putting the tray down. As Melrose started to spread the butter she lingered. "Well," she said, "you must have seen the laird. How is he? And his poor wife. Bearing up after the tragedy, I've no doubt."

"They are both deeply shocked," Melrose said. "Sir Henry's wife looks positively stricken."

"They worshipped that girl," Mistress MacDonald said. "Everyone did. The sweetest thing on God's earth. Who could possibly have wanted to harm her? You'll not have uncovered any evidence so far, I'm thinking?"

"I'm afraid not," he said. "It's not easy to surmise what happens when a boat capsizes out at sea. It could turn out to be an accident after all."

"Oh, really?" She looked disappointed. Even as he had said the words he found himself wondering if this would be the case. Stewart was a humble young man of limited means. What if he had simply borrowed an old boat, its sail already disintegrating, its ropes rotten and ready to snap, and everything had given way in the face of strong waves? How easy it would be to come to that conclusion and to go back to Glasgow.

Only one thing stopped him from coming to this conclusion. Euan Chisholm had vanished, on the night of the tragedy. And the Wild Girl was nowhere to be found. One of them either knew something or had to be involved. He could not go back to Glasgow before he found out the truth. He had no idea how he would do that. He got out his notebook and made a list:

*Need image of Chisholm to show around. Recheck ferries. Find out if his picture has been circulated at mainland ports.*

*Visit Chisholm's family on mainland.*

*Speak to villagers about what they know and what they might have seen.*

*Speak to other members of Sir Henry's household—the maid who took food to Chisholm, etc.*

*Visit governess on mainland.*

*Arrange for my transportation.*

This last item was imperative as he could accomplish none of the others without it. He went up to the front counter. "I'd be grateful if I could use your telephone," he said. "I have to arrange for the taxi for myself."

"Young Jock, you'll be needing then, no doubt?" she said. "Aye. He's a good lad. Taken over from his father, whose rheumatics are now troubling him. Verra proud of that motor car of his, you know. Keeps it spotless. Lovely just."

Melrose dialed the number, praying that Young Jock was not at this moment driving someone to a hospital on the other side of the island. The phone was picked up after the first ring.

"Jock's Taxi Service, Young Jock speaking," said a cheery voice.

Melrose introduced himself and asked if they could meet.

"I'll be over in a jiffy," Jock said, and true to his word he arrived soon after, pausing on the doormat to take off his oilskin and shake the rain from his hair.

"Aye, but it's a moist kind of day," he said. He looked as cheery as his voice, a lanky lad with dark hair and dark eyes that twinkled with amusement. He held out his hand.

"Glad to meet you, Inspector, and happy to be of assistance. Frankly at this time of year the extra money will be welcome. We've a little one on the way and the wife wants a fancy nursery—a proper cot and swathes and all. The old family cradle isn't good enough for her." He gave Melrose a knowing grin. "Are you married yourself?"

"I am not," Melrose said. "My young lady died, unfortunately. I haven't found anyone to match her since."

"I'm sorry to hear that," Jock said. He crossed the room with Melrose, and they took two armchairs near the fire. "Life's not easy, is it? We've plenty of tragic deaths on the island, you know. Not all the babies live to grow up, in spite of our good fresh air." He crossed his long legs. "So Inspector MacDonald says that I'm to drive you around wherever you need to go."

"That's right," Melrose said. "You understand that I'm here to investigate the death of Sir Henry's daughter and the man she was running away with." He broke off as a great blast of wind buffeted the window, making it rattle alarmingly. "Although I'm not sure that this afternoon is the right time for it."

"It's supposed to get worse by nightfall," Jock said. "A proper storm they're saying. My dad could have told them. His rheumatics play up when a storm's coming in. Better than the weatherman on the radio, he is."

"So tomorrow morning, if the weather has improved, I'd like to interview the villagers in Dun Akyn," Melrose said. "And speak to the household members at the castle. I've already met the family. Now I'd like to chat with the servants."

"I don't think Sir Henry will like that." Jock still looked amused. "He won't want his servants speaking behind his back."

"He'll have to lump it then," Melrose said. "This is a police investigation. Sir Henry doesn't have a say in who I talk to."

"I look forward to that," Jock said. "And what else?"

"The important thing is to find Euan Chisholm," Melrose said. "Apparently he disappeared around the same time as the couple fled in the boat. I have to think he's a major suspect. You wouldn't have any information on him, would you?"

"Not recently," Jock said. "The police from Portree already asked me if he'd used my taxi to get to the ferry. I told them he had not. I transported him to the castle when he arrived several weeks ago."

"And what was your impression of him?"

"You know what these aristocrats are like. They think God made them and then he rested. This man was definitely more stuck up than most. Thought a lot of himself. He ordered me to carry his bags as if I was his personal servant. Snapped his fingers at me and told me to 'get on with it, man, and don't keep me waiting.' I didn't take to him so much."

"So now it's imperative that we find him," Melrose said. "I'll need a photograph of him to show at the ports."

"I don't think you'll need that," Jock said. "Everyone in these parts knows the Chisholms."

"All the same he could have slipped across in some sort of disguise."

Jock nodded. "True enough, I suppose. Although anyone unfamiliar would have caught the eye of the boatmen. It's different in summer when it's tourists and mountaineers coming and going. But this time of year it's only locals going across to visit relatives or to a doctor's appointment."

"Well, that's something we can do today," Melrose said. "I don't like to be sitting idle. Let's go down to the ferry port and see what we can learn."

"Right you are," Jock said. "Best put your waterproofs on, though, or you'll be drenched."

Melrose looked out at the swirling rain. "Maybe just leave all this for the morning then."

"My thoughts exactly," Jock said.

# Chapter 22

Emma put down the pages with a sigh of impatience.

"Why are you waiting until tomorrow," she said out loud, frowning at the pages. "This is a murder mystery. Time is of the essence to keep up the tension. Get on with it. Go and get wet."

She realized if she took on this story it would need some editing and paring down. Melrose had said the same things to so many people and it didn't seem as if they were getting anywhere. Emma wondered if this ongoing rambling was Iris floundering a little, wondering herself where to go next and waiting for inspiration. She leafed through the remaining pages. There were not that many. Had Iris had a flash of inspiration, had Melrose suddenly found the clue that put him on the right track so that the story could be brought to a conclusion? Or . . . Emma paused . . . did Iris really no longer remember what she wanted to happen?

Emma poured herself a cup of tea, took the slice of Victoria sponge cake and put another log on the fire before curling up on the sofa again. She added Young Jock and Roland to her list of characters. She liked the former immediately but wasn't sure about Roland. He was already exhibiting some of his father's arrogance, but then he was recently out of university and might just have been showing off to impress a lowly policeman. And he clearly grieved for his sister. She brushed crumbs off her notebook, then picked up the next chapter.

## *The Wild Girl*, Chapter 12

The morning dawned bright and brisk, giving Melrose renewed hope that they might finally get somewhere, although where that might be he had no idea. He ate a hearty breakfast of black pudding and oatcakes as well as eggs and porridge and was ready when Jock showed up at nine.

The previous afternoon he had telephoned Inspector MacDonald to ask him if he had any photographs of the missing Euan Chisholm and was told he did not. When people are shown an actual photograph it stirs a memory they might otherwise have forgotten. He remembered that Sir Henry had shown him the snapshot including Chisholm. He'd have to ask to borrow it, although he wasn't relishing the thought of facing Sir Henry again.

He put this sentiment aside and told Jock they'd start at the castle. He'd ask for the photograph and speak with the servants there. Then he'd question the villagers and finally the boatmen at the ferry. If they had time they'd ferry across to speak with the governess. At this Jock's friendly face registered alarm. "You're not expecting me to go across to the mainland with my taxi?"

"Is that a problem? Is it not a car ferry?"

"It is, so to speak," Jock said. "But this taxi is my livelihood. I'm not taking risks with it. If the weather blows up and the vehicles are tossed around . . . No, I think I'll stay safely on land, thank you. I wasn't born for seafaring."

Melrose was amused by this as the crossing from Kyle of Lochalsh to Kyleakin was not a long one.

"Very well," he said. "I can do that on foot later. But the other thing we have to do is to search for Flora MacLeod. She'll have got wet and cold last night if she was hiding out in the hills. She might have come home, or even come back to the castle."

"The Wild Girl?" Jock said. "I don't think she'd be returning to the castle after what happened. She'd fear she'd be blamed in some way."

"Why is that?"

Jock shrugged. "She was taken on as Miss Lucy's companion, was she not. Supposed to keep an eye on her and act as her chaperon. Well then, if something bad befell the young lady, then Flora was not doing her job."

"Oh, I don't think anyone would blame her if Lucy slipped out in the middle of the night," Melrose said.

"All the same, people like Flora's father have always been wary of police matters. No doubt he's done his share of smuggling and salvaging in his time. Most of the fishermen around here have. If a few crates of whisky wash ashore they disappear rather rapidly."

Melrose smiled and nodded to let Jock know that he quite understood this. When people have so little no one can blame them for seeing washed-up treasure as a gift from the gods.

"Right," he said. "Let's get going."

After the storm the day was crystal clear. The peaks of the Cuillin stood out in the background sharp and jagged against an arc of blue sky. Today they looked almost close enough to touch. Across the strait the mountains of the mainland rose, tier after tier, one after the other, as far as the eye could see. Sgurr na Coinnich reared defiantly ahead of them as they went over the crest. The castle, as they approached it, looked as gaunt and hostile as those mountains, and again Melrose found himself wondering about why a family would still choose to live there. *No wonder Lucy couldn't wait to get away,* he thought.

They approached the castle from the rear this time, taking the track that wound around the bluff to the promontory. A high wall encircled the property but the wooden gates were open and they drove in. Ahead of them was the woodland that he had seen the day before. They drove through it, the Scots pines reaching above the drive to form a canopy and shutting out the daylight. He was glad when they came out again on the other side to see the sunlight. They crossed an area of close-cropped grass on which some sheep were grazing before coming to a halt at the gate of the keep. Here they got out and Jock opened the gate. They stepped into the forecourt. Jock looked around nervously as if he wasn't too happy about being there.

"I should keep an eye on my motor car," he said. "I would nae want a branch to fall on it."

"All right." Melrose understood. "I shouldn't be too long."

"Take your time. You're paying." Jock grinned as he turned back to his waiting taxi. Melrose took a deep breath then headed to the main door of the castle. Before he could reach it he heard footsteps, and a maid came out of one of the outbuildings. She started in surprise when she saw Melrose and froze like a woodland creature in fight-or-flight mode.

"Hello," he said before she could run off to warn anyone. "I'm Inspector Melrose. We're trying to find out what happened to Miss Lucy. Can I ask you a couple of questions?"

The girl's eyes darted nervously. "I don't know anything about it," she said.

"I can't help you, and the master wouldn't want me speaking with outsiders."

"I'm a police officer on an investigation," he said. "So I am allowed to speak with anyone I choose and ask any question I want. Is that clear? You will not get into trouble for speaking with me. Now, what's your name?"

"Morag, sir." She was looking down at her feet, not meeting his eyes.

"And what is your position here?"

"I'm a housemaid, sir. I clean, I wait at table, I make beds."

"Were you the one who discovered that Miss Lucy's bed had not been slept in and Miss Flora was gone?"

"No sir, that would have been her maid, Agnes."

"Agnes. I must speak to her. Do you happen to know what time that was?"

"Not exactly. Late in the morning, sir. I had done the sweeping."

"So Miss Lucy did not have her morning tea brought to her room like most of the fancy folk do?"

"She did, sometimes. But she let her maid know that she had a headache and wanted to sleep it off."

"I see. That would be Agnes?"

"That's right, sir. She's the maid who takes care of her and of the mistress."

"And who took care of Mr Chisholm when he was here?"

"Ian the footman looked after his clothes and shoes, sir, but I took him his meals when he did not want to eat at the big house."

"Can you show me where he was staying?"

She glanced up at the castle, afraid someone was watching her. "It's this way, sir. This cottage by the gates."

She led him to a grey stone outbuilding. The inside was not what he would have considered fit for an aristocrat, especially one like Chisholm, who sounded as if he was used to comfort. A room with a bed, a giant carved oak wardrobe, a dressing table, washbasin stand. A small desk in the window and at the back a simple bathroom, clearly added on in recent years. Adequate but not luxury.

"You took him his meals, including the last day he was here, when he felt poorly?"

"I did, sir."

"Who told you to take him his food?"

"Why, Cook did, sir. She said the young gentleman had put a note outside his door saying he was feeling poorly and would be keeping to his room that day. So Cook said the poor man should have some nourishment before nightfall and sent me over with it."

"And how was he? Did he seem to be sick?"

"I didnae get to see him, sir. He'd left a note on the door saying he was not to be disturbed. So I tapped on the door and left the food outside. But he never did take it, sir. And the next day when we looked, he had gone."

"I see." Melrose examined the room. He opened the wardrobe. A suit was still hanging there, but no shirts. He went over to the chest of drawers. They were in disarray and some items were clearly missing. Chisholm had packed a bag in a hurry and had only taken what he could carry. He turned his attention to the bed. It had not been slept in, or someone had made it.

"Was no maid called in that day to make the bed?"

"Oh no, sir. That would have been me, and I was told to leave the gentleman in peace. Ian, that's the footman, said he thought the young gentleman must have taken a drop too much whisky the night before and was sleeping it off."

"I see," Melrose repeated. He noticed the slippers, tucked under the bed. He pulled back the coverlet and found pyjamas, neatly folded. He supposed that rich people didn't worry too much about leaving items of clothing behind, but who would not want to take their nightclothes with them? He went through to the bathroom and saw that the man's sponge bag was not there, but his razor still lay on the shelf over the bathtub. Melrose tried to make sense of Chisholm's actions. Somehow Chisholm had overheard Lucy and Stewart planning to run away together. He had decided to make sure that didn't happen, so he went down to the harbour and damaged Stewart's boat. But then did he come back to the castle and pretend to be sick all day or did he pack his bag and leave as soon as he had done his dirty work, putting a note outside to say he must not be disturbed?

And where had he gone then? If the ferrymen had not seen him, had he bribed a boatman to take him to the mainland? Melrose's next task, after speaking with the members of this household, would be to have a chat with the occupants of that row of cottages on the quayside.

"So, Morag," he said, turning back to the maid, who stood patiently in the doorway, "tell me, did you ever notice Miss Lucy chatting with Mr Stewart? Alone, I mean?"

She frowned. "No sir. I never did. Miss Lucy was rarely alone. They made sure Flora was with her, especially when she went for walks or rides with Mr Chisholm. That was only proper."

"So did Mr Stewart interact much with the family?"

She shook her head firmly at this. "He did not, sir. He took his supper with them and sometimes he ate his breakfast at the same time as one of them, but usually he was out for the day long before they all woke up. I'd say he was not comfortable being amongst the fine folk. He was more like one of us, except that he'd been educated at the university. But apparently he'd been speaking with the crofters and telling them that they should refuse to move if the laird said they had to. He said it was their right. Tenancy laws."

"And the laird did not like that?"

"He did not, sir. We could hear the shouting. I was sweeping the stairs at the time. It was terrible, just. Sir Henry said, 'I want you out of my house this minute, and if you are not off the island by the end of the day, then I can't vouch for your safety.'"

"So he went?"

"He did, sir. He went up, got his bag and left."

"Did you see where he went?"

"Why, down to his boat, I presume."

"But he didn't sail back to the mainland until that night."

"Apparently not, sir."

"And nobody saw him speaking with Miss Lucy in the meantime? Did she overhear the shouting? Was she upset?"

"I don't know, sir. She might not even have been awake. It was morning and she liked to sleep late."

"What about Flora?"

"She wasn't at the house, sir. She went to take the broth to her father the day before."

"The day before? You mean the day before the row between Stewart and the laird? The day before Chisholm was feeling ill and stayed in his cottage?"

"I suppose so, sir." She looked troubled now.

"Did you see her leave with the broth?"

"Not personally, sir. I was working, and if she'd come out of the kitchen it would have been by the back door and straight down the steps."

Melrose was still trying to put together a timeline.

Flora had left the day before, carrying broth, but had never gone to her father, so he claimed. Chisholm had kept to his room, claiming to be sick, and was not seen all day. Stewart had been banished from the castle that morning. And Miss Lucy had slept late. Nobody had seen anybody. So what really happened? Surely one of the staff would know. He'd have to find a way to interview them all without Sir Henry or the family listening in.

# Chapter 23

## *The Wild Girl*, Chapter 13

Melrose did one final inspection of the room. He didn't know how much clothing the son of a laird brought with him on a visit, but he suspected it was a lot more than he, Melrose, would ever have owned. So perhaps Chisholm had taken a good amount with him and left the items he didn't care for. He looked back at Morag, still standing nervously in the doorway as if she was unwilling to come into the room.

"Morag, you say you brought Mr Chisholm his food from time to time. What did you think of him?"

She flushed bright red. "That's not for me to say, sir."

"Was he pleasant to you? Rude?"

Her face turned even redder if that was possible. "Well, sir, if you want the truth he was a little too friendly."

"Too friendly?"

"Too free with his hands, if you get my meaning. I tried to get in and out of there as quickly as possible."

"He was fresh with you?" Melrose hesitated, hoping to use words that would not upset her.

"Well, sir, I suppose you could call it that." Her face was a picture of embarrassment. Melrose had been around long enough to get her meaning.

"What did you do?"

"I tried to stop him. I said I'd scream. And he said if I did he'd tell the laird I had been rude to him and I'd be given the sack."

"So you had no choice?" Melrose fought back his anger.

"That's right, sir. I had no choice. I need my position for my family. Besides, it's what you have to get used to if you're a servant. The laird himself is that kind of a man. I expect they all are. They like to think of servants as possessions. They have the power. We have none."

"So the laird made passes at you?"

She nodded, turning away so that she didn't make eye contact with him. "He'd run his hands over my body to see if I was developing nicely. That's what he said, anyway. And once he put a hand down inside my shirt and he felt . . . you know."

Melrose did know. He'd spoken to young rape victims in his days on the streets.

There was never any use pressing charges. The courts always hint that she asked for it, wore provocative clothing. And the jurors were all male.

"I'm sorry, Morag," he said. "But at least Mr Chisholm is gone now. One of your worries is over."

She nodded.

"So would you take me up through the servant's door to speak to Agnes? I'd prefer not to encounter Sir Henry until later."

Her eyes darted nervously again. "I don't know, sir. I could get in trouble."

"I'll tell your master that I ordered you to do this, if you're worried. You will not be my coconspirator."

She gave him a nervous little grin. "Come on. Let's cross the courtyard quickly then. You can be seen from the windows."

He followed her, hugging the wall of the keep until she came to a flight of steps in the wall of the castle, went up and in through a small side door. The smell of cooking reached him, and voices speaking softly in Gaelic. Morag hurried him past the open door.

"Let me see if she's in the servant's hall or up in her room." She glanced inside, shook her head and beckoned him onward, leading him up a flight of narrow wooden stairs to a second flight, this one a spiral stair and steep. He pitied the servants who had to go up and down these with coal, water and anything else their masters needed and felt a great wave of sympathy for Stewart, who dared to speak up for the crofters.

After another steep flight Morag opened a door, and they came out onto a landing. "Agnes?" she called. "Are you up here?"

A young girl appeared, her wiry hair tucked under a cap. Her eyes were puffy as if she had been crying. Melrose put her at no older than seventeen or eighteen. She stepped back with a horrified expression when she saw Melrose. "What are you doing up here, sir? These are the young ladies' quarters."

"I want a word with you, Agnes," he said. "I'm a police detective, and we're trying to find out who killed your mistress. You'd want to help with that, wouldn't you?"

"Oh, I would, sir. I've been so upset, I've been crying my eyes out. I can't think who would want to harm that dear, sweet girl. She never did an unkind thing in her life."

"Young ladies often confide in their maids. Did she ever talk to you about Mr Chisholm or Mr Stewart?"

She squirmed uncomfortably. "She did mention Mr Chisholm, sir. She did not like him. She said he was overbearing and what sort of life would she have if she married him. He'd order her around and she'd not have a life of her own."

"So how did she plan to get out of marrying him? Was that why she decided to latch on to Stewart and run off with him?"

"I've no idea, sir. She didn't mention Mr Stewart much. I know I heard her talking about him once with Miss Flora and I heard her say, 'He's not bad-looking, but he hasn't two pennies to rub together.'"

"And what did Miss Flora say?"

"I think she said that money wasn't everything. She said, 'You'd have plenty of money if you married Chisholm.' And Miss Lucy said, 'Yes, and be a prisoner in a worse castle than this one. I'd have to grow my hair like Rapunzel.' And they laughed. They were so close, those two. They certainly enjoyed each other's company."

"Miss Flora is nowhere to be found, Agnes. Do you have any idea where she might have gone?"

"No idea, sir. Back to her father, I suppose. She went off to see him right before the tragedy."

"Miss Lucy took a bag with her when she went. You didn't help her pack it?"

"Oh no, sir. I had no idea, until we found she'd gone. And she didn't take much with her either. Only the minimum of undergarments and maybe a jumper or two. She did take her jewellery, though."

"For sentimental reasons or was it valuable?"

"Oh, quite valuable, sir, I'd imagine. She had her grandmother's diamond brooch and pearls and some other lovely things. I suppose they're all lying at the bottom of the water now." She hesitated, thinking. "Oh, and her greatcoat was missing. She must have taken that. That's probably what pulled her under. It was quite heavy to start with, and with all that water—"

"Interesting," Melrose interrupted. "She wasn't wearing a coat. She was wearing a hooded cloak and trousers."

"That is strange, sir," she said. "She did have such a cloak but she rarely wore it. Nor the trousers. She only wore them if they were going stalking in the hills and she'd have to do her share of crawling on the ground."

"Perhaps she wanted to look like a boy if necessary," Melrose said. "And the cloak was dark and hid her face."

"Of course." Agnes nodded. "Then she'll have packed her greatcoat to take with her, although it would have been heavy to carry. I suppose they didnae recover her bag?"

"Not that I've heard," Melrose said. "Perhaps it will wash ashore one day."

A puzzled expression had come over her face. "That's another thing, sir," she said. "The day before I'd had to work on that coat. She gave it to me with mud and dirt on it. She said they'd sat down to take a rest during their walk and she hadn't realized she had been sitting in some mud. So I had to sponge and brush it for her."

"Who was they?"

"She didn't say. It's not my place to ask questions."

"So it had mud and dirt caked on it?"

"It did, sir. And some pine needles stuck in the tweed."

The woodland outside the gates was composed mainly of Scots pines, he thought. She had taken a rest after a very short walk. And he found himself wondering if Stewart had been hiding out in the wood after the blow-up with Sir Henry. Had Lucy had a tryst with him there, and that was when they planned their escape? But the mud on the coat was from the day before. And the question still remained: Who knew? Who had found out what they were planning? Who had decided to stop them? On his way out he'd have to check whether Chisholm's cottage was close enough to the woods that he might have seen or overheard something without leaving his room.

"How did Miss Lucy seem the day she left? Did she seem agitated, excited?"

"She didn't want me near her that day, sir. She said she had a headache and wanted to be left alone."

"Was that after Mr Stewart was banished?"

"I couldnae say, sir. I did not hear the row with Mr Stewart from up here. Our maids' rooms are one floor above this, too far away."

"So you don't know if Miss Lucy went out at all that day?"

"Again I couldnae tell you, sir."

Melrose wondered if this was loyalty to her dead mistress or if Agnes really had been kept in the dark. He didn't think he'd get much more out of her. Lucy had kept to herself that day, feigning a headache and packing a bag while she was alone. At some stage she'd have had to slip out to meet Stewart. Had she appeared at meals and acted normally that day? That was the next thing to find out. He was about to leave when, on impulse, he asked, "Agnes, I just heard from another of the maids that the master is a little too friendly at times. Has that been your experience, too?"

She eyed him warily. "I'm lucky. I'm usually up here in my mistress's room and don't have any opportunity to encounter the rest of the family. But I have heard rumours from other servants. And not just the master. Mr Roland, too. They're all just as bad as each other."

He thanked Agnes and was directed this time down the proper staircase, this one wider but still made of plain stone with whitewashed walls. As he came out onto the landing below he was confronted by Sir Henry. Had Sir Henry been listening to his conversation? How much could he have overheard?

"What the devil do you think you are doing?" Sir Henry bellowed. "Going up to my daughter's room without my permission? Who let you in? Why was I not informed?"

"I have been to speak with Agnes, your daughter's maid," Melrose replied calmly. "I felt it was essential to know whether your daughter had confided in her and what Agnes knew. Was the escape long planned or was it a spur-of-the-moment decision after you turned Stewart out of your house."

"And what did you discover?"

"Nothing, I'm afraid," Melrose said. "Miss Lucy did not confide in her maid, or her maid is staying silent out of loyalty. I do know that she told Agnes she had a headache and wanted to be left alone, presumably while she packed a bag. But when she met Stewart to plan details, I could not say. Did she come to meals as usual that day?"

Sir Henry frowned, then he shook his head. "She did not. She pleaded a headache at luncheon and then said she wasn't hungry at dinner time and would only have a bowl of soup in her room."

"Did she actually eat that bowl of soup?"

"I gather she must have done, or it would have been mentioned to my wife that she was off her food."

"So she was still in residence at suppertime?"

"I presume so."

"And slipped out at some time after that. Do we have any idea when the boat sailed?"

Sir Henry's face flushed red again. "Look, man, does any of this matter now? Someone had the means to sabotage that boat. It keeled over. They drowned. All we need to know is who did it. And my money is on Chisholm. So don't waste any more time here speaking with my servants behind my back. Get busy and find the culprit."

"I should like to speak with your wife again before I leave," Melrose said. "Your daughter may have confided in her."

Sir Henry's face turned from red to puce. "My wife? You will not disturb my wife. She is in a very delicate state, distraught with grief, and I will not allow you to put her through more misery. But I can tell you one thing—she was all for the marriage to Chisholm. She felt it was the perfect match. So no, Mr Policeman. Lucy would not have told my wife about her plans to run away with a no-good, interfering Communist agitator."

Melrose could see he was not going to get any further with this family. Sir Henry escorted him across the landing to the main staircase, also made of stone and winding down, hugging the wall of the castle. Melrose glanced out of a slit of a window, looking back across the courtyard to the woodland and to the hills above. Surely someone would have noticed Lucy slipping out to meet with Stewart on at least one occasion? Those pine needles indicated they met in the wood. But before he had time to contemplate this, Sir Henry barked, "Come on, man. Get a move on. We haven't got all day."

And he was taken down the rest of the stair, across the foyer and out of the front door, Sir Henry leaving him with an abrupt "Good day to you, sir."

He had been dismissed.

# Chapter 24

A sudden gust of wind swirled down through the chimney, sending sparks flying and making Emma look up from her reading. Rain peppered the window, and she realized that the daylight had almost faded. If the weather did not abate she wouldn't be looking forward to going over to the main house for dinner. But she couldn't expect poor Maggie to brave the storm if she asked to have a simple meal brought over to her. And why had Iris put her here? There must be spare bedrooms in the main house, and that would have saved the maid from making the trip across in the rain. But why had Iris insisted on her staying here at all? Surely she could have travelled down to Iris for the day and then gone home again to the flat at night? Iris had plenty of money. She wouldn't have begrudged a taxi from the nearest station. Perhaps Iris wanted to make sure that Emma never mentioned to anybody what she was reading. She wanted her safely under lock and key.

It wasn't all bad, she decided. Staying in Iris Blackburn's guest cottage sounded enticing and romantic, something she could tell her friends about.

"When I was staying with Iris Blackburn and we were working on her book . . ." Emma smiled at the thought. She had never been one to give herself airs, always thought of herself as ordinary and still couldn't believe that Iris had chosen her, singled her out. She stared down at the remaining pages on the sofa beside her. Had she really decided to take on finishing this book? And what about the editing that would be needed? How would someone of Iris Blackburn's stature take suggestions or even criticism from a nobody like herself? she wondered. What if they didn't agree on an ending or what happened to a character? It could be unpleasant, and Emma shied away from drama. Her mother had been prone to it.

Oh well, she told herself, better read to the end and talk to Iris about what still needed to be done. Then she'd make her final decision. She went back to the manuscript:

## *The Wild Girl*, Chapter 14

After the heavy front door was shut firmly behind him, Melrose crossed the forecourt, heading for the main gate. He would like to have asked the kitchen staff if Lucy had eaten her soup that evening, but he decided not to chance his luck at sneaking around to the staff entrance again. He was glad Sir Henry had chosen not to accompany him on his exit as he veered off to the right and back to Chisholm's cottage. The faint odour of some kind of pomade or cologne still lingered. Now alone Melrose examined the room more thoroughly. What he observed made him conclude that Chisholm had definitely packed in a hurry.

He went over to the desk, hoping to find an incriminating note left imprinted on the blotter, but unfortunately there was nothing of interest. He then went to the back of the cottage to see if Chisholm could have spied on the lovers or overheard their tryst. But this too proved futile. The back of the cottage was built into the wall, separating the bailey from the outside world. With a sigh of frustration he rejoined Jock.

"Did ye find anything?" Jock asked.

"Not much. Only that the young lady might have been getting together with her sweetheart in the woods."

"So not the pure young thing we had thought her to be?" Jock gave a chuckle. "So what next, sir?"

"I think probably go and chat with the people in the cottages on the waterfront, see if any of them might have noticed someone damaging that boat, or witnessed what time the couple set off."

Jock nodded. "Although if it was after dark you won't be in much luck. People here keep their curtains tightly closed when the sun goes down. There is still a lot of superstition about what might be abroad in the night."

"Fairies and ghosties and things that go bump in the night?" Melrose looked amused.

"Precisely. When you live on Skye you take things like that seriously."

"Like suggesting that Flora's real father was a kelpie?" He was still grinning.

"Aye. Things like that. We don't mock the supernatural here. We've all too many stories of things we can't explain."

They drove off, bumping along the track through the woods. Melrose glanced around, wondering where the pair might have found enough privacy for a tryst. Later he'd come back and look, although he didn't see how it could help his case. It seemed to him that the one person who could help was Flora. If she and Lucy were as close as everyone had said then Lucy would surely have told her of her attraction to Stewart and of their plans. And that must have been why she was conveniently far away on that night, so that when questioned she could truthfully say that she had no idea that Lucy had run off. Somehow he had to get her the message that she was safe with him.

The wind was blowing strongly off the strait and the boats in the small harbour bobbed up and down, their ropes creaking and groaning. He must find out exactly what the sea had been like when the couple attempted that crossing. Waves lapped at the low wall along the waterfront, sometimes sending spray onto the narrow road.

"Do you know who lives in the waterfront cottages?" he asked Jock.

"Some of them," Jock said. "That first one would be Dan MacLeod, and a bit further along is Callum MacLeod."

"All MacLeods, are they?"

"Mostly." Jock grinned.

"It might be smarter for you to introduce me, if you know Dan MacLeod," he said. "Is he a relative?"

"No, just a fellow clansman," Jock replied. "I don't really know him. I've driven his wife to the hospital a couple of times. He's a good man. I doubt you'll find him at home during the day, though. He'll be out on the boat, won't he? Still Jinty will be there. His wife."

They went to the front door and knocked. It was opened almost immediately by a large man. "What's this then?" he asked. Then he spotted Jock. "Oh, hello, Jock."

"Hello," Jock said. "I didn't expect to find you at home at this time of day."

"Don't tell me you've come with designs on my wife, thinking I'd be gone." He laughed heartily. "No, I've been out five days in a row. The herring are plentiful at the moment. But the nets are needing some work, so I didn't go out this morning. It's been a good catch this week. Can't complain."

"I've brought someone to see you," Jock said.

"This is surely not a visitor looking for a room at this time of year?"

"No, it is not, Dan," Jock said. "This is the inspector from Glasgow, come about the sad accident."

"Oh aye?" Dan examined Melrose, summing him up.

"Hello, Mr MacLeod," Melrose said, holding out a hand. "Inspector Melrose. We're trying to get to the bottom of this sad business, and we were wondering if you and your neighbours could shed any light on it."

"You'd better come in then and have a wee strupak," Dan said. "Woman, we've got visitors."

They stepped into the cottage. The door was low enough that Melrose had to duck his head, and he wondered how many times big Dan had hit himself on it. Inside the small room was delightfully warm with a glowing peat fire and spotlessly clean. The opposite of Flora's father's cottage. The window was framed with bright curtains and looked out on the seawall and the mountains across the water. A youngish woman with round, red cheeks and hair back in an old-fashioned bun turned from the stove to greet them. They were seated by the fire while she poured tea from a pot on the stove and cut slices of currant bread.

"I baked that this morning," she said. "Nice and fresh. I must have expected visitors."

They ate in silence, Melrose enjoying the fresh bread and hot tea. He didn't say anything until they had put their cups down. "That was delicious, thank you," he said. "Just what the doctor ordered."

She gave an embarrassed smile and offered more. Melrose thanked her but turned it down. "I'm afraid I've still got a lot of work to do, Mrs MacLeod," he said. "The laird is desperate to find out who killed his daughter."

"I should have thought the sea did that," Dan said. "The young man was no sailor, and the tides can be tricky here for those who don't know them."

"But their boat had been damaged," Melrose said. "The sail had been slashed in many places and a rope that held the sail appeared to have been cut."

"Both could be explained away," Dan said. "If that sail was rotten a stiff wind would do the trick, and the same with sheets. Ropes don't last long with the salt."

"That's possible," Melrose said, "but I'm told the sail was fairly new. Also two people are now missing, which has to raise suspicions. There are those who did not want the couple to elope together, including her suitor, Mr Chisholm."

"He hasn't been found then?" Jinty MacLeod asked, pulling up a ladder-back chair to join the group.

"He has not. Neither has Flora MacLeod."

"Well that's no surprise," Jinty said, giving a frown of disapproval. "Flora has always come and gone on her own terms. If Miss Lucy drowned then she'd see no reason to stay at the castle and she'd be off, God knows where."

"You haven't seen her then, since?"

"I have not," Jinty said.

"Can you think when you last saw her?" he asked. "We were told that she took a bowl of broth to her father the day before there was all the drama and the young pair ran off. Did she not come this way then?"

"I didn't see her," Jinty said, "and I'm usually aware of someone walking past. The window is open most days and I hear the feet coming. We're lonely enough here to be interested in outsiders."

"So let me ask you this," Melrose said. "Did you spot anyone working on that boat during the day, anyone who shouldn't have been in the harbour?"

"Aye," she said. "I saw the young man who drowned. He went down to the boat around midday and he had a bag with him. He didn't stay long and came back having left the bag. I assumed he was preparing to leave as he had the mainsail ready to be raised."

"You didn't see him come back later, with the young lady then?"

"I did not. But I was preparing Dan's dinner and I keep the curtains closed after dark. But Callum MacLeod says he let the dog out before going to bed and saw two people, a man and a woman, walking together near the harbour. He said they walked close together holding hands so he didn't like to be too nosy. He thought it might be Alasdair and Jenny, you know, Callum's daughter and the young man who is courting her? Anyway the girl was wearing a long cloak with a hood up, just like Jenny has. So he went back inside and didn't see where they were heading."

Melrose made a note of this. Agnes had mentioned Miss Lucy's hooded cloak. "But you saw nobody earlier. Nobody working on that boat? Damaging the sail?"

Both MacLeods shook their heads.

"Were you in the harbour at all that day, or out at sea?" Melrose turned to the husband.

"I was out," he said. "I left before sunrise and came back mid-afternoon."

"And nobody was lurking around the harbour either of those times?"

"Not that I saw. But I'm fully occupied with getting the boat ready to go and then unloading the catch when we come back."

"We? You have a mate on the boat?"

"Aye. I operate it with young Robbie from number seven down there. It takes at least a crew of two to work a fishing boat."

He decided to change tactics. "Did you ever see this Mr Chisholm for yourselves?"

Dan looked across at his wife, then shook his head. "Not close up. But he did drive past here in a car once, so I got a glimpse of his face. He looked as if there was a bad smell under his nose. Rather haughty, if you get my meaning."

"But you've never seen him at the harbour."

"I have not. Him I would have remembered seeing."

"We don't get many mainlanders here," Jinty said. "No outsiders at all much. Occasionally ramblers or climbers will come wanting a room in the summer, but they usually prefer to stay where there is a good pub and some fish and chips."

"You didn't hear Mr Chisholm asking any of the boatmen around here to take him across to the mainland?"

Dan looked puzzled. "And why would he want a ride on a herring boat when there is a perfectly good ferry that takes him right to his own front door?"

There didn't seem to be much more to ask. He thanked them for their hospitality, and he and Jock were escorted to the door. He ducked to step over the threshold, turned to thank them again, then asked, "You'd have no idea where Flora might be hiding out? Does anyone know where she goes when she runs away?"

"No idea at all," Jinty said. "No one's ever been able to find her when she didn't want to be found. Like a spirit she is, a wild thing. But then who could blame her, growing up with no supervision, and her mother wild and flighty herself."

"Hush, woman," Dan said. "It doesn't do to speak ill of the dead."

"Well, she was." Jinty gave Melrose a knowing look. "Grew up in the village here and danced with all the boys but never stayed with one. Then she gets herself a job at the big house and gave herself airs of being grander than the rest of us. Then suddenly out of the blue she announces she's going to marry none other than that Angus. Can you imagine that? She could have had her pick and she chooses him, who always was free with his temper and his drinking, and lives cut off from the rest of the world. She paid for it, didn't she. Miserable and lonely, stuck out there with no one to talk to except the baby, and then she goes and kills herself."

"We don't know that it was deliberate," Dan said, but Jinty sniffed. "You don't stand on a cliff and fall off by accident. Of course she wanted out of that life, and I can't say that I blame her."

Melrose couldn't think what else to ask and bade a polite goodbye, moving along to the rest of the row of cottages. The occupants of these houses yielded no more information of use. The harbour wall shielded anyone working on a boat from casual eyes. The fishermen had gone out early, come back with their catches and gone home to a well-earned meal. None of the men had been approached by Mr Chisholm to ferry him to the mainland, and they couldn't think where he'd find a boat for several more miles along the coast. The consensus was that he'd be mad to try and walk that way.

None of the women had seen Flora pass by their homes.

"She had the mother's bad blood," one of the husbands agreed. "I don't reckon Angus was the father of that child at all. I reckon it was a sailor from one of those boats that put in here during the Great War."

His wife looked up from her knitting. "I'm more inclined to think it was a storm-kelpie."

"What exactly is a storm-kelpie?" Melrose asked Jock as they drove back along the seafront.

"It's a kind of sea-demon that inhabits the lochs and shores of these parts," Jock said. "A shape-shifter, you know. So it could appear like a handsome young man, or a horse or whatever it chose."

Melrose tried not to smile at the simplicity of the islanders. "Did you ever see one yourself?" he asked.

"No, but there's plenty of folks who will swear they saw one."

"In what shape?"

"Various. A seal who turned into a man. A horse who galloped into the sea and disappeared." Jock shrugged. He glanced across at Melrose, who was staring straight ahead, trying not to smile. "You may well mock," Jock said, "but when you live on a place like Skye, where the storms sound like banshees out of hell and the mist can come down to envelop you in minutes, you're inclined to believe a lot of things."

"I'm sorry," Melrose said. "I've grown up in the big city where we're surrounded by realism. Life is hard enough with smoke that chokes your lungs and damp that gives you consumption and gangs waiting to rob you. We don't need the supernatural to scare us."

Jock nodded.

"I think we've done about all we can here for today," Melrose said. "I don't know about you but I could do with some food. It's been a long time since breakfast."

"I wouldn't say no to that," Jock agreed. "Do you fancy fish and chips? They do a good one at the café near your hotel."

"Sounds good to me," Melrose said.

# Chapter 25

Emma realized that she had read several chapters without taking notes. The story had picked up in tempo. She was enjoying the interactions with Jock and the local inhabitants. It all felt delightfully foreign to her. She opened her notebook and started to jot down random thoughts. Chisholm had left in a hurry and hadn't taken all his things. Lucy had also left in a hurry, but with a different motive. It all seemed rather clear. Chisholm had overheard Lucy and Stewart planning to leave and slipped down to the harbour to make sure they didn't make it to the other side. Then he had grabbed a few items and made off. Maybe he had found a car to take him across to the other side of the island where he could hire a boat to take him to the mainland.

But then there was Flora, also missing. Was it possible that Emma had got it wrong, and it was Flora who overheard Lucy planning to leave and decided she couldn't bear to be left behind? She would have the facility to go down to the harbour unnoticed. She was good at it. Perhaps she had only meant to stop Lucy and Stewart from leaving, by making the sail inoperable, but when they drowned she felt remorse and went to hide out in the hills. Or was terrified she'd be blamed. But that didn't explain why Chisholm had also slipped away.

*Good.* Emma nodded with satisfaction. *Now we have a good puzzle.* She was keen to see where it was going next. She glanced up at the clock on the mantelpiece. A little more time to read before dinner. Would Iris be present? she wondered. Emma considered what she should say to her. Had she really made up her mind that she'd finish writing the book? She looked back at the unread pages sitting on the sofa beside her. She supposed it depended on how much further in the story Iris had progressed. Because if Emma had to take it on now, she had no idea where Iris could be going with it.

With a small sigh she picked up the next chapter:

## *The Wild Girl*, Chapter 15

After a satisfying meal, at which he turned down the suggestion of a wee dram of whisky, Melrose asked Jock if he could be available that afternoon. Jock had to meet an elderly lady at the ferry and take her to her daughter's house, but after that he could drive Melrose again. So Melrose took the opportunity to make notes, then telephoned MacDonald at Portree, saying that he wished to question the governess and to visit the Chisholm estate. Could MacDonald arrange for a police vehicle to drive him around the next day?

"What's wrong with Young Jock?" MacDonald asked.

Melrose chuckled. "He won't take his motor car on the ferry. Afraid it will fall off, or something. He's proud to own a new cab."

MacDonald chuckled, too. "Very well. I'll see what I can do. What time?"

"Oh, right after breakfast, I think. Shall we say ten?"

"How are you getting along?" MacDonald asked. "Found anything that we didn't know?"

"Not really," Melrose said. "I understand that Chisholm was a chap who thought a lot of himself. He could well have been furious if he knew that the girl he was supposed to marry was running off with someone else. So far I haven't found anyone who saw him making a getaway, but there is so much ground left to cover."

"And what about the Wild Girl?" MacDonald asked. "Has she turned up yet?"

"She has not."

"Do we know why she didn't return to the castle after she took her father the soup?"

"She never took him the soup in the first place," Melrose said. "That's the strange part. Why did she vanish the day before any of this blew up? Being a creature of nature did she sense that all was not well? I'd dearly like to locate her if I can. I'm having Jock drive me around the various crofts in the hills this afternoon, to see if any of them have seen her."

"Good luck with that. I'm told she could be away for weeks if she felt like it. Not so easy now, with the fancy dresses they made her wear at the castle. I heard she'd become a fashionable lady. They said they couldn't even tell her apart in her manners from Miss Lucy. She'd become a proper little aristocrat. They went around like sisters."

"So perhaps she's in mourning for a lost friend," Melrose said.

"Or perhaps she didn't want her dear friend to leave without her and decided to stop it," MacDonald said.

"That did cross my mind as well."

"You'll never be able to prove that," MacDonald said, "unless she decides to confess. If that girl wanted to move without being seen, then nobody would have seen her."

"And if Flora was the culprit, that wouldn't explain why Chisholm decided to vanish, too. Unless they went off together."

"Highly unlikely," MacDonald said. "If anyone was proud of his lineage it was he. He'd never go off with the brat of a fisherman and a trollop."

"Ah well. Back to work," Melrose said. "Talk about looking for a needle in a haystack!"

"We do have a dog on the island who is good at tracing lost climbers," MacDonald said. "If he could be any use, I'll send him down to you."

"Yes, I suppose that might show us at least which direction Chisholm took when he left the castle. Not that that would say much."

"Let me ask you this," MacDonald said. "What is your impression of Young Jock? I know he's newly married with a baby on the way. And he's purchased a new taxi. Probably needs money right now. Do you think he could be bribed to drive someone like Chisholm to the ferry and to keep quiet about it?"

Melrose paused, considering. "I don't know him well enough yet," he said. "He seems like a decent sort of bloke. But if someone offered him enough money . . . who can say? We all have the point at which we can be bought, don't we?"

"Do you?"

"I haven't reached it yet," Melrose said. "I suppose I'm not far enough up the ranks of the Glasgow Police to make it worth being bribed. But we do hear rumours of the ones at the top with their palms open and willing to look away when necessary."

"It's nae like that here, I can tell you," MacDonald said, "but of course there aren't the criminals on Skye, not folks with the kind of money to make it worth our while to look away." He laughed heartily at his own joke.

Melrose was glad to hang up. He had never really taken to MacDonald, although he had to admit the man had gone out of his way to be friendly. But then he found himself thinking about their conversation. If

Chisholm, or even Sir Henry, had offered MacDonald enough money to keep the interloper from Glasgow from finding out the truth, would he have taken it?

Jock returned at three thirty and they spent the rest of the daylight hours driving around the crofts on the hillsides, going as far as the other side of the island and checking out other small hamlets along the way. The thought that had struck Melrose when he had arrived on the ferry occurred to him again: there were very few people on this island. Each of the crofts was a smallholding with a few animals, maybe a Highland cow or two, some vegetables, dying at this time of year, and a peat stack, cut from peat beds higher up the mountain.

The journey was not an easy one: the narrow road switchbacked over hills, making Melrose close his eyes on occasion as nausea crept in. Each crofter they visited invited them in for a strupak, and they had to chat politely while tea and some kind of bread or cake was served. Most of the crofters knew Flora, but none had seen her recently.

"Let's go back," Melrose said as a narrow band of red sunlight hung beneath thickening clouds. "I don't think we're going to learn any more, and if I have to eat another oatcake I'll burst."

As they headed back from the western shore they passed over the foothills of the Cuillin, now close and etched against the fading light. For the first time Melrose was aware of the power and danger of the mountains, the steep and craggy cliffs. They might not be the Alps but they were mountains to be taken seriously. He was glad he was not a climber.

The last of the daylight faded as they came down the hill towards Kyleakin. The water in the strait was smooth as glass. A crossing ferry cast lights on the water. It was a charming sight. *What if I lived somewhere like this?* he found himself wondering. Married a good woman, settled down, did police work that involved locating lost sheep? But then he remembered that he did not speak Gaelic. And from the sounds he had heard, he was not likely to pick it up!

He ate a good dinner of shepherd's pie and peas, followed by a steamed pudding and custard and a pint of local ale, then he went to bed and slept soundly.

The next morning he walked down to the ferry and enjoyed the crossing to Kyle of

Lochalsh on a fine day and smooth sea. As they sailed he asked the ferrymen whether they might have noticed Chisholm crossing from the island. This was met with shaken heads.

"He's a tall chap, isn't he?" one said. "And he has a sort of look about him. I'd have remembered him."

At the police station he met Constable MacLean, who announced that he had been assigned to the murder investigation. He seemed to think this was a perk and was quite deferential to Melrose, who found this amusing. He was used to being near the bottom rung of the ladder.

The police vehicle was a well-worn Morris Minor, and it smelled as if the last occupant had been eating his fish and chips in it. They drove first to the governess's residence. Melrose had forgotten that her father was the local schoolmaster and was surprised when they pulled up at the school. Children's voices floated out from a classroom, repeating the four times table.

*Four fours are sixteen.*

*Five fours are twenty.*

*Six fours . . .*

"You'll find Miss Anderson in one of the classrooms," the driver said. "She's back to helping her father with the school."

Melrose approached the grey stone building and opened a door. It led straight to a classroom where about thirty small children were seated. They gaped at him as if he were a creature from another world. Then he saw the slim young woman standing by the blackboard. Her ash-blonde hair was twisted up in a bun and she had clear blue eyes. A pleasant-looking person. She was holding a pointer and looked up, startled, as he came in.

"I'm sorry to interrupt," he said. "Are you Miss Anderson?"

"I am. Who are you?"

"Inspector Melrose, Glasgow Police," he said. "I wonder if I might have a few words about Miss Lucy Hamilton?"

"Such a sad thing to happen," she said, "but I don't know how I can help you. I was dismissed before any of this happened."

"All the same, I'd appreciate some insights, if the children can be left for a moment?" He was conscious of all those pairs of eyes staring at him with amazement. A strange man did not appear very often in Kyle of Lochalsh.

She put down the pointer. "Very well. Children, turn to page twenty-three in your books. Read the paragraph about Robert the Bruce. And no talking. I'll be outside and I'll hear every word."

She gave a stern look. Heads went down as they turned the pages of their textbooks. She followed Melrose outside.

"I wondered if you could give me any insights into what Miss Lucy thought about her suitor, Mr Chisholm, and what she felt about Mr Stewart."

She shook her head. "I don't know what I can tell you. She was not pleased when Mr Chisholm came to stay. She made it clear that she did not like him and certainly didn't want to marry him." Those blue eyes held Melrose's. "I am a great believer of the freedom of women to choose, to make their own lives, not to be sold off like cattle. I told Lucy she needed to go out into the world, to experience life before she settled down anywhere."

"And what did she say?"

"Oh, she was all for it. She said she certainly didn't want to be stuck in this dreary corner of the world producing heirs for a laird. She was a bright and gifted young woman, you know. She wrote lovely poetry and plays that the girls put on. Oh, they had such fun, those girls." She paused, smiling at a memory. Melrose noticed she had dimples.

"Had you been her governess for long?"

"For about the last six years. She had been sharing her brother's tutor until he turned ten, but when he went off to school she needed a governess. At first she was a shy little thing, very quiet and withdrawn, but then Flora arrived."

"Ah yes," he said. "Tell me about Flora."

"Such an interesting child," she said. "When she came she really could be called a wild thing. No idea how to use the proper utensils, how to take a bath or brush her hair. She wasn't sure she wanted to be with us at all and resented any efforts on my part to civilize her. But it was Lucy who achieved the miracle. She took to Flora instantly, and the moment Flora had someone who cared about her, who loved her, everything changed. Those two were thick as thieves. They did everything together. Lucy wrote plays and they acted them for the family. They had this huge dressing-up chest and they were so amusing. They played every character, from Saint Joan to the old hags in *Macbeth*."

Her face lit up as she spoke, her eyes sparkling. Melrose smiled, too. "I can see they enjoyed having you as their governess."

She nodded. "Yes. We got along very well. I tried my best to encourage and educate Lucy. I wished she could go on to university like her brother, but the family was against it. I said they should at least consider sending her to a finishing school on the Continent so she could learn how to behave in society."

"And what did Sir Henry say to that?"

"He said that when she was married her husband could take her to Paris if he chose. He said there was no such thing as society in Scotland and he'd made up his mind that she'd marry Chisholm."

"Goodness," Melrose said. "That sounds very archaic."

"Positively feudal." Her eyes flickered with amusement. The absurd thought came to Melrose that he'd be happy looking at that face for the rest of his life. "If you believe in these things so strongly, why are you still here, teaching in a backwater?"

The amusement faded. "In case you don't realize, it costs money to travel. I've been saving up. That was why I took the job with Sir Henry. It paid well, and when I met Lucy I felt sorry for her. I probably have enough for a short trip abroad now, or I may look for a governess position in another country. If I can leave my father, that is."

He saw the wave of pain cross her face. "Your father is not well?"

She shook her head. "He was gassed in the Great War. His chest has never recovered. He gets terrible bronchitis every winter. One day it will turn to pneumonia and finish him off."

"And your mother?"

"Died years ago, when I was a child. She died giving birth to my sister, who also died. Life is hard up here. And life is cheap, as we see from what happened to Miss Lucy."

"I'm sorry," he said. "Life is hard on the streets of Glasgow, too. So when did you leave the laird's service?"

"He dismissed me a few weeks ago. He said I was putting rebellious ideas into Lucy's head, and besides, her education was now finished."

"Had Mr Stewart come to the island by then?"

"Oh yes," she said. "A pleasant young man, if rather earnest. I joined them at dinner sometimes, when I was invited."

"Did you notice any spark of attraction between Miss Lucy and Mr Stewart?"

She frowned. "I can't say that I did. She paid him no attention. On the other hand I could see that Flora enjoyed flirting with him. But given her background I suppose that was natural for her."

"How did Mr Stewart take the flirting?"

She smiled. "It made him quite embarrassed. He was a studious young man, I think. Not particularly one for the ladies."

"And yet somehow he and Lucy met in secret and planned to run away together?"

She paused before saying, "I've been mulling this over, and it is my opinion that Lucy was using him. She wanted to escape from Chisholm, and she wanted a way off the island. Perhaps she feigned interest in Stewart to persuade him to elope with her, or perhaps it was more mundane—she paid him to take her over to the mainland."

Melrose was annoyed that he had not thought of this himself. Of course she had paid him. It made sense. She saw a way of escape and took it.

"Had Mr Chisholm arrived before you left?"

"A week or so before."

"And what did you think of him?"

"If I had been Lucy I should not have wanted to marry him."

"So tell me," Melrose said, not wanting to end the interview. "Do you feel he was the sort of man who would rig a boat to drown a girl who rejected him?"

"Oh yes," she said, then hesitated. "No, that's wrong. I think he's more the type who would have confronted her and shot or stabbed her. He's the sort of man who would like the young woman to know who was killing her and to watch her feel fear before she died."

"Miss Anderson, you are so perceptive," he said. "I've learned more from you in five minutes than I have from every other interview."

"Governesses are like furniture," she said. "Nobody notices we are in the room. We have plenty of time for observation."

"I should bring you down to Glasgow and put you on the force there," he said jokingly.

"I wouldn't say no to that," she replied, but then blushed. "I meant I think I'd make quite a good policeman, I mean policewoman, if there are such things."

"I believe there are in London at Scotland Yard," he said.

"Then perhaps I should go to London." She smiled at him. Then a sound from the school made her turn around. "I should go," she said. "Those children have probably destroyed my entire classroom by now. They know I am reluctant to use the switch on them."

He wanted to say more, but he couldn't think of what that might be.

"Well, goodbye then," he said lamely. "And thank you for your help."

"Not at all. I've enjoyed talking to you. It's not often we get outsiders here. Although I don't think I've told you anything that will help you find out who caused Lucy to drown."

"You've shown me that it might not have been love at all, but a means to escape. That changes everything."

"Does it?" she asked. "She's still dead. So is he."

# Chapter 26

"Stone the crows," Emma muttered, putting down the chapter on top of the others. Love interest for Melrose. Was Iris explaining why he never married? This was the girl he loved and couldn't have? Or will there be a marriage in the future? A marriage that doesn't last for some reason? Suddenly the story had developed a personal nature. Now she was especially anxious to read on, but there weren't many more pages. She glanced up at the clock, hoping she could finish before she had to go over to the big house for dinner.

## *The Wild Girl*, Chapter 16

Melrose watched her walk away, noticing the neatness of that upswept bun, the daintiness of her step. *Say something, you fool,* shouted the voice in his head.

"I say," he called after her. "Is there any chance we could meet again?"

She turned back. "I'm not sure there is anything else I could tell you that would be useful," she said.

"I didn't mean that." He felt himself blushing and knew that the blush would show up horribly against his fair skin. "I meant, you seem like such an interesting and intelligent woman. I'd enjoy having a chat with you sometime, when you're not busy."

The amusement returned to her eyes. "Apart from correcting spelling tests, planning the next week's lessons and cooking the meals for my father I'm hardly busy," she said. "There is not a lot to do in a place like this."

"Is there somewhere one could have a cup of tea? Or even a pint at the pub?"

"Don't you have a case you're supposed to be working on?"

"Yes, but not in the evenings," he said. "If you came across on the ferry they do quite decent food at my hotel."

Now the humour spread to her lips and she smiled. "Go across on the ferry to a gentleman's hotel? A stranger's hotel? A man I've just met? Can you imagine the rumours there would be about that? My reputation would be ruined forever."

"Surely not," he said. "We'll dine together in full view of everybody, and I'll walk you back to the last ferry."

"All the same they'd say I was fresh or desperate, wanting to pick up a fellow."

"Does that really matter to you?" he asked.

"I have my father's reputation to think of," she said. "Look at what they say about the Wild Girl. She was really a poor little mite abandoned by her family. Now they attribute all kinds of things to her, including the death of Lucy and Mr Stewart." She hesitated. "We're a small community, Inspector. We have to live together, to get along well. We can't let the outsider rip us apart."

"I understand," he said, "but could I perhaps write to you?"

"You've only just met me."

"Yes, and I felt right away that you're somebody I'd enjoy getting to know better. Nothing improper about it, I assure you."

Now it was she who flushed. "Well, I suppose I can't stop you from writing to me."

"And if you happened to come down to Glasgow, I could show you around, including the police station."

"Now that is a bribe," she said, laughing. "All right, Inspector. But I really have to go now. It was nice talking to you. Really nice."

"Before you go, may I know your first name?"

"It's Isla," she said.

"Pretty name. I'm James."

"James." She gave a nod of approval. "I must go."

Then she turned and walked into the building. Melrose watched until she had disappeared then went back to his waiting vehicle.

"That Miss Anderson, she's not bad-looking, is she?" the constable said as they drove off. "Bit of a waste stuck in a place like this."

"Does she have suitors?" Melrose asked.

"There's several who would like to court her but she's verra picky. Too picky, some would say. You have to take what you can get when you live in a small community. And she won't leave on account of her sick father. So where now?"

*Where indeed?* Melrose asked himself. If he wrote to her and she'd never leave her father what was the point? But if he didn't try then he'd have no chance at all.

"Which way, sir? We're at the crossroads," the young policeman said.

Melrose jerked himself back to reality. "I should visit the Chisholms," he said.

"Oh my." He sounded alarmed.

"Is there something wrong with that?"

"They don't take too kindly to intruders," he said.

"I'm not an intruder. I'm a police officer of the Crown come to question them about a murder investigation." He sounded more confident than he felt.

"If you say so, sir." He turned the car to the right and set off up the hill, swinging around and following the coastline north. After a mile or so they came to the gates of another great estate. Melrose got out and opened the gate. As they drove in he could see that this estate was very different from the castle of Dun

Akyn. Dun Akyn was a veritable fortress with no attempt at adornment. This was a gentleman's residence, fortified with towers at the corners, but grand and elegant nevertheless. A place where people who had money lived. No wonder Sir Henry was keen to unite his estate with theirs.

As they pulled up at the portico a footman came out, dressed in black livery. Melrose opened the car door. "Inspector Melrose from Glasgow here to speak with Mr Chisholm," he said.

"Do you mean Lord Chisholm?" The tone was icy.

*Oh bugger,* he thought. He'd put his foot in it before he started.

"Of course. Excuse me," he said. "Would you please tell him that I am here."

"Please wait here. I shall inform His Lordship of your presence."

The man disappeared, and it seemed to Melrose that he had to wait for a long time. He wondered what he could do if they refused to speak to him. Not much without a warrant, he decided. At last the footman returned. "His Lordship will see you in his study."

Melrose stepped into a foyer decorated with suits of armour and an even more impressive display of weapons and banners than he had seen at Dun Akyn. The footman led him down a long, dark hallway and tapped on the door at the far end.

"Enter," said a voice.

The footman opened the door and Melrose stepped inside, taking a deep breath as he did so.

"Good morning, Your Lordship," he said. "Detective Inspector Melrose from the Glasgow Police. I'm here about the sad matter concerning Miss Lucy Hamilton and her companion."

"And what could you possibly want from me?" The man behind the large oak desk had wavy grey hair and an impressive grey beard. "I have already been questioned by the local police and made my statement."

"I'm sorry to disturb you again, but I wondered if you had any news about your son? It seems he disappeared at the same time as this tragedy happened."

"And you are insinuating there might be a connection . . ."

"Not at all, Your Lordship. As you can imagine, we are anxious to contact him to see if he can throw any light on this sad business."

"Not as anxious as I am, and his mother," Lord Chisholm said. "We've heard nothing from him. Nothing at all. We have no idea where he might have gone. For all we know he was in that boat too and his body has not yet been found."

"You think your son might have been in the boat?"

"Isn't that a strong possibility? He and his sweetheart decided to elope and get married and dispense with all the fuss of her overbearing parents. This Stewart character was merely the ferryman."

He could hardly say that Lucy clearly loathed Chisholm. "That could be a possibility, sir," he said. "We will keep looking. We'll have an all-points bulletin to find him."

"We understand he was not well when he left. I assume he intended to come home and be looked after by us while he recuperated. Did he try and walk back to the ferry? What if the mist had come down and he had lost his way and fallen? Or been overcome by his sickness?"

Melrose nodded. "I have the offer of a hound who seeks out lost climbers," Melrose said. "Let's see if that can help us track him down."

"Good idea," Lord Chisholm said. "Anything to find out what has happened to my son. His mother and I are sick with worry, you know. I had hoped the Glasgow Police would send up more than one junior officer. I rather hoped for men to comb the countryside. To say I am disappointed is putting it mildly."

"I'm sorry, sir," Melrose said. "I assure you I am doing my best."

The look indicated that his best fell far below expectations. "Well, I don't think there's any point in keeping you a moment longer. Get back to the island and put that dog to work."

"Yes sir," Melrose said. He had been dismissed.

"Where now, sir?" the driver asked.

"Back to the ferry, I suppose," Melrose said. "I think it's probably a waste of time to look around here any longer. If Chisholm came across on the ferry someone would have noticed."

"They would, sir. There are those who make it their business to watch who goes in either direction. Nosy old biddies, you understand. They'd have seen."

Melrose was inclined to agree that nosy old biddies don't miss much. And the ferry did not run for long after dark. As they drove back to Kyle a sudden thought struck him. He remembered Lord Chisholm's arrogance, which his son apparently mirrored. The complete assurance that he was in the right and others were merely annoying flies to be brushed aside. And Melrose agreed with Isla's theory: Chisholm was not the type who would sabotage a boat if he overheard his intended plotting to run off with another man. He'd have confronted her, dragged her off to her parents to be locked up until she came to her senses. That was exactly what he would have done!

# Chapter 27

## *The Wild Girl*, Chapter 17

On the return crossing he tried to keep his mind focused on the case, but a pair of blue eyes kept swimming into his vision, making it impossible to concentrate. Until now he would have scoffed at the idea of love at first sight, but this was it. Somehow or another he had to have that girl. While he had been at Chisholm's estate, the mist had come in, and the ferry's horn echoed eerily as the boat inched forward.

When he got back to Kyleakin he found that the dog and its owner, a Mr MacGregor, had arrived. The dog was a hound of indeterminate breed, very friendly, and immediately covered Melrose with wet kisses.

"Whist now, you silly beast," the owner said. "I offered him to the police, but you can see he'd be no good chasing a criminal. Unless he licked him to death." He chuckled, then grew serious. "But when he's on the job he's quite different. You give him a scent and he's focused until he's found something. There's several climbers who owe their lives to Whisky here. Found one lying in a cave halfway up a mountain. In a place where the men swore they had already searched. The poor wee laddie was unconscious, but Whisky found him."

"That's great," Melrose said. "I need him to trace a missing man. He left without telling anybody and no one has seen him since. But there are plenty of items of his left in the guest cottage at the castle, so we could start from there."

"Aye, that would be a good place to start," the man said softly.

Melrose sent for Jock and they set off with Melrose in the front seat, dog and handler in the back. All the way Melrose was conscious of the hot breath on the back of his neck and was glad when they finally took the turn-off winding down to the castle.

"Should we announce ourselves to Sir Henry, do you think?" the dog's owner asked as they arrived. "I don't like sneaking onto his property."

Melrose hesitated. He knew it was the right thing to do, and he had already had a slap on the wrist for sneaking in the back door to speak to the servants. He stared up at the forbidding castle, barely visible through the mist, and shook his head. "We can access the guest cottage without being seen from the castle itself. And I don't think anyone will be looking out of windows on a day like this. Let's just get on with it. I don't want Sir Henry sending someone to accompany us."

He led them to the cottage tucked into the outer wall of the keep. Luckily the door was still unlocked. Inside everything was just as he had left it. He pulled back the covers to reveal the neatly folded pyjamas. "These should do the job, don't you think?"

"Oh, excellent." The man picked up the pyjama jacket and held it out for Whisky. The dog sniffed at it with enthusiasm. "Go find," he said. He opened the door and the dog took off ahead of them, heading through the outer gate and back along the way they had come. Melrose and MacGregor broke into a trot to keep up with the dog before it was swallowed up into the mist.

"Ach, so yon man went this way," MacGregor said. "But then you have to in order to leave the castle, don't you?"

"Unless you take the steps down to the harbour."

"Well he didnae do that."

Melrose made note of that. Had Chisholm been down to the harbour earlier and then made his escape in the opposite direction? The woodland loomed ahead, the trunks of the tall pine trees rising until their branches were lost in mist. The silence was absolute apart from the crunch of their feet on the gravel drive.

"Whisky, where are you?" MacGregor called. His voice was muffled.

Ahead of them they heard a bark. A short, high-pitched yip.

"He's found something." Mr MacGregor sounded excited.

They followed the barks deeper into the woodland, stumbling over tree roots, edging between close-growing trees until they came upon the dog. He was standing, ears and tail erect, barking at the ground.

"Oh no," MacGregor said. "What did you find, boy?"

Melrose dropped to his knees, heart beating fast, and started to scrabble at the soft soil. His hand touched something and freed it from the loam. It was a sock. He scrabbled a little more. Several other items of clothing came to light. A man's white shirt. An undershirt. A wool scarf. Melrose stared at them, frowning. "Chisholm's clothing," he said. "Why did he bury his clothing?"

"Maybe he didnae want to be burdened down with carrying it if he had far to go," the man suggested. Melrose tried to understand this. Why not just leave it deep in the wood? Why waste time burying it? "Let's see where he went from here, which way he took, if we can."

MacGregor picked up the sock. "Whisky. Go find."

The dog paused, sniffing at the sock, then took off again, not back to the track itself but further into the woodland. The two men were gasping as they stumbled over the uneven ground between trees, unable to see more than a few yards ahead, trying not to lose sight of the dog. Cold, damp mist swirled around their faces. It felt like moving through a dream. Then the barks came again, this time excited and more insistent.

They came to a small clearing. An old pine tree had fallen and undergrowth had sprung up around it—bracken and blackberries, now dead and dying at this time of year. They went over to a mass of piled dead branches near the tree. Melrose hauled them aside and saw that sod had been replaced. Under it the earth appeared to have been disturbed. He dropped to his knees. He didn't have to dig far before he touched something hard and cold. He recoiled, dug on until he was looking at a human hand.

"Give me some help here." He looked up at MacGregor. The owner had been restraining his dog. He gave a command to stay, then reluctantly the man dropped to the ground. After several minutes of feverish

```
working they found themselves staring at
the face of what had undoubtedly been
Euan Chisholm.
```

"No!" Emma shouted. She was holding the last sheet of paper in her hand. She got up, looked around the room. There were no more pages. She had come to the end. As if on cue the telephone on the table rang. She went over and picked up the receiver. "Hello?"

Cynthia answered. "Oh Miss Callander, I thought I should warn you that we'll be eating in about fifteen minutes. There is sherry now in the drawing room if you'd care to come across."

Before Emma could say anything the line went dead. "This is not fair," Emma said. "She can't leave it there. I can't possibly take on her story now."

Would Iris be at dinner tonight? Emma wondered, or was she deliberately staying absent until Emma finished reading? There was only one way to find out, and that was to go over to the big house. She caught sight of herself in the mirror over the fireplace—her hair was an unkempt bush and she was wearing old tracksuit bottoms. Although Miss Morton had said not to dress for dinner, that it was "only us," she could hardly show up at dinner wearing that. She pulled the curtain aside and looked out of the window. It seemed the rain had subsided to a wet mist. The thought of the word "mist" sparked a strong reaction in her head. Melrose in the mist, in that wood, and Chisholm's body. Now she had to find out where Iris intended to go with this story. And what about the governess? How did their narrative play out?

She went into the bedroom and changed the baggy trousers for a skirt, and at the last moment opted to change the big jumper for a blouse and cardigan. Iris had been confined to her room all day, but just in case she appeared for dinner, Emma cared enough to look respectable, if not fashionable. Then she brushed her hair, held it back with a clip, and ran a lipstick over her lips. She found the umbrella, put on her mack and hurried through the darkness to the side door. Good smells were coming from the kitchen as she sidled past, hanging up the mack on the peg in the hallway and leaving the umbrella in the stand.

She could hear voices coming from an open door ahead. Iris's voice, she thought, and again her heart started racing. She wasn't quite sure what she was going to say to Iris. She found herself tiptoeing down the hall, then jumped as Miss Morton came out of the room.

"Oh, Miss Callander, there you are. I was just going to give you another ring. Mrs Fisk hates it if we're not to dinner on time. Do go in. There's sherry on the tray."

Emma went into the room, which was almost too warm. Iris was sitting in one of the high-backed Queen Anne armchairs by the fire, a rug over her knees and a glass of sherry in her hand. She looked up expectantly as Emma came in.

"Here she is, the lovely girl who is going to finish my book," she said. "How far have you got, my darling?"

"I've finished it. At least I've finished all you have written, but you can't leave it there, Iris, you absolutely can't." The words just spilled out. "Who killed him?"

"Killed who, darling?" Iris looked puzzled.

"In your book. Mr Chisholm. I've just found him dead and buried. And I have to know who killed him."

"Mr Chisholm." Iris toyed with the words, then shook her head. "I really can't say I know a Mr Chisholm, and I've no idea who killed the poor man," Iris said. "Is he in the story?"

"Yes," Emma said, fighting back exasperation. She wanted to shake Iris and say, "You must remember. Think hard." But of course one could not do that to a national treasure. "He's not a very nice character. He was supposed to marry the girl who drowned."

"Drowned?" Iris paused. "Oh yes. Drowned."

"You remember. Scotland. The Isle of Skye. The castle." Emma could hear the tension in her voice.

"That's just the point," Cynthia Morton said, coming into the room again. "She can't remember. And it upsets her to talk about it. Besides, we have a guest."

Emma looked towards the door as Tony Gordon entered. Her immediate reaction was that she should have put on a dress and done something more with her hair. Then she reminded herself that he had a girlfriend.

Iris held out her hand to him. "Tony, darling. How good of you to be at my beck and call."

He came over and kissed her on the cheek. "As if anyone could refuse your commands, Iris." He looked across to Emma, giving her an encouraging smile. "Hello, Emma."

"Hello," she said, feeling horribly self-conscious. When was she going to stop blushing like a schoolgirl?

"Help yourself to a sherry, Tony," Cynthia said.

"Oh, thanks awfully." He went across to the tray on the sideboard. He glanced back at Emma. "You don't have a glass yet. Would you like one?"

"Please," Emma said. He came over with two glasses. Emma took hers and then was going to sit when Iris said smugly, "Emma has already finished reading my manuscript."

"That was quick. And?" Tony looked at her.

"It's very exciting," Emma said, "but it breaks off in the most suspenseful place. I have to know what Iris intended and where the story is supposed to go from here."

Iris gave a tired sort of smile. "It's no use my darlings. I can't remember what I intended. So don't let's talk about it now. Drink your sherry and sit down. You've been working too hard. I thought you'd take days to get through the book."

"It wasn't that long," Emma said. "And I was just getting caught up in the story when it stopped."

"I know," she said. "So was I. I foolishly thought I'd write just one more book. Wrap things up nicely with Melrose. Wouldn't it be nice to take him back to his roots, I thought. To let people see what shaped him as the man we later knew. But then I started it and I suddenly realized 'I can't do this.' Melrose used to speak to me and now he doesn't any more. I don't really know what sort of man he was in those days. I can't think through a plot in my head any more. I've always been a great plotter, you know. My books were known for their fiendishly clever outcomes. And now . . . all gone." She sighed. Then she reached out a bony hand to Emma. "That's why I'm counting on you, dear child. You won't let me down, will you?"

Emma had been heading for the sofa. Instead she stepped forward to take the hand. Iris pulled her closer with surprising strength until she was standing right beside the chair, feeling the heat of the fire on her left side. Iris gazed up at her with such fervency that she found it unnerving.

"I'll do my best," she said.

"As if she can possibly finish it," Cynthia Morton said angrily.

When they turned to look at her, she went on. "You said yourself, Iris, that you are known for your meticulous plotting, cunning twists. And you're entrusting your work to a girl who has published one slight volume with almost no twists and turns that I know of? Of course she won't be able to do it justice, and you'll be disappointed, and the whole thing will have been a waste of time."

Emma felt her hackles rise. Cynthia was speaking as if she wasn't even in the room. She waited for Iris to say something, but then she said, "You're right, Miss Morton. I only said I'd do my best. And if my best isn't good enough, well that's that, isn't it? I'll go away and Iris can hire a more experienced writer."

"Who will want to put their own stamp on my book," Iris said. "Who will want equal billing on the cover. I do know what I'm doing, Cynthia. I saw something in this young lady's work that touched a nerve. It was like reading what I'd written in my twenties. And I thought, 'Yes, she'll understand what is needed. She'll finish it for me.'"

Emma hoped this was not misplaced confidence but did not say so.

"Well, are you coming in to dinner before it gets cold?" Cook stood in the doorway, hands on hips.

"To hear is to obey," Iris said. "Help me up."

When Tony and Emma moved to Iris, Cynthia stepped in. "Come along then," she said.

Tony and Emma followed behind. Tony drew closer to Emma, making her heartbeat quicken for a second before he whispered, "You've read the book. What do you really think? Is it all right?"

"It's only half there," Emma said, "but what she's written is great. All the atmosphere of Skye. I can't wait to see it for myself."

"That means you're taking on the task and going to Scotland?"

"I'd be stupid not to," Emma said. "It will kick me into writing again."

He paused, looking at her with interest. "Writing means a lot to you, does it?"

"It meant everything until recently. I haven't been able to write since I came to England, and I've been terrified I'll never get a good idea again."

"Of course you can't write about a place you don't know well," he said.

Emma gave a worried chuckle. "And yet I'm being asked to write about Skye, where I've never been."

Tony grinned. "That was a tactless thing to say, wasn't it? I'm sure you'll do brilliantly."

"I wish I was equally sure," Emma said, "but I'm going to give it a lash as we say."

"A what?"

"A try. I'm going to give it a try."

"Come on, you two. I know you'd like to have your tryst in the darkness, but Mrs Fisk will kill you if the food gets cold," Iris called, her voice booming, remarkably strong, down the hallway.

Emma and Tony exchanged an amused grin and hurried in. Dinner passed pleasantly enough. Iris refused any more mention of the book and did not hint at why Tony had been summoned. Emma glanced at him across the table. He was so nice, so easy to talk to, but it was no good thinking he was being any more than naturally friendly. Iris had instructed him to be nice to her. She'd invited a young person to make Emma feel more at home. That was all there was to it. With a little sigh Emma looked down to focus on her meal.

The food, as Emma had come to know, was delicious. It was a consommé with herbed croutons, lamb cutlets with mint sauce, parsley potatoes and a vegetable marrow with white sauce. There was claret to accompany it, then floating island followed by cheese and fruit. To Emma, who had lived on grilled cheese, omelette and the occasional Sainsbury's individual steak and kidney pudding since she arrived in London, this felt like heaven. It took her back to the old days growing up on the farm, a time of absolute plenty when leg of lamb, steaks on the barbie, shrimp and lobster were all taken for granted. When there was fruit to pick whenever you wanted it. And a whole cellar full of wine. She hadn't realized until now how much she missed it. Missed her dad and her pony and the life there. To her embarrassment she felt tears coming to her eyes.

"I should be getting back," Tony said, shaking her out of her thoughts. "Thank you for dinner." He started to stand up.

"So you've looked into arrangements for me, haven't you?" Iris said, making him sit down again. "Emma will need enough money to tide her through and a letter of credit to the bank in Scotland in case she runs short. Oh, and book her a berth on the night train to Glasgow. She'll want to spend at least a day in that city, seeing Melrose's home before she goes on to Fort William and Mallaig."

"Really?" Tony looked concerned. "Are you sure that line is still open? It wasn't part of Beeching's Axe?"

"They have probably axed the line from Inverness to Kyle but the line from Mallaig must still be operating. It's the only way to get the herring from the port to the cities," Iris said.

"And the lobsters and Scotch to the south. More important, I suspect." Tony smiled. "So when would you want to leave, Emma?"

Emma felt this was all a bit rushed. "I . . . I don't know. I haven't even discussed the book with Iris yet. I really can't make decisions until—"

Iris held up a hand to interrupt. "What I want you to do is to go to Scotland first, then we can talk about the book. That way you'll have a clear view in your head about where Melrose is and what happens next. So let's think. What day is it?"

"It's Thursday."

"Thursday. All right. So she goes home tomorrow and has the weekend to get ready and settle up with her flatmates about rent and things. Then she can take the night sleeper to Glasgow on Sunday night." She fastened her gaze on Tony. "You've got that, dear boy? Money. Letter of credit. Berth on the night train, oh, and find out what the best hotel in Glasgow is. She'll want to stay at least one night there, maybe more."

Tony shifted nervously. "If that's all right with you, Emma?"

He gave her a questioning stare. "Don't you think we're rushing her a bit, Iris? She's from another country. She probably hasn't had the chance to travel by train here yet. And to go to Scotland alone . . ."

"Of course it's all right with her. She's made her way from Australia alone, dear boy. And I'm sending her on a free holiday, aren't I?" Iris said loudly, and Emma realized that Iris might have consumed quite a bit of wine with dinner. "Who would turn down a paid trip to a place she's never been? She doesn't want to go back to Australia having not seen Scotland, the birthplace of her ancestors."

"My ancestors?"

"Callander is surely a Scottish name," Iris said. "Did they never talk about it?"

"My family has been in Australia since the eighteen hundreds," Emma said. "And my mum was proudly English from Kent. She even had a convict in her history, which everyone boasts about these days."

"Hmmm," Iris grunted. "Anyway, I want you to go and the sooner the better. I take it you don't object, in spite of Tony stirring up trouble."

"He's not stirring up trouble," Emma said. "It's nice of him to be concerned about me."

Tony met her gaze, making her blush and look away.

"And it is fine with me," Emma said hastily. "I'm still not sure if I can do justice to your book and help you finish it, but I'm willing to go up to Scotland and get a feel for the place. Actually I'm keen to see Skye for myself now."

"Good girl," Iris said. "You see, Tony, she's made of sterner stuff. True-blue Aussie grit." She wagged a finger at him. "Tony will make all your arrangements until you get to Skye. Then it's up to you to decide where you want to headquarter yourself."

"How do I get around?" Emma asked. "Will there be regular buses? There weren't in Melrose's day."

"Darling, I'm giving you plenty of money," Iris said. "You hire a car and a driver to take you where you want to go. It's outside the tourist season. There will be drivers wanting work. You'll figure it out." She attempted to stand up. "So off you go then." She waved them away as if she were shooing chickens. "Come back for her at lunchtime tomorrow, and you can drive her to the station."

"Very good." Tony gave a mock bow and backed from the room, as one does for the queen.

"Cheeky monkey," Iris said, laughing. "Now I think I've used enough energy for one day, and so have you, dear Emma, reading all that material. There should be cocoa and milk in the cottage so you can have a night cap. Do you want to take a glass of Scotch across with you to add to it and help you sleep?"

"Oh no. I've drunk quite enough for one day," Emma said. "Sherry and then wine. I'm not used to it. Can't afford it."

"Finish this book and you can afford whatever you damn well please," Iris said, still sounding belligerent.

"Good night then," Emma said. "I hope this trust in me isn't misplaced. I'll try not to let you down."

"Of course you won't, dear girl. It's all going to be wonderful, and we're going to celebrate a bright future together." She raised a hand to Miss Morton, who had sat silently, glaring, across the table. "You can help me to bed now, Cynthia dear. I've had enough excitement for one day."

Miss Morton came around to help the old lady stand, then offered an arm to help her from the room. Maggie was waiting at the door to assist her mistress to the stairs. Miss Morton looked back at Emma. "By the morning she'll probably have forgotten about everything she said tonight. She may have no idea who you are or why she wanted you to go to Scotland. She has good days and bad days, you know. And the bad days are happening more often."

"So what would you have me do?" Emma asked. "If working on this book, with the hope of finishing it, is keeping the darkness at bay isn't that a good thing?"

Cynthia Morton continued to look at Emma. "If you think you have a hope in hell of finishing it. I don't know what she thinks a trip to Skye is going to do for you, but she's insistent on it."

"Maybe it's a trip she wanted to take but knows she is not up to it," Emma said. "Maybe for her, finding out about Melrose's past feels like holding on to her own memories."

"You're a perceptive young thing, aren't you?" Cynthia said at last. "Maybe you'll do after all."

# Chapter 28

The wind sprang up again that night, howling around the chimney. Emma heard the clunk of a slate falling from the roof, and the windows rattled as they were buffeted. *I want to go home.* The thought echoed around the room. There was no central heating, and the fire in the living room had died down so that it sent no heat through to the bedroom. She had plugged in both electric fires, but they didn't seem to be doing much to raise the temperature. The cottage felt cold and hostile, as if it didn't want her there. Lying awake, staring into the dark, she tried to calm racing thoughts. She'd go to Scotland, because Iris had insisted on it, but what then? She'd see the scenery for herself, find out if the castle was based on a real place, then come back, none the wiser about who killed Mr Chisholm. It had to be Flora, of course. Trying to protect Lucy. But that was too easy. It wasn't the clever twist which Iris's readers expected. How could she, Emma Callander, with only one book to her name, be expected to come up with a plot worthy of a legend?

At last she drifted off to sleep and woke to a clear sky and the deafening sound of birdsong. Having grown up in the Australian Bush she was used to magpies and other local birds, whose songs were so different from the songs here, and she lay there enjoying the blackbird and thrush competing with the incessant rhythmic cooing of a pigeon. When she looked out of the window the lawns sparkled with dew. The country wasn't such a bad place in the right weather, she decided. She got up, opted against a shower as the bathroom was icy, but washed and dressed in her smart pantsuit again, ready for the trip back to London.

She repacked the suitcase, then stood, looking around the room, turning to the stack of manuscript pages on the table. If she was going to Scotland she'd dearly have loved to take them with her, to remind her exactly what happened, but everyone had made it clear that the pages were not to be taken away. So instead of going over to breakfast Emma sat down again, went through each chapter making more notes. Ferry. Armadale. Portree. Kyleakin. Mountains. Cuillin. And then on the mainland Miss Anderson and Lord Chisholm. She knew they were fictitious characters, but it would help to see where they lived. As she worked she began to feel more enthusiastic. She had been given a wonderful challenge. And Iris had said that if she completed the book she'd not have to worry about money again. That was a heady thought, but it sent a warning bell. She put down the page, thinking. Payment had not yet been discussed. She had no idea how much she would be paid if she finished the book, or if she'd get any credit on the cover. Would she have a meeting with Iris this morning before she left? At least Iris would want to meet with Tony when he came to pick her up. And she found herself breathing a little faster at the thought that she'd be riding with him to the station.

"Nonsense," she said firmly. "Has a girlfriend. Remember Simon. They always choose the one who can help with their career."

And with that she went over to the big house to breakfast.

"The mistress is having hers in bed again." Mrs Fisk poked her head out of the kitchen to greet her. "You'd better come into the kitchen."

Emma did as commanded, sat at the table and was poured a cup of tea.

"So what's it to be?" Mrs Fisk asked.

"Oh, nothing special. Just some toast would be fine," Emma said, rather afraid of the woman's glowering.

"You're a considerate little thing, I'll say that for you. And the missus has clearly taken to you. So tell me what you'd like and I'll cook it for you."

"A boiled egg if you don't mind," Emma said.

"Of course." Mrs Fisk got to work, producing an egg, thinly sliced soldiers and a toast rack full of toast. The egg, of course, was cooked perfectly. Emma spread homemade marmalade on the toast and found herself thinking that it wouldn't be so bad to return to write the book with Iris. At least she'd eat well.

She finished her meal, carried her plate over to the sink, then wondered what to do next. Tony was coming at noon, that much was set, but she'd dearly have loved to see Iris and talk to her about the book before she left. Feeling self-conscious and out of place she wandered through to the conservatory. On this bright morning the sun sparkled through the glass and there was a pleasant scent in the air from the many plants. She found the daily papers arranged on a low table, took *The Telegraph* and sat on a wicker rocking chair, reading.

After a while she heard voices down the hall and Iris came in. Today she was dressed in smart wool trousers and a silk blouse with jabot and looked quite the countrywoman.

"You're still here," she said, sounding surprised.

"Yes, Tony is coming for me at noon, remember?"

"Tony? Oh yes. Tony. Good. So how have you enjoyed your stay here?" She took the wicker chair opposite Emma and picked up *The Times*.

"Very much, thank you."

"But you still want to go home to Australia?"

Emma smiled. "It's not as if I live in a place like this. But it has reminded me that I'm a country girl at heart. I feel trapped in the big city."

"As I did," Iris said. "I tried Sydney for a while, and it's much more open and friendly than London, but even that was too much. I'd have to go and walk in the Domain, or on the waterfront every day."

"I felt the same," Emma said. "But you have a lovely place here."

"Lovely, but a bit remote, you know. I have to invite people to see me, otherwise I'd be stuck with Cynthia and she'd drive me potty."

"How long has she been with you?"

Iris considered. "She came as my secretary before the war. Then she joined up to do her part, as she said. I think she was probably something quite hush-hush, but she's not allowed to talk about it. Then when the men came home and she was kicked out of the Admiralty, she came back to me. And has been here ever since. Funny old biddy, isn't she? But alarmingly devoted to me. I really do believe she'd throw herself on a hand grenade to save me." She chuckled, then added, "Of course I've left her well provided for in my will. She won't have to worry about money when I go." A wistful look came over her face.

"Miss Blackburn—Iris . . . ," Emma said hesitantly. "Can I talk to you about the book? I really want to know your thoughts on where the story should go. You say you can't remember, but you must have some idea. Was it supposed to have a brilliant twist with a killer we hadn't thought of?"

Iris frowned. "I'm not sure that I ever knew. Melrose usually tells me himself. He finds out something, or someone says one little sentence and he thinks, 'Aha. So that's what was missing.' But I'm afraid he's fallen silent. He doesn't speak to me any more." She leaned across to Emma. "Perhaps he'll start talking to you. You'd be his type. He'd like you."

"Not as much as the governess," Emma said. She smiled. "So do you know what happened with the governess? Did they ever get together? Did they marry?"

"I suspect it was one of those loves that could never be," Iris said slowly. "Kept apart by fate. She couldn't leave her father. He got a chance to go to London . . ."

"That sounds awfully sad. If they truly loved each other they'd have made it work," Emma said.

"In that case you make it work, if you feel so strongly about it," Iris said.

Emma blushed. "I couldn't mess with your story."

"Nonsense. If you write it, it will become your story. You're the puppet master."

"I don't think so," Emma said. "I think if you've created the characters they tell you where they need to go. At least that's what I've heard you say."

"True. All right. Perhaps Melrose will show you what he means to do with Miss Anderson."

Emma felt a tight grip in the pit of her stomach at the thought of Melrose dictating a storyline to her. So presumptuous. Most likely he'd take one look at her and think that she was not worthy to carry on the tradition. Please bugger off, Miss Callander, and get Iris back here. That's what he'd say.

"So tell me, Miss Blackburn," she began.

Iris held up a hand. "Oh for God's sake, darling. It's Iris, please. We're Aussies. We don't need all this bloody formality. You and I are going to be working together. We're mates."

The thought of being a mate with Iris Blackburn made her blush again. "So I wanted to ask you, Iris, why did you choose the Isle of Skye? You must have been there because it's all so real and vivid. Did you decide when you first wrote Inspector Melrose that he'd have some kind of connection to that place?"

"I did go there once," Iris said. "When I'd been in England for a while and had made some money, I decided to see the rest of the British Isles. I hired a car and driver and went around Scotland. And the driver was from Skye. He insisted on showing me his island. I only had a day or two there but it left a lasting impression. Hauntingly beautiful. I intended to go back and spend longer, but there were other places to be explored. Then the war came, and after that I was horribly famous and invited to literary events all over the world until I got too old to travel any more."

Emma nodded, understanding. "But you decided to revisit it by writing about it."

"I always intended to set a book there, but never got round to it until now. I'm interested to see what you think of the island. Perhaps it's changed since the war. Perhaps you'll find it's all caravan parks and tea shops, but I hope not. Will you drop me a letter or a postcard from time to time to let me know how you're getting along?"

"From time to time?" Emma asked. "Aren't you only expecting me to stay for a few days?"

"Stay as long as you need to, my darling. Weeks if you need to get the feel of the place, and if it helps you to figure out the story."

"Oh, I don't think I'll need that long," Emma said. "Surely I can have a car and driver take me around the whole island in a day."

"Such an impatient person," Iris said, wagging a scolding finger at her. "The young are so impatient. First she reads the whole manuscript in one day, then she wants to do Skye in one day. But when you are a writer sometimes you have to wait and let things percolate. You can't go rushing ahead." She leaned forward, towards Emma. "So my advice to you is to take your time. Let the island speak to you. Know how it feels. It certainly spoke to Melrose, didn't it?"

"I believe it did," Emma agreed.

"Good, so go and have a bloody good time. Drop me a postcard every day then. Do you like whisky?"

"I've never really had a chance to try it," Emma said.

"You will. I understand there are distilleries on Skye now. The best stuff comes from there. It's the water, coming down from the mountains through the peat."

"Then I'll certainly give it a go," Emma said.

"Tony should be here soon." Iris looked around as if expecting him to materialize. Then she added, "He likes you. You'd make a good couple."

"He has a girlfriend," Emma said more sharply than she intended.

"I could send him to Scotland with you. A couple of weeks together in the romantic Highlands?" Iris's smile was teasing.

"Oh no, please don't," Emma said rapidly. "I wouldn't want to interfere with someone else's life."

"Just kidding, darling. No, I want you to concentrate on the task ahead. I want you to be open to what you see and learn there."

"Yes," Emma said. "I'll do my best and try not to let you down."

"Don't be so bloody earnest," Iris said. "Say 'I'll go to Skye and have a bloody good time no matter what.'"

Emma had to laugh.

# Chapter 29

Maggie had just served coffee when Tony arrived.

"Here you are, my darling." Iris held out a hand to him. "Such a treat for an old lady to see a handsome young man about the place. I might have to hire you just to sit and talk to me and cheer me up."

"That would not be a good idea, Iris," Tony said, looking a little embarrassed. "We'd soon get heartily sick of each other. You need to get out more. You've become a recluse. If you went up to a show in London occasionally . . ."

"It's so bloody difficult being famous, that's the trouble. I go to a restaurant and I'm about to take a bite of food and I hear the whispers. 'It's her, I'm sure. Go and ask for her autograph.' I can't tell you how much it puts one off one's dinner. And London—my play is still running after fifteen years. Isn't everybody bored to tears with it by now?"

"It does help to keep you in this rather luxurious lifestyle," Tony said. "Why don't you take a holiday abroad while you can still travel? I'll make the arrangements for you. A cruise?"

"Same thing, darling. I'd be on the beach in Cannes and hear, 'Ooh la la. C'est Iris!'"

"The trials of being an icon," Tony said and winked at Emma. "Anyway, I've come at your command with the things you requested and to drive Emma to the station."

"That's right. You've got her money?"

"All here in this little pouch. And the train ticket will be waiting for her at the ticket office at Euston. Oh, and the hotel in Glasgow is booked for one night with a possible extension."

"Such efficiency," Iris exclaimed. "Sit down and have a cup of coffee. Cynthia!" she bawled out. "Bring another cup. Tony's here."

"Poor Cynthia, you do boss her around," he said.

"She's used to it. Perhaps she likes it."

"I heard that." Cynthia came in, carrying a teacup and saucer. "And I do not like it, Iris. It makes me feel like the dog. I only stay out of extreme devotion and because you can no longer handle things alone."

"I certainly can."

"Who flushed her toothbrush down the loo the other day?"

"Only because it fell in by accident. I wasn't going to retrieve it."

Emma watched them. In some ways they acted like a long-married couple, she thought. There was a fondness on both sides.

"Here you go, Emma." Tony passed her the packet. "I'm ready to go when you are."

"I brought my case over," she said. "It's in the front hall."

"Right. Let's be off then, shall we?"

"Are you sure you don't want coffee?" Iris said.

"Sorry, but I'd rather get going, and I expect Emma would, too."

Emma nodded. "Yes, I'll have quite a lot to do if I'm to leave for Scotland on Sunday."

"Very well then," Iris said. "Off you go. Oh, and Tony . . . take good care of her." She looked suddenly frail and scared. "I wish you were going with her."

"She's a big girl. She managed the trip from Australia alone. I think she can tackle Scotland," Tony said. "And she won't need me getting in her way when she's trying to write."

A brief image of Tony standing with her on a rocky hillside overlooking the sea flashed through her mind. Hastily she brushed it aside. "Well, goodbye then, Iris," she said. "Thank you for everything." She was tempted to kiss Iris's cheek.

Iris grabbed her hands and held them for a long moment before she let go. "Stay safe and come home to me."

As they drove off Tony turned to her. "Iris has really taken to you, hasn't she?"

"She seems to have. I wonder if she's missing Australia and I somehow remind her of her own youth?"

"Possibly. I can tell you who doesn't adore you, and that's the Morton woman. You should have seen her glowering when Iris said goodbye to you."

"Poor Cynthia. Yes, she's very possessive about Iris. I tried to tell her I'm not a threat."

As they drove on Emma was just coming to terms with what had transpired over the past two days. It had felt like living in some kind of fantasy, and now she was back in the real world again. As they passed a village complete with village green and duck pond, a pair of ducks landed on the water and stirred a sharp memory. She glanced across at Tony.

"Could we stop for a moment, please?"

He brought the car to a halt. "What's wrong? Did you leave something?"

"No. I just want to take a look at that water. It reminds me so much of the pond at home. I used to swim in it during the summer, even though I'm sure the water was full of bacteria. And there were a pair of spoonbills . . . Have you ever seen them? Such odd but beautiful birds. And egrets. It was so lovely."

"You're really homesick."

"I must be . . . Everything here is so different. And I suppose I'm grieving that I don't have a home to go back to."

"You said your father died and your mother remarried?"

Emma nodded. "And the property went to a cousin. So I've actually nowhere to call home, which makes me very sad."

"That must be hard for you. Maybe you should try to make a new home here."

"But I miss Australia. All that sunshine and the animals. We had wallabies every evening and all sorts of lovely birds."

"If you lived outside London you could have your share of foxes and pheasants, and Iris has swans. Of course Isobel likes to hunt the poor foxes. She's quite bloodthirsty."

"You don't hunt then?"

"Me? I don't ride. I tried it once and fell off. Not a happy memory." He laughed and Emma smiled, too.

Then she took a deep breath before saying, "Tony, there's one thing I want to ask you, and I don't quite know how to put it." There was a long pause. "I'm worried about taking this assignment because I'm afraid of being let down again. I don't want to find that I go to Skye, I do the work and then Iris forgets who I am, or brushes me off and I wind up with nothing at the end."

Tony gave her a look of concern. "I suppose that is a risk you are taking, although it's the same with any job, isn't it? Some contracts work out and some don't. Writers submit manuscripts and some are accepted and others rejected. I'm sure you'd be disappointed, but you've nothing really to lose."

"You're right," she agreed. "But this means so much to me. My big chance. And I don't want another letdown."

"Another letdown?"

"I've had a couple of really hurtful letdowns in my life and they still haunt me."

He was fully focused on her, his gaze understanding. "Your mother abandoned you, just like mine did?"

"Not only that, Tony. I gave up my chance at Oxford for her, because she was in such a delicate state. I got a job, I looked after her. I had no chance for a normal life, and then out of the blue she announced she was getting married again, and the worst thing was she said . . ." Emma broke off, afraid she was going to cry. "She said it was about time I stopped depending on her and got on with my own life. After all I'd done, Tony. It hurt so much."

He put his hand on hers. "Of course it did. She sounds as if she was wrapped up in herself, just like my mother was. Two horrible women. We're better off without them."

"Yes." She managed a smile.

"And the other letdowns? Do you want to talk about it?"

Emma looked out of the car window, her gaze focused on those ducks. "I had a boyfriend until recently. My first real boyfriend, actually. A really nice English bloke. The perfect choice, you'd have said. Well educated, well dressed, funny, smart . . . a lawyer like you. We went dancing and he took me to the cinema, but I never met his family and I wondered why. He always went home at weekends and I thought, 'What a devoted son.' But then one day he said he'd have to stop dating me because of this other girl he'd been seeing . . . at home. She was more suitable than me, it turns out. Good for his career prospects. And he'd only been taking me dancing because she didn't like to dance and he did. Can you imagine what that felt like?"

"Pretty rotten, I'd think," Tony said. "But you mustn't judge all Englishmen by one bad apple."

"But I suppose you do all care about good families and good prospects and that kind of stuff?"

"Lots of people do. It's always who you know here and what they can do for you."

"Like Isobel's family?"

"I'm sure that's how my father thinks. But listen, Emma. If I'm handling this current job for you, I'll make sure you're treated fairly to the best of my ability. And I think I can say that Iris is a fair person, too. She'd never want to trick you out of anything. It will be a question of whether your name goes on a cover, but we'll talk about that later. Right now go and have fun in Scotland. You said you're a country girl. I gather there is an awful lot of empty countryside there, and grouse and stags and fish and all kinds of things to shoot and catch."

"I don't like the idea of shooting and catching," she said. "I'm not a violent person."

"No, you're quite sensitive, I can see that. And you've had a rotten deal, but now you've published a brilliant book and your future looks bright."

"Did you actually read my book?" she asked.

He grinned. "I'm not much of a fiction reader, I confess. I haven't even read Iris's books properly, only don't tell her. She'd sack me instantly."

They laughed together as he let out the clutch and they drove on.

As they approached the station Tony said, "Look, you have my telephone number. If you do need anything in Scotland feel free to ring me. I don't anticipate any problems, but just in case . . ."

"Thank you. You've been very kind."

Now it was his turn to blush. "Just doing my job, ma'am," he said in a mock police voice.

He insisted on carrying her case to the platform. "Well, goodbye then. And good luck. I think you'll have a marvelous time."

"Thank you. You've been there?"

"Skye? No, never. I went to Edinburgh once, for the Fringe. I was part of an acting troupe at university. We did these crazy short scenes—spoofs on modern kitchen-sink drama. A lot of fun."

A new side of Tony was revealed. Tony the actor. Not always the well-behaved solicitor-in-training.

"I've looked at the map," she said. "It seems very remote. Like the ends of the earth."

"Yes. Pretty remote. But they still have telephones and fish and chips so you'll be all right. Oh, and don't stint on hotels or meals. Iris has given you a generous amount. Enjoy it."

"Thanks. I will." She turned at the sound of the approaching train. "Thank you again, Tony."

"Hey, this got me out of a day of helping to draft an old colonel's will," he said. "See you when you get back. I'll want lots of good stories. And you can bring me some whisky."

"I will."

She sensed for a moment that he was going to kiss her on the cheek, but he retreated and opened the carriage door for her, handing her up her suitcase.

As the countryside flashed past she found herself smiling. See you when you get back. She must not read too much into that.

# Chapter 30

London looked surprisingly attractive as the train crossed the bridge over the Thames. The clear, bright day with puffy white clouds highlighted the Houses of Parliament, and even the Battersea Power Station looked imposing. *I needed this,* she thought. *I needed something to look forward to. And now I have it. A chance to write the book of my lifetime, to establish a name for myself. And to see Tony again,* she added.

When she entered the flat it felt as if she had been away for ages, although it was only one night. Jilly's clothes lay strewn over the back of the sofa. There was a piece of toast with one bite taken out of it on the coffee table. The scent of Jilly's latest perfume experiment lingered—too sickly and floral for Emma's taste. She unpacked, then studied her wardrobe, wondering what to take to Scotland. It would be cold and probably wet, according to Melrose. She washed her big wool jumper and laid it to dry on the ledge outside their window. The wool slacks would go with her, and the new pantsuit. She supposed she should wear the mack, but would it be warm enough? She looked down at that pouch of money. And there was the letter of credit if she needed it. Would it be too extravagant to go and buy herself a warm coat or jacket? Not Burberry or Lillywhites, of course, but perhaps Marks and Sparks had something.

She went shopping and made some modest purchases, conscious that she was spending Iris's money. She had also found three Inspector Melrose paperbacks at W. H. Smith and shoved them into her tote bag in case she wanted to read on the train. She hoped Iris wouldn't be cross with her, but it seemed that money was no object to Iris, and as she said, she had nobody to leave it to. The thought of a holiday ahead where she could eat and drink what she chose was rather heady and exciting.

That evening, when the other two came home, they listened eagerly to Emma's description.

"My oath," Jilly said. "You've fallen on your feet, haven't you? Driving all over Scotland with a car and a berth on the sleeper train?"

"I know. It feels a bit like Cinderella."

"I hope it doesn't turn into a pumpkin at midnight," Robyn said. "So you're really going to write her book for her?"

"Not write it. Finish it. She's set up the whole story on the Isle of Skye. I just have to figure out who the killer was and finish it for her."

"She doesn't know who the killer was? What writer starts a mystery book without knowing who committed the murder?" Robyn asked.

"Iris Blackburn, apparently. She says that Melrose usually figures it out as he goes along. She talks of him as if he's a real person. It's rather weird."

"She's a bit bonkers then?" Jilly asked.

"Not really. She forgets things from time to time, but then she seems really sharp again. It's just that she's spent so long with her inspector that he has become real to her. I can understand that."

"And you think you can do it? Write the book in her style?"

Emma shook her head. "I couldn't do it in her normal style, the one we're all used to in her Inspector Melrose series. But this one is softer, gentler, more like her first Miss Faversham books. Remember them?"

"With the cat? Oh yes. I liked those when I was a nipper," Robyn said.

"More to the point," Jilly said, "have you got the right sort of clothes for Scotland?"

"Probably not," Emma replied. "I've washed my big jumper and I'll wear my wool slacks, but I went to Marks and Spencer and bought a lambswool cardi and a couple of wool vests today, oh and a waterproof jacket with a fleecy lining from the sporting goods shop."

She went to retrieve it from her bed.

"Not exactly the height of elegance," Jilly exclaimed.

"How can you be elegant in pouring rain?" Emma asked. "It rains a lot, so I gather."

"But if you've been given all this money why not buy yourself a kilt while you're there. You're Scottish by ancestry, aren't you? You can wear the family tartan."

"There's a Callander tartan?" Emma laughed.

"Bound to be. Every Scottish family belongs to a clan."

Emma gave a nervous shrug. "I wouldn't like to spend Iris's money on something for me," she said.

"Stone the crows, Em, you're doing her a favour, and she's rolling in it, isn't she?"

"I suppose so," Emma agreed hesitantly. "But what if I can't finish the book to her satisfaction? She'll have put out money for nothing."

"You need a dose of self-confidence, my love," Jilly said. "Look in the mirror and tell yourself she's lucky to have found you."

"I'm afraid I don't quite believe that."

"At very worst you're going to see a place you've never seen and have a jolly good time there," Robyn said.

"Oh, and I should leave you with the rent money for next month, just in case I'm not back," Emma said.

"You think you'll be in Scotland that long?"

"Probably not, but then I'll have to go down to Iris's house and start working with her. She'll want me to be under her nose, in the guest cottage again."

"What's it like, this guest cottage?" Jilly asked. "Pretty swanky?"

"I suppose it could be quite nice but Iris's companion doesn't want me there at all. She made that very clear. She was supposed to do things like turn on the hot water and she didn't."

"Oh, it's like that, is it?" Jilly gave Robyn a knowing grin. "We're just good friends, nudge nudge."

"I don't think so." Emma frowned. "But what do I know? They've been together for years."

"Don't drink the cocoa she makes for you then," Robyn said, laughing. "That's how they get rid of people in all those mystery novels."

"Thanks for the warning." Emma laughed, too. "I don't know why she sees me as a threat, but she does."

A pleasant weekend passed. Emma treated the other two to a Chinese meal with her newfound wealth, and on Sunday night she took the Circle line to Euston. The sleeper train was already waiting on its platform, looking rather splendid. As she stood at the barrier, fumbling for her ticket, she heard her name being called. She turned around and there was Tony, running towards her.

"I'm glad I caught you," he said. "There was a holdup on the Tube, and I was afraid I'd miss you."

"What on earth are you doing here?" Emma stammered out the words.

"Iris insisted I come to see you off. To make sure you get on the right train."

"That was totally unnecessary, Tony," Emma said. "You didn't have to come all this way up to London just to see me get on a train."

She hesitated, waiting for him to say that he wanted to see her again, too, but instead he gave a nervous chuckle. "Don't worry. It gave me an excuse to come up to London for the evening. I hardly ever get the chance these days."

"Well, it's very kind of you, and I'm glad you're here," she said.

"Let me take your bag and we'll find your berth," Tony said, picking up her suitcase. "Are you packed properly for plenty of wind and rain?"

"I hope so," she said. "I bought a big waterproof jacket."

"Iris was all for sending one of her fur coats with me so you weren't cold," he said. "But I said I couldn't picture you going around Scotland in mink."

"Too right," Emma laughed. "I'd look ridiculous."

"I'm sure you'd look very elegant," Tony replied, "but you'd hardly blend in with the natives."

They walked along the platform until they came to the correct carriage.

"This is it." Tony hefted her suitcase up the steps. "Goodbye then. I hope you have a lovely time. A great adventure. And come back with brilliant ideas for the book."

"I hope so," she said.

"And whisky," he added, making her laugh. "Ring me if you need anything, all right?"

"I will. Thank you again."

"Safe trip." He leaned forward, went to shake her hand but then gave her an awkward little kiss on the cheek. She hurried up the steps, not wanting him to see how flustered this made her. A steward was waiting to escort her to her berth. It wasn't exactly glamorous—a narrow bunk-style bed with clean white sheets and a washbasin—but it was private. The steward took a look at her suitcase and what she was wearing and immediately judged her to be someone's young relative, not good for a big tip. Nevertheless he spoke kindly to her, showed her the toilets at the end of the corridor and informed her that he'd deliver coffee or tea to her as they reached Glasgow.

With the door closed she half undressed and settled down for the night. As the train pulled out of the station she lay on her bunk and put her hand up to her cheek where he had kissed it. It had been a friendly gesture, nothing more, she told herself. He had come to London because Iris had ordered him to. He was a nice, decent bloke who was doing his job, and she was being stupid to hope for anything more. She didn't exactly sleep well, with the rocking of the train and the bumping every time they went over points. There were several stops: Birmingham.

Manchester. Carlisle. She woke and peered out at each of them, seeing platforms eerily deserted. Then at first light the steward appeared with the tray of tea and biscuits. Emma washed, dressed in her good pantsuit and watched out the window as the train pulled into Glasgow Central Station. First impressions, exiting into morning rush hour beneath a grey sky heavy with the promise of rain, were not favourable. It came across as a dirty, smoky city of colourless, tired-looking people. No wonder Melrose was enchanted when he saw Skye.

She checked into the impressive Central Hotel, glad she had changed into the pantsuit and was not wearing her mack as she saw herself scrutinized. Her room was spacious, with old-fashioned furniture. The window looked out on other buildings at the side of the hotel. She tidied her hair, then she went down to the restaurant for a good breakfast before setting out to explore. She passed museums and civic buildings that had an air of faded grandeur, then came to the less impressive part of the city. Row after row of drab little houses with no front gardens, one backing onto the other, made her shudder. She pictured Melrose growing up there, playing football in the street with the other shabby boys. And yet the way Iris wrote of him, he always seemed to have an air of culture and education about him, as if he had somehow transcended his environment.

"All right, Melrose," she said. "Iris said you always spoke to her. Now you have to tell me what exactly happened on the Isle of Skye." She felt ridiculous as she said it and walked on with an embarrassed grin.

As Emma explored, the weather turned to misty rain and a chill wind. This was the final straw. She would spend one night in Glasgow and take the train and ferry to the island first thing in the morning. Dinner at the hotel was as depressing as the city had been: a grey slice of beef with cabbage boiled to a pale grey slush. It was followed by a hefty currant pudding and custard.

As she lay in bed, listening to the sounds of the city, the clank of trams on their tracks, the whistle of a policeman at a crossing, drunken shouts and singing from a pub that had been turned out at eleven, she found herself wondering what she was doing here. What could possibly be achieved by going to Skye, seeing Melrose's sights for herself? Iris had described all of them well enough. All Emma had to do was decide who killed Chisholm, sabotaged the sailing boat and wanted Lucy and Stewart dead. There was only one person that pointed to and that was Flora, the Wild Girl. But that would be a pretty lame ending. Flora would be chased, leap off a cliff to her death, and Melrose would go back to Glasgow, with or without the governess. Book finished. But surely Iris wouldn't be satisfied with that. Neither would Emma.

# Chapter 31

Emma awoke early to the street noises beneath her window. In hazy morning sunshine the city looked more attractive, and she went down to breakfast in a good mood, to find out that porridge in Scotland was eaten with salt, not sugar, and then she saw something called black pudding on her breakfast plate. She finished it all with relish, checked out of the hotel and made her way to the train station where trains headed north into the Highlands. As the train pulled out of Queen Street Station and the rows of drab houses were left behind, the track hugged the River Clyde with all sizes of boats from tugs to great cargo ships, and then civilization melted away to small farms and gentle hills, and finally they were climbing steadily into the Highlands. Hillsides covered with the last of the heather glowed purple. Streams danced down over rocks. On a distant hilltop she spotted a stag with impressive antlers. Emma had only seen a stag in paintings before and could hardly believe it was real. She stared out of the window, holding her breath as the train climbed higher and vistas of mountain after mountain spread on either side.

She had to change trains in the small town of Fort William. As she waited on the platform for the train to Mallaig she was conscious of the air, fresh, crisp and somehow different from anything she had breathed before. At home the country air was always tinged with the scent of eucalyptus from the gum trees. Here it carried a hint of tangy shrubs, juniper maybe? Ben Nevis, the highest peak in Britain, soared over the town, and there were mountain ranges as far as the eye could see. When the train to Mallaig finally came in, Emma was surprised to see it was powered by steam. The other passengers were either climbers, carrying heavy rucksacks with coils of rope, or local fishermen. If the first stage of the journey had been impressive, this part, down from Fort William to the coast, was spectacular. They passed deep blue lakes and flew over a valley on an impossibly high viaduct. Finally the sea appeared before them with the Isle of Skye in the distance. The town of Mallaig was a simple cluster of white-and-black houses, clearly a working fishing town, as the aroma of fish greeted Emma as she climbed down from the train. She headed with fellow passengers towards the small harbour. Fishing boats lined the dock, and at the far end was a bigger ship that she guessed was the ferry. At the ticket booth Emma asked if the ferry went to Portree.

"To Portree? Oh, no, miss," the man behind the counter said, shaking his head in surprise. "There hasn't been a ferry to Portree in my lifetime."

"What about Kyleakin," she asked, wondering if she was pronouncing the word correctly. She had only seen it written. Was it with the emphasis on the first syllable? Was the "a" pronounced like in "apple"?

"Dear me no." He looked concerned now. "There's a shorter ferry route from Kyle, but there's no train from Inverness any more, thanks to Dr Beeching axing all the Scottish train lines. So there's no way to get there from here apart from the road. There's big sea lochs in the way, you see."

"But this ferry does go to Skye?"

He now looked at her as if she might be a bit simple. "Oh aye. To Skye all right. But to Armadale. Directly across from us."

There was no alternative but to buy a ticket and go on board. It seemed important to take the same route that Melrose took, but as the boat left the harbour and started to rise and fall with the gentle swell, Emma wished there was a shorter crossing. Sea mist hung ahead of them, blotting out any view of the island, so she had no idea how far away it was. The boat was swallowed in the mist, and she recalled Melrose's crossing, how he had felt strangely changed and reborn, and a similar feeling came over her. Somewhere in the distance she heard the rhythmic clanging—a fog warning bell floating on a buoy. As the mist finally started to clear, the island came into focus ahead of them, a green and wooded shore and then mountains rising in the distance. The mist still hovered at the shoreline so that the island appeared to be floating, magically, on a cloud. To enhance the magical feeling a creature broke the surface beside the boat, with what sounded like a sigh, and Emma recognized it as a dolphin. Another joined it and they kept pace with the ferry, riding the bow wave. It seemed like an omen. The absurd thought came that when she stepped ashore on Skye nothing would ever be the same. It was so compelling and in a way so frightening that she half resolved to take the same ferry back to Mallaig, to go back to Iris and tell her that she was not going to work on the book.

As was the case for Melrose, Emma could see no signs of habitation until the ferry turned into a small bay. Then she saw a few cottages amongst the trees and a bigger building off to one side. She followed the other passengers, who quickly dispersed once ashore, leaving her standing alone near the dock. There was a small café and shop beside the harbour, so she went inside and asked about buses to Kyleakin.

"Oh, I'm sorry, my dear," the shopkeeper said, giving her a pitying smile. "But the bus has already gone for the day. There's one at ten tomorrow. You'll need to find a bed and breakfast for the night if you've a mind to go there. But don't worry, there's several places with a spare room. Just look for a sign in a window."

Fighting back frustration Emma turned to go. At that moment a man got up from where he had been sitting at the counter.

"You need to go to Kyleakin?" he asked. "I'm heading that way myself. I can give you a ride if you like."

His voice sounded cultured and more English than Scottish. He appeared to be in his twenties, with dark eyes and dark curly hair. Those dark eyes flashed with interest. *Not bad* was Emma's immediate reaction.

"That's very kind of you," she said. *Am I being too trusting here?* she asked herself. She knew girls hitchhiked all the time, but she hadn't tried it. Still he looked like a decent bloke, and they were on an island, after all. Surely everybody knew everybody else.

He gave her a reassuring smile. "Not at all. I welcome the company. It's lonely driving by myself all the time."

She followed him out to a van. "PATTERSON's Fine Malt Whisky" was painted on the side. This reassured her. He was making deliveries for his work.

"I've been dropping off some cases at the ferry," he said. "Hop in. I'll put your bag in the back."

He moved some papers from the passenger seat and Emma climbed up.

"I really appreciate this, Mr . . ."

"Patterson," he said. "Andrew Patterson."

"Oh, so it's your family distillery?"

"It is. I'm just back from uni at St Andrews and learning the ropes of the family business," he said. "Starting at the bottom, I might add. Delivery driver. At least I've moved up from sweeping floors." He laughed then. He had a pleasant laugh. "And what's your name?"

"Emma," she said. "Emma Callander."

"Oh, so a fellow Scot?"

"Originally, I suppose, but I'm from Australia. My family owns a winery there."

"Oh, so we have a connection in booze." He laughed again. "And what are you doing here? Not trying to sell Aussie wines to us whisky drinkers?"

She smiled, shaking her head.

"A bit late for the tourist season, and you're not a climber, or you'd have brought a ton of equipment with you."

"No, I'm researching a book," she said.

"You're a writer then?" He sounded impressed.

"I am. But I'm writing this particular book with another person. The preliminary work has been done, and now I just have to get a feel for the place and check out the locations."

"And you can do that in a couple of days, do you think?"

"No! I'm told I should stay as long as it takes. I've no idea how long that will be. Most of the story has already been written."

"It's a travel book? Historical?"

"No. It's a crime novel."

Andrew gave her an interested grin. "I wouldn't have put you down for a crime writer. You look too sweet and demure. But then all the old biddies in crime novels poison people, don't they? So you can never tell."

She had to remind herself not to make any mention of Iris's name. "My book has a detective inspector," she said. "Quite legit."

"I don't think you'll find much crime on Skye," he said. "I've lived here all my life, and I can remember only one murder. A man came home drunk and beat his wife to death. But no police work needed. He came in and confessed. Said he didn't mean it."

As they talked the road followed the shoreline for some time but then began to climb from the woods and market gardens along the bay to barren hills. These were covered in dying yellow grass and patches of bracken, ferns that were not familiar to Emma. At this time of year it was brown, dead and dying. There were still occasional streaks of purple heather but not a tree in sight.

"You say you've lived here all your life," Emma said. "Don't you find it rather . . . remote? Cut off? There don't seem to be many people."

"That's true," he replied. "But my family has been here for centuries. I did go away to boarding school and then uni, but it was expected that I come back to learn the family business, and I don't really mind that at all. Apart from the lack of eligible young women." He turned to give her a cheeky grin, then had to swerve, negotiating sheep that had wandered close to the road. "So what about you? Are you expected to go home and run the winery?"

"I'm afraid not," she said. "When my father died his cousin came to take it over. My mother and I were turned out. And now she's remarried, so I've no close ties to home really."

"I'm sorry. That's a raw deal." Andrew gave her a sympathetic nod. "I couldn't imagine not being part of my family heritage. There have been Pattersons on Skye since the time of the Vikings. In fact we probably have some Viking heritage. I don't. I'm pure Celt, but my sisters have the strawberry blonde hair and freckles, so some ancestor got friendly with a Viking."

"Like mine," Emma said. "At least I was a strawberry blonde in Australia, where I was in the sunshine. Here it's faded to a dull brown."

"Nothing dull about it," he said, making her cheeks turn pink. "So what do you need to do in Kyleakin? Is that where the book is set?"

"I'm not sure if it's set in a real place," Emma said. "That's one of the things I have to find out while I'm here. Tell me, is there a real Dun Akyn castle?"

"Oh yes, indeed," he said. "We call it Caisteal Maol these days, but that was its original name."

"And people live in it?"

He looked amused. "Not any more," he said. "I'll take you to it when we get there and you can see."

"That's very kind of you, if it's not out of your way."

"Not at all. As long as I complete my deliveries by the end of the day my time is my own. So where do you plan to stay?"

"Is there really a Kings Arms Hotel, or is that fiction?"

"Oh no. That's real enough," he said. "Oldest hotel on the island. I'd say it's a bit run down these days, but you'll be comfortable enough there. I don't know how you plan to get around, but buses are few and far between. You can always hitch. It's safe enough here. That's what a lot of the young visitors do."

"I may try to hire a car and driver," she said.

"Good luck with that," he said. "Not too many hire cars on the island."

"Then I may have to resort to hitching," she said. "I've never done it, but there is a first time for everything, isn't there?"

He gave her a teasing sort of look that made her blush. "There is indeed. So did you leave a heartbroken Aussie bloke behind when you came here?"

"Not me. Footloose and fancy-free, don't they say?"

He grinned. "And I hear that Aussie girls tend to be a bit fast and loose. Is that right?"

"Some may be."

"An Aussie chap told me that the Sydney virgin's club meets in a telephone box." He chuckled.

At this mention of sex Emma glanced at him nervously. It felt as if a line might have been crossed. She gave him a disapproving frown. "Some of us want to wait for the right bloke to come along."

"Don't wait too long. Life's short, you know."

Emma didn't quite know how to answer that, and the way the conversation was going made her uneasy. They were now quite high, going over the shoulder of a mountain, with the strait far below them. At this point the crossing was narrow, the hills of the mainland reaching out almost to touch Skye.

"So why didn't they put the ferry here?" she asked. "Seems more sensible."

"All of this coast has deep sea lochs that go far inland. It's a case of you can't get there from here. There would have to be bridges built and there is no good harbour for a town here. There's one tiny hamlet over there and that's where they used to swim the cattle across."

"Swim the cattle?"

"Yes. Taking them to market on the mainland. It was a big event once a year."

She remembered then that it had been mentioned in the book. A true fact that Iris had got right. "Gosh. I'd like to have seen that."

"Before my time," Andrew said. "Now they go in a lorry on the ferry. Progress is usually boring, isn't it?"

"But safer, I'd imagine."

He nodded. As they drove on she kept an eye out for the castle described in the book. They were far inland when another coastline came into sight. There were more mountains on the far shore, and at the tip of a promontory was a town, with a ferry leaving the port.

"That's Kyle of Lochalsh," Andrew said. "It's a short ferry ride."

"The one I'd rather have taken," Emma agreed. "But I gather the train line has been closed."

"It has. Bit of a bugger," he said. "Now you need a car to get anywhere, and not everyone has a means of transport."

"Actually this is a better idea," Emma said. "Coming to the island the same way my main character did in the book."

"He's not a local then?"

"He's a policeman from Glasgow, sent here to investigate a murder."

"And what do you know about policemen from Glasgow?" He sounded amused.

"Absolutely nothing. I was in the city yesterday and I looked around, but I know nothing about Glasgowites or how they think."

"Glaswegians," he corrected. "That's what they call themselves. And they have attitude. Edinburgh is the snooty, cultured city and Glasgow is its rough and ready neighbour. Is your policeman ready for a good fight?"

"I don't think so," Emma said. "He seems rather a quiet, bookish type to me."

"Then he should have come from Edinburgh," Andrew said. "Can you change it?"

"I can't. My cowriter has created him."

"And what does he or she know about Glasgow?"

"Equally little, I'm afraid."

"Then isn't it a bit of a cheek writing about people you know nothing about?"

"I suppose it is," she agreed. "I've been told to stay up here as long as it takes, but I doubt if I can get a good feel for the people of Skye in a week or two."

"I doubt it, too," he agreed. "They're not very open to strangers here, and you'll still find plenty who speak Gaelic as their first language." He glanced at her. "Of course I can probably find time to educate you on the locals. I usually get my evenings off."

The road was descending into the small settlement on the water. Instead of continuing down Andrew swerved off to the right, taking a tiny lane up behind the town. It came out onto a headland.

"Well here it is," he said, slowing the van to a halt. "Dun Akyn, just like you wanted."

Emma stared in disbelief. Instead of a castle as described in the book this was a veritable ruin.

Only parts of the walls were still standing and the roof was long gone.

"How long has it been like this?" she asked. "Did people ever live here?"

"At the time of the Vikings it was flourishing," he said. "The twelve hundreds. But it's been a ruin for centuries now."

"Oh." Emma fought back disappointment. So Iris had just used a name that appealed to her. Nothing in the book was real. She had created an image of Skye based on a day trip.

# Chapter 32

"Do you want to get out and take a closer look?" Andrew asked.

Emma shook her head. "It's not what I expected at all. I suppose my cowriter just took the name because it sounded exotic." She sighed. "Never mind. If you could drop me in the town, I'll find this Kings Arms Hotel and book myself in. Then I need to figure out what I should do."

"All right." He reversed the van with difficulty in the narrow area, then inched down into the town.

"That's the Kings Arms," he said, indicating a long, low white building on the waterfront. "It will be a good base for you."

He stopped the van outside the hotel, retrieved her suitcase from the back and helped her down.

"Thank you so much," Emma said. "I really appreciate this."

"You can send me a copy of the book when it comes out," Andrew replied. "And I can point out all the things you've got wrong, unless you'd let me take a look now and save you from future mistakes."

Emma shook her head. "I can't do that. My cowriter won't allow it."

"So she calls the shots, does she? Or is it a man?"

"I'm afraid I'm not at liberty to say."

He gave her a questioning stare. "Mysterious! Oh well. Good luck then." He carried her suitcase to the front door. "I have to take a delivery over to the mainland in a couple of days, so I may look you up if you're still here. There's not much to do in Kyleakin, but I expect I can find a way to amuse you." The way he said it made her a little uneasy, although she suspected he might just be acting the part for a foreigner. At least she had a good-looking chap seemingly interested in her, but as he had said, there wasn't much choice on the island.

"Thanks again, Andrew," she said.

He gave her a friendly wave and headed back to the van. She picked up her suitcase and went into the hotel. The reception area was dark with a low ceiling and the smell of woodsmoke from a fire. At one end was an oak counter and at the other a lounge area with chairs around the fireplace. It felt cosy and warm. She rang the bell on the counter and an older woman came out. She had wispy white hair and bright red cheeks, but her eyes were still bright.

"Hello, my dear," she said. "And what can I do for you?"

"I'd like a room, please. If you have one?"

The woman smiled. "At this time of year you can take your pick. Now if you'd been here in August it would have been another matter. We had quite a crowd this year, and we're getting more people from other countries, too. Germans and Americans, if you can believe it." She leaned closer. "An American woman wanted to know why the central heating was not on. I told her it was summer, and she said it didn't feel like it. I didn't have the heart to tell her she won't find central heating anywhere on this island."

Emma chuckled.

"So how long will you be staying, Miss . . ."

"Callander," Emma said. "Emma Callander."

"Oh. Callander." Emma waited for her to say she was a fellow Scot. "We had a Dr Callander staying here last year. He was from Edinburgh."

"No relation," Emma said. "I'm from Australia, although I suppose my ancestors came from Scotland."

"We've had several Australians here, too," the woman went on. "Friendly people. So are you just here for a night or two?"

"I'm not quite sure," Emma said. "Probably at least a week. It depends how long my work keeps me here."

"Oh, so you're here on business?" She leaned closer again.

"I'm doing research for a woman who is writing a book," Emma said. It seemed wiser than saying she was the cowriter.

"A travel guide, would it be?"

"No, it's fiction, but it's set on Skye so she wants to get it right."

"Of course she does. Well, you can tell her how special this island is, can't you?"

"I intend to."

"Now if you'd just register in the book here, I'll show you your room. Since we're nearly empty I'll give you the corner room at the end. Lovely views across the water. And far enough away from the bar if it should become rowdy."

She led Emma along a hallway and opened a door at the far end. The first thing she noticed was the view, across the strait to the mountains on the mainland.

"I'll leave you to have a wash and brush up then," the proprietress said. "And there will be a cup of tea ready for you in a wee while. Bathroom's just two doors down from you."

Emma put her suitcase on the bed and unpacked. The room had a cosy, homey feeling to it, with a big, old-fashioned oak wardrobe and matching chest of drawers, a small chintz-covered armchair with plenty of cushions and a handmade quilt on the bed. There was indeed no central heating but a gas fire on one wall. Emma was relieved to see it didn't require shillings in a meter. It reminded her of the way her home had looked during her grandparents' time, when the winery still belonged to them. They had both died when she was quite small, and her fashionable mother had thrown out their furniture, redecorated and changed everything. Emma hadn't thought about them for ages. She was too young to have anything except hazy memories—sitting on Nana's knee and being read to, or on Grandpa's knee and riding horsy. They had both been older parents, her father an only child of later life. He in turn had not married until his thirties.

Now she found herself wishing she knew more. Had they come out from Scotland as young people or been born in Australia? She tried to call up their voices. Had they had a Scottish accent? Or had the accent been lost through years of living in Australia? Her father hadn't spoken much about them or about her heritage. There was no point in asking her mother. She was staunchly and proudly English. And yet it gave Emma a warm feeling to know that she was part of this lovely countryside. It was in her bloodline.

After a quick trip to the bathroom she went to the reception area and found a tea tray with a toasted teacake. She ate with relish and thanked the woman when she came to collect the tray.

"At what time do you want your evening meal, Miss Callander?" she asked.

"Whenever is convenient."

"Then shall we say at seven? And if you've a mind for it, my Ruari caught a marvelous salmon yesterday. Our local salmon is the finest in the world, so they say. Would you like to try it?"

"Oh, yes please," Emma said. "What did you say your husband's name was?"

"Ruari." She spelled it out. "It's a local Gaelic name."

"That's interesting because my father was Rory. I suppose it's the same name with anglicized spelling."

"No doubt it would be."

"And what is your name, ma'am?"

"I'm Mrs Bruce. Born a MacDonald. My parents ran this place before me." She looked up with the hint of a smile on her lips. "I married an outsider, you know. From over on the mainland. I've never heard the last of it."

Emma shared her smile. "So tell me, Mrs Bruce," she said. "If I wanted to hire a car and driver to show me around the island, how would I go about it?"

"Why, that would be Young Jock," Mrs Bruce said. "He'll not be too busy at this time of year."

"Young Jock?" Emma's jaw dropped. "How old would he be now?"

The woman looked surprised. "Why, about your age, I'd think. His father owned the taxi service before him, and his grandfather had the first motor car on the island. Both of them named Jock, too. This Jock's father had been Young Jock before him. Now the grandson is Young Jock and his father is Old Jock."

So that much of Iris's story had been true, Emma thought. Had Old Jock been the one to drive her around the island? She felt an excitement that there was at least one tie.

"And how would I contact Young Jock?"

"I'll have him come round to meet you in the morning. He'll be available, I'm sure, unless . . ."

"Unless he has to drive someone to the hospital," Emma finished for her. The woman looked up, surprised. "Now that was just what I was about to say. And it's true. The only ambulance on the island is up at Portree, so Jock does a lot of that sort of thing."

Mrs Bruce picked up the tray. "I'd better get on with my work or there will be no supper for any of us tonight. Until later then, Miss Callander."

Emma watched her go, feeling strangely warm and cared for, almost as if she had come home. Since it was still light she decided to walk into the little village to see if she could buy postcards. She had, after all, promised to write a report to Iris every day. As she walked along the waterfront the sun was setting beyond the mountains, etching them sharply in silhouette and painting the water of the strait with a deep, rich glow. Above to her right the castle ruins stood out, also glowing blood red in the setting sun. Emma stood, wrapped in an emotion she couldn't describe. A place so different, so magical, and yet it somehow felt right that she should be there. This was how Inspector Melrose had felt, standing in the same place. Maybe he'd start talking to her now and she'd be able to write again.

She found a village shop, about to close, and managed to persuade the owner to let her select some postcards. There was also a post office counter at the back where she purchased stamps to go with them. As she walked back she caught the appetizing smell of fish frying, and from above music floated down from a radio—the Beatles singing "Yesterday." Again it seemed to fit the mood. *Yesterday I was far away,* she thought to herself. And who knew what tomorrow would bring. The sun sank behind the mountains and the world was plunged into sudden darkness. Lights twinkled into the harbour and from across on the mainland the ferry emerged, its lights shining on the water. Emma watched until it came into port and disgorged its passengers and cars. After a few minutes all had dispersed and the world fell silent. She went back to the hotel, sat in the lounge and wrote her first postcard.

> *Dear Miss Blackburn,*
> (She was still not comfortable with calling her Iris.)
> *I have arrived on Skye, just as Melrose described it. I'm staying at the Kings Arms Hotel (which does exist), and I've seen Dun Akyn castle which alas is a ruin. Tomorrow I'll be driven around by Young Jock—I think Melrose met his father, who was Young Jock then! More tomorrow.*
> *Emma*

The salmon was as good as promised, served with parsley sauce, potatoes and peas. After dinner she lay on her bed reading one of the Melrose novels. It was dark and gritty, and Emma found it hard going. The established Melrose was so different from the sensitive young man in the current novel. She put it away and turned off the light.

Emma slept well and enjoyed a hearty breakfast. *I'd better do a lot of walking while I'm here or I'll get as fat as a pig,* she thought. The view outside her window showed a bright and hopeful sky, and she hesitated to wear her new waterproof. Still she knew from what she had read that weather can change quickly in these parts and took it with her to the lounge to await Young Jock. He arrived at ten, a skinny young man with dark hair and serious eyes, exactly as Iris had described his father.

"Would you be Miss Callander?" he asked in a soft local brogue.

"I am indeed." Emma stood up and shook his hand. "And you are most definitely Young Jock." She was about to say that he looked just like his father had at the same age but stopped herself. That would make things too complicated.

"Aye. That's me. Now what would you be wanting? Mistress Bruce said you're writing some sort of book?"

"That's right. I'm actually helping a writer with her book, and she needs to get all the scenery correct."

"Aye. Well we can certainly do that if you tell me where you need to go."

"I thought I should first do a tour of the island so I get a feel for the place and know where everything is situated," Emma said.

"Good idea." He gave an encouraging nod. "Should I take you on the usual tourist loop that I do?"

"Why not?" Emma said. "I'm sure that's what my cowriter would have done when she visited."

"It will be quite a long day," Jock cautioned. "Skye is not exactly small and the roads are nae the best, to say nothing of negotiating sheep and cattle everywhere we go."

"It will be an adventure." Emma smiled. "And it's a lovely day, so let's make the most of it."

"So far," he said. "Ye ne'er can tell here. The weather is a tricky thing. Hope for the best, prepare for the worst here, that's what we say."

"Then I'll bring my mack just in case."

"Right then. Let's get going, shall we?" He went to stand up but she held up a hand.

"So we should probably settle how you'd like to be paid before we start. If I hire you for the day, how much would you charge?"

He quoted what Emma thought was a reasonable amount, given the price of petrol, and she nodded. "That sounds fair."

The taxi was a solid-looking blue Hillman Husky and they set off, driving out of Kyleakin and heading north along the coast. Jock drove carefully and confidently. He told her he'd been recently married and was glad of the extra work now as they were hoping to start a family.

"You're not married yourself then yet? Making the most of being fancy-free?"

"I just haven't met the right chap, I suppose," she said and explained her life in Australia. He showed immediate interest. "My wife is talking about emigrating," he said. "Lots of opportunity there, is it? A good life?"

"Yes, I think so," Emma agreed. "Sunshine and plentiful food and they really want new immigrants."

"There's other young folk I know thinking the same thing," Jock said. "Not much opportunity on the island and the shipbuilding is almost dead in Glasgow. I don't fancy London or Manchester. But a new country with plenty of room—that sounds quite appealing. So tell me, are there really kangaroos hopping around everywhere?"

"Not in the city," Emma laughed, "but out where I grew up we had wallabies on the lawn every evening. And kookaburras and maggies—I mean magpies. Lots of interesting birds. And quite a few bad things too: poisonous snakes and redback spiders. I almost got bitten by a funnel-web spider when I was a toddler. It was hiding inside my rain boot. They can kill you."

"Don't tell my missus that." He laughed, too. "She hates spiders, even the harmless ones."

"I should warn you there are also huntsmen then," she said. "Hairy spiders as big as your hand. They're fairly harmless but they look frightening."

"Then we're definitely not going." He shook his head. "If Alice saw one of them she'd be off back to Scotland in an instant."

As they had talked the road had veered inland, passing through what looked like cultivated fields, although whatever had been growing in them—some kind of grain—had now been harvested. They rejoined the coast, moved through several small settlements, then veered inland again, over a series of treeless hills, just as Emma had seen on her trip from the ferry. To their left a series of impressive mountains rose.

"Those would be the Red Cuillin," Jock said. "Not quite as challenging for the climbers as the big stuff on the other side. We've some really top-class mountains over there on the west. I spend much of my summers driving people who have fallen and injured themselves to the hospital. Of course I don't transport the bodies of the ones who don't make it." He smiled cheerfully.

"Are you a climber yourself?" she asked.

He laughed. "I don't have a head for heights. I get dizzy standing on a ladder hanging a picture."

At last the road joined a rocky shoreline, with more islands dotting the sea ahead of them. It hugged the coast, going in and out of narrow inlets, then climbing up into the wild again until they came into what looked like a bigger village.

"This is Portree," Jock said. "Capital of the island. Not exactly a metropolis, is it? And nothing happens here." Emma could have guessed that from Melrose's description. It was a pretty little place with a row of pastel-painted houses nestled below a wooded cliff and a harbour with several fishing boats tied up.

"We'll not stop here now," Jock said. "Not if we want to do the circuit of the north. That's what most of the tourists want to see, unless they are climbers." And off they went again. The countryside ahead was spectacular, with green hills on one side and a blue sea on the other. Waterfalls cascaded down hillsides, and the road passed over rushing streams on old stone humpbacked bridges. Everything felt so fresh and different that Emma sat forward in her seat, trying to take in every aspect of the view. They pulled off at a viewpoint to see a waterfall plunging from cliffs onto the rocks of the seashore and Emma took photographs. Then on again until Jock pointed out a strange rock formation rising like a jagged pillar beside steep, rocky crags.

"That's the Old Man of Storr," Jock said proudly. "On another day we can come back and you can climb up to it. There's a magnificent view, but we don't have time today." They pulled into the car park and Emma went up the trail far enough to photograph the rock.

"How do you like it so far?" Jock asked.

"It's all so wild," Emma said. "So remote feeling, so untouched. And so green. There's nothing like it in Australia."

Jock looked pleased, as if he'd handed her a present. "Are you feeling hungry yet?" he asked.

"I am, actually." Emma looked at her watch and was surprised to see it was already one o'clock.

"There's a wee café as we head over to the west side of the peninsula," he said. "I hope it's stayed open at this time of the year. If not, we'll have to go back to Portree." He paused, frowning. "We should have asked Mistress Bruce for sandwiches."

"Oh, it's fine, Jock," she said. "I'm enjoying every moment."

The café was open, and they both had ham sandwiches and coffee. As they were eating, Emma asked, "So tell me, are there really any castles that are still lived in on the island?"

"Oh aye." He nodded. "I was planning to show you Dunvegan. It's a verra grand place. Seat of the MacLeods, you know. We're not far from it."

Again Emma sat alert in her seat as they drove through a wooded area. The trees were mainly deciduous, oaks and birch with leaves already turning yellow and brown. The track was covered in a carpet of leaves, and there were puddles of water from recent rains. Then they turned into a car park.

"Are you wanting to take a tour of the house?" he asked.

"Oh, I think we should," Emma said. "Are they open at this time of year?"

"Aye, until the end of the month, I believe."

As they approached through the woods Emma got her first glimpse of the castle. It looked like something from a fairy tale, and she half expected to see knights in armour riding out.

"Oh, it's wonderful," she said. "This must have been what inspired Ir—my fellow writer."

The castle stood on a rock with the deep blue waters of a loch below it. Beside it was a tree-covered promontory with a couple of small grey stone houses on the shoreline, but no real village or harbour. They ascended to the castle, paid for tickets and entered a grand entrance hall lined with family portraits. There was a dining room with a table big enough to seat thirty, many more opulent rooms, each with more portraits on the walls going back over the generations. *Imagine living in the same house for a thousand years,* she thought. She couldn't wait to tell Iris she had seen it.

They came out and stood on the shore, looking down the loch towards the Atlantic beyond. The castle matched the description in the book, she thought, but not the location.

"Are we still at the far north of the island?" she asked.

"Northwest," he said.

"So if someone wanted to cross to the mainland from here?"

"You'd have a pretty long boat ride," he said, smiling. "You'd be wiser to drive down to the south and cross from Armadale."

"Yes," she said. "You would." No small sailing boat would have attempted to negotiate the open water of the Atlantic from here. And the location was not as Iris described it. The hills around the castle were tree covered. There was no harbour. And it seemed much grander than the fictitious castle.

"Jock." She turned to him. "Is this the only inhabited castle on the island? Is there one that juts out into the water on a promontory? Like an old fortress."

"There's Eilean Donan," he said. "That's the famous one. But it's back on the mainland. The closest thing we have here is Craigard. We could go and see it although they don't do tours. The family lives in it."

"Is it closer to the mainland?"

"Aye, it is," he said. "Right across from the mainland. But as I said, it's nae anywhere as imposing as this one."

"Could we see it on the way back?"

"Of course," he said. "It's a little out of the way but no matter. Let's get going then." He gazed out to sea. "I'm thinking the weather will be coming in soon, and this road is not one you want to tackle in a mist or a storm."

They drove off again, through mile after mile of barren hills with just a few sheep dotted on them. Not a cottage in sight. As they went south the mountain range rose ahead of them, rocky crags jutting from the smooth grass of the slopes. Clouds raced in, covering some of the summits.

"It won't be long before the rain now," Jock said. "I'd wanted to show you the Fairy Pools but that can wait for another day. They're a way off the road, and there's walking to do, so not in the rain."

"Fairy Pools?" Emma was interested. "Why are they called that?"

"Aye. They say the selkies come and bathe there, and the kelpies. The shape-shifters."

Emma tried not to smile. "Shape-shifters? An old legend?"

"Call it what you want, but most folks here take it seriously. The seals that change themselves into women and the kelpies—the sea sprites who can change themselves into anything—men or horses. Ask any family here and they've seen one."

"What about you, do you believe it?"

"I see no reason not to, if my grandfather, who was the wisest of men, swore he saw a horse run into the water and then swim away as a seal."

Emma stayed silent.

"But today is not a good day to visit. You'll likely be in the mist by the time we get there, and pretty wet, too."

He continued driving south. They finished the loop and retraced the way they had come until they arrived back in Kyleakin.

"Do you want to stop at your hotel first?"

"I'd rather get on and see this castle before it rains," Emma said.

"Right you are." He swung the car to the right, up the hill. The first drops of rain spattered onto the windscreen. The road was nothing more than a narrow lane, wide enough for one car. This didn't seem to matter as they had not passed another car for hours. Before them was no sign of habitation, just hillsides and rock and then forest closer to the coast.

"So that will be Craigard down there," Jock said.

"Is there a village as well?" she asked. "I don't see houses."

"Not really a village. A few cottages along the shore. Fishermen's houses, you know. You'll see them when we come around the next bend." He slowed as they came around a rocky outcrop, and there below them was the inlet with a string of white cottages, the small harbour at one end.

"And that would be the castle," Jock said as the road swung around the next bend.

Emma leaned forward, staring. "Yes," she said, hardly daring to breathe out the word. "This is the castle."

# Chapter 33

It was just as Iris had described: a tall tower of grey stone rising up from the rocky headland. The stone was weathered and almost looked like an extension of the rock itself. At first it seemed a solid wall until Emma noticed small slits of window sunk into it. A real fortress, a place to be defended, almost a fairy-tale castle. Surrounding it was an outer wall and at the back of the little peninsula was the woodland, Scots pine trees mixed in with birch, their leaves now turning gold.

Emma held her breath as the narrow lane eventually came down to the shoreline and the castle rose up ahead of them, looking even more forbidding than it had from first glimpse.

"So people still live in it?" she asked.

"Och aye. Same family for several hundred years. I'm not sure how old but definitely back to medieval times. They would have been defending against Vikings and Danes and then the English."

"But it's not open to the public at all?"

"I'm afraid not. The family keep themselves quite private, although you can tour the distillery."

"Distillery?"

"Aye. They are well known for their whisky. See the building up at the other side of the bay? That's it. Would you like to go and see?"

"I'd like to take some photos here first," Emma said. "Could you pull over?"

"Of course."

Emma got out, trying to shield the lens from the raindrops that were now falling faster. She took photos of the castle, the harbour and then the cottages along the seafront. She couldn't wait to show them to Iris. Surely Iris must have come here once. The description was too accurate to be made up. And she could see why Iris had chosen it as her setting. It was perfect for a murder mystery.

When she got back into the car she asked, "Tell me, Jock, did your father ever mention driving a famous writer around the island and bringing her here?"

"I don't think so," Jock said. "When would that have been?"

"I believe it was the nineteen thirties."

"He never mentioned it to me. He did drive several famous people: a film star—I can't remember which one, though—and some football players who played for Celtic. Oh, and a member of Parliament on a fact-finding mission. But he never mentioned a writer."

"Perhaps she wasn't so famous in those days," Emma said.

"So this writer of yours, she's quite well known?"

Emma hesitated. "In writing circles," she said cautiously.

"And she wrote about this place? About Craigard?"

"I think she must have, although she called it by a different name. She called it Dun Akyn."

"Must have got it mixed up then," Jock said. "Dun Akyn is the old name for Caisteal Maol. It's just a ruin."

"I know," she said. "I was shown it yesterday."

"So would you like to visit the distillery now?" Jock asked. "I think we'd have to hurry. They close earlier at this time of year."

"It's owned by the family who live in the castle?" Emma asked. It occurred to her that she might charm her way into a tour of the castle.

"Aye. The Pattersons."

"Patterson? I got a ride with Andrew Patterson yesterday. He was very nice."

"Aye, well he would be to a pretty girl. We've heard about Andrew's high jinks. He's got an eye for the ladies, so they say. A bit of a wild lad when he was off at university. His father brought him home where he can keep an eye on him, and is making him work to sober him up."

"He told me he was having to learn the business from the bottom up."

"Well, that's only right. He's the only son, so he'll need to take over one day."

Jock eased the car forward and they drove along the seafront with the cottages on one side and a wall above a rocky coast.

"Are there still fishing boats here?" she asked. The small harbour was empty.

"A couple, I believe, although these days it doesn't really pay any more. Other countries have big factory fleets, don't they? They come and sweep the ocean clean so there's no fish for the small boats. Although the lobster fishermen still make a good living, and there's still the herring fleet and the kippering sheds over at Mallaig."

Emma's brain was working feverishly. If the castle was real, and the setting was real, was it possible that any of the story was true, or had Iris merely used the backdrop for a Melrose plot?

"So tell me, Jock," she said. "This story I'm working on. It involves tragedy with the family who lived in the castle. The writer calls them the Hamiltons. But do you know of any real tragedy that happened here? The daughter of the family was drowned? She was trying to elope with an outsider?"

Jock slowed the car, frowning. "I've a mind I did hear something like that once. Although drowning is not an unusual thing here. We've all known someone who was taken by the sea. It's part of our history."

"How would I find out, do you think?" Emma asked. "Is there an island historian or something?"

"I suppose the older generation would remember," he said. "And it would have been reported in the island newspaper, would it not? How long ago was this?"

"In the nineteen thirties."

"Then I can ask my father. He was driving the taxi in those days. He'd know."

"Great. Would you do that?"

He nodded. "I could take you to visit him and you could ask him yourself, if you like."

"That would be wonderful, if you could arrange it," she said. "What does your father do these days, if he doesn't drive the taxi any longer?"

"He was injured in the war, you know. In the Royal Navy, on a boat that was torpedoed. So now he's got a bad back and doesn't like to sit behind a wheel all day. But he's also not the type to accept disability and stay home. He runs a snack bar in Portree. Does well in the summer months. Really good sausage rolls and meat pies."

"I haven't had a decent meat pie since I left Australia," Emma said. "Could we visit him tomorrow, do you think?"

Jock grinned. "You're paying for my time. Wherever you want to go. Do you still want to visit the distillery?"

Emma debated. If there had been a real family tragedy she should probably find out that first, before she put her foot in it. "Let's leave that for later."

"Right. Then I think we've done enough for one day, don't you?"

"I do," she said, "but I'm really anxious to know if your father remembers a tragic drowning of the laird's daughter."

He reversed the car and started up the hill. Emma looked back at the castle. Who would want to live in such a place? she wondered. Those tiny slits of windows couldn't let in much light. And that grim tower on the rocky headland reminded her of a prison from a fairy tale—a place where a beautiful princess was locked away. Surely it must affect the family that lived in it? Although Andrew had seemed easy-going and friendly enough—even if he was a bit of a lad, according to Jock. *Not that he'd tried anything . . . Not that I'd want to . . . ,* she thought.

She switched subjects in her brain. There was the wood behind the castle, now presumably even denser with trees than it was in the days of the story. Had a Mr Chisholm really been buried there? If it was all true, then the end of the story would have been written for her. She couldn't wait to find out more.

Back at the hotel she enjoyed a welcome cup of tea and a scone with homemade jam before writing the next postcard to Iris. She wanted to make sure it went with today's post collection. It felt important to tell Iris that she had located the real castle. As she picked up the pen to write she found herself wondering: Why had Iris chosen this setting for Melrose's first case and such a different sort of crime? Had a brief tour of the island made such an impression that she wanted to write about it, to recreate that tour, after all these years? She couldn't wait to ask.

On the postcard she wrote: *Today I found your castle. Just like you described it. Tomorrow I'm going to try to find out if your story is based on any real crime. Skye is amazing. So beautiful. So wild.*

As she wrote the word "wild" she remembered the Wild Girl. And Jock talking about kelpies and selkies as if he believed in them. Was there a Wild Girl once, whose father might not have been a human? It was too ridiculous to consider. She signed the postcard and carried it down to the postbox outside the village shop. In the fading daylight she watched the ferry heading back to the mainland. Had there really once been a beautiful young governess who had touched Melrose's heart? Would Melrose ever speak to her the way he apparently spoke to Iris? Then she reminded herself: Melrose only existed on the pages of books. He was fiction.

# Chapter 34

Jock turned up just as she was finishing her breakfast, mopping up the egg yolk with the last of the toast. It was amazing how the bracing air gave her an appetite. At home it was toast and Vegemite if anything more than a cup of tea or coffee.

"Did you speak to your father about whether he might have driven the writer around?" she asked excitedly.

"I'm sorry. I did nae have the time. We had my wife's parents over last night, so I was fully occupied and on my best behaviour." He glanced up shyly. "They don't fully approve of me. They wanted something more than a taxi driver for their daughter."

"That's silly. You like what you do and you make a good living, don't you?"

He shrugged. "It's a bit sparse in the winter," he said. "And I married a girl with big ideas. Oh well. Not your problem. Almost ready to go then?"

"Are we going to see your father?"

"If that's what you want. He's up in Portree."

"Oh, so we've got another long drive ahead of us?"

"But a beautiful one. It's a lovely clear day so far. You've been lucky with the weather. At this time of year we can have a week of rain or mist."

They set out on the same route they had driven the day before, sometimes driving along the edge of the water, sometimes cutting inland as the road climbed over another hill. Yesterday Emma had enjoyed gazing at the scenery. Today it seemed to take twice as long, and she fought back impatience. She couldn't wait to find out if the story was in any way true. As they finally approached the little town of Portree it sparkled in the bright slanted sunlight, looking most appealing today. A fishing boat was returning to port, followed by a flock of seagulls, their harsh cries echoing in the crisp air.

"Not much going on at this time of year," Jock said, "but if you'd come in the summer holidays you'd have found it bustling. That's when my dad and I both make our money. Although if you'd come in the summer you'd have had the midges."

"The what?" Emma wondered if these were more fantastical creatures like kelpies.

"Midges. You don't know what they are? Like little mosquitos, and they bite something terrible. We're plagued with them all summer here on Skye."

"Then I'm glad I timed it perfectly." She smiled at him.

He left the taxi in the car park and they walked along the waterfront to a row of shops. Next to a souvenir shop, a wool shop and a fish-and-chips shop was a sign that said "Bide a Wee." In the window was a smaller sign that said "Coffee, Tea, Hot Snacks and Ice Creams." A bell jangled as Jock pushed open the door. The place smelled of roasted coffee and was empty apart from an elderly couple sitting in the window. A man appeared from the back.

"Hello, boy," the man said, smiling. Emma could tell immediately that this was Jock's dad. "Brought me a customer, have you?"

"I have, Dad. She's Australian and she's pining for meat pie."

"Aussie, eh?" The man gave her a friendly grin. "If you wait a few minutes I'll have a pie warm for you."

"I haven't quite got over breakfast yet," Emma said, "but I'd like a coffee now please and maybe a pie later. And what about you, Jock?"

Jock also asked for a coffee. "So two coffees, please."

When he delivered the coffee Jock's father joined them. "Not much business at this time of year," he said pulling up a chair to their table. "I'm thinking of closing for the winter, but then what would I do at home? Sit around and annoy the wife all day."

"You could do one of those Caribbean cruises you were reading about," Jock said.

His dad gave him a playful slap. "Get out of here with your nonsense. What would I be wanting with a Caribbean cruise? I've got boats right here if I want to go out on the ocean."

"But not many palm trees," Emma said, and Old Jock laughed.

"She's got a ready wit about her," he said.

"She's a writer, Dad," Jock said. "At least she's helping a writer with her book that's set here on Skye."

"Oh yes?" Old Jock eyed her with interest.

"I'm wondering if you might have driven her around, years ago," Emma said. "She's an Aussie like me, and I think she came here in the nineteen thirties."

"The thirties." Old Jock paused, thinking. "That might have been my dad. I only took over in thirty-six. Before then I was working on one of the boats. I've driven some Aussies around in my time, but I don't remember a lady writer. What sort of book is it?"

"It's a mystery, but now that I'm here I'm wondering if it could have been based on a true event back in the thirties. Maybe something to do with the family at Craigard? Their daughter was in a boat that capsized and she drowned? Someone tampered with the sail?"

Old Jock was frowning now. "Now you mention it that does sound familiar," he said. "But it certainly wasn't in the thirties. It was something I heard my dad talk about, from his youth, in the early nineteen hundreds."

"The beginning of the century?" Emma considered this, not sure what to say next. "So do you reckon I could speak to your father and see what he remembers? He might also remember the lady writer."

Old Jock shook his head. "I'm sorry, lass, but he's not with us any longer. He passed away last winter. Been fit as a fiddle all his life, then he got pneumonia and he was gone in a couple of days. You'd have enjoyed meeting him. A right character, wasn't he, Jock?"

"He was," Young Jock agreed. "And he had so many good stories. He'd probably have been able to tell you more about this one."

Emma gave a small sigh. "So if I wanted to find out more, but I'd rather not ask the family in question, how would I go about it? Do you know other old people on the island who would remember that far back?"

"Oh aye. There would be plenty," Jock's father said. "Who might know, lad?"

"She could try the newspaper first," Young Jock answered. "They'd have written about it, wouldn't they? Especially a laird's daughter."

"You're right. They would."

"So there was a newspaper going in those days at the turn of the century?"

"Aye. There was. It's been going since the time of Queen Victoria. Maybe even before. We're quite proud of it on the island. It's been struggling recently, so who knows how long it will continue."

"And it's here in Portree," Young Jock added. "I can take you there now."

"All right." Emma stood up. "Lovely meeting you, Mr . . ." She realized she didn't know his last name.

"Jock will do just fine," the man said. "That's how we're known here."

The newspaper was housed in a small white-painted shop a couple of streets back from the water, nestled between a hardware shop and an estate agent. Young Jock walked her there while his father handled an arrival of customers at the café. Emma glanced at the estate board to read *Fine gentleman's residence for sale* as she passed. *What would it be like to live here?* she wondered.

In the entry of the shop, a stack of this week's papers sat on the front counter, and advertisements on the walls announced a dance at the church hall this Saturday and a sale of cattle. A young woman appeared from the back room, brushing off her skirt.

"Hello, Jock," she said, smiling at him. "Can I help you? Do you want to increase the size of your advert in the paper? We're looking for extra advertising at the moment."

"No, not that. It will do just fine as it is," Young Jock said. "I've brought this young lady to go through the archives, if you don't mind. She's writing a book about the island, and she thinks there might be a true story behind the one in her book."

"Och aye?" The young woman gave Emma an encouraging smile. "If you'd like to come with me, I'll take you back."

"I don't know how long I'll be, Jock," she said. "If you'd like to wait at your father's place, I'll come and find you."

"Oh, I've got some shopping to do," Jock said. "I'm putting up shelves in the kitchen, so I'll be at the hardware shop."

Emma followed the young woman into a cluttered room with type being set and pages being laid out. Having worked for a publisher this looked familiar if rather primitive. Two men, one old and one younger, were busy at work. They looked up as Emma went past.

"She's come to see the archives," the young woman said.

"What year, my dear?" the older man asked.

"Early years of this century," Emma said. "You might be able to help me. It was a tragic drowning that might have been murder. A laird's daughter, possibly the Pattersons?"

"I'm pretty sure I recall reading something like that." The man got up from his seat. His fingers were ink stained. "Not sure of the year though. We could start with nineteen hundred and work our way through. Nellie will take you, won't you, my dear?"

"Yes, Dad," the girl said.

So it was all in the family, Emma thought. That was how it seemed to go on the island. The back room smelled musty and damp and was quite dark, even with the lone electric bulb hanging from the ceiling. Not the most appealing place.

"We'll get the volumes you need and take them somewhere brighter," the girl said. "You'll nae be able to read the small print in a hellhole like this."

She climbed a step stool and pulled down a large volume of bound newspapers, handing it to Emma. "This is nineteen hundred. Start with that and I'll get the subsequent ones down for you."

Emma went through to the main room and found an empty desk in the corner. She sat, almost trembling with anticipation as she opened the book. The articles were in small type, crammed onto two sheets with half a page of advertisements at the back. *Wanted: stud bull for my new cows.* Emma smiled and forced herself not to go on reading. She skimmed headlines. *Turn of the Century. Our Hopes. Our Dreams. When Will the First Motor Car Come to Our Island? First We'll Need Some Decent Roads.*

As the year went on: *Sir Harry Patterson Speaks for Skye in the English Parliament. Requests Investment in Scottish Products. A Summer Festival. Record Herring Catch. New Way to Send Lobsters South—What the Railway Means to Mallaig.*

As Emma read on she got a real feeling for the life of the island, and the close-knit nature of its community. She also became aware of the fragile nature of life on the island. *Diphtheria Claims Life of Crofter's Children. Terrible Accident as Cart Is Swept Off Bridge in Downpour. Fisherman Falls Overboard.* She moved on to 1901. The big news in January was Queen Victoria's death and then her son becoming Edward VII. Articles followed on the queen's fondness for Scotland, her visits to the Highlands. There was little local news of interest, apart from an outbreak of foot-and-mouth disease that was killing sheep and cattle.

By the time she got to 1902 she was inclined to skim. *New Ship Built on Clydeside Puts Scotland on the Map. New King's Coronation.* The articles were a revelation of a long distant time, but she reminded herself that her father had been born not long after these events. If her grandparents were indeed Scottish immigrants, they must have come to Australia at least twenty years before this. These were their stories. She read on, realizing that this was taking a long time. At least Jock could go to his father's snack bar when he'd finished shopping and could have a coffee whenever he wanted. This thought had just passed her mind when young Nellie came in bringing a cup of tea.

"I thought you might be fair parched by this time," she said. "I hope you find what you're looking for. If you don't have time to find it today, you can always come back tomorrow. You're not planning to leave the island soon, are you?"

"No. I can stay as long as it takes," Emma said. "It's all so fascinating that it's hard not to read all the stories."

The girl shrugged. "I think most of what happens here on Skye is fair boring," she said. "Nothing exciting ever happens if you ask me. I can't wait to get to the city, but my dad says I have to earn enough to pay my own way and be self-sufficient. The amount he pays me here, it's going to take forever. So are you from London? Have you ever seen the Beatles?"

When Emma said that she lived in London but was from Australia, the girl looked as if she had come from another planet. "But that's halfway around the world. Aren't you scared to be so far from home?"

"I do miss my home," Emma said. "But I'm having an adventure."

"That's what I want," the girl said. "An adventure. I can't wait."

Emma thanked her for the tea and got back to work. In 1903 there was a tragic loss of a fishing boat in a storm. That made the headlines for a month. And a terrible winter with blizzards that killed cattle. She moved on to 1904. A motor car had come to the island. A real road was started between the ferries and Portree. And Jock MacLeod was starting the first taxi service. Emma smiled. MacLeod. The same last name as the Jock who drove Melrose in Iris's pages.

Then in a September issue she saw what she had been seeking: *Laird's Daughter Missing in Tragic Boating Accident.*

"It was true," she said out loud. "It really was a true story!"

Holding her breath with excitement she read on:

> *Miss Lily Patterson, daughter of Sir Harry Patterson of Craigard, is reported missing after a boating mishap. Miss Patterson, aged eighteen, was apparently attempting to cross to the mainland with a Mr Thomas Blaine when their boat capsized. Mr Blaine's body was recovered, trapped under the boat. Miss Patterson is still missing. Search parties are under way.*

"Blaine!" Emma said out loud. "That was my father's name. Rory Blaine Callander. Not Blake." She gave an embarrassed smile when the other occupants of the room looked up.

"Sorry. I just found out something important." Emma stared at the newspaper. How strange that the man who drowned had the same name as her father. But then she concluded that Blaine was a common enough Scottish name, and in any case it was only her father's middle name. She went back to reading.

> *Mr Blaine was a visitor to the island, a guest of the Patterson family. It now appears he was also a labour instigator and was secretly stirring up trouble with the crofters. Sir Harry had asked him to leave. It is not known why he took Miss Patterson with him or whether she went willingly. Anyone who saw the couple that night or has any knowledge of the situation is asked to contact the police in Portree.*

Emma's heart raced. This was Iris's story, exactly. Only the names had been changed. Lucy was really Lily. She turned the page to read the next week's headline.

*Body of Laird's Young Daughter Recovered Miles Down the Coast.*

*The whole of Skye in mourning. Miss Lily Patterson was brought home to be buried in the family crypt. Attempts to contact Mr Blaine's next of kin have been unsuccessful. It seems he was a young man from Edinburgh with no family. Not much more is known about him, except he had bought the sailing boat two months previously in Mallaig and had used it to sail to the island. He was clearly not much of a sailor and the breeze had been a stiff one that night.*

No mention of sabotage, Emma thought. Or of the suitor who disappeared. She suspected Iris had used the real event and turned it into fiction. Then Emma moved on to the next edition:

*Foul Play Suspected in Death of Laird's Daughter.*

*When Miss Lily Patterson and Mr Thomas Blaine met with tragic deaths at sea two weeks ago it was assumed their deaths were due to Mr Blaine's inexperience as a sailor. Now the boat has been recovered and examined by police brought in from Inverness and it has been found that the sail and one of the ropes controlling the boom had been damaged enough to make controlling the boat impossible, but also the rudder was missing. The police state that both the slashing of the sail and the breaking of the rudder appear deliberate. Inspector Cummings states that it seems the rudder was partially sawn through, and the force of the waves must have snapped it off once the boat was in open water. Both indicate malicious intent by person or persons unknown. Anyone with any information on this dastardly event should contact the local police.*

*The police also wish to speak to Mr Alistair Graham, son of Sir Hector Graham on the mainland. Mr Graham had been staying with the Pattersons and was considered to be the future bridegroom of Miss Lily. It is now known that he disappeared around the same time that the couple fled to the mainland. Anyone with information on his whereabouts should contact the police. Word has been passed to the police in both Glasgow and Edinburgh and at train stations along the line to try to trace him. It is not known what his connection was to the boating accident or if the two events are quite separate. Also missing since the accident is a young girl called Catriona MacLeod, daughter of a local fisherman, who had been taken in by the laird's family as companion to their daughter. It is not known whether Catriona was also in the boat, and her body has not been found. Any information on her whereabouts should be reported to the police in Portree.*

"The Wild Girl." Emma gave a small satisfied sigh. So she had been real, too.

Emma turned the pages but there was no more mention of the incident. No information on Miss Catriona MacLeod. Had she also been on that sailing boat? Emma wondered. If not, why had she fled? And most troubling of all, no mention in subsequent editions of the discovery of Alistair Graham's body buried in the woodland. Now she knew she had to speak to the Patterson family. Andrew had mentioned that he might show up again to take her out. She'd definitely take him up on that. It would be a good way to gain entrance without seeming intrusive.

"Are you finding what you need?" the older man asked, passing by her desk.

She looked up. "Why, yes I am. It's all here, just as the author wrote it. She must have come here to this newspaper. And read the account. It would have been in the thirties. Would you remember if a famous woman author had visited you?"

The man shook his head. "I can't say I remember one. There have been writers, of course, but as to famous . . ."

"She might not have given her proper name," Emma said. "She was Australian, like me."

"If it was the thirties I'd probably not have been here," he said. "My father ran the paper in those days, and I went off to work in Edinburgh for a while. I was expecting to be a proper journalist, you know. Big city scoops." He chuckled at the thought of it. "But then the war came and I was called up and nearly sent home in a box. So there was no question of me running around getting scoops any longer. I helped my dad here, just like Nellie is doing now, until he retired."

"Could I perhaps talk to your dad?" she asked. "He might know more."

"I wish you could, my dear," he said, shaking his head sadly. "But he's gone. He was always a heavy smoker, you know, and in the end his lungs couldn't take it any more. It was a sad end, fighting to breathe."

Emma nodded in sympathy.

"So are you a journalist of sorts yourself?"

"Actually I'm a fiction writer," Emma said, "but this is turning into a true crime story, so I'm not sure where we are going with it. I'll have to interview the Patterson family."

"The Pattersons? You'll not find them easy. They keep themselves to themselves. A bit high and mighty if you get my meaning. Both the old laird and his son have been our MPs and they don't socialize much on the island. So I wish you good luck."

"Thank you," Emma said. "I may be back but I think I've been through every edition that mentioned the crime."

"A crime was it then? I was thinking it was an accident you were speaking about."

"No, definitely a crime." Emma stood up. "I'll help you put these back, Nellie."

"Och, the girl can do it herself. Give her an excuse to build up muscles," her father said, chuckling.

"Then I should be going." Emma started for the door. "I've kept Young Jock waiting long enough."

"If you're paying him, I doubt he'll mind. His new missus has expensive tastes, so we've heard. Got a new three-piece suite shipped across from the mainland after their wedding." He gave Emma a knowing nod. "Next she'll be wanting a fancy nursery, no doubt."

As Emma left the shop and headed back for the waterfront, the sea mist gathered, turning the buildings into indistinct shapes and completely blotting out the hillsides beyond. From somewhere out on the water came the rhythmic chiming of a bell and a distant foghorn. It was all very eerie and unreal. She pictured the boat capsizing in the mist, its passengers clinging to the side, maybe, calling for help that never came. And there was still the question of the missing Mr Graham. A disturbing thought came to her. Did the Patterson family know where he was buried but choose to keep quiet about it? And who were they shielding?

Iris said that Inspector Melrose used to talk to her.

"I wish you'd speak to me, Melrose," she said. "You must have figured out who the murderer was. You always do."

She stood there alone in the mist, listening for a voice that didn't come.

# Chapter 35

Emma found Jock back at his father's snack bar and treated them both to a hot meat pie.

"It's good," she commented. "And we Aussies know about meat pies."

"So did you find what you were looking for at the newspaper?" Jock's father asked.

"I did. It was pretty much as the author has written it." She did not add "with the exception of the buried suitor." Was that a figment of Iris's fertile imagination? There would be no way of finding out until she had a chance to talk to Iris . . . and then would she remember?

"I'm wondering if I should have a talk with the local police," Emma said. "They were involved at the time. They'd have records, wouldn't they?"

"Likely they would," Jock agreed. "So I'll take you to the police station, if that's what you want."

They came out into cold dampness and Emma followed Jock across the waterfront again and then turned up a side street. The police station was not far, an unassuming whitewashed stone building. The constable at the desk listened patiently but then shook his head. "I'm sorry to disappoint you, but there was a fire sometime in the twenties and all our records were burned, so I can't really help you there."

"Oh well. That's that then," Emma said as they came out. "I don't know much that I didn't know before."

"But you said it was a novel she was writing. Fiction, right?"

"I now think it was entirely based on this real case," Emma said. "I want to speak to the Pattersons."

The drive back took longer, with the car going through patches of dense mist as the road hugged the shoreline and then rose above it on the crests. Jock dropped her off at the hotel with the promise to come at nine the next day. Once she was back in the Kings Arms she started another postcard.

She wrote: *The story is real, but I suspect you knew that. I'm going to visit the Pattersons tomorrow. (The name of the real family.) I can't wait to find out more. Sincerely, Emma.*

Lying on her bed, looking out at the mist swirling outside her window, she had time to think. So Iris had come here in the nineteen thirties when there were people around who still remembered the drowning of the laird's daughter. Presumably she had been shown Craigard, and perhaps the driver said, "There's a tragic story associated with this castle." Iris's ears would have pricked up, and she'd have wanted to know more, probably interviewing local people to get the details and maybe going to read the newspaper archives. Back in the thirties she would not have been so famous and thus not recognized, so perhaps nobody would remember her now. Had she made up the murder of Mr Chisholm to make the story darker and more complicated? Emma had to talk to the Patterson family and find out what they knew or didn't know.

Close to dinner time there was a tap on her door, and Emma opened it to find Mrs Bruce standing there. "If you don't mind, my dear," she said, "I'll serve you your meal in the lounge tonight. We've got a big, rowdy party taking up the dining room, and I don't think you'd feel comfortable there. Football players, you know. The local team having their kickoff celebration for the upcoming season."

"Thank you." Emma smiled. "I think I'd probably not want to join a room full of football players."

"But you'll be pleased to know that it's roast beef tonight, on account of the number of men we have to feed." Mrs Bruce delivered this parting shot as she closed Emma's door again. Knowing that the place was full of young men made Emma touch up her make-up and tidy her hair before she went out to dinner. She admitted to a certain amount of vanity, after all. Loud male voices came from the bar and dining room, followed by raucous laughter. She took a seat at the far end of the lounge near the fireplace and waited for Mrs Bruce to find her, rather than going up to the bar for a sherry. A large plate of roast beef, roast potatoes, Yorkshire pudding, roasted parsnips and cabbage was delivered to her place, and Emma asked for a glass of red wine. Then she settled in to eat alone.

A trifle followed and Emma was feeling rather full and content as she finished the last of her wine. The noise level had dropped while the men next door attacked their own meals, but clearly they too had finished now as somebody broke into song, and there was more laughter and shouted insults. Emma had decided it might be wise to retreat to her room when the door to the dining room opened and Andrew Patterson came out, a glass of something in his hand. He saw her and a big smile spread across his face. Her own pulse quickened at seeing him. He really was an attractive man. A vision of Tony flashed into her mind but she dismissed it. *Tony has a girlfriend, a very suitable girlfriend, remember.*

"Hello again," he said. "I'm glad to find you here. I've had enough of that rowdy bunch."

"Are you a football player then?" she asked as he came over to her.

"Not me. I played rugby at school. But my family sponsors the team, so I had to be present to give the official blessing, since my father claimed he was too busy to do it—lazy bugger."

He took a seat beside her. "Can I get you a whisky?"

"I hate to say it but I've never tried it."

"Well, we must remedy that. Patterson's Fine Malt is the best, though I say it with all modesty." Andrew winked at her, laughing, as he went to the bar. He really was quite attractive, she thought, followed by the realization that a nice chat with Andrew could get her the invitation to the castle so she could find out more details. He returned with a glass for her, his own refilled. She took a sip, gasped as it went down her throat, blinked and coughed.

Andrew laughed.

"It's strong," she said.

"Aye. They say here it's guaranteed to put hair on your . . ." He broke off. "Chest," he finished, making her smile, too. "Now take another sip and tell me that you sense overtones of smoky peat and juniper with a bouquet that is almost chocolate."

"All I'm tasting is fiery liquid," she said.

He leaned closer. "I have to admit that I don't notice all these supposed overtones and undertones, but that's what we have to tell the people who come to taste. It makes them feel superior." He laughed again. "So what have you been doing so far? Have you done the required tour of the island yet?"

"I have," she said. "Everything is spectacular."

He nodded. "You're right, and we take it all for granted. Our mountains are as challenging as anything in the Alps, you know. I've been doing a little climbing since I came home. I'm not sure that I'll take to it—frankly it scares the pants off me—but I have to admit the views are amazing. You don't climb, I take it?"

"No. Never tried it," she said. She decided to test the waters. "We did the tour of Dunvegan Castle. It is very impressive, isn't it?"

"It is," he said. "Those MacLeods, they've taken good care of it. Always had plenty of money, of course, whereas we just hang on by our fingertips. Have you had a chance to see our family seat yet?"

"I did," she said. "Jock drove me there. It's also quite impressive—scary but impressive. What did you feel about growing up in a place like that?"

He shrugged. "I took it for granted. When I went away to school I was quite surprised that other chaps didn't live in castles. And when I brought a friend home for the hols once and his jaw dropped when he saw Craigard, I realized I was living somewhere quite different from most."

"I'm interested in your family history," Emma said cautiously. "This writer I'm working for has included things I thought were fiction, but must have learned about them when they visited the island back in the thirties. The drowning of Lily Patterson? You know about it, presumably?"

"I was told something about it," he said, waving a dismissive hand. "My great-aunt, I believe. Something about running off with a servant? And the boat capsizing?"

"That's right," Emma said. "Only it wasn't a servant. It was a man who'd come to the island to tell the crofters their rights. A labour instigator. I gather your great-grandfather threw him out and he went, taking your great-aunt with him."

"I suppose a Communist rabble-rouser would appeal to a young girl raised in a castle. We all grew up so horribly sheltered. Very sad, huh?"

"More than sad," Emma said. "It appears, from what I read in your newspaper, that their boat was deliberately sunk."

"I didn't know that part."

"That's what it said in the newspaper article." Emma thought it wise not to admit that's what Iris had concluded, too. "So I wondered, if my writer wants to include this in her story, whether I could speak to your family and make sure I get the true facts. I don't know whether the writer will want to use them or not, but I'd like to get it right."

"I don't see why not," Andrew said. He took another swig of whisky.

"So your grandfather would be Lily's brother. Is that true?"

He thought for a moment. "Must have been. He didn't have any other siblings."

"Is he still alive and with you?"

"He is, but rather frail, I'm afraid. He keeps to his room these days and is a bit vague. Not batty, you know, but out of it sometimes. He is eighty-eight, after all. And he went through the First World War. Four years in the trenches. That was enough to break many men."

"It was," Emma agreed. "My grandfather was luckily too old to fight and my father too young, but plenty of Aussies volunteered to go off to Europe, which I've always thought was so brave—fighting for a country that wasn't theirs, half a world away."

"It was brave," he agreed. "Or bloody stupid." He laughed.

"Do you think I could meet your grandfather and get a tour of the castle tomorrow?"

"I suppose so," he said. "Come up to the distillery and I'll give you the tour of that first, then we can go over to Craigard. So how about coming for a drive with me now?"

"Where?"

He shrugged. "I don't know. Around. There's a good viewpoint not far away."

"It's awfully misty tonight. I doubt we'll see anything at a viewpoint."

"You never know. Come on. If we sit here any longer all the football blokes are going to be coming out, and I assure you, you don't want to see that drunken mob."

Emma hesitated. Jock's words echoed in her head. "A bit of a lad." Still, it was just a drive in a car, and she did want to get into that castle.

"All right," she said.

"Drink up then," Andrew said. "You can't waste good single malt."

Although she wasn't at all sure that she liked it, she did as she was told, gasping again as the liquid went down her throat. Then she stood up. "I'll go and get my coat," she said.

Emma climbed up beside Andrew in his Land Rover. It was still quite misty, with eerie halos around streetlights and buildings hovering as indistinct shapes. There would be no views tonight, she thought.

"Are you sure this is a good idea?" she asked, hearing the tremble in her voice.

"Where's your sense of adventure?" He gave her a grin as he started the motor and drove off, rather fast. They went along the one lighted street and then up the hill until suddenly they were in a world of mist and darkness.

*Am I being naïve again, going off with a strange bloke in his car?* she asked herself. But then she thought, *Why not? A good-looking chap from a rich family is attracted to me. I mustn't think every bloke has bad intentions just because I've met a dud or two.*

"So where are we going?" she asked.

"You sound nervous. You don't have to be. I'm a good driver and I know this road like the back of my hand."

She didn't say any more until he pulled off the tarmac onto a gravel area. She only knew this from the scrunch of tires. The Land Rover came to a halt. Andrew switched off the motor. "This is the viewpoint," he said. "Not much of a view after all, I'm afraid. Still never mind. I'm sure there's something we can do to keep warm, isn't there?"

He put one finger under her chin, drew her towards him and kissed her. The kiss was warm and gentle. The Scotch, following a generous glass of wine, had dulled her inhibitions, and Andrew was an expert. She found herself melting into the kiss. His hand came inside her jacket and felt for her breast. It was all very nice until a faint alarm started to ring in her head. She sat up suddenly.

"I know," he said. "It's rather cramped in here, but it will be okay if we move to the back seat."

The desire to see the castle wrestled with her moral compass. She grabbed his hand. "Andrew, no. Look, I'm sorry, but I hardly know you. I'm not the sort of girl who . . ." She broke off, unwilling to finish the sentence.

"Oh, come on. Relax. I assure you I'm quite good at—"

"Andrew no. Stop." She grabbed at his hand again and attempted to move away. "Please take me back now, or I'll get out and walk. I'm sure I'm horribly old-fashioned, but I don't . . . I mean, I'm probably one of those girls meeting in the Sydney telephone box."

"You mean you're still a virgin?"

"Afraid so."

"You haven't had boyfriends who wanted to?"

"Well yes, at least I had this boyfriend in London and we dated for quite a while." A vision of Simon swam into her head. Simon's flat. Simon saying, "We've finally got the place to ourselves." And Simon expertly guiding her through to the bedroom and her not resisting. She wanted to move to the next step, to seal their relationship as it were. But something had stopped her. And soon after that Simon had broken it off. If she hadn't said no, might he have stayed?

"What happened to him?" Andrew asked.

"He found someone more desirable," she said bitterly.

"I find you quite desirable," Andrew said, starting to stroke her thigh. "So if you wanted to have a go now . . ."

"You're very tempting," she said, "but I'd want to know and love a man before . . . I am sorry. I do find myself attracted to you, but I'm only here for a few days. I'll go home and never see you again and I'd never forgive myself."

"And leave me broken-hearted?"

Now she laughed. "I'm sure you've never been broken-hearted in your life, and you'll soon find another tourist for the back seat."

"Not in the off-season," he said, but he was smiling, too. "Oh well. I suppose I'll drive you back. Pity, you were a good kisser. I bet you'd like it if you tried."

"I probably would," she said. "And later I'll probably tell myself I'm stupid to have turned you down. But I'm far from home and trying to behave the way I was raised." This wasn't quite true, as her mother was so self-absorbed that the subject hadn't really come up, but it seemed to work. Andrew started the motor again, and they drove back down the hill in silence.

"I'll see you tomorrow then," Andrew said as he dropped her off at the hotel.

"You're sure it's all right still?"

"Don't worry. I'm not going to ravish you in a castle bedroom," he said, laughing. "I too have a family that is horribly old-fashioned and strict. Come to the distillery."

"Thank you. I will."

As she headed for her room she wondered if she had been an idiot to stop him. Would Jilly have done so?

# Chapter 36

It was cold and blustery when Jock arrived the next morning. Emma was glad of her new waterproof and tied a scarf firmly around her hair.

"So where to today?" he asked. "I don't think this is the right time for the Fairy Pools. It will be raining by the time we get there."

"To the distillery at Craigard, please," she said. "I met Andrew Patterson last night, and he's going to give me a tour and then take me over to the castle."

"Is he now?" Jock looked a little concerned.

"Don't worry, we've had a talk," Emma said. "He'll behave himself."

"I hope so," Jock said. "Things we've heard would curl your hair. Still gossip always gets exaggerated, doesn't it? People hear one tiny fact and embellish it when they retell."

Was that what had happened with Lily Patterson's drowning? Emma wondered. A simple accident, but someone suggested a deliberate sabotage and someone hinted that the suitor, Mr Graham, had disappeared? She was itching to find out more.

The car was buffeted by great blasts from the north as they drove over the high country on the way to Craigard. The mountains beyond had their summits hidden in cloud. It was the sort of day to sit by a fire and read a book, she thought. Theirs was the only car in the visitor's car park, and the wind took her breath away as she opened the car door.

"I think I'll stay put here, if you dinnae mind," Jock said. "I've seen what they have in there, and I cannae have a wee dram myself while I'm driving or I'll lose my license."

"That's fine," she said. "I don't think I'll be too long."

She went into the tasting room. Inside was warm and well lit, a bright space with the walls decorated with posters of Skye, the crest of the Patterson family and various award certificates. *Best Whisky, Highland Games of 1935, Festival of Britain Award for Merit, 1951 . . .* lots of them. The Pattersons had been successful Scotch makers for many years. A young woman was standing at a bar with bottles on it. She gave Emma a welcoming smile.

"Good morning, miss," she said. "You're our first customer of the day. Are you wanting to take the tour or just do the tasting?"

"Is Andrew Patterson here?" Emma asked. "He offered to show me around."

"Aye, he's here," the girl said, her expression changing almost imperceptibly. One of Andrew's conquests, the look said. "I'll go and fetch him."

Andrew came out, wearing a big seaman's jumper and old cords, making him look too handsome. Again she felt a fleeting regret that she had turned him down the night before.

"Hey." He came over and kissed her cheek. The receptionist frowned. "Did Jock bring you?"

"He did. He's waiting outside in the car."

"You could tell him he's free for a while. I'll drive you over to the castle and he can pick you up there later."

Emma nodded. "Thank you. I'll go and tell him."

She went out to find Jock scribbling in a notebook. "Done already?" he asked.

"No." And she told him what Andrew had suggested. "Will you be able to find something to do instead of waiting around?"

"Oh aye. I got the wrong size screws for the new kitchen cabinet," he said. "I'll pop back to the nearest hardware shop in Broadford."

She left him and found Andrew chatting to the woman behind the bar, who was blushing.

"All set? Come on then, let's have a tour."

They set off, going from room to room. Andrew explained that they used water from the small stream that came down from the mountains, laden with peat. That's what gave it its dark colour and the smoky taste that made the whisky distinctive. Emma tried to be fascinated, but she wasn't that interested in whisky making and was dying to get to the castle. They finished up with the tasting, where frankly she couldn't tell the difference between twenty-year-old and three-year-old malts.

"Do you think we can visit your castle now?" she asked, having thanked him for his time.

"Give me a few minutes. I need to grab my oilskin. It's coming down quite hard," he said. "I've parked the Land Rover as near as possible."

The rain was now falling in great squalls. Emma took a deep breath before she ran out and climbed into the passenger side. The windscreen wipers went madly as the car came down along the waterfront. Waves splashed up against the sea wall, and the water beyond looked black and angry. Even that short crossing would be dangerous at a time like this, Emma thought. It didn't say in the paper how the waves had been that night. They passed the cottages and the harbour and then took the track up to the castle. As they entered through the darkness of the wood with trees creaking and groaning as they swayed in the wind, Emma couldn't help glancing around. Where had the body been buried if that part was true?

"Was there always a wood here?" she asked.

"As far as I know," he replied.

"I suppose it helped keep attackers at bay."

"Definitely. We held off the Vikings and God knows who else back in the day."

"Was it always this thick?"

"How would I know?" he said. "The trees haven't changed much in my lifetime. In fact I don't know why my father insists on keeping it. It's useless. None of the trees grow big enough for commercial timber. I've suggested we get rid of it and plant some kind of crop, or fatten up the Angus beef here. My dad claims it was planted as a shield against the worst of the northerly gales, but frankly I don't think it does any good at all. It only adds the risk of a branch falling on the car as we drive past." He swerved to avoid a small branch that lay across the track. "Why all the interest in trees?"

"Nothing, except it feels like a gloomy forest that might be good for atmosphere in the book."

"Ah yes. The book," he said. "Is it going to be gothic?"

"A mystery," she said. "But it's always good to have creepy things in a mystery."

He turned to look at her. "Is there something mysterious about my great-aunt drowning, or is that just an incident in the story?"

Emma hesitated. "Just an incident," she replied, looking away from him.

They came out of the other side of the wood and saw the castle ahead of them. It looked dark and menacing through the rain-soaked windscreen. She felt a shiver of fear as they passed through the archway into the courtyard.

"Abandon hope all ye who enter here," Andrew said cheerfully. It was exactly as Iris had described it: The guest cottage where Mr Graham had stayed on one side. The outbuildings where the bodies had been laid out and ahead of them that grim, studded front door up a flight of steps.

"I'm afraid we're now going to get a bit wet," Andrew said.

"I came equipped," she said, retying her scarf. Andrew went ahead and she made a dash for the front door, almost slipping on the wet granite of the steps. She hurried into the foyer and Andrew closed the door behind them, plunging them into darkness. Another frisson of fear shot through her. It was like one of those horror films, trapped in the castle of the mad count.

Then Andrew said, "Who turned the bloody lights off? My mother being thrifty again, I suppose. She's been complaining we waste electricity. As you can imagine it costs a lot to keep a place like this going."

As he talked he crossed the wide space and flipped on a switch. Light flooded from a chandelier above their heads, revealing an oak-panelled wall adorned with weapons and hunting trophies. About the grimmest and least welcoming place she had ever seen. She tried to picture living here, growing up here. On one side a stone stair ascended into darkness. Andrew looked around. "I don't think my father is home," he said. "I believe he had a meeting over on the mainland today, but my mother should be here. Let me find her."

"Do you have lots of servants?" Emma asked.

"I gather we used to," Andrew said. "Since the war it's been impossible to get people to work in domestic service. We have an older woman who cleans, a gardener/handyman and a nurse who comes in to help with my grandfather. That's about it. Mummy does much of it and cooks."

"You said you had sisters?" she asked.

"I've three sisters who wisely fled the coop as soon as possible. One is doing her PhD in Newcastle, one is married and one went to Canada. Mummy is still hoping for grandchildren. Of course I'll have to do my bit and provide the heir one day." He said it seriously and Emma saw he wasn't joking.

There was the tap of heels on the stone floor and a woman came into view. She was wearing slacks and a wool twinset and her hair was permed and set in the way of the older generation. She stopped in surprise when she saw them.

"I thought I heard voices," she said. "What are you doing here at this time of day?"

"I've brought a friend, Mummy. This is Emma Callander. She's helping to write a book set on the island."

"Really?" Andrew's mother looked interested. "A travel guide?"

"No, a story from the island's past," Emma said. "It includes your family, which is why I asked Andrew if he could let me meet his grandfather."

"Oh, I don't know if that is wise." Her smile had faded. "You never know if he's having a good day or a bad one. What did you need to know about us? How many generations back?"

"The turn of the century," Emma said. "The book includes the tragic drowning of Lily Patterson."

"Oh yes." She nodded. "I did hear that story once. So sad. She was eloping with an unsuitable young man, wasn't she? And he was no sailor and the boat capsized."

"That's right," Emma said.

"Would that be Grandpa's sister?" Andrew asked.

His mother frowned. "Yes, I suppose it would. Well you could go up, Andrew, and see if he's in the right frame of mind to receive a visitor. Would you like some coffee, Miss Callander?"

Emma remembered that Andrew's mother had to run the kitchen by herself.

"Oh, no thank you. I had some at the distillery. Andrew gave me a tour."

"It's frightfully interesting, isn't it?" Mrs Patterson said. "I don't understand half of it, and I'm not a big fan of Scotch, but I have to admit that those vats are quite fascinating." Her voice was smooth upper-class English, no trace of a Scottish accent, but then Andrew did not have one either. She turned to Emma. "Would you care to come into the sitting room and wait until Andrew sorts things out?"

"Thank you." Emma followed her into a room with a fireplace that took up half of one wall. A fire was glowing. "Thank heavens we have the woodland to supply us with endless logs," Mrs Patterson said. "Otherwise the cost of heating this place would be untenable."

She indicated Emma should sit by the fire. "Are you also from this part of Scotland?" Emma asked.

"Me? Oh, good Lord no. I'm from Suffolk," she said. "About as far away as you can get. I met my husband at university at Cambridge. When he said he lived in a castle I was intrigued. If I'd been wise I'd have backed off then." She laughed.

"Do you find it very remote living here?" Emma asked.

"Of course it is, but I tend not to stay here year round," she said. "Or at least until my husband's father needed looking after. We have a small place in the south of France, and I used to retreat there for the winter. Now I'm pretty much stuck here." She smiled at Emma. "But you are used to the warmth and sunshine, I suspect."

"I am. I'm from New South Wales. My family owns a vineyard so I know all about vats of liquids. And I have been seriously considering going home again. This weather can be so depressing, can't it?"

"It most certainly can. But I'm sure Andrew wouldn't want you to run off."

"Oh," Emma said blushing, "we're not . . . involved. He was just being friendly."

"Really?" Andrew's mother gave a knowing smile.

Andrew's steps echoed down the hallway. He came in, breathing hard as if he had hurried. "Grandpa is awake, if you want to come up. I didn't tell him why you wanted to see him. I'll leave that to you to explain."

"Don't tire him too much, remember," his mother called after them.

"We'll only be a few minutes," Emma replied as she followed Andrew out of the door. They climbed the first flight of steep stairs, then a second. Emma could see why Andrew was breathing hard. She was too at the second landing.

"In here." Andrew tapped on a door and then opened it cautiously. An old man was lying propped up in a high four-poster bed. He watched Emma approach with interest.

"You've brought your latest young lady to get my blessing, have you, boy?" he asked. "It's about time you settled down and stopped sowing wild oats."

Andrew looked uncomfortable. "She's not my young lady, Grandpa. She's a girl I've just met and she's on the island because of a book she's helping to write. She thinks you might be able to help her."

"Really?" The old man attempted to sit up.

"So let me make the proper introductions. Grandpa, this is Emma Callander from Australia, and Emma, this is my grandfather, Sir Robert Patterson."

"How do you do, sir," Emma said shyly, taking the old man's hand.

"I'll leave you two to get on with it," Andrew said. "I've got to grab a bite of lunch before I'm due back at the distillery. I bet you didn't have to work like this when you were my age, Grandpa."

"You forget, I started the distillery," Sir Robert said. "I worked a damn sight harder than you. The family thought I was crazy to have such big ideas. But it turned out all right in the end, didn't it? One of the finest in Scotland."

Although his voice was faint and frail his eyes were remarkably alert, focused on Emma as he spoke. "Go on then, away with you. I'd like to speak to this young woman." He patted the bed beside him. Emma sat, perching on the edge of the bed.

"So you're writing a book about the island?"

"I'm helping the writer," Emma said. "Not my story. I'm just filling in facts she doesn't have yet. It has to do with the death of your sister, Lily. I wonder how much you can remember. Was it a complete shock when she ran off with this Mr Blaine? Did you know she was interested in him?"

He was no longer smiling. He was glaring at her. "Of course we didn't know. We had no idea. I was her brother. I was supposed to be close to her, but she never said a word to me. In fact I had no idea that she'd ever consider . . . Do you think for a moment if I had known . . ." He did manage to sit up now. "Who are you and why are you here? Do you think we haven't suffered enough? All these years trying to forget, and you open old wounds again. My God, do you think I haven't paid?"

His voice had risen to a screeching wail. A nurse came rushing in. "It's all right, Sir Robert. Calm down. She doesn't mean any harm. Lie back. There. I'll get your tonic."

She frowned at Emma. "He gets agitated very easily these days. You'd better go."

"I'm sorry," Emma said. "I didn't mean to cause you any distress."

"We didn't know," the old man said, his voice shaking. "How could we know?"

Emma retreated, feeling guilty and uneasy. As she went down the twisting staircase she noticed a slit window in the wall that looked out onto the woodland and the hills beyond. And she remembered that Iris had described Melrose doing this, wondering if anyone had seen Lucy and Stewart together. Now the bigger question arose: Had anyone seen Mr Chisholm, or Mr Graham in real life, being murdered?

Both Andrew and his mother were kind and understanding when she apologized. They reaffirmed how easily the old man became upset these days.

"Anything to do with the past can set him off," Mrs Patterson said. "His wife's death, the war . . . but he's never spoken much about his sister's drowning. Clearly he was close to her and it was a huge shock."

"I didn't get a chance to ask him about the man Lily was supposed to marry," Emma said. "He vanished at the same time. There is no more mention of him in the newspaper. Is it possible that the family knows anything more?"

"Don't look at me," Mrs Patterson said, chuckling now. "I've stayed well away from Patterson family history. I find it all horribly boring and violent. Battles and being hacked to pieces! It was Alistair Graham, wasn't it? Well, the Grahams still live on their estate on the other side. You could always visit them and find out what they know. I'm afraid I can't tell you anything."

So, Emma thought, either they didn't know that Alistair Graham was buried in their woodland or Iris had created this part of the story.

And if the former was indeed true, she had no way of finding out where in that woodland he had been buried or who might have killed him.

"I presume you didn't find out anything of use," Andrew said as he walked her to the front door. "I don't think it would be wise to talk to my grandfather again. You can tell me what you wanted to know and I might be able to find a good time to ask him."

"That would be kind," she said. "Thank you for your time today, Andrew."

"Not at all. I enjoy your company, even if you did bruise my ego by turning me down in the car last night." He was smiling as he said this. "Maybe we can see each other again before you go. When it's not raining quite so hard." He peered across the forecourt. "I see your trusty driver has arrived. I'd make a run for it if I were you."

"I will. Thank you again," she said.

"You might talk to me, Melrose," Emma muttered as she hurried towards the main gate. "Surely you would have found out the truth by now." She waited. But the only sound was rooks cawing from one of the big trees.

# Chapter 37

Emma was glad to find Jock waiting for her, engrossed in reading his newspaper. The wind had dropped, but there was still continuous rain. Emma took off her headscarf and shook it out as she got back into the car.

"Creepy sort of place, isn't it?" he asked as they drove off. "Mind you, I've never been inside. What's it like?"

"Equally creepy," she said, laughing as the tension melted away. "I met old Sir Robert, the grandfather. I'm afraid I upset him, asking about his sister's drowning."

"Poor old fellow. He's not long for this world now, is he, so I hear?"

"He did seem pretty frail," Emma agreed. They had entered the wood again. Drips thudded onto the roof of the car and the place felt eerily still. The wood stretched as far as she could see in both directions. Surely Mr Graham could not have been buried too far from the track? But how could she ever suggest this to the local police?

"So I'm thinking you'll probably be needing something to eat now?" Jock said. They emerged from the trees and began the descent to the road. "I take it they did not offer you a wee strupak there?"

"I was offered coffee but declined," Emma said. "After the old man got so upset I felt it was wise to beat a hasty retreat."

"They always keep themselves to themselves," Jock said. "So should we head back to Kyleakin for you to have a wee bite? It would be no use going sightseeing on a day like this. The mountains are hiding inside the clouds."

"All right," Emma said, then changed her mind. "Wait. Jock, you must know most people on the island. Are there other old people around here who might remember the incident? Any of those families in the cottages here?"

He slowed the car, thinking. "Aye, well there's old Mistress MacLeod, the grandmother. She must be close to ninety. We could go and speak to her, if you've a mind to."

"Yes, let's," Emma said. "Is she a relative of yours?"

"Just a clanswoman," he said. "Most people around here are."

Jock came to a halt outside one of the cottages. He left Emma in the car while he went to the front door. She watched him speak to a young woman, a baby at her hip. Then he returned. "You can come in. She says Granny will welcome the visit."

The young woman brought them into a spotless little kitchen with copper pans hanging over a stove, lace curtains at the window. A peat fire was burning in the hearth, giving off a pleasant, herby smell. A tiny old woman sat by the fire, a hand-knitted shawl around her shoulders, a lace cap on her head. She almost looked like a caricature of an old-fashioned grandmother. Her face was withered like a dried apple and when she smiled it was clear she had no teeth.

"Granny, this lady has come from London to ask you some questions," the young woman said patiently. She turned to Jock. "Her English is not always so good. Maybe you can translate if necessary."

"Aye, if I can remember my Gaelic," he said, pulling up a wooden chair.

"You'll be taking a wee something?" the young woman said, putting a kettle onto the stove. As Emma sat opposite the old lady the young one put biscuits and cake onto a plate and set about making tea, all the while balancing a hefty baby on one hip. At last she popped him into an old-fashioned cradle while she poured the boiling water. Emma watched, fascinated. The woman was clearly no older than she was, and yet she did all these tasks so effortlessly.

It was only when they had eaten and finished their tea that Emma asked her questions. She mentioned the tragedy and the old woman nodded. "Aye, I remember it clear enough," she said. "Elspeth MacLeod remembers seeing them, a young couple, she said, going to the harbour after dark. And she with her hood up and he with a hat on so she couldnae see their faces, but afterwards she reckons it was the laird's daughter right enough." She gave a knowing grin. "And then one of the fishermen came in next morning and said a boat had been found, floundering on its side. And the men went out and found the poor wee man's body and afterward they found her, too. Such a terrible thing to have happened."

"I read in the paper that the boat was deliberately disabled," Emma said. "The sail slashed, a rope cut and the rudder broken. Did the men notice that?"

"I can't say that I heard that," the old woman said. "Who would have wanted to do such an evil deed?" She shook her head. "Ach well. We'll never know, will we? At least their bodies were recovered so they could have a Christian burial. Better than never knowing."

"Tell me," Emma said. "Did you ever see Mr Alistair Graham when he was staying here?"

"I did not," she replied, "but my friend Morag did. She said she and another girl were out for a walk one evening when they met him and he commented that she had a nice round little rump. He was overly friendly, Morag said. But that was the way with aristocrats in those days. They thought they could do what they liked with our sort of people. We were nothing. At least things are a bit better in that direction now, wouldn't you say?"

Emma thought of Andrew offering sex in the back seat, or the men she met in London who only wanted one thing. Would that ever change? she wondered. Another thought came to her. "So was there really a Wild Girl? Did you know her?"

"Oh aye." She smiled, recalling a memory. "That would be Catriona, Fiona's child. We could never understand why Fiona married Angus MacLeod and went to live out there, all alone in that cottage by Allt Dubh."

"Did they really call her the Wild Girl?"

"They did, and she was. Off on her own over the heather and rocks from the time she was a wee thing. Well, her poor mother died, probably from being married to that man. He liked his drink too much, you know, and got violent. So the wee girl learned to stay out of his way. We tried to keep an eye on her, you know. My mother would put out food, just like you would for a stray cat, and it was always taken, but you never saw Catriona come for it. Sometimes she'd show up at the school and then she'd be off again."

"But she was taken in by the laird's wife, was she not?"

"Aye, and it was a remarkable transformation, too," the old woman said. "She turned into a fine lady, so we heard. Gave herself airs, just like the laird's daughter. Wore her clothes, studied with her governess."

"And then she vanished," Emma said. "Did you ever see her afterward?"

"I did not," the old woman said. "We never saw her again. We all wondered, you know . . ." She paused. "We all wondered whether she'd had anything to do with sinking that boat. She did not want Miss Lily to go and leave her, so she made sure she didn't."

"And where do you think she went after that?"

The old woman shrugged. "Certainly not back to her father. Maybe somewhere up in the wild hills. She knew how to take care of herself. Or perhaps she managed to get to another island, or even the mainland. We'll never know that either, will we? It's such a long time ago." Her face became wistful and she stared into the fire.

Emma couldn't think of anything else to ask. Everything she had learned confirmed what Iris had written. But nobody knew the fate of Graham or the Wild Girl. He liked women, she thought. What if he and Catriona had run off together?

The rain eased to a fine drizzle as they drove back to Kyleakin. They stopped for fish and chips on the waterfront and then Jock deposited her at her hotel.

"Will you be needing me tomorrow?" he asked.

Emma considered. "I'm not sure what I still need to do here," she replied, "apart from you showing me the Fairy Pools."

He smiled. "Aye. I'm not letting you leave without seeing my favourite part of the island. But we'll need to wait for good weather."

"Is it supposed to clear up tomorrow?"

He shook his head, still smiling. "If the weatherman says it will be fine, that means rain for sure. I don't know how they earn their money, always being wrong."

Emma went into the hotel, went to her room without encountering Mrs Bruce and wrote another postcard to Iris. *Have been to the castle and met the old man who was Lily Patterson's brother. He got very upset when I wanted to talk about his sister, and I was forced to leave. So I haven't learned anything new. One thing I do know: it rains a lot here.*

She put on her waterproof and walked down to the postbox. When she came back she lay on her bed, wondering how long she should stay on the island and what there was still to find out. Eventually the warmth of the gas fire made her nod off to sleep. She was woken by tapping on her door and sat up, confused about where she was.

Mrs Bruce opened the door. "Ah, Miss Callander, sorry to disturb you, but you have a visitor, and I didnae like to let him come to your room. That would not have been correct."

Her first thought was that it must be Andrew. Mrs Bruce would not have had problems with Jock. She got up, splashed water on her face and brushed her hair before going into the lounge. A strange man was sitting by the fire. He stood up as she approached. He was tall, middle-aged, grey hair slicked into neat waves, distinguished-looking and wearing a dark suit.

"Miss Callander?" His voice was smooth upper-class English. "I am Ross Patterson. You came to visit my father this morning."

"Yes, I did," she said.

"May we talk somewhere private?" He glanced around the lounge. Mrs Bruce still hovered by the counter. "It's a matter of some importance."

"I suppose you can come to my room," Emma said.

"That will have to do then." He followed her along the hall. She hastily pulled up the covers on the bed and took her coat from the one chair. "If you'd like to take a seat? Do you have more information to give me about your family tragedy?"

He sat in the chair while she perched on the bed.

"You came to see my father . . ." His stare was cold.

"We've already established that," she replied.

"And you upset him. You upset him greatly. His nurse had to sedate him to calm him down."

"I'm really sorry, Mr Patterson," Emma replied, "but I had no idea that a tragedy that happened all that time ago would still have such a powerful effect. I'm sure it was devastating to lose his sister, but I lost my father only six years ago and I feel sad when I think about it, but I've got on with my life, and it certainly doesn't make me break down to speak of him."

"My father is an old and sick man. Things play on his mind and you've stirred up an old wound."

"As I said, I'm sorry. I had no intention of causing grief. I won't trouble him again."

He crossed his legs, still staring coldly at her. "So tell me, Miss Callander, this book that you are writing—what on earth gave you the idea that you could write someone's family history without asking permission first?"

"Let me clarify," Emma said, annoyed by his tone, "I am not the writer. I am merely an assistant. I was told this was a novel. I had no idea it was linked to real family history until I came here."

"Who is this writer? And why did she decide to write about our family?"

"I'm afraid I can't give you her name," Emma said. "She values her privacy. But she came on a visit to Skye years ago, before the war she said, and I can only deduce that while she was doing research for her books somebody told her about this sad story. And she jotted down the details and put them aside for a future book. That's what writers do. They come to a place and have antennas out for any sort of story. I don't know if she spoke with your family at the time, or interviewed the police . . ."

Mr Patterson stood up suddenly. "Whatever she did it is a damned cheek and an invasion of our privacy. You will tell this woman, whoever she is, that my family history is not for public consumption. If she dares to proceed with this harebrained scheme, we will see her in court and do everything in our power to prevent this book from ever seeing the light of day. Do I make myself clear?"

"Absolutely, Mr Patterson, although I assure you she intends it to be a novel. The castle is fictitious, the names and dates are changed. Only the story about the drowning is taken from reality."

"My dear girl, what on earth good do you think changing the names will do? Everybody will know it's us. I am a member of Parliament. I do not want my family name dragged through the mud."

"Hold on a minute." Emma stood up, too. "Nobody's dragging anyone's name through the mud. It's a love story that ends tragically. A young girl runs off with the man she loves secretly and their boat capsizes. What is so awful about that? It is the stuff of Scottish ballads."

"It's more complicated than that, as you know. You've been poking your nose where it's not wanted—trying to drag up sordid details. So I'm not going to tell you again: you pack up your things and go home and tell this blasted writer to set her stories somewhere else. She is not wanted on Skye and neither are you."

He gave her one last glare then opened the door and stalked from the room. Emma sank onto the bed, her heart pounding. What could have triggered that outburst? What had made that man so angry that the veins stood out on his temples as he yelled at her? Then she began to wonder: Did they know that a person was buried in their wood? Did they know who killed him, and would the revelation rock their family reputation?

# Chapter 38

Emma sat on her bed, staring out of her window. The rain had stopped but there was no sunset, and the last of the grey light was fading early. She had been threatened, told to pack up and go home. She should report this to Iris immediately, but she realized she did not have Iris Blackburn's telephone number. This was a case where a postcard would not do. It dawned on her that on an island like this information on a postcard could easily have been passed along to the Pattersons. Had she been too naïve in what she said?

Then she remembered that she did have Tony's card. With luck he'd still be at the office. She went out to the front desk and rang the bell for Mrs Bruce. She came out, wiping her hands on her apron. "You caught me in the middle of making a cottage pie with the last of that beef," she said. "What did Mr Patterson want with you? He looked fit to burst."

"I went to see his father today," Emma said. "And apparently what I asked him really upset him, so I was told not to bother them again."

"What a rude person. Those Pattersons think that they own the island. Never mind, if you wait a wee while I'll make you a nice cup of tea. That's the only way to calm the nerves."

"I was wondering, Mrs Bruce, where I could make a trunk call down to England? Would I have to go to the post office?"

"The switchboard can connect you from here, if you like. And we'll find out the cost of the call and add it to your bill."

"That would be very kind," Emma said. "But the call is rather private, so I wondered . . ."

"Och, dinnae fash yourself about that, lassie," she said. "I'll be back in the kitchen and I'm nae an eavesdropper. I'll dial the operator for you and you can give her the number you're wanting."

Emma waited, Tony's card in her hand. She heard Mrs Bruce exchange pleasantries with the operator. Then she said, "And the wee lassie needs to make a call down to England." She handed Emma the receiver, then retreated. Emma gave the number, held her breath, waited and then a crisp voice said, "Gordon and Tate, Solicitors."

Emma identified herself and asked if Mr Tony Gordon was there.

"I don't think he's left yet, Miss Callander," the voice said. "Let me see."

Emma waited again and then Tony's voice came on the line. "Emma. What a surprise. How is everything?"

"Tony, listen," she said. "I think we're in trouble here. You haven't read Iris's book, have you?"

"Of course not. She wouldn't let anyone see it."

"Well, it turns out to be based on a true story, and the real family has now threatened to sue if we go ahead with it. The father of the family came and was so aggressive and awful to me. I was told to leave the island, so now I don't know what to do."

"Bloody hell. That's awful. I'm sorry, Emma. You must be really upset."

"It was rather beastly. This Mr Patterson got in my face and shouted at me. So I need you to talk to Iris as soon as possible. I need to know what I'm supposed to do. Frankly I've done all the research I can, so should I just pack up and leave?"

"Let me go over and talk to her right now," Tony said. "Stay put until I pass on instructions." He hesitated. "Emma, you're not in any kind of danger, are you? Are we talking about a real crime that was committed?"

"Yes, but ages ago. I can't see why anyone should be upset now."

"Don't do any more snooping," he said. "Stay in your hotel until you hear from me, and if you must go out, go somewhere safe and touristy with your driver."

"Right," she said.

"I suspect Iris will tell you to come home tomorrow, then she'll have to decide what to do with the information you've found."

"That's just the trouble," Emma said. "I haven't really found out much that she didn't already know. The only surprise is that everything about that story is real, apart from Inspector Melrose being sent up from Glasgow. Oh, and that the boat actually had the rudder damaged. Not just the sail."

"I don't know the story, remember. But I'll pass that along to Iris."

"I already told her on a postcard," Emma said. "Looking back, postcards probably weren't the best way of communicating."

"Probably not," he said. "All right. I'm off to see Iris now. Give me the number you're calling from and I'll report back to you with instructions."

"It's KYL 3254," she said.

"Right. Got it. And Emma . . ."

"Yes?"

"Please take care of yourself. I have to assume this man was only trying to intimidate with bluster, but you never know."

"I will. Thanks, Tony. I'm so glad I caught you before you left the office."

She hung up, feeling sick and scared inside. Then she gave herself a good talking to. Tony was right. The man was a bully. She'd stay in the hotel until she heard from Iris and nothing bad could happen to her. As she walked back to her room she went over the scene with Mr Patterson, and then his father before him. There must be something about the story that had not come out yet, something that would look bad for the family. She suspected that it was the murder of Mr Graham. Had Lily's brother Robert killed him because he was horrible to Lily and she didn't want to marry him? Obviously she couldn't ask the Pattersons now. But if Mr Graham was killed and buried in the woodland, how on earth did Iris know when it didn't appear in the newspapers?

She gave herself the answer to that. Iris had been to the police station. One of the officers was old enough to have worked on the original case and could have told her about finding a body in the woods. Or perhaps she had got it wrong: there was no body. Mr Graham damaged the boat and took off for the mainland. Iris had decided to embellish the story.

Emma managed to eat a helping of cottage pie that night, but she found it hard to sleep. She kept waiting for the sound of a telephone, but none came. What had Iris said to Tony? That she should stay on? Not worry about offending the Pattersons? Go to the wood and see where the body might be buried? No way, she told herself. She would not go near the Pattersons again. If she heard nothing by morning she'd pack up and leave. The Pattersons could keep their secrets.

Having not fallen asleep until well past midnight, she awoke late to find a brilliantly sunny day. The water in the strait sparkled, the dewdrops on the grass glinted like a thousand diamonds. Emma found that she felt better. The gloomy weather had contributed to the atmosphere yesterday. So Mr Patterson had warned her to stop asking questions. She would heed the warning and go home. End of story. Nothing more to worry about. She bathed, dressed and went out to find breakfast.

"I was wondering if I should wake you," Mrs Bruce said. "You've been an early riser until now."

"I didn't sleep well last night," Emma said. "I was waiting for the phone call from Kent. I don't suppose it came while I was sleeping, did it?"

"There were no telephone calls last night." Mrs Bruce shook her head. "Now, if you'll take a seat I'll see about your breakfast."

"Oh, Mrs Bruce," Emma said. "I think I'll be leaving today. Perhaps you could have my bill ready. I'm just waiting to get my instructions, but I don't think I need to stay on any longer."

"Well, I'm sorry to hear that." She reached out and touched Emma's shoulder gently. "I've enjoyed having you here, mo ghaol."

Emma chuckled. "What does that mean?"

"It's the Gaelic. It means 'my dear, my love.' Our form of affection, you know."

"So you speak Gaelic, do you?"

"I do. It was the first language spoken in our house as I was growing up. In fact I didn't really speak English until I went to school. Now there's not many that still have the old tongue, more's the pity."

"I wish I were staying longer. I'd like to learn a little of it," Emma said.

"You can always come back on holiday sometime. But I can't stand here talking. There's a breakfast to be cooked."

Emma sat down and with remarkable speed Mrs Bruce delivered the food to her, as appetizing as ever. She ate with gusto, thinking that it would be the last time she had such a meal in the mornings. The breakfast at Iris's had also been rather good, but would she return there? Wouldn't the whole project now fold? Iris surely couldn't be rash enough to proceed with a book that could get her sued and give her such bad publicity. Emma had just finished the last of her toast and wondered whether to telephone Tony again. She had to know. She picked up the phone, spoke with the operator and asked to be connected to his number in England. The same efficient office manager answered. "I'm afraid Mr Tony has not come in yet today," she said. "Would you like to leave a message for when he appears?"

Emma fought back disappointment. "Can you tell him that Emma Callander is still waiting for instructions on what to do next?" she said.

She put the receiver down, staring out at the ferry crossing to the mainland. Should she just go? Why hadn't he called? Perhaps Iris had not been well last night, perhaps she had not been coherent and he'd had to go back this morning. Emma did not want to pack up and go without approval. It occurred to her that she might want to visit the Graham family on the mainland to find out more about their missing ancestor. Would Jock drive her across, and would he get into trouble with the Pattersons for doing so? It was such a difficult situation. In any case she did not want to stay indoors on such a glorious day. Perhaps she'd ask Jock to drive her to those Fairy Pools he kept talking about. That would be a normal touristy thing to do and wouldn't arouse any anger. Or perhaps she should visit the place where the Wild Girl had come from. There had been little mention of this Wild Girl, and she wished now she had asked the Patterson grandfather about her before he became upset. Was she also an embellishment of the story by Iris? She was scarcely mentioned in the newspaper, but the grandmother in the cottage remembered her. She had mentioned the place she had come from. Allt Dubh, wherever that was.

"Mrs Bruce," Emma said as the woman came to clear the table, "you speak Gaelic. There is a place called Allt Dubh. What does that mean?"

"Well 'allt' means a little river, a stream or burn as we call it. And 'dubh' means black. So it's the black burn."

Emma froze. She felt the hairs on the back of her neck prickling. The black burn. This place had held a special meaning for Iris. She had delved into Skye history and this story and it must have made a big impression on her because, whether intentionally or not, she had used it as her pen name. But surely she was using the pen name before she came to England? Or was the name simply a coincidence?

"And where is this black burn?" she asked.

"It's been diverted now, this stream. Those Pattersons diverted it. It's the water they use for the distillery."

"Thank you." Emma was still shaken. She should definitely ask Jock to drive her to see where the Wild Girl's cottage had been and how far it was from the castle.

As she went to get Jock's telephone number the door opened and Andrew Patterson came in. Emma gave a little gasp and took a step back. Andrew laughed. "Hey, I don't bite, you know. Well, not often." He approached her. "Look, Emma, I came to apologize for my father. He told me what he'd done yesterday, and frankly I was horrified. He always is a bit of a bully, but that was unforgivable. To be honest, I don't know what all the fuss was about, but he had no right to be so damned rude to you. So I thought I should make it up to you if I can. I'd like to take you to lunch."

Emma hesitated. "You don't have to do that. Anyway, I've just had breakfast."

"So we'll do a bit of sightseeing first," he said. "It's a lovely day, isn't it? Make the most of it before you have to leave."

"It's fine, Andrew. I have Jock to drive me. I was about to ring him."

"Don't worry, I passed Jock on the way and told him I was taking you out for a while."

The thought flashed through her head that those Pattersons had damned cheek. They took a lot for granted. She was about to say that Jock needed the money and she'd rather go with him, but Andrew said, "He was about to turn down another job because of you. One of the old women had to be picked up from the hospital after some kind of procedure."

"Oh, in that case I suppose it's all right," she said.

"And he told me I had to show you the Fairy Pools."

She laughed now. "He seems obsessed with my seeing those pools. They better be good."

"Oh, they are," Andrew replied. "Top attraction on the island. And then we'll have lunch at the new hotel on the other side of the island, on Loch Brittle," he said. "I haven't had a chance to try it yet, but I've heard rave reviews. They catch their own lobster and crab."

"That does sound good," she said.

"Great." He gave her a beaming smile. "Get your coat and off we'll go."

# Chapter 39

Andrew was waiting by the Land Rover as she came out and opened a door for her.

They drove away.

"So does your father know you've taken a day off?"

"It's Saturday. I normally get weekends off. Besides, my father had to go across to the mainland today. What he doesn't know can't hurt him." He grinned. Then he asked, "So you said you're doing the research for another writer?"

"That's correct."

"And it's a crime novel but it includes what happened to my family?"

"It seems to." Emma was wary now. "I suspect this writer read about the story when they browsed in the newspaper archives and thought it could be adapted to a good novel."

"So who is this writer?" he asked. "Someone famous? Would I know him or her?"

"I can't tell you. I'm bound to secrecy."

"How intriguing. So it probably is somebody famous. I'm always amazed at the number of famous people who decide to write a book, or think they can write a book. So she's hired you to ghostwrite for her?"

"I don't think I mentioned it was a woman." Emma felt quite uncomfortable now.

"It's usually women who decide to tackle crime novels, isn't it?" he said. "So did you telephone her to report your encounter with my father? What did she say? Are you ordered home?"

"I'm still waiting to hear," Emma replied.

"And did you manage to uncover any of my family's deep, dark secrets? I can't imagine what made my father so upset. And I'm dying to learn." His tone sounded light but she sensed he was determined to find out.

"No deep, dark secrets at all. That's what's so strange," Emma said. "Nothing more than what was in the newspaper—and that was just a tragic love story. A young girl trying to run off with the man she had fallen in love with and they drown. I can understand that your grandfather had felt his sister's death so much at the time, but why now?"

"He's been dwelling on the past a lot lately," Andrew said. "Going over things he did and things he should have done. Almost as if he's punishing himself. It's sad in a way. I suppose his brain is getting scrambled."

"Well, I'm sorry I upset him," Emma said.

"You didn't mean to. Relax. Let's enjoy the day."

"So how far away are these Fairy Pools?" she asked, anxious to change the subject as they left the village and headed north along the shore.

"A good way," he said. "Over on the other side of the island, amongst the Cuillin. Those are the mountains, you know."

"Yes. Jock did point them out to me."

After they had reached the settlement of Broadford they headed west and inland, the mountains coming ever closer. The road narrowed to a single lane, but they had passed no other vehicles. The only sign of life was some shaggy red cows with huge outwardly turned horns.

"Oh, look at those cows!" Emma exclaimed. "Aren't they adorable?"

"Highland cattle," he said. "Adorable is not the word I'd use. But they are native to here and weather the winters well. My father runs them on our land."

Emma remembered the crofters being turned out so that the laird could run cattle but said nothing. The terrain became harsher, windswept grass leading up to bare rock, and ahead of them the sheer granite faces of craggy mountains, one behind the other. At last Andrew turned off the paved road and bumped along a track. A sign announced the Fairy Pools. All Emma could see was grassy hillside rising to a rocky summit. As they got out of the car she noticed a small stream beside the road, bouncing over pebbles as it ran downhill.

"Oh, that's annoying," Andrew said. "There are other people here. I like it to myself."

Emma observed that there were two other cars, but no sign of their passengers.

"We have to walk a wee bit," Andrew said. "Not too far."

They started up a trail and Emma heard the sound of rushing water. That little stream had cut itself a small gorge with a waterfall cascading into a deep, clear pool.

"Oh, it's lovely," she said.

He nodded. "The pools go on like this, one above the other, all the way up the hillside," he said. "People come to swim in them. The water is supposed to give you magic powers. Would you like to try it?"

"I don't have my cozzie." She gave him a disapproving smile. "And besides, it must be cold."

"It's absolutely bloody freezing." He laughed. "But people still do it. For the magic powers, you know. And all sorts of creatures come to swim in the pools. Even the seals come up from the ocean, so they say, but then they are shape-shifters—kelpies, you know."

"Shape-shifters!" She smiled.

"Hey, here on Skye we take such things seriously."

"I hardly think that seals can make their way up from the beaches." She was still smiling.

"You'd be surprised what can happen on Skye. It is a place of magic, you know. Come on. The pools get better as we go up." And he took her hand as if it was the most natural thing in the world. "It's a shame . . . that you have to go," he said, looking at her, almost tenderly. "I think that you and I . . ."

"I'm probably going back to Australia," she said. "I'm missing the sunshine."

"It's sunny here today," he pointed out.

"Yes, but not warm and sunny. I miss being warm. Besides, I'm not sure that Britain is the right place for me."

"And Australia is?"

"I'm not sure of that, either. The truth is I'm not sure where I belong any more."

He didn't answer. She had half hoped that he'd ask her to stay on in Skye or promise to come down to London to visit her, but he didn't. They followed the stream uphill, as one pool, one waterfall appeared after another. The water sparkled in bright sunlight. It truly was magical, and Andrew's hand in hers felt somehow right.

"Be glad you're here now and not in the summer," he said. "We'd have been eaten alive by midges in the summer months."

They looked up as a pair of hikers, earnest types with rucksacks, came up the trail behind them.

"Time to go and see that hotel," Andrew said.

They turned and made their way down again to where they had left the Land Rover.

"Now I can tell Jock I have seen the Fairy Pools," she said, wondering if and when she'd have a chance to see Jock again and how she would manage to pay him.

They drove on, towards the western shore. The mountains now rose all around them, dark, rugged and stark as the road zigzagged upward. The coastline came into view far below, a narrow finger of bright water surrounded by mountains, and beyond it the open sea.

"There's the hotel where we'll eat," Andrew said. "See, down there on the shore."

Emma picked out the lone white building, perched on the shoreline and surrounded by trees. "It seems a strange place to build a hotel. So remote. Who'd come to stay there?" she asked.

"Climbers, and ramblers. And those who want to get away from it all," he said. "I'm told it's quite posh." He glanced at his watch. "We're still a bit early for lunch and you said you'd had breakfast late, so why don't I show you my favourite view on the island. It will be spectacular on a clear day like this."

"All right," she said. She picked up on his excitement. He really was enjoying sharing his home with her, which she found endearing. After a while he turned onto a rocky track and the Land Rover lurched forward uphill until they arrived at the foot of a crag. Andrew parked on the grass beside the track. The mountain rose before them, cutting off the view to the west coast.

"Right." Andrew took her hand again. "It's up here. Not far at all."

They started upward. Grass grew between rocks, making the going treacherous. Then the path, if it could be described as that, came around a buttress and Andrew stopped, pointing upward. "There," he said. "See that ledge up there? That's the best view on the island."

Emma stared up at a narrow ledge that jutted out from the mountain face. High above a bird of prey was circling. "Up there? I'm not climbing up there, Andrew. I don't climb. I haven't got boots. I'm not equipped."

"It's really only a scramble," he said. "Lots of people do it. It isn't hard. Look—you come around the side here and just go up a series of rocky steps really."

"No," she said again. "I don't want to try it. I'm scared of heights."

He put a hand on her shoulder. "Oh, come on. You can't miss this. You can see out over all the islands. It's breathtaking. I'll go first and help you up each of the rocks. It really isn't as hard as it looks. Just a giant staircase. I've seen little kids go up there. In fact in summer there is a veritable queue."

Emma stood still, staring up at that ledge, telling herself not to be a coward. Surely she could make it up there, if only to please Andrew. Then over the gentle sigh of the wind there came a small voice in her head. "Dinnae do it, lassie." It was Melrose's voice. He was finally speaking to her.

Andrew's hand was digging into her shoulder and trembling. She realized with sudden clarity why she had hesitated and what his suppressed excitement was for. Andrew was going to kill her. She tried to dismiss this thought as ridiculous nonsense, but it refused to go away. Why else would he have shown up this morning, looked at her tenderly, taken her to the Fairy Pools, except to gain her confidence. She could picture it as she stared up, trying to hide her horror. They'd reach that ledge. He'd point something out to her. She'd look outward and he'd give her a push. There was nobody around to see. She'd plunge hundreds of feet to her death. He'd rush to the nearest settlement, distraught. Such a tragic accident. He'd say she lost her balance in a great gust of wind. That he couldn't save her.

As the scene played out in her head she realized if she refused to go up, he'd find another way to kill her. There were plenty of chances to get rid of an unwanted woman in this sort of country. His father had probably ordered him to do so. She looked around. Not a single sign of human habitation. No cottage to run to. No car coming up the road. She was quite absolutely alone. But Melrose had warned her. Now she was prepared.

"All right," she said, giving him an encouraging smile. "I'm willing to give it a try."

"Good girl," he said and she read the relief on his face.

"But only if you go up first so I can see that it's not too hard. You show me how you go up and then I'll know."

"All right," he said. "If you insist. So we start right here and we go up this rock and then it's quite simple until we get to . . ." He climbed as he gave the running commentary. He was now well above her, moving easily. "This is the only tricky bit," he called down. "You have to grab on here and . . ."

He turned to the rock face above him, looking away from her. As he hauled himself up Emma took her chance and ran. The ground was uneven and unstable. Fallen rocks lay amid the grass. She was terrified of falling or twisting an ankle. She reached the Land Rover and glanced inside. He had taken the key with him. Damn. She scanned the scene ahead. Not a tree in sight. But she heard the sound of running water over to her right. She followed the sound. Just like at the Fairy Pools a stream had cut its own little channel. In a second she was down over the side into the streambed. Ice-cold water rushed over her feet as she flattened herself against the bank. She heard him shouting out.

"Emma? Where are you? Don't be silly. Come back. We don't have to go up if you don't want to. Emma—don't be a bloody fool. Look, I'm sorry if you got scared. We'll just go down to lunch at that hotel, okay? Please come back . . ."

She heard his voice, echoing from the rock face, getting closer. She moved along the bank to an overhang, then spotted a bush growing out. She eased herself under it, squatting amongst its roots, and waited. He was getting angry now. "Damn you. I don't know why you're acting so crazy, or where you think you can go from here . . ."

She heard his feet crunching on rock as he came close, then he moved on.

"Where the devil are you, you stupid bitch. Don't think you can hide forever." Until this moment she had questioned whether she was completely overreacting and Andrew meant her no harm. Now that she heard the cold anger in his voice she knew he had meant her harm. He did mean her harm. She remembered his annoyance when there were other cars at the Fairy Pools. Perhaps he had intended to shove her over one of the higher waterfalls onto the rocks there.

She peered up through the foliage of the bush. He was heading around the mountain where there were rockfalls, places to hide and wait for her at the bottom of the cliff face. She had two choices: to hide under the bush until he gave up and went away, or he found her, or to follow the stream downwards in the hope that she'd get to the road and a car might come. Perhaps those tourists whose cars were parked at the Fairy Pools might decide to come in this direction. She ran through possible scenarios in her mind. If she came to a spot further down the stream where there were more shrubs or even trees, she could hide then hit him over the head with a rock when he came near. But even the thought of doing that made her feel sick. How hard did you have to hit someone just to knock them out?

She peered up again. Andrew had disappeared amongst the rocks. Emma took her chance and moved down the stream. The icy water had now numbed her feet and legs, and she was shivering as she stumbled over slippery rocks, but she kept on going. At last she neared the road and she saw that a small stone bridge passed over the stream. This was her chance. She glanced up, could not see Andrew, then darted under the bridge. She would be quite safe here unless he looked underneath. And she could hear any approaching car, climb out and wave it down. Standing in damp darkness, shivering in the cold, time seemed to stand still. How long before Andrew gave up and left without her? Or would he wait here, by the road, knowing she had to appear eventually? It was a chilling thought.

She looked down at her watch. One o'clock. There was no indication that the Land Rover had moved. How long could she hold out here? Wouldn't he think of checking under the bridge when he came past? But she had no other choice right now and surely some sort of vehicle would come past before the end of the day. At last she heard the sounds she had been dreading. The crunch of tires coming down that rocky track. The Land Rover. But at the same time she picked up the sound of a car approaching from the other direction. Cautiously she peered out from under the bridge. Yes. A car was coming up the hill towards her. And the Land Rover? It was driving slowly down the track, presumably looking for her. Which one would arrive first? That was the problem.

It was a chance she had to take. If she let this car go by, how many more would pass by today? She climbed up onto the road and stood waving her arms. Then she recognized the vehicle. It was a blue Hillman Husky. She ran towards it, waving like a crazy person. The car sped up as it came towards her, then screeched to a stop as she collapsed, gasping, onto the bonnet.

"Miss Callander. Are you all right? Thank God I found you." Jock got out and took her into his arms. "Are you hurt?"

"Get in," she said. "Let me in quickly before . . ."

The Land Rover had reached the bridge and turned onto the road. Jock opened the passenger door for her then gave her a questioning look. "What the devil was going on here?"

"Don't wait, just go," she said.

He didn't hesitate but jumped into the driver's seat, gunned the engine and swerved past the Land Rover. Emma heard Andrew shouting but he did not give chase.

# Chapter 40

Emma sat hunched over in the passenger seat as Jock drove away, the engine roaring in protest on the steep road.

"What was that all about?" he asked. "Did that man touch you? Hurt you?"

"He was going to," she said. "I got scared and ran away. He was trying to find me. I hid."

She looked up at Jock. "How did you find me? How did you know to come looking for me?"

"I had to drop off a woman on this side of the island," he said. "And seeing that you hadn't telephoned me this morning, I stopped by at the hotel. Mrs Bruce told me you'd be going to the Fairy Pools and then to lunch with Andrew Patterson. Knowing his reputation with the ladies, I thought I'd just keep an eye out for you."

"Thank God you did," she said. She paused, thinking. "But he told me he'd spoken with you and you'd recommended the Fairy Pools."

"That's a damnty lie," Jock said. "I'd nae had any contact with him this morning. He just wanted to get you alone, I can see that now." He looked across at her. "He's nae a good man, Andrew Patterson. In fact he was charged with rape when he was a student on the mainland. But his father has powerful connections. They got the best lawyers and absolutely trashed that poor girl's reputation. Made her out to seem like a proper tart who'd go with anyone. So Andrew got off and that poor girl was completely broken. She killed herself, you know."

The thought flashed through Emma's head that Andrew might have killed that girl, as punishment for taking him to court. She took this a step further. Had there always been bad blood in the Patterson family? Had one of them killed Mr Graham, and the family knew about it and didn't want it revealed? She realized that the sooner she left this island the better.

"I think I should go back to London," she said. "Nothing good has come out of this visit—apart from meeting you, of course."

He smiled. "Those Pattersons, they don't play by the rules. You know a century ago they drove crofters off their lands so they could run sheep and cattle. Turned them out. Burned down their cottages and burned their crops."

"What happened to them?"

"Some of them became fishermen, but many more went abroad—to America or Australia. Everywhere was looking for settlers in those days."

Australia. Emma toyed with this thought. Had something similar happened to her grandparents that made them leave their homeland? When she got home she'd ask her cousins about the family history. When she got home. Those words bounced around her head. Suddenly she had an overwhelming desire to escape, to go back to somewhere safe and familiar. She'd give her report to Iris and then book a passage on the next boat. Having made this decision she felt a sense of calm. She'd go back to the hotel, pack up and leave whether she had heard from Iris or not. Surely Iris would not have anticipated that Emma would stir up a hornet's nest when she came to Skye?

Jock glanced across at Emma. "You're shivering," he said. "Let's find somewhere to get you a cup of tea."

Emma nodded. "That would be nice. I was standing in a freezing-cold stream."

She thought she heard Jock mutter "Bloody man."

They came into Broadford and stopped at a café where Jock ordered her tea and a bacon sandwich. Then, feeling refreshed and warmer, they continued on to Emma's hotel.

"If I were you I'd lock your door," Jock said. "Just to be on the safe side. I don't think those Pattersons take defeat lightly." He paused, thinking. "If you like I could stay around for a wee while."

"I'm sure that's not necessary," Emma said. "Mrs Bruce is there and I should be safe in a hotel. Besides, I'm just going to pack and then leave."

"Should I wait to drive you to the ferry?"

"Oh, I can walk. It's not far," she said.

"No. That's not right. You give me a call when you want to be picked up, all right?"

"You've been very kind, Jock," she said. "I can't thank you enough. And let me settle up how much I owe you."

She paid him more than he had asked, waved and went into the hotel. She didn't see Mrs Bruce and was glad that she didn't have to explain her soaking wet trousers and shoes. There was no note on her door or in her room, so presumably there had been no telephone call from Tony or Iris. Emma felt annoyed by this. Why was any communication taking so long? Had Iris's dementia suddenly worsened? Was she unable to make a decision? Then surely Tony would have phoned to tell her to hang on for the moment. It was clear she didn't matter at all. An annoying whisper in her head said that Iris must have known this trip could be dangerous, and that was why she sent a nobody to do her work for her. A nobody who didn't matter.

Emma took down her suitcase from the top of the wardrobe and started to pack. This story had clearly affected Iris. Why? She had made it seem that she had only toured Skye for a day or two, but she must have done a good deal of research here. How much had she known? Unless she had turned the newspaper articles into fiction she knew a murder had taken place. Did she know who had killed Alistair Graham? Did she know where he was buried? And what was her motive for stirring this up now?

Emma froze as there was a tap at her door.

"Miss Callander?" Mrs Bruce's soft voice. "Are you in there? There's a young gentleman wanting to see you."

Andrew Patterson was here at the hotel. She looked around the room in panic, eyeing the window.

"No," she blurted out. "Tell him I won't see him. I'm not seeing anyone."

She couldn't hear a conversation but Mrs Bruce said, "He says he's come up from London to see you. He came as quickly as he could."

Emma opened the door a few inches. Tony was standing there, a worried frown on his face. "Emma, are you all right?" he asked. "I tried to telephone you but for some reason I couldn't get through. Maybe I copied the number down wrongly. So I decided to come myself. I took the night train and then drove down from Inverness. I'm sorry I couldn't get here sooner."

"Oh Tony," she said, "you don't know how glad I am to see you." She choked back a sob as she opened the door.

He came to her and enveloped her in his arms. "It's okay. Everything's going to be okay," he said. She remained there with her head on his shoulder as he stroked her hair, feeling the tension melt from her body.

"You had a shock," he said. "It's never nice to be threatened. Iris didn't seem to be too concerned. Her thought was that if you'd been warned to go you must be onto something good. But I heard the upset in your voice, and I decided to come and get you."

"Thank you," she said. "It was horrible. Much worse than just being threatened."

"What?" He held her away from him so that he could see her face.

"I can't tell you here. I can't talk about it until we're safely far away. I don't know what to do, Tony, but I do know I want to get away from here as quickly as I can."

"All right," he said. "You finish packing and we'll go. Although . . ." He looked back. Mrs Bruce was still hovering behind them. "I haven't eaten since last night. I grabbed a cup of disgusting coffee and a stale bun in Inverness but nothing since. Is there any chance for a sandwich?"

"I can do better than that," Mrs Bruce said. "I don't know what's upset the young lady so, but I can see that you've made her happy coming here. You're her young man, are you?"

Tony glanced at Emma. "In a way," he said.

"Yes," Emma said. "He's my young man, come for me from London."

Tony flashed her a surprised glance but said nothing more.

"Then I can find you a bowl of my cock-a-leekie. That will do the trick."

She went, leaving Tony and Emma alone.

"I'm sorry about claiming you were my young man," she said, "but I thought it was important to show that I wasn't alone, that I had backup."

"What on earth happened here?" Tony asked, perching on the end of the bed as Emma took items out of drawers.

She shook her head. "I can't tell you now. I'll tell you later. Go and have your stew, then we'll catch the ferry. I presume you came across from Kyle?"

"I did. Only a short crossing. The other one seemed too long."

"It was," Emma said. "And hard to get here from Armadale." As she said it she remembered Andrew offering her a lift, the pleasant chat as they drove, then the subsequent night when he had kissed her and wanted more. How easily he had switched from Prince Charming to someone who would not have thought twice about pushing her off a ledge.

Emma stowed the last items in her suitcase, double-checking the drawers and shelves. When she carried her suitcase out she found Tony rapidly wolfing down a bowl of soup, and Mrs Bruce stood up.

"I have to say I'm sorry to see you go so soon, my dear," Mrs Bruce said as Emma asked to settle up with her. "I was enjoying your company, but I can see that something has not gone according to plan, and I understand that you have to leave. I wish you every happiness."

She looked over at Tony, now cleaning the last of his bowl with the crust of bread.

"He seems like a nice young man. Anyone who comes up to Scotland to take care of you is worth keeping."

Emma blinked back a tear. If only he were her young man. If only there was no Isobel, so suitable. But he was here now, he'd take her back to safety, and suddenly everything seemed all right.

# Chapter 41

As the ferry pulled away from the dock, Emma looked back and felt a profound sense of relief. The horror of the day no longer seemed quite as real and raw, and she found herself questioning whether she had let her imagination run away with her. But the tone in Andrew's voice when he couldn't find her gave him away. A concerned friend would have been worried, scared that something had happened to her. He was furious. She looked back to Tony. He had taken it upon himself to come all this way. That had to mean something, didn't it?

As if he sensed her looking at him, he asked, "So tell me now. What happened that made you so frightened?"

"Andrew Patterson tried to kill me," she said.

"Andrew Patterson?"

"Ross Patterson's son."

"He tried to kill you?" The horror on his face was real.

She took a deep breath. "He turned up this morning and offered to make up for his father's rudeness. He took me out for a lovely drive then wanted to show me the best view on the island. It was on this ledge halfway up a mountain."

"And he tried to push you off?"

She shook her head. "No, but I sensed that was what he was going to do."

"Are you sure, Emma? You weren't letting your imagination run away with you?"

Emma's face flushed with anger. Coming from Tony it felt like a betrayal. "You don't believe me?"

"Of course. I'm sorry. I can see you're really upset."

"It's okay. I asked myself the same question," she said, calming down, "but I picked up his feeling of suppressed excitement all morning, and I realized he'd orchestrated the whole thing—holding my hand, saying he was sorry I had to leave, gaining my trust and then insisting I climb up this bloody rock face. I confess I did wonder if I was overreacting, but then I heard his voice when I ran away. He was furious, not worried. Absolute blind rage, Tony."

"But why would he want to do that?"

"I have to presume I'd uncovered something detrimental to his family."

"And had you?"

She hesitated before saying, "Tony, I know Iris didn't want you or anyone to read the manuscript, but it's all true, and in it there is a murdered man buried in the wood behind the castle. There is no mention of this in the newspaper accounts of the time. I don't know if Iris told you that her fiction turned out to be a real event—a couple fleeing together died when their sailing boat was tampered with. Only Iris doesn't mention the broken rudder, which was the worst part."

Tony was frowning. "If they died in a sailing accident who was buried in the wood?"

"The young woman's suitor, a local aristocrat. But the newspaper only mentions that he had disappeared, and hinted that he was responsible for the boat capsizing."

"I see."

"So I don't know whether Iris made that part up to embellish the story and make it more suspenseful or if she somehow found out about it, although I don't know how. So I'm wondering if there really is a buried body and the Patterson family wants to stay mum about it."

"It would appear so," Tony said. "Although if this all took place long ago, why would they worry now? Surely none of the participants are still living?"

"Only the grandfather and he's . . . shall we say . . . fragile."

Tony was silent for a moment, then said, "Do you think we should go to the police?"

"Oh God no," she said. "No good would come of messing with that family any more. It's their island. I'm sure they have a lot of clout here. They'd dismiss me as a hysterical woman."

Tony reached across and put his hand on hers. "Well, you're safe now. But in a way I wish we hadn't had to leave in such a hurry. I'd like to have seen this castle and given Andrew Patterson a punch in the nose."

Emma gave a nervous chuckle. "I don't think that would have ended well."

"You don't think we should tell anyone about the body buried in the wood? It's a pity we didn't have a chance to check for ourselves."

Emma shook her head. "After dealing with Andrew and his father I don't think I'd want to have been caught in their grounds. They'd probably have shot at us. And I wouldn't have wanted to go to the local police either."

The ferry came into the dock. Car motors started up as the ramp was lowered.

"So do you want to drive straight back to Inverness?" Tony asked.

Emma considered. "I had been planning to speak to the Graham family. In Iris's book, it was their ancestor who was buried in the Patterson's wood. I wonder if they know more."

"You can't just descend on someone and tell them a family member was murdered if they don't know."

"In real life he may have fled and contacted his family later. I don't understand how Iris could possibly know that a murder took place thirty years earlier unless she spoke with someone who had seen it happen, but why would they share this information with a stranger, a foreigner? If anyone knew, why not go to the police?" Emma sighed. "None of this makes sense, Tony. She says she came here on a brief visit years ago, then suddenly decides to write about it now. Why? And how did she find out so much on a brief visit?"

Tony shrugged. "She's a brilliant woman, and perhaps old people become fascinated with reliving their past. Or . . . she's been going through all the ideas she never used and thinks are too good to ignore . . . or . . . she'd wanted to write about this but it had never fitted into her series."

All of these ideas made sense. "I suppose so," Emma agreed.

Their turn came to drive off the ferry and they followed the stream of cars into Kyle of Lochalsh.

"Can we at least find out where the Graham family lives?" Emma asked.

"You don't think we should just leave this now, go back to Iris and see if she wants to proceed or not?" Tony looked worried.

"Tony, we could be looking at another murder. I'm not sure who we tell or what we do, but at least we should check on the facts. Maybe I'm worrying over nothing."

"All right," he said. "How do we find out where the Grahams live?"

"We could ask at one of the shops. He was supposed to have an estate nearby."

Without hesitating Tony pulled up beside a newsagent's. Emma got out and went inside.

"The Grahams?" The man at the counter scowled. "Snooty lot they are. Never come and shop here. Have everything sent up from Edinburgh or even London, so I've heard. Of course the laird never was one of us."

"Do they live nearby?"

"Bloody great pile up on the road towards Plockton," he said. "You can't miss it."

Emma relayed the news and they set out again, this time heading north and hugging the coastline. The newsagent was right. It was a bloody great pile, and they couldn't miss it. As they came around a curve in the road they saw it on the hillside above. It reminded Emma of Dunvegan, the seat of the MacDonalds on Skye. One of the gates was open and they drove up a driveway to an impressive grey stone house.

"Do you want me to come, too?" Tony asked.

"If you don't mind," Emma said. "I'm still a bit shaken up."

"Of course." He got out, came around and opened the door for her. Together they walked up steps to an enormous front door. A bell tolled somewhere deep inside and the door was opened. Emma had expected a footman or butler but instead a middle-aged man in corduroy trousers and a baggy, hand-knitted cardigan stood there.

"I'm sorry," he said. "We don't do house tours at this time of year."

"We are not here for a house tour," Emma said. "I just want to ask the current laird a couple of questions about his ancestors for a book I'm helping to research."

"Oh, right. Well, I'm Alexander Graham, the current laird, and you'd better come in."

Emma looked around a hall with banners hung from the ornate wooden ceiling and family portraits around the walls. Again she found herself wondering how anybody felt comfortable living in a veritable museum.

"Come through to the morning room," the man said. "We have a fire in there. The rest of the place is bloody cold."

It was a small, pleasant room with a view out over the coastline to Skye. The laird invited them to sit.

"I'm sorry to trouble you," Emma said, "but for this book I'm researching we can't find anything out about your grandfather, it must be, Alistair Graham. The newspaper reports on Skye say he vanished about the time of a tragic boat accident. Do you happen to know more?"

"Sorry, but he's not my grandfather," the man said. "The direct line died out with him. My father was a third cousin or something and got dragged away from a pleasant suburban life in London to look after this monstrosity. I went off to university and was also enjoying a pretty normal life until he had a heart attack and died young. Now I'm stuck with it."

Emma gave a sympathetic nod. "So Alistair Graham died?"

"That was a problem for years. As you say, he vanished. It was assumed he went abroad and met with a bad end. But he couldn't be declared legally dead for years after. From what we understood he was a bad lot, and we were told he'd caused the boating accident then made his getaway. So I'm sorry. I know no more than you do. I only wish he'd been found alive and sired heirs for this place. It's not easy keeping it going while it falls to pieces around us." He gave a sad little laugh.

"I'm sorry." Emma stood up. "Thank you for your time," she said.

He escorted them back to the front door and they drove off. For a long while Emma was silent.

"You're very quiet," Tony said. "Are you writing the book in your head?"

"No," Emma replied. "I'm thinking that Alistair Graham was killed and buried in the Patterson's estate and they know about it, but nobody else does." She paused, staring out as the spectacular scenery of the coastline swept past. The sun was now sinking into the bank of cloud on the western horizon and the sea was like navy blue velvet. "I don't really know what to do, Tony. If there was a murder, do we report it, after so long?"

Tony glanced across at her. "In the end it's up to Iris, I presume, but I'd say we leave well alone," he said. "It was so long ago that those involved are dead. There's nothing we can do to see justice served, and what's more, the Patterson family has shown that they are prepared to stop at nothing to keep the truth from being found out."

"You're right, I suppose," Emma said. "I hate to just walk away and admit defeat, but the book can never be published the way it is written."

"There's one thing that's troubling me," Tony said. "If the police and the rest of the population didn't find out about it, how the hell did Iris Blackburn learn of it in her few days as a tourist in Skye?"

# Chapter 42

For a while they drove in silence, retracing their steps back into Kyle of Lochalsh. Then Emma said, "In answer to your question, I suppose she read about it in the newspaper's archives or heard the story when she was being driven around the island. Then her fertile writer's brain could have invented a clever plot based on what she read, and by sheer luck she hit upon what really happened."

"Yes, you may be right," Tony said.

Emma stared out of the window, looking back at the island. "She's going to be angry when she learns that she can't use her plot."

"So we should head for home now?" Tony asked.

"I suppose so," she said.

"It will be too late for me to return the hired car tonight, so we'd better drive until it gets dark, then find somewhere to stay along the way."

"All right," she agreed. She still couldn't shake off the tension after the events of the day. Getting back to the safety of London and the south seemed like an excellent idea.

They came into Kyle, and as they were negotiating the narrow streets, Emma looked around and saw an old-fashioned grey stone school building. She thought she heard Melrose's voice again. "Isla. That's a pretty name." The governess who had returned to look after her father and Melrose had fallen for. Was she a real person?

"Hold on a minute, Tony," she said. "There was a governess whom Lucy's father dismissed a few weeks before she died. It's unlikely she's still alive, but in Iris's book Melrose falls for her, and Iris never got far enough for us to know whether she left to go to Glasgow with him. I'd love to know if she was real or not."

"And you think she might be here?" he asked.

"Her father was the schoolmaster and that's the old school building."

"I doubt he's still in residence all these years later." Tony grinned. "He'd be about a hundred and twenty-nine."

"All the same . . ."

"All right," he said amiably and turned into a narrow lane that ended at the schoolhouse. It was a sorry sight, with weeds growing up through the playground and a broken window.

"Clearly not in use any longer," Tony said.

A man came towards them, wheeling a bike. Tony hailed him. "What happened to the school?"

"They built a new one, all steel and glass—primary and secondary all in one," the man said. "That's progress for you."

Emma summed up the man. Aged fifty or more.

"Would you remember the schoolmaster here, when you were a boy? Did he have a daughter?"

"Mr Anderson?" The man's face brightened up. "Aye, who could forget him, or his cane? Many's the stroke I got on my backside."

Emma's pulse quickened. Anderson. Iris had used the real name, the only other real name in the story, apart from Jock. "He had a daughter?"

"Aye. He certainly did. She who taught the school herself for years until she retired."

So she hadn't gone to Glasgow. "She's not still alive, is she?"

"But she is. And still hale and hearty at ninety. Walks her dog every day."

"Where would we find her?"

The man swivelled around. "You see that row of cottages on the waterfront. She lives in the white one in the middle, the one with the green front door."

"Thank you." Emma beamed. The man nodded and continued to wheel his bike away.

"The governess is still alive." Emma gave an excited glance to Tony. "She may be able to fill in a missing piece."

They drove down to the waterfront and knocked on that green door. A slim and gaunt elderly woman opened it, blinking in surprise at two strangers standing there.

"Are you wanting a bed and breakfast?" she asked. "Because then you'd need Mistress MacClean's at number twelve."

"Are you Miss Anderson?" Emma said. "I wanted to talk to you. About Lily Patterson and what happened to her."

A shadow of pain crossed the woman's face. "That poor dear girl," she said. "What is your interest in her after all these years?"

"I'm helping to research a book," Emma said, "and going through newspaper archives I found the story mentioned."

"You'd better come inside then." Miss Anderson opened the door. They stepped into an immaculate but tiny living room. A fire was burning in the hearth and a Skye terrier lay on the rug. He stood as they approached, tail wagging, and came to greet them.

"This is Hamish," Miss Anderson said. "He loves visitors, especially when they feed him cake. Sit yourselves down and I'll make us a cup of tea."

The ancient rocking chairs were covered in crocheted rugs. There were china dogs on the mantelpiece and a photograph of a man with white hair—the schoolmaster father, Emma supposed. There was a crocheted cloth on the table and a bowl of fruit. A warm and friendly room. Hamish the dog came to Emma and curled up at her feet. Tony stood as Miss Anderson carried in the tray. "Can I help?" he said.

"Ach no, it's no trouble," she said. She had a soft, gentle voice. "I'm not quite the invalid yet." She smiled and Emma could see that she must have been pretty once. She still had the fine cheekbones and hardly any wrinkles. She poured tea and handed them each a cup. Emma drank hers before speaking.

"You were the governess to Lily Patterson?" she asked.

"Aye, I was. Miss Lily had taken her lessons with her brother's tutor until he was sent away to school, so I was hired then, and such a bright little girl she was, so willing to learn." She paused, savouring memories. "And she liked having me there, not that much older than her really. Another young woman to giggle and gossip with. It was lonely for her, sure enough, shut away in that big, cold place. I spoke to her father about sending her off to school, too, but he said there was no point in educating females. They'd make a match for her and she'd be gone." She looked up at Emma, eyes still bright. "That was how men thought in those days, didn't they? We were a chattel to be traded. You're lucky to be living now."

"Yes," Emma agreed. "But then her family brought in a companion for her?"

"They did. Catriona MacLeod, the fisherman's daughter, she who had grown up with no mother and had been running wild." She looked up at Emma. "Now how on earth did you know that?"

"It was mentioned in the newspaper clippings," Emma said, avoiding her gaze. "And I interviewed an old lady living near the castle. She said they called her the Wild Girl."

"Aye, they did and she was. When she first came to us she was like a wee savage, grabbing food off the table and disappearing out onto the shore when she felt like it. But soon she got the feel of being a young lady. She wore Lily's dresses and she came to love learning as Lily did. They became really close. They adored each other. Like two peas in a pod they were, inseparable."

"The sister Lily never had?"

Miss Anderson leaned closer. "Aye, well, that may not be so far from the truth. I heard on good authority that she really was the laird's bairn, you know. He was known to be free with his favours, so to speak. None of the maids were safe from him, and Catriona's mother, well, she was the flirty type by nature so I suppose it was inevitable. Anyway they married her off rapidly to Angus MacLeod, and they couldn't have given her a worse fate. He was an awful man, a drunk, a bully. No wonder she killed herself."

"So she really killed herself? I wasn't sure."

"Aye. Threw herself off a rock into the sea and drowned."

"Poor Catriona," Emma said.

"Aye. Poor wee scrap. But her life had really turned around before the tragedy happened."

"So tell me about the tragedy," Emma said.

"There's not much I can tell since I had been dismissed shortly before. Told I was no longer needed as Miss Lily was going to marry Mr Graham."

"What did you think of that?"

She shook her head. "I didn't have much to do with him, but what I saw I did not like, and I thought he was wrong for Lily. I told them so and that's partly why I was dismissed. Lily certainly didn't take to him. She said to me, 'Andy, you have to help me run away if they're going to force me.'"

"And she was trying to run away."

Miss Anderson sighed. "Aye, she was."

"Do you know whether she was in love with that Mr Stewart or was she just using him to take her to the mainland?"

"I wouldn't have said she was attracted to him. She thought he was a nice man, kind, wanting to do good, but that would have been enough for her. I remember Catriona once said she thought he was handsome, and Lily said, 'Oh no. Rather ordinary-looking.' Of course that could have been to hide her true feelings. You never know with girls. They can be quite tricky and secretive."

Emma was phrasing questions in her head. "You had gone when Lily drowned," she said. "What do you think really happened?"

"They say that Mr Graham did not take kindly to losing his future bride to a commoner and took his revenge," she said. "But I'd be more inclined to think it was Lily's brother."

"Her brother?" Emma stared in surprise.

"He was always so possessive about his sister, unhealthily so, if you want my opinion. If he found out she was sneaking away he'd have stopped her."

"You think he damaged the boat then?"

The old woman stared past Emma, out of the window where seagulls were now whirling, their screeching cries echoing. "I don't know what to think any more. I've asked myself over and over could I have foreseen it and been able to stop it."

"So what do you think happened to Mr Graham?" Emma tried to keep her voice even.

"The dear knows." She shook her head. "If he was guilty he took off. If he wasn't, then Lily was no longer available, so he went elsewhere."

"And Catriona? Did she come to see you after the tragedy?"

She shook her head, more fiercely this time. "I never saw her again. I've always wondered if she was responsible for it. Those rips in the sail. An angry person did that. Did she damage the boat and then regret it and kill herself? It would not have been entirely out of character. She was certainly dramatic and unpredictable enough. She loved Lily and Lily was going. What would become of Catriona after that? She wouldn't be welcome to stay on at the castle. Maybe she went back into the wild and died there eventually, away from people, like some wounded animal."

"I'm sorry to have brought back painful memories," Emma said. "We shouldn't keep you any longer."

"It's all so long ago now," Miss Anderson said. "It feels like a book I once read. But it was a strange case that baffled the police, and now we'll never come to the truth."

"You've been here your whole life, and never married?" Tony asked. He had been silent until now.

"There was my father to look after," she said softly. "He was never a well man and I couldnae leave him to take care of himself. He lived into his nineties and by then . . . I was already an old maid. But I got great joy from teaching the children here until I retired, and the people are very kind. They all keep an eye on me."

"There was never a handsome policeman?" Emma asked, almost shocked that she had said it.

The old woman looked surprised. "What a strange thing to ask." She paused, examining Emma's face. "There was a young man once, but I could nae leave my father."

"His name wasn't Melrose?"

Miss Anderson shook her head. "It was Thompson. And he was a painter, come up here for the summer. My father was quite frail by then." She gave a sad little smile.

*What a disappointing life,* Emma thought and wondered if Iris had intended to make things right for Miss Anderson, at least in a book. She wanted her to marry Melrose and live happily.

"One last thing," Emma said. "Do you remember a lady writer coming to visit you before the war? An Australian?"

Miss Anderson's face lit up. "You mean Iris Blackburn, don't you? Yes, she did pay me a visit when she was up here, doing research for one of her books. I read a lot and I recognized her right away from her book jackets. She wasn't as famous in those days, and she was surprised I knew who she was. She was very kind and left me a nice check for the help I had given her. Not that I could tell her anything that wasn't in the archives. But the money was much appreciated."

# Chapter 43

"Did you learn anything from her that you didn't already know?" Tony asked as they got back into the car.

"Only one thing, that she suspected Lily's brother. How strange. That would account for his behaviour when I asked about her. He got very upset and said, 'Do you think I haven't paid?'"

"If he was so possessive of her, could he also have killed Alistair Graham?"

Their eyes met. "Perhaps the old man had kept the secret all his life, and my questions made him tell his family the truth. And that's why they were so keen to get rid of me." She hesitated, thinking this through. "So what do we do? Tell the police what we suspect? Say nothing?"

"It's Iris's story," Tony said. "We report to her and she decides what to do from now on. We're paid employees, Emma. It shouldn't be your worry. In fact I'm rather angry with Iris for sending you up here. She must have known it could be dangerous."

"I still wonder whether she really knew any more than the newspaper story," Emma said. "Whether the buried body was her creation."

"We'll ask her when we get back," Tony said. "Who knows if she'll still remember."

He let out the clutch and they drove off. "It's already getting dark, this far north," he said. "No point in lingering around here any longer. Since I can't turn in the hired car until morning, we should probably spend the night in Inverness. It's a big town, plenty of hotels."

"How long is the drive?"

"It took me a little over two hours, but I drove rather fast. I was worried about you."

Emma turned to him. "That was so sweet of you. You've been really kind."

Tony blushed with the normal English embarrassment after a compliment. "Not at all. I'm glad I came, even though I would have enjoyed to see a bit of Skye first, had the situation been different."

"Oh Tony, I'm sorry, you missed your chance to see it. It really was a lovely island. But I can't imagine having stayed. Who knows what the Pattersons might have done?"

"You're right. Best to get away and put this behind you. Do you think we should grab a bite to eat here, in case there is nothing open along the way?"

"Actually I'm starving, and you probably are, too," Emma said.

He gave her a quick grin. "All right. I saw fish and chips on the quayside. Not elegant but it's probably the freshest fish we'll ever get."

They picked up two portions of haddock and chips, wrapped in newspaper and well salted and vinegared. Then they sat in the car eating, staring out as Skye faded to blackness across the strait. One by one lights twinkled on, reflecting in the calm water. *So beautiful,* Emma thought. *I'm glad I came, even though it turned out the way it did.* They rounded off the meal with a pint in the pub, then set out, heading east. Immediately they left all signs of human habitation behind, driving first along the edge of a sea loch then into wild, mountainous country. Their headlights strafed the darkness as they swung around bends and climbed over crests. It seemed to go on forever.

"Are there any towns along the way?" she asked.

"Nothing really," Tony said. "I remember passing the odd cottage, but there's not much before Inverness. There was one town but don't ask me to pronounce it. It was on Loch Ness."

"Loch Ness?" Emma perked up. "Where the monster lives?"

"The very same. It's very long. Goes on forever."

"Gosh, I'd love to see it," Emma said. "I'd like to get a glimpse of the monster—take a photo, sell it and make my fortune."

Tony chuckled. "So would half the world." He was silent but then said, "Does it matter to you? Making a fortune?"

"My word, yes," Emma said. "I'm tired of living hand-to-mouth, making just enough to get by."

"But I thought your family was well off. Owned a winery?"

"They did." She sighed. "I told you my father was killed. It turned out that he'd invested in a lot of new equipment, made some bad decisions, and we were in debt. It took all his savings to pay off the debt and wiped us out. Then his cousin inherited the property, and I had to support my mother instead of going to university."

"You're bitter about that."

"Too right," she said. "My mother grew up rather spoiled and used to luxury. She did nothing but complain about the way we were forced to live, as if it was my fault. I tried my hardest and she didn't seem to realize that I was giving up my own life for her. I didn't get a chance to make friends in Sydney, or to date, or to do any of the things you should do at eighteen. Then she found a new husband, and off she went without a second thought."

"That's rough on you," Tony said. "I'd say you've done remarkably well, considering. And you've a bright future ahead of you. Your second book will be a hit. You've a good future in publishing . . ."

"I'm not staying here, Tony," she said. "I'm going back to Australia. I don't think London is for me. If writing with Iris had worked out, then I'd have stayed at least for a while. But now this book can't be written, so I want to find somewhere where I belong. I don't really have anybody these days."

He took a hand off the wheel, reached across and squeezed hers. "It will all work out, I'm sure. And you should write that second book. The first one was really good."

"You finally read it?"

"I did. I have to be up to date with my clients, you know."

"And you liked it?"

"Liked it? It was brilliant. Such a fresh voice and sympathetic characters. Don't tell anyone, but I cried at one point."

"Crikey. I didn't think Englishmen ever cried."

"Only in secret," he said.

They lapsed back into silence. *Why can't I meet someone like him,* Emma thought. *Will there be someone like him waiting for me in Sydney?*

Emma was beginning to feel a little carsick; the greasy fish and chips was not agreeing with her. She was about to ask Tony to stop for a while when he said, "Ah, here we are. The famous Loch Ness."

The headlights picked out black water ahead of them.

Emma sat forward in her seat. "Can we stop somewhere so I can get out and see it?" she asked, not wanting to admit to the weakness of feeling sick.

"Of course." He pulled into a lay-by at the edge of the lake.

Emma got out, buffeted immediately by the strong wind coming in from the west. She walked to the rocky shoreline and stepped up onto a flat boulder. As her eyes accustomed themselves to the darkness, she picked out whitecaps on the black waters and waves splashing against the rocks.

"Too dark to spot a monster." Tony came up behind her. "There could be one looking at you right now, wondering if you'd make a good dinner."

"Don't." She shivered, sensing the cold menace of the place, the complete isolation, the moan of wind through pine trees. Then as she looked at the dark waters something long and black rose up in front of her, coming towards her.

"Oh." She gave a startled cry, stepped back, teetered, flailed, about to lose her footing on the slippery rock.

"Careful." Tony pulled her back, steadying her. "I've got you. Iris wouldn't forgive me if I let you fall into the loch."

"I thought I saw the monster," she said, conscious now that he was holding her.

"It was a big log that the wind drove against the rocks. See, there it goes."

"Oh yes. How silly of me. I guess I'm still shaken up by what happened today."

"You're quite safe now," he said gently. "Don't worry. I won't let anything happen to you."

Then he pulled her towards him and kissed her. It was so unexpected that it took her breath away, but then she found herself responding to him as his arms came around her, pressing her to him.

"I'm sorry," he said when they eventually broke apart. "I don't know what got into me. I'm not in the habit of grabbing girls and kissing them. I think I got carried away. I hope you're not offended."

She had to laugh. "Tony, you're so British. Of course I wasn't offended. It was wonderful. But now I'm going to feel guilty. What will Isobel think?"

"Oh yes. Isobel," he said. "I'd rather forgotten about her."

"Don't worry. We won't tell her. I'm sure it was only a spur of the moment reaction," Emma said, still a little breathless. "You saved the lady and got your reward."

"No," he said. "It wasn't a spur of the moment thing. I've wanted to do that for a while. In fact I felt an attraction to you when I first met you."

"You did?"

His arm was still around her. "I tried not to show it. You know how it's drummed into us that we have to keep emotionally distant from a client. But chatting with you felt so natural. I didn't have to think what to say in advance. It was as if we'd known each other for ages."

Emma nodded, gazing up at him.

"And when I felt you might be in trouble up here, I couldn't get to you fast enough."

"But what about Isobel?"

"We're not engaged or anything. I suppose we just fell into the relationship because it's what our families want. Nice, steady girl, good family, also in law. Perfect choice. It's pleasant, comfortable."

"Then I shouldn't get in the way," Emma said, regretting the words as she said them. *Shut up, you dope.* The comparison to what had happened with Simon was too strong. Was the nice girl from a good family always going to win in the end, and she couldn't bear it if . . .

Tony's arm tightened around her. His breath was warm on her cheek. "But she's never made me feel what I felt just now, Emma. When I kiss her she stands there, as if she's doing it for England." He laughed. "Then she starts talking about horses again."

"You'll never hear the end of it from your father if you try to break up with her."

"Probably not. But I'm not going to live my life to please him. I don't really want to be a country solicitor, doing wills and conveyancing. It's just his physical condition makes me feel beholden."

"Just like the lady teacher we met who wasted her whole life looking after her father."

"I suppose so," Tony said. "I sort of feel responsible for him, even though he can still take care of himself, and we do have a housekeeper who watches over him like a hawk."

"You shouldn't give up your own life for someone else, Tony. I did and I wasn't even thanked for it."

He nodded with understanding. "Well, let's not think about it now. It feels like it's starting to rain and that wind is picking up. Let's get going before it's worse."

With his arm still around her shoulder he steered her back to the car.

# Chapter 44

The weather rapidly deteriorated as they drove onward in total darkness. Wind buffeted the car while rain drummed on the roof and the windscreen wipers worked frantically to keep the view clear.

"This is awful," Tony said. "I don't fancy going all the way to Inverness in this. I think we should try and find somewhere to stop. I did notice a few bed and breakfast inns along the lake as I drove."

They drove in silence. Emma's thoughts whirled, the memory of Tony's lips against hers so wonderful and so right. Could it really be happening? Could she really dare to hope? Now the dreadful driving conditions put all other thoughts from her head. She sat up, tense and alert, gasping as small rocks bounced down the slope beside them and onto the road.

"Don't worry." Tony reached out and covered her hand with his. "I'm sure it can't be too far now."

They plunged ahead through total darkness. At times waves splashed over onto the road and tree limbs swayed in the wind. At last they spotted lights ahead and came into a small settlement.

"This is it." Tony sounded relieved. "The place I couldn't pronounce." He tried to sound out the sign beside the road. "Drumnadrochit. I'm sure I saw a hotel here."

"Yes, look over there." Emma pointed excitedly. "The Highland Inn."

It was an old granite building, almost like a miniature castle, and the lights were on. Tony parked as close as he could to the front door.

"Let's see if they've got rooms first," he said, "then I'll come back for the cases."

Emma didn't argue. The rain was a torrent now, and as she opened the door she was met with a river of water rushing towards the lake. She made for the entrance as quickly as possible, swept along by the wind. She had almost reached the door when there was a flash of lightning followed almost instantly by thunder.

"That's close." Tony came up beside her and took her arm. "Let's get inside."

They stepped into an empty entrance hall, dark and gloomy and lit by one anaemic lamp. There was a counter with a bell on it which Tony rang. Footsteps came from a side passage and an older woman appeared.

"Good evening," Tony said. "We rather got caught in the storm."

"Aye, it's fierce enough out there tonight," the woman said. She looked from Tony to Emma. "You'll be wanting the one room, I'm thinking?"

Tony hesitated before saying, "No, I think it better be two rooms, please."

"Very well, that will be thirty shillings," the woman said.

Tony paid and the woman handed them two keys. "Next door to each other on the second floor," she said. "But I'm thinking you might need a wee dram before going up. Go into the parlour by the fire and I'll bring you one."

They didn't argue and went through to a small room in which a fire was glowing in a river rock fireplace. They sat on either side of the hearth, holding out cold, wet hands to the warmth.

"That was quite a drive, wasn't it?" Tony said. He looked at Emma. "Are you all right?"

"I'm fine." She smiled at him. "I was quite surprised she immediately offered us one room. She looked old and prim."

"I have to admit it was a tempting offer." Tony gave her a cheeky grin. "But I don't think this is the right time or place, do you? And you have had more than your share of excitement for one day. You need a good night's sleep."

"Yes." Emma noticed how his eyes glowed in the firelight, and crinkled at the sides when he smiled. She wondered what it might have been like if Tony had said yes to the offer of one room.

The landlady appeared with a tray with two glasses of whisky and a plate of shortbread. Emma took a sip and gasped.

"I don't think I'll ever get used to this," she said.

"It's good for you. It will warm you up. You've been through an awful lot today." Tony took a sip of his own and coughed a little. "But it's certainly strong." He looked up. "Listen to that wind. Thank God we found this place."

Emma watched him as he put down his glass, the events of the day flashing through her mind. But she realized if she hadn't been through so much, Tony would never have come to rescue her, and if the night had not been so wild and black he'd never have kissed her. She thought she heard Melrose's voice. "Everything happens for a reason, lassie."

Tony looked up and his smile said everything.

"Are you ready to go up?" he asked.

"I am. I think I've certainly had enough excitement for one day."

Tony made a dash for the car to retrieve the suitcases and insisted on carrying hers up the stairs. The first flight was broad and carpeted, but the second was a twisting tower stair, not unlike the one in the Patterson castle. When they were halfway up another flash of lightning appeared as Emma looked out of a narrow window. It was followed by another great crash of thunder. She gasped, shivered and hurried after Tony.

"Well, good night then," Tony said after he had put her suitcase in her room. "I'm right next door if you need anything."

They stood looking at each other, now feeling a little awkward. "Thank you for everything," Emma said.

He put his hands on her shoulders and kissed her again, then gave a nervous chuckle. "I think I'd better go before I get any more ideas," he said. "Sleep well." He planted another quick kiss on her forehead and left her alone.

The room was cold, but Emma found an electric fire and turned it on. It wasn't likely to warm up the room before she went to bed. She undressed hastily and lay between cold sheets, hoping to warm up. Wouldn't it have been nice to have Tony's arms around her, she thought. And Tony making love to her? She had never gone all the way. She almost did with Simon until that inner warning bell made her back off, and other men had not made her feel loved and secure enough to trust them. But she knew she could trust Tony. Of course there was still Isobel. She mustn't forget her. Would he be able to walk away when it came to it? Emma tried to put aside the nagging doubt.

She lay there but sleep wouldn't come, the events of the day playing in her head like a newsreel. Something was bothering her, something hovering at the edges of her consciousness. Something she had seen . . . Her eyes shot open, realizing what it was. That slit window in the stair. Like the one in the castle. How had Iris ever known about that unless she had been in the castle herself? Had the Pattersons let her in? That seemed unlikely.

A strange thought crept into her head, a thought that seemed impossible, but she toyed with it. Iris said she'd come to Scotland on a tourist visit, a brief tour. But she knew Jock's name. She had sought out the governess. She knew all the details of the actual drowning. She knew how the people spoke and sounded. And she knew about the black burn where Catriona lived. Emma got out of bed, put on her robe and slippers and went out onto the landing, tapping softly at Tony's door.

"Tony, are you awake?"

The door opened. "Emma, what's wrong?" he asked. "Or have you decided you don't want to take it one step at a time after all?" He was making a joke of it.

"I need to speak to you," she said. "It's important. Something I've just thought of about Iris."

"Well come in then." He opened the door for her. "The room is bloody freezing but there is an electric fire." She sat on the bed and he pulled the fire closer. "Here." He took the eiderdown off the bed and wrapped it around her shoulders. "Now, what's worrying you?"

"Tony." She hesitated. "Do we know that Iris is Australian? Actually know that she was born there?"

"We know she was writing books there in the twenties and came to this country in the thirties," he said. "Everything we know about her background is what she's told us."

"So she could have gone to Australia as a young person? And invented a background for herself?"

"I suppose so," he said. "What are you getting at?"

"She knows too much, Tony," Emma said. "Now that I've been to Skye and heard the people talking, I can tell she's got their speech just right. Can you do that as a tourist in a couple of days? And she had all the details of the tragedy right and, what's more, she seems to know what happened to Alistair Graham and where he's buried." She turned to look at him. "I'm wondering if she could be the Wild Girl herself."

"The Wild Girl? Remember, I haven't read this book."

She explained to him. "She's given herself the pen name Blackburn. 'Allt Dubh' means black burn, and it's where the Wild Girl grew up. Isn't that a giveaway? And she knew about the window in the castle."

"What window?"

"I realized it tonight because there's a similar one here. As you go up the twisty staircase there's a slit window in the wall just like the one in the castle, and she says Melrose looked out the slit window and spotted something. I saw that window in the Patterson castle. How would she know about it unless she'd been there?"

"They might have invited her in," Tony suggested.

"Not likely, considering the way they treated me." She shook her head. "Listen, Tony. The Wild Girl vanished and was never seen again. What if that was Iris and she didn't want Lily to leave. So she slashed the sail, which was the sort of wild, impulsive thing the Wild Girl would do, and then when she found she'd actually caused their deaths, she escaped to the mainland and somehow got to Australia. Do we know what her real name is?"

"I heard once that it was Rose Byrne. Irish. But she changed it legally to Blackburn before she came to England."

"Before she came to England, you see!" Emma gave him an excited stare. "Before she could ever have visited Skye."

He nodded. "I see what you are getting at."

Emma was frowning now. "There's an awful lot of flower names involved in this, aren't there? Lily and Rose and Iris? I wonder if there's a way of finding out? I have a friend who works at Australia House. Perhaps she can look up Iris's birth certificate and find out who she really was."

Tony gave a nervous laugh. "This is almost too much to take in, Emma, but what you say is quite compelling. And it might explain why she wrote the story now. She feels guilty and she wants to get it off her chest before she dies. She might have wanted you to find the truth."

"Yes," Emma said. "But why me? Why bring me in? Why not you, for example? Why not just confess to your father?"

"Who knows with Iris. She's never been straightforward to deal with. Always wanted things done her way. And she was impressed with you as a writer. She chose you to finish the story. Didn't she say she admired your spirit of justice? She wants justice served."

"She must really know the end of the story," Emma said. "Does she want it told?"

"I don't know," Tony said. "But I do know I'm freezing right now, and so are you. Let's talk about this tomorrow. Come on. Come into bed with me."

When she shot him a nervous look he added, "I promise I'll behave like a gentleman tonight, but I'd rather we both don't freeze to death."

She gave him a shy smile as she climbed in and he pulled the covers over them. She lay with her head on his shoulder and his arm around her.

"Comfy?" he asked.

"Perfect." She gave a small sigh of content.

# Chapter 45

When Emma awoke the next morning sun was streaming in through a high window and she was alone in the bed. As she sat up and looked around, the door opened and Tony came in, fully dressed and having bathed and shaved.

"The storm has blown over and it's a perfect day," he said.

It was, Emma thought. A perfect day. But then reality crept back into her thoughts. She had to find out the truth about Iris, and if her suspicions proved to be correct, then she'd have to confront her. She felt a tension gripping her stomach, but then she told herself that Tony was with her, an ally she could count on.

They breakfasted on scrambled egg, toast and marmalade, then set off again, returning the car and then going to the station. The train south seemed to take forever. Emma sat beside Tony, anxious to find out the truth and get the whole thing over with. She still couldn't fully comprehend what would make Iris write this story, if she really was part of the tragedy. Why not stay silent and remain the famous author from Australia until her death? Why had she sent Emma to Skye knowing that she might well uncover the truth? She shifted uneasily in her seat. Tony gave her a reassuring smile and took her hand. That small gesture made everything worthwhile. If she hadn't gone to Skye he wouldn't have come to rescue her, and she might never have known that he cared about her. But there was still Isobel.

"Tony, we need to talk," she said softly, as soon as the people in the seat opposite got out at Newcastle. "I don't suppose you've had a chance to think this through yet, but if this isn't going to work with you and me I'd like to know sooner rather than later. I don't want to be let down again."

"I was doing some thinking when you were asleep last night," Tony said. "Only it wasn't about you and me. It was about my relationship with Iris. If I'm her solicitor then surely it's my job to protect her. We shouldn't dig into her past if she doesn't want it known. If facts came out, they could ruin her reputation, and if she was in any way connected to a murder . . . well, she could wind up in jail, and I couldn't allow that."

Emma considered this. Until now she had been so caught up in getting to the truth, excited when she had put two and two together and made four. Now it hit her with full force that it was Iris Blackburn's life they were talking about. A real person and real consequences. "Don't worry," she said, "I'll report to Iris what I've found out, and it's up to her what she does with it. I wouldn't dream of telling anyone else."

"But you are involving someone else," Tony said. "If your friend at the High Commission finds out about her past, what's to stop someone there from selling her story to the tabloids?"

Again Emma hesitated, but then she said, "Nobody need know we're looking into Iris Blackburn. You said you'd heard her real name, but you said she changed it legally before she came to England. So I'd just be asking about Rose Byrne, not Iris Blackburn."

"I suppose so," he said. "But what is all this going to accomplish? If we confront her with a shocking past she won't thank us for it. She'll fire you on the spot and probably drop us as her solicitors for helping you."

"Then why did she send me if she didn't want me to find out the truth?" Emma heard her voice rising. "We can't stop now, Tony, whatever the consequences. We have to know."

"It's up to you, I suppose," he said. "But if she turns on you, you do realize it could affect your own writing career. She could tell your publisher to drop you."

"Golly, this is getting so complicated." Emma stared at him. "Would she do that?"

"She doesn't like to be crossed."

"Tony, I swear I'll only present her with what I've discovered and leave it at that."

He put his hand over hers. "I'm sorry. I didn't mean to upset you. You've been through a lot for her. She owes it to you to fill in the final pieces of the puzzle."

"Thank you."

"And about the other thing . . ." He paused. "That's complicated, too. You said you wanted to go home to Australia. Remember, I know what it's like to be abandoned, too. I don't want to find I've fallen in love with you only to learn that you're leaving me in a month or so."

"Tony, if I had something worthwhile to stay for, I wouldn't go," Emma said. "If I had someone who loved me, it would make all the difference. I wouldn't want to leave." She turned to look at him. "Would you really be happy with Isobel?"

"Maybe," he said. "We've grown comfortable with each other. I'm sure we'd have a nice, pleasant marriage. We'd have the requisite two children. She'd make me breakfast and we'd go on walks on Sundays, or watch the children ride their ponies, and probably I'd accept that this was what one did."

"Then I shouldn't get in the way." She looked away from him, at the scenery that was rushing past.

"But you have got in the way, don't you see?" His gaze was intense. "You've upended things and made me realize that I shouldn't be content. Content is a feeling for old people. I should bloody well be living and feeling excited about the person beside me."

"And do I make you feel excited?"

He shook his head, smiling. "Do you know how hard it was to behave myself last night, not to wake you and . . . you know."

She blushed. "I don't think I'd have objected too much."

"It wouldn't have been right. You were emotionally overwrought, and that sort of thing is a decision we should make together, isn't it?"

"Yes. Yes it is."

"But I do look forward to getting to know you better." He put full meaning into the words, then broke off as the compartment door opened and two elderly women came in.

It felt strange and otherworldly when the train arrived at King's Cross Station and they emerged into London crowds. On the train they had agreed that Emma would go back to her flat and wouldn't come down to Iris's house until she was ready. They took the Tube, with Emma getting off at Earl's Court and Tony continuing on to Victoria.

"Ring me when you find out," he said. "Only don't leave it too long. It won't be easy stalling with Iris."

"If we don't find anything soon I'll come down and present what I have," Emma said. "I don't want to be away too long."

"I don't want you to be away too long either." He smiled and gave her a final kiss as she left the train. She came up into a breezy autumn evening, the taste of his kiss still on her lips. It had all happened so rapidly and felt so heady that she found it hard to believe. After years of just existing she had felt fear and excitement and love, all in a few days. She had experienced scenery that had taken her breath away, and now she carried with her a great and terrible secret and wasn't sure how she would dare find out the truth.

It felt as if she'd been away for years, not a few days, when she let herself into the flat. Jilly's shoes were in the middle of the floor. Coffee cups were on the low table. Nothing had changed. It didn't seem possible when Emma's own life had been turned upside down. She hadn't been back long when Robyn came home. She stopped in surprise when she saw Emma, sitting on the sofa with a cup of tea in her hand, eating toast and Vegemite.

"Stone the crows, you gave me a shock. We didn't expect to see you for ages," she said. "What happened? Did Skye not work out?"

"But it did. I've done my research and now I have to follow up here," Emma said. "And I need your help." She explained that she needed to know details about a woman called Rose Byrne who might have emigrated to Australia around 1904. "Find out if she really was born in Australia or not," she added. "Do you think you can do that?"

"Should be easy enough to find out if her birth certificate was registered in New South Wales, or Victoria," Robyn said. "And I think they can check immigration records that far back. I'll give it a go tomorrow."

"Thanks. You're brilliant."

Robyn went over to the teapot and poured herself a cup. "So who is this Rose Byrne woman? I thought you were dealing with a fictitious story."

"So did I," Emma said. "But this real person may be connected to it and I'd like to know."

"Righty-oh." Robyn came to sit beside Emma. "So did anything exciting happen on Skye? What was it like? Cold and gloomy?"

"It was . . . magical," Emma said. "And quite a lot happened."

Jilly came home late, having been to a photoshoot with a modelling agency. She was bubbling with excitement. "And they think I may have the look they want. The photographer said I was a natural," she said. She asked Emma briefly about Skye then declared she was exhausted and went to bed.

The next day Emma waited impatiently, feeling in limbo. She toyed with going to Barlow and Barlow, but that would require giving explanations. As far as they knew she was with Iris. Robyn came home that evening saying that she'd managed to get the message sent through on the telex, but she didn't know how long it would take. Emma debated whether to telephone Tony but decided to wait. She wondered whether he'd spoken to Isobel yet. She agonized over whether he'd change his mind once he was back in his own world and realized how sensible it would be to stay with Isobel. She sensed he was not the sort who would enjoy rocking boats. But she remembered the feel of lying beside him, the warmth of his arms around her, and still couldn't believe that it actually happened. She was not going to share this with Robyn and Jilly until she was quite sure.

Then on the next evening Robyn came home waving a piece of paper from a printout. "I've got what you wanted," she said. "There were several women called Rose Byrne, but only one who came to Australia in 1904. She came on the agricultural immigrant scheme and was sent to work on a property in the Hunter Valley. They kept records on these mostly Irish immigrants at that time, wanting to see if they turned into productive citizens. It seems she was only there a few months, and it says she quit unexpectedly, and they couldn't find her location. A note was made to possibly return her to England or Ireland. But then later she shows up, working as a maid, at another property called Fairview."

"Fairview?" Emma said. "That's the estate next to my family's. How extraordinary."

# Chapter 46

Emma rushed to telephone Tony with the news. He was waiting at the station for her the next morning, and his beaming smile when he saw her coming off the train made her heart race. Nobody had looked at her like that before.

"So you're sure this is the correct Rose Byrne?" he asked. "They didn't find a birth certificate for the approximate date she was born?"

"They did not. And it has to be the right person, Tony. A ship from Liverpool arrived about the same time in 1904. Golly." She paused. "She must have known my family. Do you think that's why she chose me?"

"It does begin to make sense," Tony agreed.

"I'm not sure how I'm going to say any of this to Iris." Emma chewed on her lip. "She may hate me for finding out the truth, if it is the truth. I suppose it's possible that everything she has told us is true after all. Rose Byrne is quite a common name, isn't it? Perhaps she really was born in the outback and never had a proper birth certificate registered. But it all fits together so well."

"I'd tread carefully if I were you," Tony said as he ushered her into the car.

"Are you coming with me?"

"I think I'll stay well clear."

"Coward." She grinned at him.

"No, being expedient. She won't want to think that her solicitor was going behind her back. I don't think we'll even mention that I went up to Scotland to you, and definitely not that you and I . . ."

"Have you spoken to Isobel yet?" she asked tentatively.

"No. I'm still working out what to say, but don't worry, I will. When this business is all sorted out and we know where we are."

"All right." A small sliver of doubt crept in. He'd decide that Isobel made more sense after all. So suitable. Just like Simon.

He reached out and stroked her cheek. "I don't want to lose you, you know. You're the best thing that ever happened to me."

"Me too."

He took her hand, squeezing it before he had to let go and negotiate the next bend in the road.

It was a rare sunny autumn day and the leaves glowed in russets and gold. Slanting sunlight made the sky look like a blue arc. They drove mainly in silence until they reached Iris's expansive grounds. As they pulled up outside Cynthia Morton appeared, just as she had done the first time. "You're back quickly," she said, not looking pleased. "I expected you to be away for weeks."

"I have some news and updates for Iris," Emma said. "May we come in?"

"She's out in the walled garden," Cynthia said. "Come on, I'll take you there."

"I'll be waiting in the car," Tony said. "Come and get me after you've spoken to Iris."

Emma followed Cynthia across the grounds to the walled garden. Rose petals lay on the ground and the creeper on the wall had turned blood red. The air still hummed with bees. Iris was sitting on the marble bench by the fountain, a rug over her knees. She looked up in surprise when she saw Emma.

"But you're supposed to be in Scotland," she said.

"I came down because I've found out some interesting facts," Emma replied.

"Well, come and sit down then. Cynthia, love, bring us some coffee, I'm still a bit chilly."

Cynthia shot a look of dislike at Emma then left.

"Now, what was so important that it made you leave a nice holiday in Scotland," Iris said as Emma sat beside her.

"Did you get my postcards yet? The one in which I found out that the story you had written was all true?"

"I did see that one, yes. You found the details in the newspaper, did you?"

"Some of them. Others I put together for myself."

"And what was your conclusion?" Iris's face was bright and alert, and she looked like a much younger woman.

"You may be very angry with me, but I have to know," Emma said. "Iris, are you the Wild Girl?"

Iris did not look either astonished or angry. If anything she looked amused. "An interesting conclusion, but no, I am not she." She studied the disappointment on Emma's face, then she said, "You seem to be on the right track, and you've worked out a lot. Good for you. I can't leave you hanging, not when you've come so far. But if you want to know who I am, you should think of my name. And the name I went by . . ."

She had a challenging little smile on her face. Iris Blackburn. Rose Byrne. "So many flowers," she had said to Tony. Emma frowned, shaking her head. "The only other person was Lily Patterson."

"Precisely." Iris beamed. "Well done."

"But you can't be Lily. Lily died in the boating accident." Emma stammered out the words.

"No, dear. It was Catriona who died. We always did look alike. She was wearing my clothes, as usual, and by the time they found her the fish had nibbled at her face, so they assumed . . ."

"Catriona ran off with Mr Stewart?"

"She did, and I've found it hard to forgive her. She ruined everything."

When Emma looked surprised at this outburst, Iris went on. "We had done everything for her. I had done everything. Given her everything. Treated her like my sister. And then I found she was going to slip away and desert me. Leave me behind."

"So you slashed the sail. Did you also damage the rudder?"

It was Iris's turn to look surprised. "Rudder? I never knew anything about the rudder."

"It says so in the newspaper. The sail was slashed but the rudder was deliberately sabotaged. The police said it had been partially sawn through."

"Oh," Iris said. Emma could see she was processing this.

"That's what left the boat at the mercy of the waves," Emma said. "Not the sail. Who do you think did it? Was it Alistair Graham?"

"No, it couldn't have been him," Iris said. There was a long pause, then she added, "He was already dead."

Emma looked startled, and Iris said in a calm voice, "We killed him, Catriona and I."

Emma stared at her.

"Not deliberately, although he deserved it," Iris went on. "He was a vile, repulsive man. I hated him from the beginning. I didn't want to marry at all, and my parents were throwing me at him. He took me for a walk in the woods . . . 'So you two can get to know each other better,' my mother said. And once we were out in the forest he tried to kiss me and fondle me. I pushed him away and told him I didn't want him and I wasn't going to marry him. He was laughing. He said I'd soon come to appreciate the delights of the flesh and he couldn't wait to teach me. I said not with him. Never. Then he got angry. He threw me down to the ground, lifted my skirt, and he raped me, quite brutally. Then he was smiling again and he said I'd have to marry him now because nobody else would touch me. I was spoiled goods. He'd let the world know."

"Oh Iris. How awful," Emma said. She was about to take Iris's hand when she reminded herself that this was the famous Iris Blackburn.

Iris nodded. "I was still lying there, battered and terrified, when Catriona stepped out behind him. She saw what he'd done. She hit him over the head with a rock and screamed, 'You leave her alone, you monster.'" Iris paused again. She had been staring out, watching the water splash into the basin of the fountain, but then she turned back to Emma. "She killed him. He fell forward, across me, dead. We didn't know what to do. There was no way I'd go to my parents and tell them what he had done to me and say it was an accident. So we dragged him further into the woods, away from the path, and we buried him. Cat went to find spades from the gardener's shed and we dug the hole. It was hard work, but in the end he was buried, and we piled branches and leaves over the grave. We sneaked back to his cottage and took some of his clothes to make it seem that he'd left in a hurry, and we buried them, too."

She paused, reflecting on what she had just said. "But we both felt it was only a matter of time before someone found him and we'd be arrested and hanged. So we planned to get away. We had big ideas, Cat and I. We'd already talked about running away. We decided to disguise ourselves from the dress-up box. Two old women with grey hair. We'd make our way down to London, where Cat would be a dancer and I'd be a writer. We had no idea what we'd do for money, but it was a lovely dream.

"We packed bags and hid them and waited for the right moment. Cat pretended to visit her father and hid out. Then I found out she was escaping with Stewart, without me. I overheard them. She'd been seeing him behind my back. They were going off together. It was the ultimate betrayal. I crept down to the harbour and slashed the sail. That would teach them, they wouldn't get anywhere. They'd be trapped there.

"But that was when I got the courage to escape, on my own. If anyone was stuck and caught for the murder it wouldn't be me. Remember I was only eighteen. I wasn't thinking clearly. I was in a rage and a panic. So I sneaked down to the boathouse and rowed myself across to the mainland. Nobody would notice one of the old rowing boats missing.

With the grey wig, the shawl around my head and dirt on my face, I didn't think anyone would look at me twice. As I made my way to the train at Mallaig I learned that they had both drowned. Then I knew I had to get away. I was a murderess."

"But you didn't kill anyone, Iris," Emma said. "The damaged sail didn't capsize the boat. It was out in the sea with no rudder. That's what made the boat capsize. Also one of the ropes, the sheets that held the sail, was cut. You didn't mean to harm them," Emma said.

"No, I didn't." Iris squeezed her eyes shut as if trying to shut out the memory. "I loved her. My darling Cat. I didn't want her to leave me alone. And when I heard . . . Well, I was desperate."

Emma nodded with understanding. "If I'd been in your shoes I'd have been desperate, too."

"Anyway, I took train after train south until I got to Liverpool. I could lose myself in a big city, I thought. Then I saw the notice on a lamppost. Immigrants wanted in Australia, especially Irish workers for agriculture. Free passage in return for two years of labour. I went to the docks and signed up."

"As Rose Byrne," Emma said with a tiny smile of satisfaction.

"You found that out? Good for you." Iris looked pleased. "I registered. So many Irish didn't have birth certificates in those days, and you didn't need a passport. So I went to start a new life in Australia, only halfway through the voyage I discovered I was pregnant. Alistair had raped me and left me with child. Now I was really glad Catriona had killed him, but I was desperate. What colony would want a pregnant unmarried girl?"

Emma nodded again, wanting to reach out and take the old woman's hand.

"Anyway, they sent me to a farm in the Hunter Valley. I told a young farmer's wife about my plight, and she took me to some nuns. They ran a home for girls like me. My baby was born, a beautiful boy. He was taken from me, but by chance I learned where he had been placed. I got myself a job as a maid at a nearby property so I could watch him grow. He never knew I was his mother, but I followed his progress. He did very well and he had a beautiful daughter."

She was looking at Emma now, with tenderness and pride.

"I was allowed to name him," she said. "Before they took him away. I named him Rory Blaine in honour of Thomas Blaine, the man I had killed. A good man with a good heart, good intentions."

"My father?" Emma could hardly say the words.

"Your father."

Emma stared at her, trying to digest this. Of all the things that had happened in the past week, all the revelations, and dangers, and unexpected love that she had found, this was the one that completely bowled her over. Conflicting emotions surged through her. That this elderly, birdlike woman was related to her, her grandmother, was hard enough to comprehend. But that she had known about Emma all the while and let her suffer through that bleak time in the room over the bookshop, when she felt she had nobody in the world and no hope, was hard to understand. Hard to forgive.

"You knew about me," she said in a clenched voice.

Iris nodded. "I watched over you and your father from afar—I had my spies by the time I came to England, and I had money. I thought all was well. I bided my time. Your family was flourishing. You were happy, so I didn't want to interfere, but I wanted to make sure you had every opportunity. I arranged with a friend who was the dean of St Anne's College for the scholarship to Oxford for you."

"It was you?"

Iris nodded. "And I can tell you I was really miffed when you didn't take it. I thought, 'Screw her. She doesn't want me.' Then I learned the reason. That your father had died. My son—my lovely son had died. It was an awful shock."

Emma blinked back tears. When she said nothing Iris went on. "I wanted to reach out, but I found that you and your mother had moved away. I lost touch for a while. I had people searching for you. And when I finally found you, you were having a rough time, living above a bookshop. I wondered how I could help, and then I learned that you had written a book. I made sure it got to the right people."

"Oh," Emma said, recoiling as if it were a slap in the face. "You got it published. So it wouldn't have been good enough without your help?"

"Absolutely good enough," Iris said angrily, "but first-time authors have a tough time getting looked at. I made sure you got a smooth entrance to the world, and a job in London."

"And then you sent me to Skye because you wanted me to find out the truth," Emma said. "Why didn't you just tell me? Why the pretence of writing a book you can never publish and asking me to finish it?"

"I suppose I wanted you to understand why I acted the way I did, and what I went through," Iris said. "Maybe I wanted someone to finally find out the truth that had haunted me all these years and to make me accept the punishment for what I had done." She looked up sharply. "They never found him, did they?"

"Mr Graham? Not as far as I can tell," Emma said. "I assumed one of the Pattersons had killed Mr Graham because they were so hostile and tried to scare me off. But I realize now that they were protecting the old grandfather, your brother. I saw your governess, and she said she'd always suspected that your brother sabotaged the boat. He was too protective of you, she said."

"Robert? Yes, he always was very possessive. So he tried to kill me for running away?"

"Maybe he just tried to stop you, and then, when he thought you had drowned, he felt great remorse. He still shows it."

"Poor man." Iris, sitting silent and unmoving, looked down at her hands.

"You know, I wonder now whether he even realized you were on that boat," Emma said. "It's possible that your father had told him to make sure Mr Blaine never came back to the island and he took this literally."

"Yes. That could be true." Emma saw relief on Iris's face.

"When you went to Scotland in the thirties did you not want to see your family?" Emma asked. "You didn't try to see them?"

"I did," Iris said. "Oh, I wasn't stupid enough to show up on their doorstep and announce that the prodigal daughter had returned. I certainly didn't want to be taken into the fold again. But I had the driver take me to look at the castle. While we were sitting there a big car drove out of the gates. A Bentley, I think, or a Rolls? A man was driving. Youngish. In his thirties, I suppose. And two small boys were kicking a football around on the grass. It went into the road. This man, who I presume was my nephew Ross, the one who threatened you, rolled down the window and shouted at them. 'Keep that damn ball off the street. Do you want to cause an accident?' They were little kiddies. They looked terrified. And he sounded so arrogant. I decided then and there that I was well rid of them."

"You're right," Emma said. "He was definitely arrogant and unpleasant to me. Really threatening. And his son, Andrew . . ." She broke off, unable to share with Iris those awful last moments fleeing from Andrew Patterson.

"They're a bad lot, the whole family," Iris said. "The best thing I did was to escape. I wanted to forget all about them, about everything, but I couldn't put it behind me. The guilt has haunted me all these years. I killed a person I loved. That's why I wanted to write the book. It's my confession to the world, so they'd know what really happened. Melrose would tell them."

"You can't publish the book, Iris."

"Why don't you call me Granny now? I'd like that." She squeezed Emma's hand.

"All right," Emma said, feeling her own hesitancy. This was all so sudden, so overwhelming. How could she be expected to feel love and warmth for this stranger? It would take time for her to process everything that had happened.

"So Granny," she said, forcing out the word, "we can't finish the story with the truth. The Pattersons would sue you, for one thing.

You could even be arrested as an accessory to a crime. You could go to jail."

Iris gave a long shuddering sigh. "I suppose you're right. But you know the truth now. So what are you going to do with the information you have gathered? Are you going to tell the police about Alistair Graham, buried in the wood?"

"It's your story, Iris, I mean Granny. All I know is what you have written. Fiction. I don't know if anyone is buried in a wood. You didn't kill Alistair Graham, or Thomas Blaine, or Catriona. And you've certainly paid the price all your life."

"Oh my dear child." Iris took Emma's hands into hers. "You don't know what this means to me. The burden I've carried alone all these years, and finally you've lifted the load from my shoulders. You've shown me I'm not a murderer."

"No, you're not. You were a victim, too. And as for telling the police about Alistair Graham, what would be the point now? He deserved to die. Let him rest there."

"Your grandfather," Iris said. "How strange it sounds to say that, but it's true."

"Gosh, I hadn't thought of it like that." Emma was still staring at her. "My grandfather, that horrible man. How weird to think of it. And it's hard enough coming to terms with you being my grandmother. My extended family must have known that my father was adopted. I remember that I overheard the cousin who took the estate saying it was only right that it went to the bloodline and not to interlopers. Now I understand. Oh well, it's all water under the bridge. I couldn't have run the winery myself anyway. I had no interest, and my mother . . ."

"Has already moved on to pastures new." Iris smiled.

"So what do we do now?" Emma said.

"Well, as you are my granddaughter, I'd be delighted if you'd make this your home. I'll encourage you to write your next book."

"And Inspector Melrose? It's a pity we can't finish that book."

"It is a pity. It was a good story."

"And you wanted Melrose to find love with the governess. I liked that. He shouldn't have been alone all his life."

"No. That was a mistake of mine. I created his character to be like me. Alone. And now I'm not." She reached out and patted Emma's hand. "And I don't want you to be either. Find a nice bloke for yourself, darling. Bring him to live here. I want to enjoy watching your children run about the grounds and to know what it feels like to be part of a family."

Emma felt tears stinging in her eyes. "Yes," she said. "Oh yes."

"Anyone in mind?" Iris asked innocently. "You know you could do worse than young Tony. That's why I requested him instead of his father when I summoned you. But he's got an awful, boring girlfriend. We'll have to do something about her."

"Iris, I mean Granny, Tony can handle that himself, I'm sure." Emma laughed.

"Oh, so it is moving in the right direction." She gave a knowing nod. "I was sure of it, and I'm seldom wrong when I get a hunch."

"Can I tell him the truth or do you want it kept a secret?"

"I think that officially it's better if we say you're my old friend's child, so that we don't have to go into details," Iris said. "That might make things too complicated. Maybe you can share with Tony eventually. If things progress with him as they should. The boy is quite trustworthy, I'm sure."

"Cynthia will want to know."

"She already does. I told her everything."

"Everything? About Skye and what happened there?"

Iris shook her head. "Not that. I've never told anybody that. It's been my secret. But while you were gone, I told her that I'd brought you here because you were my long-lost granddaughter. She was being so hostile because she didn't want an outsider brought into our lives. She's still a bit worried that you'll come and take her place in my life."

"I won't take her place. She'd be welcome to stay, wouldn't she?"

"As annoying as she is, yes, she can stay."

They both looked up as Cynthia appeared with a tray.

"Two coffees and some gingersnaps," she said. "And you don't want to stay out here too long. You'll catch cold."

"Don't fuss, woman. I'm perfectly fine, and my granddaughter will take care of me," Iris said.

"So she knows?"

"Yes, she does and it's all going to work out splendidly."

"I see." She glared.

"I won't get in your way, Miss Morton," Emma said. "I'll just come to visit for a while, until I map out my future."

"Well, I suppose it will work for the best," Cynthia said. "By the way, there is a young man sitting in a car. Should I bring him in?"

"Yes," Iris said. "Bring him in."

When she had gone Emma examined Iris. No longer lounging on the chaise, but sitting upright. "All right, Granny," she said. "All those details of your life in the outback, finding a dead sheep on the doorstep and having to skin it, that was pure fiction, was it?"

Iris grinned. "I am a bloody good fiction writer, after all. Always did have a flair for the dramatic. I had to invent a past for myself that couldn't readily be checked on. And the dead sheep did happen to a girl I worked with as a maid. She told me the whole story in grisly detail." She reached out and took Emma's hand again. "We're going to write wonderful stories together."

"Tell me, Granny," Emma said hesitantly. "I don't want to lose you again now I've found you. Do you really have dementia, or was that put on as a ruse to get me here?"

"What do you think?" Iris asked.

"I think you're sharp as a tack."

Iris threw back her head and laughed. "I like to think so. My doctor says I probably am in the early stages of cognitive decline. I do confess to not remembering where I've put something or why I came into a room and I do mix up names, but I think I could have finished that story if I'd wanted to."

"And they all lived happily ever after? Melrose married the governess?"

"Possibly. I do like happy endings." They looked up as Tony came towards them, a big smile on his face.

# Epilogue

## From *The Call of the Isles*

## *Inspector Melrose's Last Case*

### By Iris Blackburn and Emma Gordon

As the train bore him northward, Chief Inspector Melrose let out a long sigh of relief. He had done it, he had walked away from Scotland Yard. They hadn't wanted to see him go. They had begged and pleaded, offered him more money, even offered him a promotion that would have meant a desk job. But he'd turned them down and done what he'd wanted to do for years. To go home to Scotland, back to a place where life made sense, where he felt free, with the chance to be reborn.

The letter, of course, had made all the difference. They had exchanged correspondence all these years, polite but friendly letters with a sprinkling of news. But this latest letter had said that her father had died. She was thinking of leaving Kyle and doing a bit of travelling. Was he still in London, because she'd love to visit him sometime. His pulse grew a little faster at the thought.

"Be reasonable, laddie," he told himself. "You're a fifty-year-old man. She's a middle-aged woman." Too late for romance and passion. But it was worth a try, wasn't it? To come back to a place that had called to him so long ago and maybe find her there. He glanced out of the train window, willing the journey to go faster.

# Author's Note

Anybody who has been to Skye will recognize the topography and places. However Craigard, the home of the Patterson family, is fictitious. I needed a castle in the right sort of place to make an escape feasible. It is, however, based on real castles in the area that are still inhabited by local lairds. And the name Craigard is Gaelic, meaning "high rock."

You'll also find odd phrases of Scottish Gaelic:

"Mo ghaol" means "my dear" or "my love" and is a term of affection.

A "strupak" is a bite to eat and drink, offered to any visitor as a means of polite welcome.

"Mo ghràidh" also means "my love," a term of endearment.

"Tha i fliuch" means "it's raining."

"Fash," as in "dinnae fash yourself," means "don't get upset about it."

"Whist" is a common Scottish term that means "to know."

# Acknowledgments

As always, I want to thank my entire team for making this such a smooth and easy process, for being my biggest cheerleaders. Former editor Selena James, current editor Pippa White, Jodi Warshaw, and everyone at Lake Union; Meg Ruley, Christina Hogrebe and the gang at Jane Rotrosen Agency; and last, but not least, my husband John and my brilliant family. I am so lucky.

# About the Author

*Photo © Douglas Sonders*

Rhys Bowen is *The New York Times* bestselling author of more than sixty novels, including *Mrs. Endicott's Splendid Adventure*, *The Rose Arbor*, *The Paris Assignment*, *Where the Sky Begins*, *The Venice Sketchbook*, *Above the Bay of Angels*, *The Victory Garden*, *The Tuscan Child*, and *In Farleigh Field*, the winner of the Lefty Award for Best Historical Mystery Novel and the Agatha Award for Best Historical Novel. Bowen's work has won sixteen honors to date, including multiple Agatha, Anthony, and Macavity Awards. Her books have been translated into many languages, and she has fans around the world, including more than seventy thousand Facebook followers. A transplanted Brit, Bowen divides her time between California and Arizona. For more information, visit www.rhysbowen.com.